THE SWEETEST THING

Books by Elizabeth Musser

FROM BETHANY HOUSE PUBLISHERS

The Sweetest Thing

Words Unspoken

The Swan House

*The Dwelling Place**

*Searching for Eternity**

OTHER BOOKS

Two Crosses

Two Testaments

*Two Destinies***

*available as e-books only

**coming in 2012

THE
Sweetest Thing
a novel

ELIZABETH MUSSER

BETHANYHOUSE
Minneapolis, Minnesota

Published by Bethany House Publishers
11400 Hampshire Avenue South
Bloomington, Minnesota 55438

Bethany House Publishers is a division of
Baker Publishing Group, Grand Rapids, Michigan.

Printed in the United States of America

Library of Congress Cataloging-in-Publication Data

Musser, Elizabeth.
    The sweetest thing / Elizabeth Musser.
        p. cm.
    ISBN 978-0-7642-0831-7 (pbk.)
    1. Upper class—Fiction. 2. Preparatory schools—Fiction. 3. Teenage girls—Fiction. 4. Atlanta (Ga.)—Fiction. 4. Georgia—History—20th century—Fiction.
I. Title.
    PS3563.U839S94   2011
    813'.54—dc22

                                                                    2011008204

This story is dedicated to four amazing women:

Valerie Ravan Andrews
Margaret Coggins DeBorde
Kim Levy Huhman
and
Laura Hendrix McDaniel

We've laughed and cried together through
grade school, high school, college, and adult life;
we've shared secrets and dreams with each other;
you've challenged me, inspired me,
prayed for me, believed in me, and loved me.
Friendship doesn't get any sweeter than that.

Merci! I love you all.

Perri

I met Dobbs on the day my world fell apart. It was 1933 and most everyone else's world in the good ol' United States of America had fallen apart years ago. But I had survived virtually unscathed for four years. The Depression, as far as I could tell, had hardly invaded my niche of paradise.

And then it came to a screeching halt, along with Herbert Hoover— on the last day of his presidency. The banks died, and so did my world.

It didn't start off as a terrible day. In fact, it felt as if there was electricity in the air. I slept in late that Saturday—I had gone to a fraternity party over at Georgia Tech the night before, and I was worn out. Mamma woke me at ten, as I'd asked, and after gobbling down my grits and eggs, I joined my whole family in the dining room, where our radio sat perched on the buffet.

The announcers were in a ruckus of excitement, describing the scene there in Washington, D.C. "There are crowds and crowds here stretching across ten acres of lawn and pavement, all awaiting the president-elect. . . ."

Mamma and Daddy and my younger siblings, Barbara and Irvin, and I scooted as close as we could to the radio. Jimmy and Dellareen, our servants, were there, too, with their five children. Mamma had invited them over on that Saturday—they usually only worked for us on the weekdays—to hear Mr. Roosevelt being sworn in.

It was as if America were holding her breath, waiting to see if maybe this new president could save us from ourselves. I felt a nervous anticipation and Mamma kept her society smile plastered on her face, but Daddy did not try to hide his dark mood. That very morning, March 4, 1933, every last bank in America had closed its doors, and Daddy was a banker. The country was afraid—or maybe *terrified* was a better word.

As we waited for the speech to begin, Mamma went over to Daddy and pecked him on the cheek. "Holden, I believe Mr. Roosevelt is going to get us back on track."

"It's too late, Dot" was Daddy's reply.

Typical, I thought, irritated that he might spoil the drama of the moment. I guess Daddy had every reason to be pessimistic. As one of the heads at Georgia Trust Bank, he looked at the economic situation with little hope for a miracle cure—no more reliable than the fancy elixirs that Jacobs' Drugstore proposed at the soda fountain.

"He's simply a charmer, that Mr. Roosevelt," Daddy said to Mamma. "He's never said one practical thing about how he is going to change things. His speeches are optimistic rhetoric with a little humor mixed in. No one knows the man."

Mamma patted Daddy's hand and gave a little shrug. We could hear music in the background, and every once in a while the announcer cut away to a commercial about Coca-Cola or Sears and Roebuck Company or Haverty's Furniture. Finally it was time for the new president to speak. Dellareen hushed up two of her little boys who were squabbling on the floor. I sat on the dining room table, my feet propped in Irvin's lap, and no one told me to get down.

I think we were all praying for a miracle. Everybody in the United States needed a miracle. Bankers and servants and everybody in between. Republicans and Democrats, old people and young. Personally I was happy to see Herbert Hoover leave office. I'd had enough of "Hoovervilles" and a hundred other things we had mocked the poor president for. The thought of change excited me.

Mr. Roosevelt's voice crackled across the radio lines, and we all leaned forward a little more.

. . . This great nation will endure as it has endured, will revive and will prosper. So, first of all, let me assert my firm belief that the only thing we have to fear is fear itself—nameless, unreasoning, unjustified terror which paralyzes needed efforts to convert retreat into advance. . . .

We all listened, enraptured—except perhaps for Daddy—by the voice of Mr. Roosevelt, his paternal tone reassuring, confident, pronouncing words I thought could produce miracles.

"And he embodied that strength and optimism by pulling himself out of the wheelchair and making his shriveled-up legs walk across the stage to the podium," the announcer ranted after the speech ended.

I hoped that the new president's speech had buoyed dear Daddy's spirits. I had watched his mood grow more and more morose over recent months. My father often confided in me—things about his business, which I found fascinating. But lately he'd spent a lot of time alone in his study, and the night before I had overheard him arguing with Mamma about the banks closing.

Mamma had a positive outlook on life, which helped soothe my brooding father. His moods were as dark as his hair—hair that was black without a trace of gray. I thought it odd that my father, so often melancholic, looked young and vital, while Mamma had rings under her pretty green eyes, and her dark blond hair needed dyeing every other month, an extravagance that we had never thought extravagant until Daddy had come home the month before angry and forbidden poor Mamma to go to the beauty parlor.

Mamma was resourceful and figured out a way to get her hair cut and dyed on her own—Dellareen knew lots about fixing white ladies' hair. I'd watched Dellareen preparing her concoction and hoped to heavens it worked, so my Atlanta friends wouldn't think that the Singleton family had fallen on hard times.

That Saturday in early March, Mr. Roosevelt had soothed the nation with his words, and I actually felt hopeful. I had friends, parties to attend, and dates galore, and now the new president was somehow going to fix the nation's economy. And the banks. Oh, please, the banks, especially Daddy's.

"Perri, I'd really like for you to go with me to the train station in a little while," Mamma said after lunch. Irvin had scooted out to play baseball with friends at the park, Barbara was over at her friend Lulu's house, and Daddy had retired to his study.

I wanted to walk down the street to see my friend Mae Pearl and ask her what she thought of Roosevelt's speech. I made a face. "Aw, Mom. Why?"

"Josephine Chandler is going to pick up her niece who's arriving from Chicago. She'll be staying at the Chandlers' for the rest of the year and is going to attend Washington Seminary."

"Starting school now—in *March*?"

"I think her family's come on hard times, and Mrs. Chandler has offered for the girl to live with her and get an education."

Everyone has fallen on hard times, I thought, a little frustrated with Mamma for ruining my afternoon plans. But this girl was lucky. The Chandlers lived in the biggest house in the neighborhood and had parties almost every week in the summer, and loads of girls I knew would have given up iced tea in August to spend time in the Chandler home.

"Holden, we're gonna take the Buick to the Chandlers'," Mamma called back to Daddy. He must have grunted his approval because the next thing I knew we were driving down Wesley Road toward Peachtree in Daddy's two-door Buick Victory Coupe. Daddy was so proud of that car that he hardly ever let Mamma drive.

He's in a good mood on account of Mr. Roosevelt, I thought.

Mamma, always a little nervous behind the wheel, made me nervous, too, but I tried not to show it. Mrs. Chandler was waiting for us, her driver ready to take us in the Pierce Arrow convertible to the train station. Oh, it was an elegant car! She climbed in the front passenger seat, and Mamma and I huddled together in the back as the breeze of early spring tousled our hair, lifting and twirling it like new leaves on a dogwood tree.

"Her name is Mary Dobbs Dillard. She's sixteen or seventeen and will be in your class at school, Perri." Mrs. Chandler turned in her seat to speak to us, and her perfectly coiffed hair blew slightly in the wind. "I hadn't seen her in years, and then I went up to Chicago last fall and found her there with my brother and his wife and their other children in a very difficult situation. I insisted she come down here. She's quite intelligent and deserves a good education.

"My brother, Billy, bless his soul, he means well. All kinds of benevolent ideas to help others, but it seemed to me like his family was starving while he handed out his charity. I wanted the two younger sisters to come as well, but Billy's wife, Ginnie, said they were too young to live away from home."

I pictured Mrs. Chandler's niece in my mind—skinny, hollow-eyed, meek, hungry—and imagined that Mrs. Chandler's brother looked something like the subject of the masterful photograph by Dorothea Lange—my heroine in those years—called "White Angel Breadline." It showed a group of beat-up men, old-looking but probably not old, waiting in a breadline, and it focused on one man, facing the camera, a worn hat on his head and a tin cup cradled in his arms. He was leaning on a fence, and he looked completely destitute.

We pulled up to the elegant Terminal Station, with its arches and tall towers, and Mrs. Chandler, Mamma, and I hurried into the station and found the track where the destitute girl of my imagination was scheduled to arrive. A few minutes later, in a mist of steam and fog, Mary Dobbs Dillard stepped off the train, and I gasped.

My first sight of her was spellbinding. Mary Dobbs was the most gorgeous girl I had ever laid eyes on, but in a strange, unorthodox way. She had softly tanned skin—not at all the perfect pale that we considered stylish—and thick, wavy black hair that she wore loose to her waist. Her eyes were black—truly, big black oval onyx stones—and her face was a perfect oval too, with high cheekbones and skin that had never known a blemish, I was certain. She was small-boned and not particularly tall, but she looked strong, a determined kind of strong.

She wore a faded dark blue cotton dress that hung all wrong on her thin, thin frame.

Maybe her family had fallen on hard times, but she did not look meek. She stood straight up, shoulders back, and had an expression of wonder on her lovely face.

"Hello, Mary Dobbs," Mrs. Chandler said, giving her niece a friendly pat on the back.

Mary Dobbs set down a small suitcase, off-white, scuffed, and well used, to say the least, and threw her arms around Mrs. Chandler and hugged her tightly. "It is so, so good to be here, Aunt Josie!"

Wearing a startled expression, Mrs. Chandler politely undid herself from Mary Dobbs's embrace and said, "I'm so glad you made it safely." Then she turned to Mamma and me and said, "Mary Dobbs, I want you to meet dear friends of mine, Mrs. Singleton and her daughter Perri."

Mary Dobbs surveyed us, gave a warm smile that showed a perfect row of teeth, and reached out and took my hand, shaking it up and down forcefully. "Nice to meet you," she said, and added in a whisper to me, "I've dropped *Mary*. I just go by *Dobbs* now."

Our eyes met, briefly, and I felt my face go red.

"Well, Mary Dobbs," Mrs. Chandler said, "I'll get my chauffeur to retrieve your bags."

She motioned to the driver, but before he could start up the steps to the train, Dobbs shook her head, pointed to the worn suitcase, and said, "This is all I have."

Again Mrs. Chandler seemed surprised, but she recovered quickly and said, "Well, if this is all, then I suppose we can be going." The driver picked up the suitcase and headed out of the train station, with us following.

On the way home, I sat in the back seat with Mamma on one side and Dobbs on the other. I watched, fascinated, as Dobbs's long black mane flew out behind her like a flag in the May Day Parade. I didn't know another girl with long hair.

Mamma gave me a little nudge in the side, which meant, *Say something, Perri!* So I asked, "Have you ever been to Atlanta?"

"Once or twice, a long time ago. I don't remember much, but my father has described parts of Atlanta to me."

"He's from here?"

Dobbs looked at me with suspicion. "Well, yes. My father is Mrs. Chandler's brother. He grew up in the house she lives in now."

My face heated. *Of course. What a stupid question!*

I wanted to tell her she was amazingly lucky to be living in that huge house, but that would not have been polite. For whatever other faults I had, I did know I must be polite, especially with Mamma sitting in the seat beside me. I also wanted to ask Dobbs about her life in Chicago, but considering what Mrs. Chandler had said about their situation, I didn't think that would be polite either.

So we sat in silence.

Mamma turned to me and tried to make conversation. "Perri dear, why don't you tell Mary Dobbs a little about your school, the girls in your class? I'm sure she's eager to hear about it."

I scowled a little. She didn't seem eager; she seemed *overeager*, her eyes wide with enthusiasm, and that annoyed me. "Washington Seminary is the name of the school. I guess you know that—"

Dobbs cut in, "Oh yes! Washington Seminary—and it's not a seminary at all. It's 'an efficient and beautiful school for girls'—something like that. There are thirty experienced teachers and four courses leading to graduation, and you have a French club and a Spanish club and all kinds of sports—basketball and field hockey and a swim team—and May Day festivities . . ."

I stared at her with my mouth open. She sounded like an advertisement for the school as she spoke with an accent that was certainly not Southern.

She gave me a warm smile and said, "Aunt Josie sent me last year's yearbook. I've read it through. *Facts and Fancies*."

"Oh. Well then, I guess you know everything there is to know. Nothing much I can add."

Mamma glanced at me with disapproval in her eyes, and I shrugged.

"No, I don't know everything," Dobbs said sweetly. "Of course not. Tell me something about yourself."

I did not want to talk to this effervescent girl, but Mother nudged me in the ribs. I rolled my eyes. "I'm seventeen, in the junior class—there are thirty-two of us—I write for *Facts and Fancies,* and I'm a photographer. I head up the Red Cross Club, I'm vice-president of the junior class, and I'm in the Phi Pi sorority. I love parties and my circle of friends attends two or three a week. Dances, you know, and all the swell boys are there from the boys' high school, which has the most boring name in the world—Boys High—and from the colleges in Atlanta—Georgia Tech and Emory and Oglethorpe. And several girls in my class are pinned.

"After school we go to Jacobs' Drugstore and order Coca-Cola or something else from the soda fountain. I love to ride horses. Fox hunting is my favorite. Let's just say I'm rarely bored."

Dobbs stared at me the whole time with a tiny smile spreading across her lips. She cocked her head and just kept staring—jet black eyes looking straight through me—and said, "Well, thank you for that monologue, Perri Singleton. But I'm sure there's a lot more to you than that. It will be nice to get to know who you *really* are."

I glared at her, stuck my nose in the air, and turned to Mamma, who always said that when I was mad, lightning bolts flashed from my eyes, "seeking someone to sizzle."

Dobbs did not seem to notice but leaned forward and said, "Aunt Josie, wasn't Mr. Roosevelt's speech fabulous! *We have nothing to fear but fear itself!* He's going to bring this country around! I just know it! The way he said we have enough, but that we just haven't been using our resources the right way, is the plain truth!"

Dobbs sat beside me in her rags and talked on and on about the "religious tone of Mr. Roosevelt's address" and how he put words to the feelings of the American people. Mrs. Chandler nodded politely but looked as if she were more worried about getting a crick in her neck as she twisted around in her seat to look at Dobbs.

She's just trying to impress Mrs. Chandler, I thought.

I finally shot Dobbs my lightning-bolt look, and she smiled back at me, completely unfazed. "What did you think of the speech, Perri?" When I didn't respond, even after Mamma elbowed me twice, the three of us sat in silence again.

Thank heavens we arrived at the Chandler place a few minutes later. I mumbled, "Nice to have met you," and Dobbs said, "Likewise. See you on Monday at school."

"What a strange person," I said to Mamma as she drove the Buick toward home and turned onto our street. "She's a bit dramatic, wouldn't you say? Babbling on and on about the new president as if she knows it all, in her potato-sack dress and pitiful suitcase. I'm glad we wear uniforms at Washington Seminary. At least the girls won't have to see her wardrobe. Yet."

"*Shh* now, Perri. Yes, she is a bit different, but I think she's simply very excited to be here, considering where she came from. She'll fit in fine, I'm sure. Please try to introduce her to a few girls on Monday. And don't judge her too soon."

Sweet Mamma, she always gave people the benefit of the doubt.

Dobbs to me spelled trouble.

We got back home, and Mamma parked the car in the driveway. "Holden, dear. Holden," she called out lightly once we were in the entrance hall. "I made it just fine in the coupe. Not one bump or scratch. But I left the car in the driveway, as you like. I'll let you maneuver it into the garage." She chattered along, walking back to Daddy's study.

I had turned to go upstairs when Mamma uttered a tiny shriek and came into the hall with one hand over her mouth and holding a piece of Daddy's stationery in the other. "Your father . . ." she started. "We've got to find your father!"

She ran out the back door toward the garage.

I felt my heart pumping strangely in my ears, and my vision went momentarily blurry, taking in the horrible expression on Mamma's face. Then I followed her out the door and took off at a dash in the opposite direction from Mamma—across the back lawn to the stables where Daddy kept his horses. Riding and fox hunting were his favorite hobbies, and I imagined he had gone on a trail ride. I flung open the door to the stable. The long hallway was empty, save a few strands of hay probably dropped by the stableboy from the morning feeding. The horses, all five of them, were pacing nervously back and forth in their stalls, nickering.

"What is it, fella?" I asked, as I ran my hand along the forehead of Windchaser, Daddy's favorite. Then I caught sight of something out of the corner of my eye. I turned and went into the tack room, and there I saw it—Daddy's tasseled leather dress shoe turned on its side where it had fallen amidst a few strands of hay and shavings. I looked up to see . . .

Daddy's lifeless body was swinging from the rafters, a lead shank around his neck, his long legs in their dark gray business slacks, moving almost imperceptibly, one foot hanging shoeless. The guttural scream that issued from inside me seemed to go on forever.

Then I fainted.

That was where they found me, Jimmy and Dellareen and Ben, their oldest son. Ben splashed water on my face, and as I came to, I looked to the side and saw tall, thin Dellareen running out of the stable gate to where Mamma was approaching, grabbing Mamma around the waist, and pulling her away from the stable door. Mamma fought with her, but Dellareen's strong dark arms engulfed Mamma, dragging her away while Mamma's stricken face looked at me and screamed, "Holden, Holden, Holden."

I remember the fierce determination on Dellareen's face, and I remember her words too. "You ain't gonna see none of it, Miz Dorothy."

Then Jimmy, who was as thin as Dellareen and not any taller, picked me up, carried me back to the house, and laid me down on the sofa in the sitting room, and Dellareen placed a damp cloth on my head.

I guess Jimmy and Ben got Daddy down.

The afternoon became a blur of people parading in and out of the house. I was thankful that Barbara and Irvin were still gone. I sat petrified—like a piece of old wood—on the sofa, watching people in a type of fog. Mrs. Chandler and her servant showed up first, then Daddy's business partner from the bank. Later his good friend and accountant, Mr. Robinson, stopped by, and Mr. Chandler came off the golf course, dressed in his plaid knickers and polo shirt. Little by little the house filled up with people, and the stench of body odor—all of ours, all of our grief let out from the pores of our body—permeated the downstairs.

Evidently, after some discussion, Mrs. Chandler called Lulu's house, where Barbara was playing, and the coach of Irvin's baseball team, and asked if the children could stay over until after dinner.

After a while, Mrs. Chandler took Mamma upstairs, and at one point, I heard Mamma wailing, "Poor Perri! And how am I going to tell Barbara and Irvin?"

I was still sitting on that sofa, arms wrapped around myself and just plain numb, but when I heard Mamma's stricken voice, I said to Dellareen, "I'll tell them."

She looked at me, startled, and shook her head. "No. No, Miz Perri. It ain't yore place."

"I want to. I *need* to. Mamma can't do it. You know that." I still had not shed a tear, but my face was burning with the fever of tragedy, and I could feel the red splotches on my cheeks.

Dellareen squeezed my hand, her brow wrinkled with worry, her face shiny with perspiration, her servant's uniform, usually impeccable, soaked under the arms with her sweat. She took my face in her calloused hands and looked me straight in the eyes.

Dellareen had known me from the time I was "knee high to a grasshopper," as she always put it, and that day she read my mind. "It ain't your responsibility, Miz Perri. You understand that? I know you loved your papa and he loved you, and he wouldn't want you carryin' this on yore shoulders."

The tears came readily, and I let Dellareen pull me into her arms while I cried. Finally, I whispered through the ball in my throat, "I wanna see Mamma."

I found her propped up in her bed with Mrs. Chandler beside her. Mamma's pretty powdered face was smudged with mascara as she wept softly. She reached out to me. "Perri, Perri." Then she whispered to Mrs. Chandler, "Perri's the one who found . . . who found . . ."

I squeezed Mamma's hand, and Mamma pulled me into her arms. I stood there leaning down over Mamma for a few seconds, feeling her tiny arms around me, the weight of her body, so frail, holding on to me, it seemed, for life. I held her tight, and from somewhere outside of myself, I pronounced the words, "It's gonna be okay, Mamma. Somehow it's gonna be okay."

But in my mind, I was thinking, *Nothing will ever be okay again unless I make it okay. It's up to me now.*

CHAPTER
2

Dobbs

Some things I just know. For sure. Don't ask me how. I just know them. And from the moment that Mother (and eventually Father) insisted I leave for Atlanta—Atlanta! A southern town!—I knew that my life had just bifurcated in a way that would have repercussions for my whole family.

At first I resisted, of course. I like to do things *my* way. "Aunt Josie means well," I told my parents. "Certainly, there are benefits to a good education. Certainly, it can be a wise investment for the long term. But what about you? How can I leave both of you and Coobie and Frances up here in Chicago, wondering where the next meal will come from, while I gallivant around in Atlanta?"

Father pronounced the words that always convinced me. "It is for the larger cause, Dobbs. You need this."

A larger cause! I loved causes, and especially the one Father referred to: propagation of the Word of God. So off I went on the train to Atlanta with one measly suitcase in my hand and my head swimming with ideas of adventure, possibilities, a whole new world to conquer! I was bursting with excitement inside over Mr. Roosevelt's inauguration. I'd listened to his speech on the radio when I'd changed trains that morning—in fact the conductor had postponed our leaving so that everyone could hear it. So on the last leg of my two-day trip down to Atlanta, I kept thinking, *Franklin D. Roosevelt is God's man for such a time as this. He will help pull America out of this mess!*

Father always said we were in this mess—otherwise known as the Depression—because of man's greed and God's judgment and a whole bunch of other things mixed together. He was probably right, but with Roosevelt in office, America could mend her evil ways and start over again!

So I stepped off the train with a big smile on my face, anticipating a new beginning for me and for America. Aunt Josie and her chauffeur met me at the station along with Mrs. Singleton and her daughter Perri.

The first thing I felt was a stare of disapproval. Aunt Josie's eyes said it first and then Mrs. Singleton's and Perri's too. Astonishment. Then pity. They recovered quickly, and we rode home in one of the fanciest cars I'd ever seen. Aunt Josie sat up front with her chauffeur— his name was Hosea—and I was in the back with Mrs. Singleton and Perri. I started rattling on, as I always do, to Aunt Josie, and she politely listened. I talked a lot, but I could tell pretty quickly what someone else was thinking, and Perri Singleton's face told me that she didn't like me one bit. Yet.

Hosea turned the car into a long private drive, framed on either side with stone posts, which would have fit nicely in a Roman piazza, I imagined. Father had tried to prepare me for the Chandlers' home, describing it to me and even showing me an old photo, but as Hosea drove around the bend, I stared, my mouth almost hanging open, at a sprawling—and imposing—white stucco house, something fit for English nobility.

Hosea pulled the car under a covered driveway to the right of the house. My aunt called this the "porte cochere," which I later realized was French, except she pronounced it in long, drawn-out syllables— po-wart co-share, which meant absolutely nothing to me.

When we stopped, Perri almost jumped out of the car. Perhaps she thought I had lice or some other terrible ailment that came with poverty, but she got in their car with her mother, and they drove away without a glance back at me.

I got out of the Pierce Arrow and followed Aunt Josie as she walked me in a circular tour around the property. Acres and acres of open land surrounded the house. To the left of the mansion were the garages for cars, and off behind the garages, a stable that Aunt Josie said was filled with horses as well as a cow and a pig, and farther out, in the fields behind, beautiful vegetable gardens, and the servants' quarters off to the left of the stables.

Then she shaded her eyes with her hand, squinted, pointed, and said, "Down the hill to the right by the little lake is the summerhouse. It's such a lovely spot. The orchestra plays there when we have lawn parties."

She said this without a hint of pretension, so I nodded as if I were used to staying at a mansion with property that spilled out everywhere and attending parties with a live orchestra playing.

I had arrived in Atlanta at the pinnacle of spring. The dogwoods and azaleas were beginning to declare the joy of rebirth, the air was mild, the daffodils were swinging their happy yellow heads back and forth, the sky was a soft pastel blue, and the scent of hyacinths tickled my nose. I twirled around with my hands outstretched and soaked it in. Fresh air and rebirth! I twirled around one more time. Aunt Josie's face once again wore a regard of disapproval, so I stopped and followed her back to the porte cochere, and we walked inside.

The best word for Aunt Josie was buxom. Or well-endowed. Or sturdy. She had the same Dillard nose as Father, straight and pointed down, and eyes like Father's too—dark brown—but they weren't nearly as flashing and passionate as his. Her hair was a pretty cherry-brown color, like Father's had been before he lost half of his and the rest turned gray.

Overall, Aunt Josie was a large, striking woman, dressed in tailored silk and pearls. She seemed to me the kind of woman you'd like to have around if you were inviting a hundred people to your house for a fancy affair, but not so much the person you'd want to confide in about a boy. Which I did. I was fairly exploding to tell someone about Hank. But I kept my mouth shut.

I'd seen Aunt Josie for the first time in years when she'd come to Chicago to visit us—her baby brother and his family—back in October.

It turned into a disastrous visit, to say the least. She saw where we lived, that there was no food in the icebox, and the state of our clothes, and she was livid at Father.

"You're preaching to others and not taking care of your own family. Haven't you read the Scriptures? Saint Paul calls you an infidel!"

Father was all torn up about her saying that, but Mother stuck by him and said that they weren't called to speak to the people who had means, but to those who had nothing, and he wasn't going to pass around the offering plate to people fallen on such bad times. God would provide.

The day after Aunt Josie left for Atlanta, a man came to the apartment and handed Father an envelope with twenty dollars in it. We whooped and hollered. Just like every time, God had provided for us; money came out of nowhere. And besides that, before she returned to Atlanta, Aunt Josie left a bag of clothes for Coobie and Frances and me, and she bought us enough groceries for two whole weeks. I wondered if she realized that God was providing through her too.

The front hall in my aunt's mansion was paneled from floor to ceiling in some kind of dark, gleaming wood, and the ceiling was sculpted like something I'd seen in a history book of the European Renaissance, and there was an enormous stone mantelpiece above the fireplace. I wanted to stop and take it all in, but Aunt Josie had already turned to the right and started upstairs. The staircase was split in two sides that wound around above the porte-cochere entrance, and the dark walls leading to the second floor were decorated with big oil paintings of what must have been family members. Most were portraits of somber-looking people, but I recognized one of Father as a child with a little dog in his lap.

"Well, here's your bedroom, Mary Dobbs. I hope you'll find everything to your liking. You've got the bathroom right there to yourself, and there are fresh towels and sheets in the linen closet. Parthenia, the servant girl, changes everything twice a week. You can put your clothes away in the chest of drawers and the closet. I've put a few other things in the closet that you might need.

"The upstairs telephone is in my room. If you need to make a call, just tell me. Your uncle Robert doesn't like us to call long-distance very often, but I'm sure your parents want to hear you've arrived safely." She ruffled her nose, frowned slightly, and said, "Your parents don't have a telephone, do they?"

"No, that's correct."

"We'll send a telegram."

At that moment, the telephone actually began to ring. "Let me go get it," Aunt Josie said and hurried down the hall.

Walking into my new room, I surmised that God had very generously provided again. The bedroom seemed almost as big as our whole apartment in Chicago. Large-paned windows overlooked the property out back. I could see the stables and the servants' quarters, and if I opened the window and stood on my tiptoes and leaned out as far as I could—which, of course, I did—I could see the summerhouse down the hill perched beside the little lake. I closed the window, twirled around again, laughed, let myself fall backward on the big bed with its fluffy comforter, and stared up at the white-laced canopy overhead.

Then I deflated, thinking about Mother and Father with my little sisters, Coobie and Frances, huddled together in that small apartment. Mother had cooked the last of the chicken three days ago, and before they took me to the train station, we'd picked every scrap of meat off the bones and boiled the bones to make broth. I imagined them hungry, and it made me want to go right back to Terminal Station and catch the next train to Chicago.

Suddenly Aunt Josie hurried back into the hall, calling down the stairs, "Hosea! Hosea! Come quickly. Yes, yes. There's a problem. A big problem." Almost as an afterthought, she stopped by my doorway. Her round face was pasty white. "I have to leave. There's been, there's been a terrible . . ." She didn't finish the sentence, and I heard her pumps making a racket on the stairs as she rushed down them.

I sat there bewildered. My practical, competent aunt had looked as if she had just been clobbered over the head and was seeing stars.

I waited to hear the news of what had happened, but Aunt Josie didn't come back upstairs. After a few minutes of a general state of commotion, with Aunt Josie calling out to Hosea and someone else, the front door slammed. I heard the roaring of a car engine, and then the house fell silent.

I tried my hardest to imagine what could possibly have happened to fluster my aunt to such an extent. Had Uncle Robert had another heart attack? Originally, I was supposed to come to Atlanta in early January, to start the new term at Washington Seminary, but on the day after Christmas, Uncle Robert had keeled over in front of the Christmas tree. Massive heart attack. It had taken him two months to recover, and hence my arrival in March.

Something downright horrible had happened, but there was no use in my trying to figure it out, so I turned my thoughts to Hank. Hank! Working in the steel factory, hurrying to night classes, preaching at the little church with Father. I wondered if he really meant it—that he would wait for me. Surely he did. Some things I just knew were supposed to be.

I had wanted to tell Mother and Father about Hank. I felt sure they had noticed something, and then I wasn't at all sure.

Coobie, my bratty little sister, noticed though. She whispered to me before I got on the train, "Has he ever kissed you?"

My face turned red, and my expression must have given me away, because she clapped her hands together and squealed, as only Coobie can, "I knew it!"

I closed my eyes and remembered our first meeting. I saw Hank standing in the alleyway behind our apartment, dressed in a white cotton T-shirt and overalls and a smile. That first time he smiled at me, I started coughing. I couldn't stop staring at his eyes, periwinkle blue, as if the brightest cloudless sky had floated down and drifted into them, filling them with life and laughter; and his hair, a blondish brown, was straight and needed a trim, but the bangs falling over his eyebrows made him all the more delectable.

"Hello, my name is Hank Wilson," he said. "I'm looking for Reverend William Dillard." He smiled again and then looked down at a piece of paper he was holding in his hand.

I giggled nervously, recovered, and said, "You're at the right spot. Come on in, and I'll take you up to meet him." I motioned for him to follow and then added, "By the way, I'm his daughter, Mary Dobbs."

"Nice to meet you, Mary Dobbs."

We walked into the apartment building and climbed the steps to the second floor, and right before I opened the door to our apartment, I turned to him and said, "Everyone calls my father Reverend Billy."

At that first encounter, eighteen months earlier, when I had barely turned sixteen and he was already twenty, I had wanted to say, "I'm gonna marry you." But I refrained. I could keep my mouth shut when needed.

"Henry 'Hank' Wilson," I said out loud to the empty Chandler house. He had promised he would write as soon as I left, and I wondered how long it took a letter to get from Chicago to Atlanta.

After I unpacked my little suitcase—all of my clothes fit into two drawers in the chest—I opened the closet. Hanging inside were three school uniforms and two other dresses—pretty, feminine dresses, the kind I had never even dreamed of owning. Had Aunt Josie bought these for *me*? I giggled, touching one of them, feeling the cool, fancy fabric. The lovely slim day dress with a tailored bodice was bright pink with tiny white flowers and had an oversized belt, a white ruffled collar, and cuffed sleeves! The absolute newest fashion.

I took it off the hanger, quickly undressed, and slipped it over my head. It fit perfectly. I buckled the belt and stared at myself in the full-length mirror on the other side of the bed. I was glowing! I looked like a woman, with curves in all the right places. I wished Hank could see me in this dress! The price tag was still on it, and as I glanced down, my eyes grew wide. My family could eat for two months on what the dress had cost.

I wanted to waltz from room to room, barefoot, in the elegant day dress, but I feared that someone might find me strutting around like a movie star. Embarrassed, I changed back into my humble attire, caught a glimpse of myself in the mirror and realized just why the Singletons and Aunt Josie had regarded me with pity. The plain dark blue dress, stained and faded, did look pitiful. Mother had wanted me to wear the pale green suit she wore at Father's revival meetings, but I had refused to take that from her.

"You can be so stubborn sometimes, young lady! Aunt Josie will faint when she sees you in that old thing," Mother said, but I didn't change my mind. Turned out Mother was just about right.

I ventured across a very wide hall with numerous doors opening into different rooms. The walls were papered in beautiful floral colors, and gold sconces hung on either side of a small table at the top of the stairway. Another portrait, this one I recognized as Grandma Dillard, hung above the table. On the table lay a beautiful oversized book called *Birds of America* by John James Audubon. I started turning pages, enraptured by the gorgeous paintings of birds.

Later, I peeked in my aunt and uncle's bedroom—even bigger than mine—and went immediately to the vanity chest with the little mirror above. Silver-framed family portraits sat neatly on the vanity along with my aunt's silver comb-and-brush set. I peered down at one photograph. Sure enough, it showed Father sitting in Aunt Josie's lap when he was a baby. I felt a gentle relief that although Aunt Josie disapproved of Father's vocation, she nonetheless had enough affection for her little brother to keep this picture in her bedroom.

Going downstairs, I stepped into the fancy hall with its dark wood walls. Off to the right of the hall was a room with high ceilings and a grand piano, another fireplace, and more fancy furniture—winged chairs and sofas the likes of which I had only read about in novels and seen in magazines that my school friends passed on to me.

I wandered from room to room, each elegant in its own way, until I arrived in the kitchen at the back of the house. What a kitchen! The white Frigidaire stood almost as tall as me, the oven looked big enough to bake five chickens at once, and the sink was made of porcelain! No one was there, although evidence of dinner preparations lay along the shiny dark green counter.

I was leaning over to see what was in the sink when I heard, "Hello. I guess you'd be Miz Chandler's niece."

I turned around to see a colored child staring at me. She was about eight or nine, her hair all in braids that were attached with bright little ribbons, and she was wearing a blue servant's dress with a white pinafore over it.

"Hello. Yes. I'm Mary Dobbs Dillard."

"Uh-huh. I'm Parthenia Jeffries. My mama and papa work here for the Chandlers. We live down there in the quarters." She threw a skinny arm out toward the backyard.

"Nice to meet you, Parthenia." Then, "Where is everybody?"

"Ain't ya heard?"

"All I know is that my aunt received a phone call and got very upset and left the house. And it seems like everyone else did too."

"Mr. Singleton passed."

"What?"

"Yep. He's done passed, and Miz Chandler went over ta help and Papa and my brother, Cornelius, went too and I was told ta stay here, so I did."

It slowly registered. "Do you mean that Mr. Singleton *died*?"

"Yep."

"Would that be the Singletons who have a daughter named Perri?"

"Yes, ma'am, and Miz Singleton is Miz Chandler's best friend. A tragedy." She stared at me when I didn't say anything. "I'd best be gittin' dinner ready now." She went to the counter where carrots and potatoes lay and then opened the Frigidaire and took out a hunk of meat.

I stood there, shocked, thinking about Perri Singleton with her pretty see-through green eyes and her blond hair, cut in the latest bobbed style, and the way she had disliked me right away, and I hurt for her. Right then and there I started crying for a girl I had only just met.

I started to leave the kitchen, but Parthenia said, "You don't have ta go. I'm not embarrassed by you crying. I just stopped crying myself." She handed me a white handkerchief that she retrieved from a frilly pocket on her pinafore. "Mr. Singleton was the handsomest, nicest man you'd ever want to meet. He always brought me cherry candy when him and Miz Singleton came over to play bridge." Parthenia sniffed loudly, as if to prove she had been crying.

"Was he sick?"

Parthenia's eyes flew open wide, the whites showing around her dark face. "No, he wasn't sick. The picture of health. Miz Singleton's the one who's all scrawny. But Mista Singleton wadn't sick at all, s'far as I know." She hesitated. " 'Cept for mebbe in his head."

I didn't know what to do with that information, so I asked, "Can I help you with anything?" She stared at me as if I were standing naked in front of her, then went back to peeling carrots. "I can do something. I know how to cook."

"Ain't proper for guests to help with the meals. We's hired help."

"Oh. But no one's around to see me helping."

Looking almost fearful, she shook her head and said, "Ain't proper."

I left it at that. She concentrated on every movement as she sliced first the carrots and then the potatoes.

"How old are you, Parthenia?"

"Eight and three-quarters," she stated proudly.

"I have a little sister who is seven and two-thirds."

Parthenia looked up with big puppy-dog eyes and frowned slightly, trying to hide a smile. She failed. "What's her name?"

"Coobie."

"Coobie? I ain't neva' heard of a girl named Coobie."

I almost remarked that I had never met another Parthenia but resisted. "Her real name is Virginia Coggins Dillard, but that somehow got shortened to Coobie."

"I don't have any sisters, but I got my brother, Cornelius. He's gettin' near to fourteen, and he's a genius with his hands, but he kain't talk none. Neva' said a word in his life, he hadn't."

"Ah." Once again, I wasn't sure how to respond. "Well, I have another sister named Frances. She's thirteen going on thirty."

That made Parthenia laugh out loud. "Mama always sez I's eight going on eighteen."

Somewhere in the house a clock chimed four times. Parthenia looked startled. "Uh-oh. I'm late. I got to get the water boiling."

"Are you in charge of dinner?"

"Well, it used ta be my mama, but she's ova' at the Alms Houses for stealin'. . . . She didn't do it, though, and everybody knows it." She made a face and added under her breath, "I knowed it most of all."

"She's in jail, but she's innocent?"

Parthenia frowned and said, "Well, it's not exactly jail, but it's where the destitute live. And then they keep the colored prisoners there to work the fields. My poor mama wishes she could come back home. Every day she prays that the Good Lawd would let someone find those silver knives, and then she could leave."

"Silver knives?"

And right away, Parthenia spun her sad tale. "Mama was accused of stealin' Miz Chandler's silver knives, but she didn't do it. They was knives that specially meant a lot to Miz Chandler, from her granny and all, and they wuz worth thousands and thousands of dollars, and one night after a big party, they went missing. We looked all ova' everywhere for them, with no such luck.

"And then Miz Becca, she prances in all high and fancy and starts accusing Mama, saying she stole 'em."

"Becca—my cousin? The Chandlers' daughter?"

"Yep, she's the oldest one, and I don't care for her a bit."

"Ah."

"We searched high and low and o' course we let them come into the servants' quarters and look and look, and they neva' found none of those silver knives, but they found the silver serving spoon that went missing too, and so Mama had to go to the Alms Houses anyway on account of a white lady accusing her and then the evidence they found."

"That's horrible!"

"Sho' is! And the way my mama done he'p raise Miz Becca from the time she was born an' all." Parthenia shook her head and, scowling, said, "Jus' goes to show you kain't trust nobody."

"How long has she been there?"

"She's bin there almost one whole month. Those things went missing after the big Valentine's party the Chandlers had."

"How much longer does she have to stay?"

"'Til we kin earn enough money to pay for the five knives, but ain't neva' gonna be able to do that 'cuz, like I said, they's worth a whole bundle of money. So me an' Cornelius'll always be workin' and neva' be able to go ta school no more. And it ain't Mama who did it."

"You know who stole those knives,, Parthenia?"

Her face went blank, and then she looked fearful as she backed away from me.

"I don't know nuthin', nuthin' at all, Miz Mary Dobbs. I promise I don't know nuthin'." She turned her back and said, "I gots ta get this dinner made."

I didn't ask any more questions, but as I stood beside the big iron stove, I wondered at the story I'd just heard, and I wanted to help Parthenia and her family. I had no idea how I could help, but maybe God did.

With her back to me, Parthenia said, "So Papa and me and my brother, we do the best we can. I'm a pretty fine cook, I am. Bin heppin' my mama since I was five." She grunted slightly as she leaned down and lifted a heavy pot from under the stove.

"Here, let me help you." I filled the pot with water from the faucet, and then Parthenia struck a match and got the gas eye going, and before long she had a pot roast in the oven and vegetables cooking on the stove. The aroma of good food cooking in the kitchen wrapped around me, and I relished it for a moment, almost tasting it. The Chandlers' kitchen represented bounty to me.

When six o'clock came and still no one arrived home, Parthenia asked, "Do ya wanna see the stables?"

I shrugged. "Why not?"

We went out the back door, passed the garage—big enough for five cars—and walked into the stables, where we stood in the hallway looking at the horses and ponies, their fine arched necks and velvet muzzles sticking out over the wooden half doors to the stalls. Parthenia patted one. "This here's Red. He's my favorite."

"Do you ride him?"

Again that shocked look, the whites of her eyes lighting up her face like two big exclamation points. "No! But sometimes I he'p Cornelius feed 'em." As we walked through the stables, the smell of fresh hay and oats greeted me. "And ova' there is the pig and the chickens and the cow."

We had just left the barn and were halfway down the hill to the lake when we heard a car engine rumbling in the driveway. "Uh-oh. We's gotta git back to the main house, quick!" Parthenia took off at a gallop with me following behind. We rushed in the back door, letting the screen door slam shut, and hurried into the kitchen, out of breath.

A few minutes later, the man who had driven us home from the train station came into the kitchen. He nodded to me and said, "Hello, Miz Mary Dobbs." He had a serious expression on his face, and he was big—not just tall, but big in every way, and every inch of him seemed to be muscle. I thought I would never want to make Hosea mad. But then he knelt down, and Parthenia ran over to her father and hugged him tight around the neck, and he didn't seem threatening at all.

"Is it really true? He's dead? And did ya haveta cut him down, Papa? Did you and Cornelius haveta do it?"

He glanced at me with a worried expression, patted Parthenia's braids, and said, "*Shh* now, little one. You be askin' too many questions, and they's not appropriate for a child. Sho' does smell good in this kitchen. Who done fixed such a delicious-smellin' meal?"

Parthenia beamed. "It's me, Papa."

He picked her up, hugged her close, and swung her around, and then he took the roast out of the oven, sliced it, and ladled meat and potatoes and carrots onto two plates for us. "We gonna take the rest of this dinner out to the car. The Singletons gonna be needin' as much food as they can git."

In five minutes he was gone.

I spent the first evening at the Chandler house picking at the pot roast and vegetables at the little kitchen table with Parthenia. I had lost my appetite.

Later that night, I lay on my bed and thought of my friend Jackie, her wavy brown hair, the naughty eyes; I could almost hear her robust laughter. And inevitably I saw the coffin in my mind's eye. Saw Mother in tears and Father standing by the grave, his round face so pasty white, unable to speak, and Jackie's mother all doubled over with grief.

The room started spinning, and I half expected the canopy above me to float down and tangle me up in its fluffy folds until I suffocated. Clutching my stomach, I sat up and waited for the dizziness to pass.

Then I closed my eyes and saw pretty Perri Singleton disapproving of me, her eyes flashing defiance—albeit a very quiet and respectable defiance—as well as a fierce kind of pride. She seemed like a girl who had determination and spunk. I wondered if she had enough to get her through this tragedy. And as I imagined her sitting somewhere in her house, tears running down her cheeks—those cheeks that had two perfect crimson spots on them when I'd embarrassed her—I just felt my heart rip in two, and I *knew* what she needed.

I went to the chest of drawers and opened the top drawer where I had put my pitiful lingerie. Underneath a pair of panties I retrieved a thin, light-blue hardback book. "*Patches from the Sky*," I read out loud, remembering when Hank had handed me that book all those months ago. Just thinking of it made my heart soar and then beat hard.

I was sitting in one of the back pews of the church, hunched over a history book and fiddling with my hair, making a tiny braid and then letting it unravel.

"Hey there, Mary Dobbs!" Hank came and sat beside me. "You doing all right today?"

I shrugged.

He stood there for a moment, then said, "You don't look so good. Something's wrong. Do you want to talk about it?"

Hank had been helping Father for two or three months, and we had struck up several conversations, but today what was bothering me was a lot deeper.

"Do you ever doubt?" I asked him.

"Doubt what?"

"Everything. The faith you were raised to believe, the purpose of being alive and human—just everything."

He sat down on the pew in front of mine and turned to face me. "Only about every other day."

His answer took me off guard. "Really? You, a Bible college student. You have doubts?"

"Sure. Sometimes."

Hank Wilson struck me as a solid young man, not flirtatious, not overly ambitious, not obnoxious. Level-headed. We sat there in the back of the church without saying another word. I don't know what was going through his mind, but I was thinking about Jackie and how she had died at the age of eighteen and how horribly much it still hurt, even a year and a half later.

Finally I whispered, "Someone I cared about died, died quickly, young, and it wasn't fair at all."

"I'm sorry to hear it." He didn't say anything else, just let me sit in the silence. He stayed with me for probably a half hour, never saying a word. Still his presence calmed me.

The next day, Hank showed up at the church. He had one hand in the pocket of his pants and held out a small book in the other. "This is for you."

"What is it?"

"Just a book I think you might like. It was my grandmother's."

As he gave me the book, our hands brushed together, and I felt a flush come to my face. I hesitated. "I can't take this."

"My grandmother told me to pass it along to someone else who needed encouragement, who was hurting down deep."

"Oh." I blushed again and turned my face down so he wouldn't see the tears that had suddenly glazed my eyes. I had told him about Jackie, and he was trying to help. "Thank you" was all I could choke out.

"She said God used that little book to help her, as part of her pathway through grief." Hank gave me a half smile. "You don't have to keep it if it doesn't help you. My grandmother gave it to me after my father died. I was having a real hard time accepting his death and was mad at everyone living and dead. Especially God."

I glanced up at him, took the book, and again said, "Thanks."

That had been months ago. Now I was absolutely sure I needed to pass the book along to Perri Singleton. It happened the same way every time. I just *knew*. Father called it the "nudging of the Holy Ghost" and Mother laughed at him and said, "It's good ol' woman's intuition."

It didn't matter. I knew.

I sank to my knees beside that bed and said the Lord's Prayer out loud and then prayed for my family and Hank and the Chandlers and the Jeffries. I finished by saying, "And please watch over the Singleton family and be very near to them in their grief."

I was about to get off my knees when I thought of something else. "Oh, and Father, thank you for Perri Singleton. I think we're going to be good friends. Amen."

Just another one of those things I knew.

CHAPTER
3

Perri

At first, I blamed Mr. Hoover for Daddy's death. I needed someone to blame, someone besides my father, to help me keep the rage and grief from strangling me. I blamed Herbert Hoover, and then I got busy with the thousands of details surrounding a funeral. Weddings are planned a year in advance. Funerals, at least Daddy's, rushed up from behind and knocked us over. And as we struggled to get back on our feet, the urgent matters kept me focused, kept me swallowing that hard ball of hate that had lodged itself in my throat.

Late in the evening on the day of Daddy's death, Ben, our servant boy, brought Barbara and Irvin home. Mamma was in the rocking chair on the screened-in porch, and my siblings and I were sitting on the wicker sofa, across from her. Barbara was swinging her skinny legs back and forth. My thirteen-year-old sister, with shining blue eyes and auburn hair all primped and curled, looked up at Mamma with disdain. "Why did I have to come home? I thought I was going to spend the night at Lulu's." Her eyes flashed impertinence.

"I know," Mamma whispered. "I know that, Barbara, but something bad has happened."

Irvin, ten and small for his age, had a big frown on his freckled face, and his arms were crossed tightly across his chest, his toes pointing down so that the tips of his baseball cleats touched the porch floor. "Yeah, I figured that," he said, "when Ben came to get us and wouldn't say a word. Just stared right ahead the whole drive home. That's not like Ben."

"What happened?" Now Barbara sounded worried.

Mamma closed her eyes briefly, and I thought she was going to break down. She lifted her hand to her eyes and dabbed them with a handkerchief. "Daddy is . . . is gone."

They stared at her, not understanding.

Mamma must have realized she had chosen the wrong words. "Your father . . . your father had an accident."

I chewed on my lip and felt the tears spring in my eyes.

"Where is he?" Barbara squealed. "What do you mean? Is he okay?"

Mamma shook her head and tears spilled down her cheeks.

Barbara stared at me, horror-stricken. "What happened? What happened to Daddy?"

I got off the sofa, knelt between Barbara and Irvin, and grabbed them both toward me as Mamma said, "I think that Daddy felt so very sad in his heart and his mind about all the pressure he was under and he didn't know what to do, and so . . ." Silence. "He took his life."

I don't remember what else was said. I remember Barbara squealing again and Irvin wiggling out of my embrace, his face such a deep shade of red I thought he had a fever, and Mamma trying to console us.

And I remember the rage inside of me. *How could you, Daddy? Why didn't you tell me?*

I think I stayed there with Mamma and Barbara and Irvin, but I wasn't really there. I was taking a walk with my father, discussing his business and stocks and money. My mind worked like my father's, and he often confided in me.

But he hadn't this time.

I pushed the thought away, but it came back, bombarding me with intensity. *It's up to me to provide for the family now.*

———

The next day blurred before me. Dellareen spent hours cooking and also organizing all the food that people brought by the house. I held on to Barbara and Irvin while they cried and then helped pack their bags. Lulu's parents asked if they could keep Barbara for two days, and Irvin stayed with his buddy Pete. That left me with Mamma and Dellareen and a mountain of decisions that Mamma was in no shape to make.

We had heard the stories of the big finance men jumping out of windows on Wall Street after the crash of '29. I'd heard from Lisa Young, whose father owned an insurance company in Atlanta, that over twenty thousand people had committed suicide in 1931—way exceeding the figures during the stock market crash.

But my father? I guessed Mamma, for all her seeming naiveté, had known of our financial troubles, perhaps even more than I had. She had tried, in her sunny, optimistic way to talk Daddy out of his morose moods, had probably begged him to talk to his doctor friends. I think she would have offered him opium if she thought it would have helped—no matter that all kinds of people were addicted to it.

But Daddy chose another way.

I stood there in our church—St. Luke's Episcopal—on Tuesday, March 7, dressed in black, tears refusing to run out of my eyes. The church was jam-packed, and for all her courage, Mamma looked completely destroyed. She kept her lips pressed together, her forehead an accordion of wrinkles, and nodded, shook hands, and thanked people. Interminably.

Everyone from Washington Seminary was there—the students, the teachers, the principal.

Girls from my class paraded up to me, not knowing what to say. After all, "I am so sorry that your father killed himself" lacked a bit of sympathy. Peggy Pender squeezed my hand with her white glove and whispered from under her black-veiled hat, "It's horrible." That was all she could get out before biting her lips and turning away. Peggy's own father had suffered a stroke two years earlier, and the doctors equated it to the stress of the financial world.

Mae Pearl McFadden grabbed me in a tight hug. "Oh, Perri! Whatever is going on in this world?" Emily Bratton—the Brat—didn't say a word, just held my hand in hers for a long time. Macon Ferguson did what she always did—she talked with her hands, turning them over and over and then up and down. I followed them as in a silent movie. I didn't hear a word she said.

At Oakland Cemetery, where we buried Daddy, people stood around in little clusters, and I heard them whispering among themselves about the bank holiday imposed by Mr. Roosevelt and the Congress. That silly title made it sound like a vacation.

We're on a bank holiday too, I thought. Never again would Daddy walk through the doors of the Georgia Trust Bank. Never again would I go meet him there after school, cross Peachtree Street at Five Points, and walk with him to Jacobs' Drugstore, where he'd buy me a Coke.

At the graveside, Mrs. Chandler came up to Mamma and hugged her tight. I was surprised to see Dobbs there beside her, dressed in black, with her black hair and eyes, her head covered in a black scarf. She came over to me and grabbed me by the shoulders. I thought she might shake me. Instead, she whispered, "I am so very sorry for your loss." Her eyes were filled with tears, and it occurred to me that this girl was somehow familiar with deep pain. She pressed a small book into my hands and whispered again, "I will be praying for you." Then she was gone.

Patches from the Sky was written across the front of the book. For some reason, I looked up and saw exactly that—patches of blue sky peeking through the big white billowy clouds. A sun ray pierced the scene, descending in a see-through stream of light. I clutched the book more tightly and whispered, "Thanks."

Somewhere deep inside, I felt a momentary flicker of hope. Then it faded. But I held tightly to the memory of how that fleeting glimmer of hope had felt.

———

The day after the funeral, Mr. Robinson, Daddy's good friend and our accountant, came by the house. He knocked on the door, and when Mamma opened it, he stood there, timidly holding his hat in his hand, his head bent down. He was a small man, slim with graying hair and thick wire-rimmed glasses. I had always thought of him as stiff and boring, but on this day, he looked bent over with grief, completely stricken.

As soon as I saw him, I felt fury. *You knew Daddy. You knew all about his finances. Why didn't you do something to help him? Surely you could tell. It's your fault!*

And to Mamma I wanted to scream, *Why did you always try to make it seem okay? It wasn't okay! It's your fault!*

"Bill," Mamma said, obvious relief in her voice.

I knew right away this wasn't a call for condolences. Mr. Robinson had come to the house with his wife several times over the weekend and attended the funeral. He had come on business. I stuck right beside Mamma, because if we were going to talk money, I needed to be there.

Mamma didn't know a thing about the finances. Figures confused her, but I loved math. Daddy always helped me study for my tests, and when I was twelve or thirteen, he started showing me the financial books. A pain seared me with that thought. Did my dear Daddy, the one who was my confidant, did he know all along he was planning to leave us? Is that why he had patiently trained me over the years? I clutched my stomach.

"Anne Perrin—are you all right?"

"It's nothing, Mamma. I'm just having a hard time."

"You don't have to stay with us." But her eyes told me differently.

Mr. Robinson painstakingly went through the books, explaining each holding, each stock, each piece of property. And after each one, he'd remove his glasses, look up at us, and say the same phrase—"I'm afraid this isn't worth anything now."

Mamma nodded every time, but I could see she didn't understand.

I did. I understood exactly what he was trying to say in the most delicate way possible. We'd lost everything. Everything.

At one point, Mr. Robinson laid his ledger down and looked at Mamma, pushing his glasses up on his nose. "Dot, I assure you that we are going to do everything in our power to keep the house from being repossessed."

I felt my stomach lurch again. *Repossessed!*

The doorbell rang, and Dellareen went to answer it. A moment later, she came in the room. "Miz Singleton," she said softly, and Mamma got up, as in a trance, and went to the foyer.

"We're ruined, aren't we?" I asked Mr. Robinson.

He frowned, wrinkled his brow, and said, "Perri, your family's holdings have been greatly compromised."

"What are we going to do? Mamma can't work—she doesn't have a skill."

"Your father was well loved and well respected. We, his friends, will not let you down."

I didn't believe him.

Mamma came back in the room, clearing her throat. "Perri dear, Mary Dobbs Dillard is here to see you."

"Me?"

Mamma nodded.

I got up and met Dobbs in the entrance hall.

"Hey," she offered.

"Hello."

She was wearing a crisp white blouse and riding jodhpurs that hung on her skinny frame—clothes Mrs. Chandler must have lent her—and her hair was pulled back in a ponytail. She glanced down at her tall leather black boots, reached out and took my hand, and as if pleading with me, said, "I was wondering if you would go riding with me."

"Riding? Horseback riding? Now?"

"Yes. Yes, Aunt Josie said we could ride her horses—that they need exercise—and I've heard you're a splendid equestrian."

"But . . ."

Mamma came beside me, placed her hands on my shoulders, and said, "Go on, Perri. It might do you good to get out of the house."

I wouldn't have gone except for one thing. *Patches from the Sky.* The first thing I'd seen when I'd opened that book the night before was a handwritten message in faded blue ink on the inside cover: "*An artist's eye can take the spiritual and bring it down to earth. Remember that the eye is the window to the soul."* I had closed the book and let my tears fall. Somewhere deep down I felt that maybe Dobbs Dillard was a prophet.

When we got to the Chandlers' barn, the stableboy had already saddled and bridled the horses. I hopped up on Red, a pretty chestnut that I'd ridden before, and watched as Dobbs struggled to pull herself onto the bay mare, Dynamite. When she finally made it on, the stableboy looked at me in his worried way—he couldn't talk—trying to tell me something with his eyes. I frowned, not understanding.

Dobbs gathered up the reins and gave the horse a kick, and Dynamite trotted off with Dobbs giggling and tottering this way and that on the mare's back.

The stableboy turned to me again, shaking his head, his big hands motioning, and then I got it. "She doesn't know how to ride, does she?" He nodded.

Worried, I clucked at Red and cantered after her. Dobbs was already out of sight on a path in the woods. "Dobbs!" I called out. I found her around the bend, jerking the poor horse's mouth as she bounced around in the saddle. Then she suddenly leaned forward and grabbed onto Dynamite's neck.

"Dobbs! What are you doing?"

She shot me a look. "What does it look like I'm doing? I'm hanging on for dear life."

"Why didn't you tell me you didn't know how to ride?"

"I didn't want you to worry." And with that, she kicked Dynamite hard in the barrel, and off the mare went at a canter that turned into a gallop.

"Dobbs!" I hated her in that moment. Impetuous, unwise, over-confident! "You're gonna kill yourself!"

She ignored my yelling as I galloped after her for five minutes, zigzagging along the trail and dodging low-hanging limbs.

I came around a turn and found Dobbs, feet out of the stirrups, lying with her head on Dynamite's rump. The mare was breathing heavily and munching on grass in an open field that looked like it belonged in a child's storybook: wildflowers everywhere on a little hill, a lake off in the distance behind a pretty little white cottage, trees surrounding the field offering shade.

Dobbs glanced over at me, shaded her eyes with a hand, and smiled. "Nice, isn't it?"

Annoyed at her, I said nothing.

She sat back up, nudged Dynamite, and began walking the mare out.

I followed her. Finally I managed, "I've been here before—it's the Chandlers' summerhouse. But how'd you find the trails?"

"Parthenia showed me."

"Who's Parthenia?"

"You know . . . Parthenia. Cornelius's little sister."

"Who's Cornelius?"

Dobbs stared at me, perplexed. "You don't know who Cornelius is? He's the Chandlers' stableboy. He just saddled up the horses for us."

"Oh. The boy who can't talk. I've always felt a little sorry for him."

She headed over to the lake and without a second thought waded in, the water reaching up to near the horse's belly. And before I knew it, Dobbs had slid off the horse and was laughing and splashing water around her while her teeth chattered. I brought Red down to the bank and watched, fascinated.

She was twirling around and saying in a singsong voice, "Water! Isn't it wonderful? Smelly lake water."

Then she turned toward me and sent a long arc of that water right into my face.

"How dare you!" I squealed. "I don't want to get wet!"

Eyes flashing, she laughed. "It's too late for that."

Infuriated, I gritted my teeth and kicked Red, and we descended into the lake. I took off my riding hat, dipped it into the creek, and drew it up full, then came beside Dobbs and turned the whole hatful of water onto her head.

She let out a bone-chilling scream and burst into laughter, and for some reason, I slid off into the water and started splashing her for all I was worth.

Before long, we were soaked to the bone and my sides ached from laughing. We collapsed on the side of the lake and shivered as the chilly March breeze rippled over us.

I looked over at Dobbs—her eyes were shining with pleasure—and whispered, "You're the strangest person I've ever met."

"Thanks."

A little while later, Dobbs pulled out a sack of food from the saddle-bag and laid a blanket on the ground. "Eat up. Yummy picnic made by Parthenia. The kid's only eight, but she sure knows how to fix food."

We nibbled on pimento-cheese sandwiches and deviled eggs, neither of us saying a word, but all the while I observed Dobbs, with her long black hair, wet and pulled back into a ponytail, and her slim legs tucked into sopping wet riding breeches.

When she stretched out on her back and stared up into the sky, I spoke. "You know how to ride, don't you?"

"Sure. My father taught me a long time ago. He told me that he used to ride all over this property when he was a boy."

"So why'd you act like you didn't know a thing about riding?"

She kept staring up, and I thought she might not answer. But finally she said, "Just wanted to help take your mind off of things. And I wanted to hear you laugh."

She paused, and I said nothing.

"I don't mean to make light of your tragedy, Perri. Not at all. The Bible says to 'rejoice with them that do rejoice, and weep with them that weep.' But I've grown up watching my parents help people who are hurting inside. And one of the things that seems to bring a little relief to people's deepest pain is for others just to be there and help get their minds on something else for a while."

It struck me later that Dobbs Dillard knew exactly what she was doing. No matter how impetuous she seemed, she had a plan in her overactive imagination. Her plan on that spring day was to make me laugh, and amazingly enough, she succeeded.

CHAPTER
4

Dobbs

Mother always said that I had boundless enthusiasm and a love of the spontaneous. Perhaps that was why I got the idea in my head that Perri needed to come riding with me on the day after the funeral. When I had an idea, I tended to be very convincing, and even though Perri looked at me as if she were seeing the Loch Ness monster when I invited her over that day, she eventually came—and we rode and we laughed and we got so wet in the lake that I knew I couldn't send her back home looking like a perfectly beautiful drowned rat.

Cornelius put up the horses for us, and we traipsed back to the house with the water squishing up in our riding boots. "Don't let Parthenia see us," I whispered to Perri. "She'll have a fit." We left the boots by the back door and climbed the stairs, leaving puddles of muddy water on the tiles and on the wooden stairway.

"Your aunt is gonna kill you for this!" Perri said, but she was smiling and her eyes had a sparkle in them. Her teeth were chattering too.

I went into my bathroom, quickly threw off the riding clothes Aunt Josie had lent me, and dried off with a big fluffy towel. Then I put on a thick yellow robe. Coming out, I handed another towel to Perri. "You take a bath first," I instructed. "I'll find you something to wear."

She took the towel and giggled a little.

I began going through my drawers and closet, and then with an exasperated sigh, I said, "I don't think any of these clothes are going to fit you. You're not skinny like me." I held up the bright pink day dress for her to inspect.

"It's a lovely frock, but you're right. It wouldn't fit me."

I started down the hall to the bedrooms of Uncle Robert and Aunt Josie's two daughters, both grown now.

Perri followed me. "What in the world are you doing?"

"We've got to find you something to wear. Otherwise you'll come down with the croup or worse."

"Well, it isn't proper to search through the house. You don't just look into other people's private affairs."

Hands on my hips, I retorted, "If my aunt were here, I'd ask her permission. But she isn't, and you're freezing to death. Now go draw a bath, and I'll find you everything you need."

Obediently Perri disappeared into my bathroom.

I found a dress in my cousin Becca's closet, which was twice the size of the bedroom I shared with my sisters in Chicago and filled with the most gorgeous dresses and evening gowns. Rummaging through Becca's drawers, I found a clean pair of panties—I wasn't about to lend Perri any of my moth-eaten ones—and a brassiere that just might fit her. It was certainly too big for my pitiful excuse for a chest.

I had laid the clothing out on Becca's bed and was searching the closet for a pair of pumps when I came across three photo albums. I opened the first one's brittle pages and found a journal of sorts with a few photos adjoined with little gold corners. I stared at a picture of this house long ago, a horse and carriage in front and a woman—my grandmother, I recognized from the one photograph we had of her— holding on to a little boy's hand. My father! He was dressed in a lacy white outfit that looked more appropriate for a girl than for him, and he was smiling his famous smile, which showed an array of teeth. I sank to the floor, enthralled.

I wondered about my father. Why had he left such opulence? How could my aunt and uncle have so much and my father have so little? It didn't make sense to me.

I don't know how long I'd been sitting there, wrapped in the robe and nothing else, slowly turning the yellowed pages and squinting to read the faded black-ink notations written underneath the old photos, when I heard a noise coming from down the hall. I paid no attention for a while until, the noise became louder and I recognized Perri's voice.

"Dobbs! Mary Dobbs Dillard. Yoo-hoo! Where in the world are you? I'm standing here buck naked under this towel. Hurry up, for goodness' sake."

I left the album, determined that I'd come back to it later, retrieved Becca's clothes, and presented them to Perri in my room. She hurriedly pulled on the panties and bra—giggling, "Where in the world did you get these old things?"—and the dress, surveyed herself in the full-length mirror, and said, "I look like a complete disaster. Heavens! What will Mamma say, and with everything else on her mind?"

"I doubt she'll notice."

"You don't know Mamma. This is precisely the kind of thing she would notice."

I quickly bathed and then put on the blue dress I'd worn that first day and ran my fingers through my hopelessly tangled hair.

Perri had little bobby pins in her mouth and was busy pinning back her hair and muttering to herself. Finally she said, "I've got to get home! Can you try to find Mrs. Chandler's servant and get him to drive me back?"

"Is that an order?"

She looked around at me, creased her brow, and grinned. "A request. Please."

"Why do you need to get home?"

"Why? Don't be an idiot! To help Mamma! To care for Barbara and Irvin. To do a thousand other things." She pinched her cheeks twice, looked in the mirror again. "I'm as pale as a ghost. And I've got things to do for school—getting ready for the yearbook meeting and the May Day celebration and the Phi Pi tea and . . ."

"Are you crazy? Your father just died. No one in the whole wide world expects you to do anything at all about school. And my aunt and loads of other people are there with your mother. She'll be okay for a while. You should just stay here."

She turned on me suddenly. "Mary Dobbs Dillard, I don't know what planet you come from, but nothing will ever be 'okay' again. Don't you see that?"

"I see that's what you believe."

"What I *believe*?"

"Perri, it's not up to you to work everything out for your family!"

"And who will do it, I ask you? Have you looked at my mother? She is pretty and kind, and she knows how to serve tea and sit with her legs crossed and fix a good pot roast. None of which will earn us a cent."

"It will work out. I just know it."

"You just *know* it? Excuse me, but your father didn't watch his fortunes evaporate in front of his eyes. And your father isn't dead. You have no idea!" Now two perfect crimson spots appeared on her cheeks. "Call the servant!" she ordered.

"His name is Hosea," I said under my breath as I left the room.

"I heard you, Mary Dobbs Dillard!" she called after me. "Don't you act all condescending, you of all people in your potato-sack dress!"

I turned around, eyes wide open, and I could tell Perri was horrified by what she had just said.

The crimson spots turned to a deep red stain, and she mumbled, "Heavens! I'm sorry. I can't imagine why I said such a thing."

I went over to her, grabbed her by the shoulders, and put my nose to within an inch of hers. "You said such a thing because it is absolutely true. This *is* a potato-sack dress. A lovely Idaho-potato-sack dress, the finest and newest style. All the swell girls are wearing them." I began wiggling my hips and twirling around, with my hands making circles over my head as I spun and hummed the theme from *Madame Butterfly*.

Perri gave a little whimper of a laugh. "You're insane."

"Perhaps."

"Are you trying to get me to laugh again?"

I shook my head and stopped. With one last shake of my hips, I said, "No. This time, I actually think you need to cry."

"Cry?"

"For your father." To my astonishment, she sank onto my bed and burst into tears. Mother always said that tears were a healthy part of grieving. I knew what grieving looked like, from accompanying my father to all his revival meetings and from our own family's troubles, and I could see what was brewing under the surface in Perri Singleton. Rage. Horror. Fear. And just about anything else that went along with tragedy.

I certainly didn't understand all the waves of emotion she was feeling, but I did know how the death of a loved one cut a person in two, and I did know what a father looked like when he saw his family hungry, and I did know the horrible faces of grief and loss that paraded before Father at his tent meetings, and I had seen Mother take the meal she'd prepared for us across town to the family whose daughter just died—and felt my stomach growling because we suddenly had nothing to eat.

And I'd seen something else. I'd seen God show up and provide again and again and again.

But I didn't know Perri well enough then to tell her that, so I whispered, "You're right, Perri. There's no way I can understand everything you feel. I only wish I could help you."

She turned her see-through green eyes to me and whispered, "I hate him! I hate him! Why did he do this? Why did he leave us? Leave me with all of this!"

I sat down beside her. "I don't know. I'm just so sorry."

She threw her arms around me and began to cry again. In between her gasps for breath and her sniffles, she sobbed, "I h . . . ate him for doing . . . this to us. For leav . . . ing us with n . . . othing. He'll k-k-kill Mamma too."

Then she collapsed on the bed, arms still around my waist, and began to moan, "I loved him so much, Dobbs. I can't begin to tell you how much. So, so much. He was . . . He was a great father. He really was. Now everyone will think badly of him. I can't bear that, Dobbs."

Stunned, I whispered, "*Shhh.* No one thinks badly of him. They're just hurting for all of you."

She didn't hear me but continued talking to herself. "He was . . . He was my friend. I understood him and he understood me. And now he's gone."

That is how she fell asleep that day, holding on to me. I sat there for a long while, gently rubbing her back. Later, I carefully unwrapped myself from her embrace, slid off the bed, and left her there, covered with a worn quilt and her grief.

Perri spent the night at the Chandler house, right there in my bed, sleeping straight through the night. I stayed in Becca's room, carefully turning the pages in the brittle album, watching my father grow up before my eyes and wondering about the life he lived in Atlanta and how he could have left the wealth, sophistication, and security all behind. And why?

When the postman came, I hurried out of the house, before Parthenia could even set down the feather duster she was using in the downstairs library. I galloped down the driveway and met the postman at the curb. He nodded to me with a smile. This was my third day to greet him with anticipation in my eyes.

"Hello, Miss Dillard."

"Hello, sir. Any mail for me?"

"I do believe there is."

He handed me a letter, and I immediately recognized Hank's handwriting. "Oh, thank you, sir! Thank you!"

The postman's face broke into a grin as he tipped his hat and said, "My pleasure, Miss Dillard. All my pleasure."

I had the letter opened before I got to the porte-cochere entrance, and I began devouring it with my eyes. The letter was a balm for my soul and ended with the most wonderful declaration.

> *. . . I am already missing you, and I just told you good-bye. . . .*
> *Do you think your father suspects my affection for you? He*

has never said a word to me. . . . Coobie, the little stink, as you
call her, hangs on my every word. She is the perfect spy. . . .
I feel compelled to speak frankly with your father soon. . . .

With my love and prayers for
you, dear Dobbs,
Yours, Hank

"What are you doing?"

Perri's voice shocked me. She was standing at the bottom of the circular stairway, all cozy under the thick yellow robe that she had found in my bathroom. Her feet were tucked into two yellow slippers.

I stupidly thrust the letter behind my back, as if she hadn't seen it, hadn't read the delight on my face. "I was just getting the mail."

"Yes, I see that. And from the way you look, you must have heard from Mr. Roosevelt himself."

"Oh no." I shrugged, embarrassed.

This time Perri surprised me and let out a cackling laugh. "It's written right across your face, Mary Dobbs Dillard. You've heard from your steady, haven't you?"

I squinted at her, frowned a little, and wondered if I could trust her. I looked at the circles under her eyes and their red rims. She must have been crying, but in those hurt green eyes sparkled a hint of mischief.

"Oh, come on, Dobbs! I bawled my eyes out in front of you. Surely you can tell me about your steady."

I brought the letter from behind my back, looked down at it again, soaking in Hank's handwriting, running my fingers across the paper, as if in so doing I could touch the hand that had written those beautiful words, and then whispered to Perri, "Would you like to hear about him?"

"Would I ever!"

I stuck the letter in the pocket of my skirt, grabbed her hand, and whisked her through the foyer and down the hall to where I found Parthenia in the kitchen. I screeched to a halt, let go of Perri's hand, and said, "Parthenia, I'd like you to meet my good friend Perri Singleton."

Parthenia's eyes grew wide, and she curtsied a little. "Nice ta see ya, Miz Singleton."

Perri nodded. "It's nice to see you too."

I went to one of the cabinets, opened it, and retrieved two tall glasses. "I came to get us each a glass of iced tea. We're going to sit out on the back porch."

Parthenia showed the whites of her eyes, stopped cutting an onion, and said, "She ain't even had breakfast yet, Miz Dobbs. She's still in her robe."

Perri laughed again, a light, delicious laughter. "It's okay, Parthene . . . Parthenia. I'm not hungry for breakfast. Iced tea will do just fine."

Before Parthenia could make her way to the Frigidaire, I'd taken out the glass pitcher filled with tea. I pulled open the rack underneath where the ice was kept and, with a blunt knife, chipped off two pieces of ice and plopped them into our tall glasses.

As we walked out of the kitchen, Parthenia muttered to herself, "Ain't proper for guests to serve themselves like that."

A few minutes later, Perri and I sat cuddled under an old quilt on the sofa on the screened-in side porch that gave a view of the stables and the servants' quarters and the hill leading down to the summerhouse. We sipped our tea in silence until Perri finally asked, "What's his name?"

"Henry Wilson. But everyone calls him Hank. I met him eighteen months ago when he came looking for my father. Father is a preacher, and Hank was at Moody Bible Institute and wanted to see if he could help Father with his tent meetings."

"Oh." Perri looked a little confused. "Your Hank wants to be a preacher at tent meetings?"

"Yes. He's devoted to the Sawdust Trail."

"The Sawdust Trail?"

"That's what my father calls preaching the Gospel and touching the world for Christ—it was a phrase used by the famous evangelist Billy Sunday."

"Ah."

"You know—at tent revivals there's always sawdust on the ground, and when someone converts, well, he walks down the sawdust trail to the front and meets with the preacher."

Perri looked at me blankly. "If you say so."

"And Hank will make a fine preacher with his deep bass voice and the prettiest blue eyes. He dreams of going all over the world, inviting people to walk the Sawdust Trail."

Perri took in this news with a cocked head. "Is that what your father does?"

"Well, not exactly. He doesn't travel around the world—just the States, primarily the Midwest and the Southeast."

Perri scooted closer on the sofa. "What's it like? Going to those cities and seeing those people?"

I closed my eyes and saw my father holding up his big black Bible, his face all red with passion, beads of perspiration running down his face, as he pled with people to find Jesus. I was sitting there in the audience of ten measly looking people. One man had dozed off; another was mumbling under his breath—Coobie said way too loudly that he didn't have all his wits about him—and a little woman all decrepit and bent over was searching in her purse for something.

I kept wanting the people to pay attention to Father, to call out "Amen," but they didn't. Father went right on preaching as if he were standing before a crowd of five hundred.

But I didn't want to tell Perri that, so I just said, "It's hard. The people don't have money. And they look hungry. Sometimes they just come to the tent meeting to get free food."

"Your parents give out free food?"

"When they can."

"They go and buy food for people before the tent meeting?"

"Oh no. Mother just prays and asks God to provide, and people usually turn up with some food and stuff—because they don't have any money to leave an offering. And whatever the people give Mother, she gives to others who are in worse shape than we are."

"Goodness. That's, that's . . ." Perri seemed to struggle with a word to give to what I had just described. "That's interesting." She paused, took a sip of her tea, and looked out over the back property, her fine feminine nose turned slightly upward, her eyes closed, as if she was trying to picture my parents handing out food to the destitute. Then she turned to me and asked, "Are you ever hungry? I mean, if your mother gives away all the food that was to be your father's pay for his services."

"Sometimes I am. But we just trust God to provide."

"And He does?"

"Every time. I haven't starved to death yet."

She shook her head slowly. "I couldn't live like that. I *wouldn't* live like that. Never knowing where my next meal is coming from."

"You would if you had to," I blurted out before I thought through what I was saying. "I mean, I guess it might take some getting used to for someone like you who generally has plenty of food to eat. But it isn't hard for me."

I stood up, spread my arms out wide, and looked across the fields. "Imagine that you are part of something big and wonderful, Perri. Imagine that you're going to help feed all the poor people in Atlanta. Yes, it means you'll have to give up certain things, but it will be worth it. Imagine lines and lines of people out back here and us serving them soup and bread and pies and wonderful cakes and iced tea—imagine the laughter on their tight, drawn faces. Just having a full belly would bring joy to them. Imagine that!"

Perri set down her glass of tea and came to stand beside me. She leaned her arms on the back of a chair and stared out into the Chandlers' property as if she was indeed imagining the scene I had just described. "I'll have to admit that sounds, *hmm*, like a very kind thing to do," she said.

"Kind! Jesus called us to proclaim freedom to the captives. It's not kindness; it's truth. I've seen it happen in other cities. I promise I have! It's what we Christians are to be about."

Perri backed away from me. "You really get worked up about this stuff, don't you? You're a fascinating person, Mary Dobbs Dillard."

"The other day you said I was the strangest person you'd ever met."

"Well, they're both true. Strange and fascinating." She walked to the other side of the porch, putting distance between us. "And so that's what Hank wants to do. Help the poor and never have any money for his family?"

"He wants to obey the Bible. And watch God provide." This, I'll admit, I said a bit defensively. Then I walked over to Perri, grabbed both of her hands, and squeezed them tight. "And I know your situation is different and everything, but honestly I feel it rumbling down in my soul. God is going to provide for you and your family too."

She let go of my hands and folded her arms tight across her chest. Her face became dark, and her eyes swelled with tears. "I've never heard anyone speak like you do, Dobbs. It sounds absolutely crazy to me. But one thing I do know. Your God may provide for you, but here in this part of Atlanta, everyone works hard and provides for himself and his family. And that's what I'm gonna do now."

I realized in that moment two things: I hadn't really gotten to tell her anything about Hank, and it might take a while to convince Perri Singleton that I was right. God would provide.

While Aunt Josie practically lived at the Singleton house, Perri stayed with me at the Chandlers'. I don't think that Aunt Josie realized that I didn't attend Washington Seminary at all that first week I was in Atlanta. The enormity of the tragedy just sucked her in, and she spent every ounce of her energy taking care of details. She'd reappear at the house long enough to fire out orders to Hosea and Cornelius and disappear again. I watched my aunt with deep admiration for her endless energy and determination.

Dearest Mother,   *March 9, 1933*
Well, I have been here in Atlanta for almost a week, and because of the tragedy I wrote you about, I have hardly left the Chandlers' property.
Perri Singleton has spent the last two days with me at the

Chandlers'. I think the fact that I have nothing to do with Atlanta and that I knew virtually nothing about her life and family and school before the tragedy, somehow makes me more approachable.

I have tried to tell her stories about the Lord providing for us, but she looks at me as if I have two heads, and it makes me feel quite stupid.

But don't you believe that the Lord will provide for them, Mother?

Please keep praying. I will write again soon.

All my love to Father, Coobie, and Frances . . .

Perri

I stayed with Dobbs at the Chandler home for two days and nights, and honestly, sometimes Dobbs succeeded in making me forget the horror of what had happened to my family. She had an endless supply of stories about her family's life on the road—going from town to town, her father preaching and her mother handing out food that she didn't have but which miraculously appeared, and of children healed of sickness and a bunch of other farfetched things that I wasn't sure were quite true, but they sure were entertaining.

And Dobbs did practical things to help too. On Thursday afternoon, Hosea—I learned his name as well as those of his children, Cornelius and Parthenia—drove us back to my house, and we picked up my siblings. My, were they thrilled to ride in that Pierce Arrow convertible! Barbara laughed the whole way over to the Chandlers' house, and Irvin just kept fiddling with every gadget he found in the car, and Hosea didn't say a word to stop him. Irvin and Barbara stayed with us the whole afternoon, riding the Chandlers' pony—none of us had dared to go near our barn where the tragedy happened—and playing silly games that Dobbs seemed to invent out of nothing.

I had never before felt the tightening in my soul that I felt for Dobbs. Most of my friends I'd known forever, but my bond with Dobbs came swiftly, desperately, born from all the things breaking inside me. She had a kind of intuition that read my mind and peered deep into my soul. I found that I needed to be near her.

On Friday afternoon, Dellareen called me at the Chandlers' and said that Jimmy was coming over in the Buick to pick me up. "Your motha' wants you to spend some time at home now, Miz Perri."

By the time Jimmy showed up, I had gathered my belongings and made a decision. "Dobbs, you're coming home with me."

She was standing in that grand entrance hall, talking to skinny ol' Jimmy as if they were good friends. She turned to me and, with a huge smile on her face, said, "I just *knew* you'd invite me. Yes, of course I'll come! Let me get a few things." She spun around in a circle and then hurried up the stairs.

Jimmy raised an eyebrow but said nothing. Dobbs came back downstairs with her pitiful suitcase and called out to Parthenia, who was down the hall in the kitchen, "I'm going over to the Singletons' with Perri."

The little girl came into the hall, holding a wooden spoon, her hands on her hips. I laughed behind my hand, seeing the colored girl in her pinafore walk up to Dobbs—she didn't even come to her shoulders—and challenge Dobbs with her big black eyes. "Ain't proper to impose yourself on people who is grieving," she said.

Dobbs was unperturbed. "It's none of your business, Parthenia. You just relay the message to Mrs. Chandler when she gets back."

As Jimmy drove us up the long, winding drive that led to my house, I marveled at the heaviness that came over me. I stared at the home that had been called an architectural treasure of Atlanta, a house that Daddy had helped his father build when Daddy was a young teen.

Eventually, when Margaret Mitchell's *Gone with the Wind* was published in 1936, everyone started calling the house Tara because it fit that description, but this was 1933, and we had not heard of Tara or Scarlett O'Hara at the time.

Perched high up on a hill on Wesley Road, with a driveway that climbed and twisted around, our house appeared from behind a forest of trees as if in a dream—a three-storied white-brick mansion with six white columns out front and black shutters on the big windows, with front and back porches and big magnolia trees that surrounded the house. Everything that had at one time meant home and comfort and beauty now looked gray, as if a thin layer of ash had swept in on the breeze and settled on our house and yard.

A sickening feeling hit me hard in the stomach, just as real as if my little brother had punched me there, which happened occasionally. Dobbs noticed—she noticed everything—and looped her arm through mine as we walked up to the house. She called back to Jimmy, "Thank you kindly for the ride."

Mamma met me at the front door, and she looked just as ashy gray as the house, and I thought no amount of makeup would have been able to cover up her grief. She grabbed me and held me tight, strangling tight, for a long minute.

Struggling out of her embrace, I asked, "Mamma, is it all right if Mary Dobbs stays with me tonight? I'd really appreciate it."

Sweet Mamma, thin and bone weary, reached out her delicate hands, took Dobbs by the shoulders, looked her straight in the eyes, and said, "It would be our great pleasure to have you with us tonight, Mary Dobbs." What I read on Mamma's face was a whole lot of gratitude.

I found I couldn't grieve for long with Dobbs around. Life for her was such an adventure, and she found excitement in every detail. Upstairs in my room, which she proclaimed "extravagant," she waltzed over to one of the walls where four photos of our house and yard, taken at different seasons, hung in simple wooden frames. She stared at them and then at me and then at them again. "These are magnificent. Perceptive. They're yours, aren't they?"

I gave a little nod. "Yes. I took the photographs."

"I *knew* it! The minute I set eyes on you, I knew you had potential."

"Potential?" Honestly, Dobbs talked in enigmas sometimes.

"To see the world from a different perspective. You know—'the eye is the window to the soul.'"

I nodded, recalling the words written in that little blue book, and said, "Oh yes. I suppose I see what you mean." But I didn't.

"So you have a camera? A real camera?"

"I do. My . . . my father gave it to me for my fourteenth birthday."

She didn't let me dwell on that. "Can I see it?"

I opened my closet and pointed to where the camera sat, neatly arranged on a shelf. Beside it was a stack of albums in which I had classified my photos. Dobbs ran her slim hands over the camera's red leatherette box.

"It's an Eastman Kodak Rainbow Hawk-Eye," I said. "It was a really nice camera for me to receive as a beginner."

"It's absolutely marvelous. And you're no beginner now. You're practically a professional. Look at all these photo albums! You're amazingly organized, Perri." She stood up and turned to where all my dresses hung on the other side of the closet. "And you have wonderful taste in clothes."

I wondered how in the world she knew anything about clothes, but I didn't say a word. No need to risk another gaffe like calling her one dress a potato sack!

"It's a splendid closet, and you've arranged it so well."

I shrugged. Arranging things, keeping order, came very naturally to me, for whatever it was worth.

"Do you have a darkroom here where you develop your pictures?"

"Not at home. Mrs. Carnes, the fine arts teacher at Washington Seminary, lets me use the darkroom there, since I'm one of the photographers for the school yearbook."

Dobbs had squatted back down in my closet and was carefully leafing through one of my albums. "You're very gifted!" she enthused.

I'd soon learn that Dobbs seemed almost always enthusiastic, but on that dark and dreary day, I believed her. I took the compliment like a cool splash of water on my face, wiping away the ash residue that had settled there.

But Dobbs's compliment didn't come without its requirements. She began calculating immediately. "With talent like this, you should be taking photos of reality."

"Reality?"

"Not just shots of your friends for the yearbook and wonderful photos of your house, but life—real life."

I stared at her, thinking briefly of "White Angel Breadline."

"You should be showing this snippet of Atlanta society how the rest of the world lives. Why"—I could tell an idea was brewing—"you could put together booklets to raise money for the poor, for the prisoners, a hundred different causes."

I plopped down on my bed and glared through the closet door at Dobbs Dillard. "Don't you think I have enough worries of my own right now—how to help Mamma and Barbara and Irvin deal with the grief, how my family is going to pay the bills, how to keep this house? I don't have time to get involved in some lofty idea of helping the poor. Right now, Dobbs Dillard, the poor is *us*!" I jabbed a finger into my chest to emphasize my point.

She came out of the closet holding a copy of the Washington Seminary yearbook, *Facts and Fancies*, plopped down on the bed beside me, and gave me an impulsive hug. "You're right, Perri. Forgive me and my big mouth." She sounded truly sorry.

I shrugged. "It's okay."

"So show me which photos you took for last year's *Facts and Fancies*."

We opened the hardback black annual, and I leafed through the pages, turning them quickly. "All the head shots of the girls were taken by a professional photographer. He also took the ones of the May Day festivities, but I took these."

She peered closer. "You took all these pictures of people in action? Why, they're just grand! You've caught people in the midst of real life—not posing."

She was pointing to one photo in particular that was part of a collage I'd put together of the sophomore class. In the photo, my dearest friends, Peggy Pender and Mae Pearl McFadden and Emily Bratton, were standing by the columns out front of Washington Seminary, gossiping about something and completely unaware that they were being photographed.

"You've got talent, girl," she reaffirmed.

I appreciated her confidence in me, but all I could think about, being back in my room, were the words that Bill Robinson had pronounced on the day after the funeral to Mamma and me, *We are going to do everything in our power to keep the house from being repossessed.*

I awoke in the middle of the night from dreams of dangling feet and voices screaming, my body sweaty and fresh tears on my face, my heart pounding. I switched on the little lamp beside my bed and breathed a thankful sigh for the diffusion of light in my room. I rolled over, disoriented.

Climbing out of bed, I walked to the window and pressed my nose against the cool pane, wishing for a ray of sun to pierce the cold darkness outside and the chill in my soul. All was black, but a thought seared through me. *Patches from the Sky.* I remembered the way the clouds had parted at Daddy's funeral and the snatch of hope I had felt when that happened.

At length I found the little volume under a stack of papers on my desk and brought it into bed with me, as if this small hardbound book could console me, chase away my nightmares with a sunbeam. I opened the book and once again read the handwritten message on the inside cover:

> *An artist's eye can take the spiritual*
> *and bring it down to earth.*
> *Remember that the eye is the window to the soul.*

Then I turned the page. Above the book's title, I found another inscription in the same handwriting.

> *To Hank, Easter 1925*
> *Love, Grandmamma*

Dobbs had given me Hank's book.

It was a collection of well-known poems and Bible verses, many of which were familiar to me. Interspersed between the poems and verses were occasional photographs of clouds, flowers, a field at harvesttime, a child in his mother's lap—each exquisite in its simply beauty. I turned the pages with trembling fingers, not bothering to read the poems, but instead eager to glimpse the next photo.

On one page, there was a photo of the night sky, lit up with stars. I ran my fingers across the page and wept. This was a picture of what Dobbs called reality, a beacon pointing to all that pushed and strained inside of me, longing, needing to escape. Drying my eyes with the sleeve of my robe, I stared at the photo and wished deep within me that I would someday take a picture as beautiful as that.

At last I read the poem on the opposite page, "The Night Has a Thousand Eyes" by Francis William Bourdillon. I had never heard of this poet, but his short poem touched me deeply:

> The night has a thousand eyes,
> And the day but one;
> Yet the light of the bright world dies
> With the dying sun.
>
> The mind has a thousand eyes,
> And the heart but one;
> Yet the light of a whole life dies
> When love is done.

I fell asleep clutching the book to my chest, the pages opened to that poem and a whisper on my breath. "Oh, Daddy. I miss you, Daddy."

———

The next morning, I awoke with gratitude to the sun filtering through the window. Dobbs had slept in Barbara's room—my sister was over at Lulu's again—and I went down the hall to find her. The bed was made and the room empty. I located Dobbs downstairs in the library, which was attached to my father's study, reading in his big leather chair.

She sat up straight when she saw me. "I hope it was all right to come in here. No one else was awake."

"It's fine. Would you like some breakfast?"

She shrugged. "There's no hurry." Then she narrowed her black eyes and said, "You had a bad night, didn't you?"

When I nodded, she stood up, took my hand, and squeezed it hard. "Give yourself time, plenty of time."

Again I had a feeling that Dobbs understood heartache very well.

She saw that I was holding *Patches from the Sky*. "Have you been reading this?"

I nodded again. "Some . . . in the night. It's lovely—so simple, so profound."

"I knew it would be meaningful to you."

"But how did you know, Dobbs? You gave it to me before we were friends, before you knew I loved photography."

She looked me straight in the eyes, and I wanted in that moment to peer through the sparkle and deep intensity straight into her soul. "Mother calls it woman's intuition and Father calls it the moving of the Holy Ghost."

I tended to agree with Dobbs's father. Something about her was deeply spiritual. I thrust *Patches from the Sky* into her hands. "I can't keep this book. Hank's grandmother gave it to him, and he must have given it to you."

"Yes. Yes, that's right." Pain flittered right behind her black lashes. "Hank gave it to me when I was having a hard time. I found the poems, Scripture, and photographs somehow soothing." She placed the volume back in my hands. "I thought you might too. I know Hank wouldn't mind my giving it to you. I don't want it back."

I didn't argue at all. I was immensely relieved. Dobbs said the poems and Scriptures were soothing, and oh, how my soul needed to be soothed.

Dobbs

No one was expecting me at Washington Seminary—except perhaps Miss Emma, the school principal—so they didn't miss me when I did not show up that first week. And given the circumstances, no one expected Perri to attend school either. But by the next Monday, I was itching to start school, and I knew Perri needed to return to a semblance of routine. She'd spent the whole weekend looking over accounting books with her mother and Mr. Robinson, and I worried she'd slip into a depression if she didn't reintegrate into school life. Perri acquiesced, with her only request being that she and I ride to school together on my first day at Washington Seminary.

People grieve in different ways. Perri's way was stoicism. Her pale, pale face was expressionless as Jimmy let us out in front of Washington Seminary on that Monday morning in March.

I'd seen pictures of the building in the yearbook, but living color changed my perception. It looked like a governor's mansion with its white Corinthian columns—twelve of them—that gracefully curved in front of the redbrick building. Out front, dogwood trees were blooming in pink and white bursts of color, and hedges of flowering azaleas lined the entrance to the school. Just walking into the building, I felt completely out of place. Thank heavens I was wearing a uniform instead of my potato sack! Yet I also felt something else. I squared my shoulders and stood up a little straighter, and I literally felt a passion rush through me. It was my responsibility to educate the girls at Washington Seminary about how the rest of the world lived. My cause!

I thought about my high school in Chicago—the soot-covered brick building, the boys and girls dressed in the most nondescript clothes, all just crowded into the place with absolutely no distinction, and how half the teachers had been let go and the rest hadn't been paid in months. But here, in their crisp white uniforms with dark blue piping, the stylish skirts that fell just below the knee, these girls seemed set apart, elite, girls becoming women, girls who were perfectly aware that they came from somewhere and were headed somewhere else. Washington Seminary had a fresh, hopeful smell so unlike the odors from the streets of downtown Chicago that drifted into my high school.

Perri directed me to the principal's office, where I met briefly with Miss Emma, a thin, serious-looking woman with gray eyes and gray hair that she wore just below her ears. She welcomed me warmly, handed me the *Catalogue of Washington Seminary*, which listed my classes and other information, and encouraged me to come see her with any questions.

She explained that every school day started with chapel, and we walked together to a beautiful room with polished mahogany pews, a crystal chandelier hanging from the ceiling, and a stage with a thick velvety dark green curtain drawn across it. I found Perri waiting for me at the back.

"Hey, quit staring at everything like a little kid," she whispered rather loudly. I followed her to where she slid into a row beside a group of girls who greeted her with outstretched hands, kisses on the cheek, and forlorn faces. A few minutes later, Miss Emma went up on the stage and stood behind a sturdy wooden podium.

"Girls, we are reading today from John 16:33. Jesus says, 'These things I have spoken unto you, that in me ye might have peace. In the world ye shall have tribulation: but be of good cheer; I have overcome the world.'

"We are thankful to have our dear Anne Perrin back with us today." Miss Emma nodded to Perri. "Our prayers have been with her and her family during this very difficult and dark time. I encourage you all to be respectful of Anne Perrin's needs. And on behalf of the girls at Washington Seminary, we again want to offer you our deepest condolences."

Then two teachers presented Perri with a beautiful bouquet of white lilies and roses. She stood up and awkwardly took the flowers with a thank-you that seemed stuck in her throat. I saw she was struggling hard not to cry.

Miss Emma allowed a time of silence before making her next

announcement. "We're pleased to welcome a new student, Mary Dobbs Dillard. She comes to us from Chicago and is the niece of Josephine Chandler, whose daughters both attended Washington Seminary a few years back. Mary Dobbs, would you please stand up."

Mortified, I obeyed.

"I want everyone to be sure to welcome Mary Dobbs," Miss Emma added.

The girls gave polite applause as I sat back down, but I was pretty sure I read a familiar evaluation on their faces: disapproval.

Perri used me as her shield from the stares of her classmates. To avoid answering horrible questions about her father and her family, she shoved me in front of her and introduced me to every girl we met in the hallway. In each class she stood up and did the same, always emphasizing the Chandler name, as if my association with them gave me the necessary clout to attend Washington Seminary. And she introduced me as Mary Dobbs. I think Perri had decided that *Dobbs* was her name for me—a secret, a privilege, an honor no one else had yet earned. I went along with her. I figured it was part of her grieving.

Even though we all wore the same uniform, I stuck out for many reasons. First of all, the school was small enough that everyone knew everyone else. I was the newcomer. Also, I didn't sound one bit like the other girls, who spoke slowly and drew out their words, adding extra syllables in the oddest places. And then there was my long hair. No other girl at Washington Seminary had long hair. Every one of them wore her hair short; they looked fashionable, sassy, confident, at ease in their world.

I remembered Mother dabbing her eyes years ago when money got too tight for her to go to the beauty parlor. She had let her thick and shiny black hair grow long, and now it was streaked with gray. She wore it in a bun. Wouldn't she have loved these styles! Mother knew style, even if she couldn't follow it. She appreciated beauty.

At noon, Perri led me into the lunchroom and stopped in the

doorway. She pointed to one of the round tables where the three girls she'd sat beside in chapel were already seated. "Voilà—my gang. We like to stick together."

"That's Emily Bratton on the left, but everyone calls her Brat. Because she is." Perri flashed me a smile. Brat had dark brown hair that she wore so short she could have been mistaken for a boy. She had a square frame—her face, wide shoulders, and arms that looked muscular even under the uniform. "She's our star basketball player and a great swimmer too. We've been friends practically since we were born. She's half crazy and not afraid of anything, and she tells the corniest jokes. I think you'll like her."

"Next to her is Mae Pearl McFadden."

I wondered if Mae Pearl's parents had had a premonition of what a beauty she'd grow up to be. She had the face of a pearl—perfectly round and so very white, porcelain white, whiter than Perri's face, and glimmering, almost luminous, almost translucent. Her hair was almost white too, a platinum blond—perfectly natural, Perri assured me. She wore her hair slick and close to her head and had pale blue eyes.

"Her mother and mine have been in the Garden Club together for years—president and vice-president—and the Junior League too, of course," Perri confided as we walked toward the table, "and they made their debuts together, and we've gone to the same church forever. She lives just down the street from me, so we do most things together. She dances beautifully and has the voice of an angel. We all think she could be a movie star or be in one of those musicals on Broadway, but she doesn't listen to a word we say.

"And that's Peggy Pender next to Mae Pearl. Oh, she's a stitch. She looks all prim and proper, but don't be fooled. She's got a mind of her own!"

I thought that Peggy looked very sophisticated, the way her dark brown hair curled slightly below her ears and several strands tickled her right eyebrow.

"Hi, y'all!" Perri called out as she pulled out a chair and gestured for me to sit next to her.

The girls waved, and each mumbled a "Hi, Mary Dobbs" to me.

We ate in what seemed much more like an elegant private dining room than a school cafeteria. The room was decorated with pretty pink wallpaper and fancy draperies, and it was filled with twenty or so round tables covered with white tablecloths. Our lunch—a hot lunch with meat and vegetables and rolls and dessert—was served to us on china plates, and the food was delicious. But every meal I ate in Atlanta, no matter what it was, reminded me of my family in Chicago, probably down on their knees praying for tomorrow's daily bread. So I chewed my food with a deep thankfulness in my heart, and a pang there too.

Brat and Mae Pearl and Peggy jabbered about a homework assignment that Perri had missed and about some tea party they had attended last week—also missed by Perri. I was only half listening when Mae Pearl turned and asked me, "Do you want to come with us to the Saturday matinee at the theater?"

"The Saturday matinee? What do you mean?"

"You don't know about the Saturday matinee? It's the best thing since ice cream. Everyone goes. We watch films like *Betty Boop* and *Tarzan*. It only costs a nickel for all morning long." Then she added breathily when I didn't answer at once, "I don't think Perri's allowed to go on account of the grieving. But I'll come by and get you. We can just ride the streetcar down there."

For all of my life, I'd grown up hearing Father talk about temptations that affected people. Things like alcohol and cigarettes and dancing. And movies. My parents never went to movies, and Frances, Coobie, and I were not allowed to either.

I'd never felt bad about it. But on that Monday afternoon, as Mae Pearl McFadden smiled at me with her porcelain face and her pale blue eyes and described it all, I wanted to go. I hesitated, just the slightest bit, shook my head, and said, "Thank you for the invitation, Mae Pearl. It really means a lot to me, but I won't be able to attend."

Brat spoke up, "Why in the world not?"

"I don't go to movies."

The girls stared at me as if I had spoken to them in Chinese. "Ever?" Perri choked out.

"Ever," I said.

Mae Pearl creased her brow and shrugged. "Suit yourself, but it really is swell."

"Americans are spending time going to movies and dances and all such things, and forgetting Bible reading and prayer. We're being sucked into the evils of entertainment," I said, without thinking, and I realized I sounded just like Father. My voice trailed off. Mae Pearl looked like the picture of innocence, and I could not imagine the movies corrupting her.

Peggy sneered. "Well, if you think *Betty Boop* and *Tarzan* are evil, I say you've got a screw loose."

Mae Pearl smiled sweetly again and said, "Oh, let's not argue. Everyone's got a right to her opinion." She took a bite of chicken casserole and said, "Mary Dobbs, I just love your long hair. It's beautiful. I don't know another girl with long hair. You're so brave to go against the style."

"I've never had much choice. We certainly couldn't afford to go to a beauty salon."

Mae Pearl's white face got two little pink splotches on it. She recovered and said, "Well, I'd never thought of it that way. That must be hard. But you're very fortunate that long hair becomes you ever so well."

Perri just stared at me, looking annoyed. We sat in strained silence for a moment until Perri found a safer topic. "Y'all, I missed out on who has been nominated to be the May Day Queen. What happened?" And they were off chattering about another event of which I had no idea.

By the end of the school day, I felt exhausted. Every girl had stared at me as if I were an alien they'd seen at a Saturday matinee. I escaped from the building without even telling Perri good-bye and was thankful to see Hosea waiting for me by the curb in the Pierce Arrow. He drove me home in silence, and I jumped out of the car, mumbling my thanks, and ran up the stairs before anyone could see me. I collapsed on the bed and burst into tears.

I missed my family. I missed reading in bed on Saturday mornings before Mother and I went to help serve a hot lunch to the many people in the streets. I missed the way Coobie braided my hair on Sunday mornings before church, her fingers almost always sticky from eating one of Mother's delicious cinnamon rolls. It became a joke, me admonishing her, "Coobie, for goodness' sake, wash your hands before you put them in my hair." Mischievous as she was, I always felt surprised when she obeyed.

I thought fleetingly about going home—just getting on the next train to Chicago. Immediately I recalled Mother's argument from a few months ago convincing me to attend Washington Seminary. "There's forty percent unemployment in Chicago, Mary Dobbs. A hundred thousand families are on relief rolls. The board of education has fired fourteen hundred teachers. You can't get a good education here. Later, perhaps, but not now. You're bright, Mary Dobbs. Your father has got to put away bitterness and pride and take his sister's offer. That's all there is to it."

I sat on my aunt's beautiful canopied bed, dressed in perfect white, and somehow felt dirty. Dirty amidst Atlanta's elite, and dirty for abandoning my family and my city. I went to the little desk and reached for a piece of stationery and a pen to write Hank all that was in my heart.

Immediately Father's zeal-filled face flashed in my mind, and I saw him holding his Bible high in the air, pleading with a group of weary spectators. "It's much easier to reach for a human hand first when we're in need. The Good Lord provides us with sisters and brothers to help in our times of trouble. But never forget, never forget, never forget"—and then his voice would crescendo until his face was a deep dark red and his booming voice almost hoarse with passion—"you must go to God first. We humans don't have the answers. God has the answers. Look in here"—he pounded his free hand onto the black leather cover of his Bible—"first!"

I set down the pen and stationery and took my own leather Bible from where it sat on the desk under a pile of new school books. It opened to where I had placed several small photographs. Mother and Father in front of the church, all smiles. Frances and Coobie and I standing by a snowman we had made in the park. And one with my sisters and me with Jackie. We were sitting on the old sofa in our apartment, and every single one of us had our mouths open, we were laughing so hard.

I miss you, Jackie.

Then all thoughts of Bible reading disappeared as I stared at her face in that photo.

Jackie Brown was another example of my parents' charity. I did not know exactly when they met Jackie's mother, doubtless at one of Father's revivals, but I remembered the first time I saw Jackie. I was four or five, Frances just a toddler, and Coobie not yet born. Mother had come into our room one night and said, "Mary Dobbs, I have someone I'd like you to meet." And there was Jackie. She was about eight or nine at the time, a pencil-thin girl with long, unkempt brown hair and deep brown eyes that seemed too big for her thin, pale face.

"Would you mind sharing your room with Jackie? Her mother is working in another town and unable to care for her." Mother never said anything about Jackie's father.

I had always dreamed of having an older sister. I was thrilled.

Jackie, whom her mother described as "sickly," flourished under Mother's loving care and fine meals—in those days, we all had plenty to eat. At first, I thought that her mother had not taught her proper manners, with her vulgar language and complete disregard for rules. But she learned quickly, and soon she was singing the hymns at church with gusto—she had a lovely voice—and helping Mother with cooking and sewing, for which she had a knack too.

I followed her everywhere, and she treated me as a true friend. We became inseparable.

At times her mother would come to get her, determined that she could take care of her child. Mrs. Brown never looked to me like she could even take care of herself, much less a child. She was as thin as Jackie, but she had her face all painted up and wore tight, poorly made clothes and talked in a quick, nervous way, her eyes darting back and forth to Mother and Father and Jackie.

Those days when she came back for Jackie were heartrending for me. Mother and Father and Frances also missed her terribly.

Inevitably, weeks or sometimes months later, Mrs. Brown would bring Jackie back, and she would join our family again. Jackie was often sick—she had weak lungs—but she was strong on the inside. She never really embraced salvation, for her mind was wild and she wanted to try on all of life. More than a few times when I was about eleven or twelve, I sneaked out of the house with her in the middle of the night. The Holy Ghost always grabbed my heart before I got too far away from home, and I'd go back, despite Jackie's protests that I was going to miss out on a lot of fun. Jackie usually didn't return to the apartment until a day or two later, after worrying my parents half to death. She never told me where she'd been, but by the look on my parents' faces, I knew it wasn't good or proper.

Jackie graduated from high school in Chicago and found a job right away. She sent most of the money she earned back to Irene Brown. She had confided to me that she felt responsible for her mother. By that time, at fourteen, I understood what no one had ever told me. Mrs. Brown was what my father referred to in his sermons as a "woman of ill repute." Jackie hoped to earn enough money to help her mother find a new line of employment.

But it didn't work out that way.

When Jackie suddenly grew ill again, she had to quit her job. Mother cared for her night and day. But then she went to the hospital, and I watched the beautiful young and vibrant woman wither up and look again like the starving child with sunken eyes too big for her pale, drawn face.

I sat by her bed, night and day. I read the Scriptures to her and whispered prayers, and the day before she died, she reached out and touched my hand and whispered through parched lips, "Mary Dobbs. Don't you worry anymore about my soul. I'll be with the Almighty when I go. He's forgiven me." Those were the last words I heard from her.

Knowing of her salvation was of some comfort at first, but afterwards came the rage and the questions and the deep, deep grief. That was why I understood Anne Perrin Singleton so well. I did not want to hear her doubts about God's ability to provide, because, although I never let myself admit it, I had the same doubts tickling the back of my mind, and I was terrified that one day they would come out and strangle all the faith in my soul.

CHAPTER
6

Perri

I'd been back at Washington Seminary for four days when Mae Pearl and Peggy caught up on either side of me after French class, directed me outside, and sat me down on a stone bench.

Mae Pearl was first to speak. "Perri, you know you mean the world to me. You really do, and I love you like a sister." Her pretty face clouded and she took my hands. "I've missed you these past two weeks. I mean it's been the hardest time in the world for you, and well, it seems you've been mighty wonderful to Mary Dobbs, but I just don't think you should feel responsible for her, not with all you've been through."

She stopped abruptly, and I knew it was torture for Mae Pearl to get up the nerve to say anything even slightly negative about anyone. She squeezed my hands and added, "I surely hope we can go for lunch at the Driving Club tomorrow. I hear there's a marvelous buffet."

Before I could say a word, Peggy said in her blunt way, "Listen, Perri. Mary Dobbs is a very interesting and enthusiastic person, but we just don't want her to run you over with her . . ." She searched for the right word. "Her *zeal*. Why, just today in history class—where were you anyway?—Miss Spencer was talking about women's suffrage, and Mary Dobbs just up and launched into a speech about how in 1913 women in Illinois won the right to vote and that Chicago was the first city east of the Mississippi to allow such a thing and the importance of being involved in the cause to support women's rights. She went on and on, and everyone felt so awkward and Miss Spencer got flustered and Mary Dobbs seemed completely oblivious until finally Brat tugged on her skirt and she came to her senses and sat down. She'll never make friends like that."

"She is a bit overly enthusiastic." I weighed my words. I had, in fact, already heard from Brat about Dobbs's impromptu speech in history class, a class I'd skipped because, in spite of my resolve to be strong, I had needed to cry alone for an hour. "I'm awfully sorry I haven't been good company, Mae Pearl. Of course we can go to the Driving Club."

But I had nothing else to say. I kept my mouth closed, because if I tried to explain the truth to my two dearest friends, I would injure them deeply. How could I tell them that I enjoyed spending every possible minute with Dobbs Dillard, that I *admired* her zeal, and that, although I had only known her for twelve days, she already seemed closer than any other friend I'd ever had in my whole life?

———

Saturday morning, Mr. Robinson came over and sat with Mamma and me as we once again went through the endless paper work that had become our responsibility. I didn't want Mr. Robinson to come visit us on business. I wanted things to be the way they used to be.

Mamma and Daddy had often had the Robinsons and the Chandlers and the McFaddens over to play bridge. I'd always thought the men made a funny quartet—Daddy all tall and thin and dark; Mr. Chandler, big and boisterous with thinning hair and a thick belly; Mr. McFadden with his pale blond hair, taller and skinnier than Daddy; and little Mr. Robinson, prematurely gray, bookish-looking with his thick glasses. But they laughed, played bridge with their wives, and then retired to the library, where I imagined they puffed on cigars and sipped brandy and talked business. Pretty, petite Mamma sat in the garden with Josephine Chandler and Patty Robinson and Ellen McFadden, chatting gaily, sipping on a drink, and occasionally breaking into melodious laughter, like the trill of a flute.

Oh, how I longed for those lazy summer evenings, my windows wide open and the sound of Daddy's low rumbling laugh and Mamma's trilling. It seemed like another life, a strand of music that I would never hear again.

But Mr. Robinson was definitely at our house on business and, true to his word, was determined not only to educate Mamma about the state of our affairs but also to help her find solutions, specifically to allow us to keep the house.

Mamma shocked both of us that morning by announcing in the midst of looking at the accounting books, "I plan to go to work."

I dropped my pencil.

"John McFadden's brother works down at the capitol and has found me a job in the tag department." Mamma's brow creased a little. She cleared her throat, sat up straight, and said, "I'm sure it will be just fine. It's nothing hard, a little monotonous, perhaps, but I feel lucky to have this prospect so quickly." She smiled at me, reached over, and patted my hand. "And if we have to sell the Buick, well, I can ride the streetcar to the capitol. You can even bring Irvin and Barbara to see me after school if you want."

I could not imagine Mamma working at a job, but Mr. Robinson looked awfully pleased. He took off his glasses and said, "Why, that's wonderful news, Dot!"

"Yes, isn't it? I'll be starting right away." Mamma sounded as excited as if she had been asked to set up all the floral arrangements for the Garden Club's annual fund-raising event—something she adored doing.

She gave me a sad smile. "Don't look so distraught, Perri. It'll be okay. You and Barbara can still attend Washington Seminary, and Irvin will be fine at Boys High. Really, the only thing that will change at all is that I've told Ellen McFadden I'll have to step down from being president of the Garden Club for a while. She was disappointed, of course, but said I was doing the absolute right thing, considering the circumstances."

I felt proud of Mamma and relieved for her job, but I made up my mind right then that no one would look down their noses at us. Somehow we'd keep our house and our membership at the country club and our car and our position in society. We came from a well-respected family, and there was no way Daddy's horrible death was going to turn us into a family to be pitied. Not if I could help it.

When I returned from lunch at the Piedmont Driving Club with Mae Pearl, I found Dobbs waiting for me on my front porch. She was dressed in the pretty bright pink dress that Mrs. Chandler had bought for her and looked as if she were ready to go to the Driving Club herself, all fresh and glowing. As soon as I stepped from the car, she rushed down the steps and across the yard, her face all aflame with excitement.

"Oh, Perri! I thought you'd never get home! I've the most wonderful news. The absolute best in the world."

"What are you talking about? And why are you all dressed up?"

"Well, I don't have anything else except my school uniforms and my potato sack." She flashed me a smile. I expected Dobbs to start twirling around, but instead she grabbed my hand, pulled me back to the car, and said so sweetly, "Jimmy, can you please take us to the Chandlers'?"

Jimmy gave her another one of his suspicious looks but nodded.

We hopped in the back seat of the Buick, and Dobbs started explaining, "Well, it came to me in the middle of French class yesterday. After that I could not pay one bit of attention, and when I got home, I went straight to Aunt Josie and told her my idea and she thought it was fabulous, and we have already gotten Hosea and Cornelius working on it out in the barn, and even Uncle Robert smiled when I told him—and you know he can be quite a sourpuss. He said, 'Mary Dobbs, I believe that is a very sensible idea and may even prove to be helpful in a financial way,' and so anyway, it's almost as good as done. So I—"

She would have continued, but I was not particularly in a mood for her wild tangents. "Slow down, will you? What in the world are you talking about?" I thought of Peggy's criticism of the way Dobbs launched into her speech in history class.

"The darkroom!" she said.

"The darkroom?"

"*Your* darkroom! For you to develop your photographs." She said this as if her words made the most perfect sense.

"I've told you I already have the use of the school's darkroom."

"But that's so inconvenient. You can only go there when the school is open. This is going to be all yours. A little room built right in the Chandlers' barn, right next to Dynamite's stall. You can come any time of the night or day. Pretty soon—I've got it all figured out—you'll be selling your prints for a nickel apiece, and then, well, who knows? You'll establish yourself in the community, and it will be money for the family. I just *know* it will work!"

I wanted to be mad at Dobbs. I wanted to ask her who in the world she thought she was, waltzing into my life and making plans for how I could help my family. I had always been perfectly competent at planning, and I liked to do things in an orderly way. But as she rattled on with her cockamamie idea about a darkroom in the Chandlers' barn and the freedom to work there anytime night or day and the fact that perhaps I could *sell* my photographs, something in me perked up, so that by the time we arrived at the Chandler property I was truly excited about the possibility, and I hopped out of the Buick and let Dobbs pull me along to the barn. Then I actually felt butterflies flittering in my stomach as I watched Hosea and Cornelius hammering away, building a little room right beside the stall of a small bay mare. And eventually I felt the slightest twinge of hope settle in my soul.

———

Two weeks after Daddy took his life, Mamma let boys start coming to see me again. Up until his death, on weekdays, when I'd get home from school, I'd sit in the formal living room in cold weather, or on the front porch of the house when it warmed up enough, and entertain several young men from Boys High or college boys from Emory and Oglethorpe and Georgia Tech. And on Sunday afternoons, many girls at Washington Seminary, like me, had front porches filled with boys.

Pop-calling was the term we used. We didn't have a date; boys just "popped in" to see us.

On that Sunday, I heard the doorbell ring, and I leaned out my upstairs window in just the right way—no one could see me, but I could see them down below—as Mamma opened the front door. I felt a little hiccup in my heart when I recognized the young man as Spalding Smith, a junior at Georgia Tech. He was holding a huge bouquet of flowers, which he presented to Mamma, and said, "We have been so distressed about your tragedy, Mrs. Singleton."

"Thank you, Spalding. These are lovely. Your mother's been an angel, helping organize meals and making phone calls. Come on in. I'll call Perri."

I came down the stairs slowly after checking my reflection in the long mirror in my room. I wanted to look just right for Spalding Smith. Just about every girl at Washington Seminary had a crush on him. He had black hair cut short and parted on the side, thick black eyebrows, charcoal eyes, and a smile that could knock you over. He played quarterback for Tech, one of the stars on the football team, and he was twenty-one! I had met him at the Chandlers' Valentine's Dance, and we had talked a little, but I never expected him to come for a visit. I felt light-headed to have him sitting on my porch.

He stood. "Hello, Perri."

"Hi, Spalding. How nice of you to come by." I sat down on the little wrought-iron bench covered with a beautiful yellow-and-red cushion, something Mamma had bought on one of her trips to Provence. I ran my hands along my legs, straightening my skirt.

Spalding sat in one of the Westport chairs. "I wanted to express our condolences in person. I hope you received my card."

We had, in fact, received almost four hundred sympathy cards, and I had not yet read them all. "Yes, thank you," I said. Nothing else came out of my parched mouth.

Thank goodness Mamma came onto the porch and offered us iced tea, which we accepted, and I gulped down several swallows.

After pleasantries, Spalding asked, "Perri, would you consider being my date for the SAE formal on April 15?"

I was speechless. Every girl at Washington Seminary had heard about the formal—it was a special dance given by the Sigma Alpha Epsilons, one of the best fraternities at Georgia Tech—but none of us expected to attend.

I sat up a little straighter, cleared my throat, and tried to sound very sophisticated. "Why, thank you, Spalding. I think that would be delightful."

I could hardly wait to tell Dobbs. I called the Chandlers' residence, hoping to heavens not to wake Mr. Chandler from a nap. "Hello, this is Anne Perrin Singleton," I squeaked out when he answered the phone. "I'm so sorry to bother you on a Sunday afternoon. I was wondering if I may speak to Mary Dobbs."

Mr. Chandler mumbled something, probably to his wife, and she came on the phone. "Perri? Yes. Hello, dear. Could you please hold a moment? I believe Mary Dobbs is in her room. I'll let her get the telephone upstairs."

I waited, impatiently tapping my foot and gnawing on a fingernail. Finally Dobbs came to the phone. "Perri, is it you? Are you okay?"

"Hey, there! I'm swell. Just swell! I hope I didn't interrupt you. Are you busy with pop-calling?"

"With what?"

"With boys at your house?"

"Boys? The only boys around here are Uncle Robert, Hosea, and Cornelius, and I have no idea what you mean about 'pop-calling.'"

In the midst of the shattering events, I had forgotten to educate Dobbs on this very important part of Washington Seminary protocol. "It's just how things work around here." And I explained the process to Dobbs. ". . . And in fine weather, you sit out on the porch and drink lemonade or iced tea or even coffee, if you're allowed. I'll bet Mrs. Chandler would allow it. I serve tea cakes and cookies and all kinds of delicious things that Dellareen bakes for us. We girls like to kid each other and say that the house with the best food gets the most boys."

"Well, there's no one around here, and I can't imagine a boy showing up unannounced at this house. And anyway, I'm not interested in the least. I've got Hank."

I was frowning into the phone, accustomed by now to Dobbs's blunt retorts. "Yes, of course you do, but he's not here, and we aren't dating. It's just social and fun." Then I asked, a bit timidly, "Are you completely against fun?"

"Silly girl, of course not! You've seen me have fun! I guess we just have different interests."

"Boys don't interest you?"

"I told you! I have Hank."

"But you're going to be so awfully bored around here if you don't go to movies or to parties or have boys over. Poor you, Dobbs."

She let that sink in without a word. I imagined her curled up on her bed with a book and rolling her eyes at me.

Finally I blurted out what I'd wanted to tell her in the first place. "At any rate, I love boys, and I've just been invited to a fraternity formal by the handsomest boy on the Georgia Tech football team. Isn't that swell?"

"Oh, Perri! I'm so happy for you!" That's when I heard Dobbs's contagious enthusiasm bubble up. "What's his name?"

"Spalding Smith. His father is a millionaire—made his money with Coca-Cola—and apparently the Depression hasn't hurt them at all. Anyway, Spalding is over the top, and I can't believe I'm lucky enough to be going with him. Now, I just have to find an appropriate gown. I cannot possibly show up in a gown I've already worn."

Dobbs listened to me jabber for a few more minutes, but I had the distinct impression that in her mind she was miles and miles away, maybe as far away as Chicago, Illinois.

Dobbs

After talking to Perri I made my way to the kitchen for a glass of tea. I found Parthenia there, clutching a white basket in her arms. She had a little bonnet on her head and was wearing a pretty dress instead of her servant's uniform.

"Where are you going dressed so nicely?" I asked.

"I'm going to see my mama ova' at the Alms Houses."

"Oh, good for you. I'm sure that will make her happy."

"Yep. Papa takes us on Sunday afternoons after church 'cause we have the day off and on account that Mama has off too. We goes in the ol' Ford Mista Chandler lets us use. I try to make some of her favorite things to take to her. We ain't gone last coupl'a Sundays on account of Mista Singleton's passing, but today we git to go." She nodded forcefully, and gave me a weak smile.

I watched her walk out the back door and across the lawn to the garage where Hosea and Cornelius were waiting in the Ford. Parthenia put her basket in the back seat and climbed up front with them. I thought of the fear that I'd seen in Parthenia's eyes when she'd first told me about her mother being at the Alms Houses. I was sure that little girl knew something, but someone had scared her enough to keep her from telling it to anyone else.

Later that afternoon, while Uncle Robert napped in the big drawing room downstairs, snoring softly as the radio played an episode of *Amos and Andy*, I turned to my aunt, who was busily knitting a sweater for one of her grandchildren, and asked, "Aunt Josie, what exactly are the Alms Houses?"

"The Fulton County Alms Houses have been around since before the Civil War, but about twenty years ago, they built new houses out past Buckhead on Powers Ferry and West Wieuca Roads—to house the county's poor. Wonderful work done there, really. A white Alms House and a black Alms House. Both of them have more inhabitants

83

than there's room for right now—very understandable. I do believe this is the worst year yet of the Depression."

She frowned slightly and squinted as if she were concentrating hard on her knitting. "And just recently, Mr. Chastain sold Fulton County about a hundred acres of land out there, and they made a prison camp around the Alms Houses. The colored prisoners live in the rear of the black Alms House. Mrs. Clark—the superintendent—is the one who looks after them. There must be forty or fifty of them there, and the women are in charge of fixing meals, cleaning, tending the gardens. The colored men prisoners run the farm across the street."

"Parthenia told me about her mother being at the Alms Houses for stealing some of your silver knives. What happened?"

"Ah, that's why you've asked." Aunt Josie continued her knitting, relating the facts without so much as a glance my way. "It's a horrible story, but I suppose you deserve to know." She kept her head bent down, a look of deep assiduity on her face.

"Women like Anna are serving time for offenses such as steal-ing clothing from department stores, playing the 'bug'—you know, gambling—and, of course, stealing from their employers." Aunt Josie had regained her composure and reported this matter-of-factly.

"The women work in the Alms Houses, and on the prison farm, rais-ing vegetables for the complex and for other prison camps in the county." Stitch after stitch she moved her needles in an effortless rhythm.

"Wait a minute, Aunt Josie! Wait a minute!" I jumped off the sofa and startled her so that she snapped her head up, met my eyes with a stunned look in hers, and set down her knitting. "There's something I don't understand at all. Parthenia told me about the stolen knives—that they were never found. She said everybody knows her mother's inno-cent, but that she had to go to the Alms House on account of being accused by a white lady."

I did not want to mention that I knew the white lady was Aunt Josie's daughter. "Couldn't you do something? I mean, do those five knives mean so much that she'd have to stay out there for months?"

"Of course not." And Aunt Josie looked, for an instant, vulnerable. "Heavens, dear Anna was the one who reported it to me in tears right after the party. She knows very well what a stickler I am for making sure nothing gets lost. And she knew how much those pearl-handled knives meant to me—my grandmother's favorite possession. Oh, they came from France in the sixteenth century. Priceless—they're worth a fortune—thousands of dollars, if you can believe it. I should have never used them at the party. It was foolish of me, but heavens, if you have beautiful things and keep them hidden away, what's the point?" Another sigh. "So Anna came and told me right away.

"We searched everywhere, and Anna and Hosea, of course, opened their servants' quarters. I didn't call the police, didn't report a thing. But later, Becca found the silver serving spoon that was also missing right among Anna's things—in a drawer hidden beneath her undergarments. We never found the knives, though."

"Becca turned her in? Didn't Anna *raise* Becca?"

"She did. It's complicated, Dobbs. Terrible and complicated."

"Couldn't you pay to get Anna out?"

"We've tried."

"Parthenia says her mother will never get out until Hosea pays back what the knives are worth!"

"Mary Dobbs"—this she said a bit harshly—"you'll be doing well not to believe everything that Parthenia tells you."

I felt as if Aunt Josie had reached across the room and poked me with one of her long knitting needles. She frowned, looked at me for a long moment, opened her mouth as if she were going to say something else, and then closed it. She turned her head back down to her knitting project and said, "Mary Dobbs, I'll be needing you to help me get supper fixed. Hosea and his children have the evening off."

So I guessed that was as much of an explanation as Aunt Josie was going to offer me. I knew that every family had its ugly bruises—those places that stayed raw and tender in hearts, places no one on the outside knew about, places kept hidden and locked deep inside a family's history—but somehow, the way Aunt Josie glossed over Becca's accusation, the way her face varied between stoicism and crushing vulnerability, I knew another thing. It came to me as I watched Aunt Josie finish up her knitting and stick the needles forcefully into the yellow ball of yarn. The Chandlers' story went a lot deeper than a daughter accusing her servant of a theft she didn't commit.

———

When I returned from school on Monday afternoon, three letters were waiting for me on the little desk in my room. Of course I tore into the one from Hank first:

> . . . You'll be happy to hear that I got up all my courage and talked with your father last night. He had known for a time, I believe, and he gave me his blessing, all the while reminding me that you are still a minor and that there's no need to rush and that you intend to finish high school in Atlanta and hopefully pursue higher education.
>
> I'm planning to come down to Atlanta the last weekend in May. I've saved the train fare. And I promised I'd bring Frances and Coobie too. Don't worry about your parents paying, because I've been saving for their fares too. We're all excited about visiting Atlanta and then bringing you back with us to Chicago.
>
> We were bolstered by Mr. Roosevelt's Fireside Chat last Sunday night. I was impressed with the way the president explained the banking crisis and the reasons for the banking holiday in such simple terms. . . .

I found myself smiling—Hank had talked to my father about us and he was coming down in two months.

> Dear Sis,
> Thank you for your letters. We read them over and over and it all sounds so wonderful. Except the part about that poor girl's father dying.
> Last night Hank talked to Father about you. I wasn't home,

but you know Coobie. She followed them to the church and hid
under a pew and heard the whole thing. But don't worry. She
said Father was real happy about it.
 I can't wait to come down to Atlanta.
  Missing you.
  Bye, Frances

There was a short one, too, from Coobie, in her seven-year-old
scrawl.

I folded the letters and closed my eyes, picturing Hank and Frances
and Coobie, feeling an ache to be there with them. At least they'd be
visiting in May, and then I'd have the whole summer back at home
with them in Chicago.

Uncle Robert and Aunt Josie and I had listened to every word of
President Roosevelt's Sunday night speech on the radio, and at the end
of the first Fireside Chat, Uncle Robert had sat back in his armchair,
puffed on his cigar, letting his lower lip stick way out, and grunted,
with his hands resting on his ample belly, "The man seems to have a
good head on his shoulders. God help him."

Not long after I read the letters, Perri came over, and we jabbered
about pop-calling for a while. Then she said, "Can I ask you something,
Dobbs—something that isn't very polite?"

I grinned at her. "You think you have to be polite to me—the rudest,
biggest-mouthed girl who has successfully shocked all of your friends
in just one short week?"

She looked surprised with that statement.

"Yes, I know what the girls are saying about me, and it's probably
true. I do have a big mouth. Anyway, I'd love to hear you be impolite,
Perri, if that's possible."

"It's just very personal." Perri attempted a half smile that failed
miserably. "The thing I keep wondering is this: Why didn't your father
get a big inheritance like your aunt did? I remember my mother helping
Mrs. Chandler care for her parents and the way she did everything for
them, and then when they died, everyone said that Mrs. Chandler was

a saint and they were glad she would keep the house and have plenty—more than plenty. Gobs and gobs of money is what everyone said.

"So where was your father, and why didn't he receive any money? I can see him choosing to live frugally and preach and do God's work—leading people down the Sawdust Trail, or whatever you call it—but I just can't imagine him letting his family go hungry when he could have money. Have you ever thought of that?"

She took a breath and looked like she might cry. "I'm sorry for asking. It's none of my business, but it's just hard to think of your family going without."

Perri had dared to voice the question that had been brewing inside of me for days and days. How *could* Father not have any money? I understood that he might turn his back on Atlanta society, but surely he had not refused to take the money from the inheritance? With it, I imagined he could keep us well fed and then hand out his charity with greater gusto.

It made my stomach cramp to wonder.

"I've asked myself that a hundred times. And I don't know, Perri. It's one of those things I guess I'll never understand."

"Like why my daddy killed himself," she whispered.

I bit my lip. "Yes, I guess it's like that."

CHAPTER
7

Perri

Sure enough, Mamma started working down at the capitol sorting license plate registrations. It sounded like the most boring job in the world, but it paid real money, which was what we needed. She came home exhausted and cranky, and Dellareen tried extra hard to fix her favorite dinners and have them ready when she walked in the door.

I kept Barbara and Irvin from arguing when Mamma got home, which usually involved giving them a treat and sitting them in front of the radio to listen to *Little Orphan Annie* every afternoon at 5:45.

I was proud of Mamma, but I knew from our accounts that she'd need to be making a lot more money than what the license department was paying her if we were going to keep the house. Mr. Robinson assured me the bank would give us a grace period, since Daddy had been such a well-respected employee, before they stepped in to repossess the house. But how long would that grace period last? I worried, too, that we'd not be able to pay Jimmy and Dellareen, and I couldn't imagine letting them go with their five children to feed.

I thought a lot about the darkroom at the Chandlers' barn and checked out three books on photography from the school library. Soon I knew more than enough to equip my darkroom. I needed developing trays, an enlarger, a light box, and a deep vat for holding several rolls of film at a time. Once a week after school, Mrs. Carnes walked me through the whole process of developing my film, and she applauded the idea of my personal darkroom, but she didn't know that I had no idea how I was going to afford the supplies.

———

Apart from Dobbs, if anything could help me forget about my poor Daddy and all our family's problems, it was taking part in, and often leading, several of Washington Seminary's committees and clubs. So I spent the spring days of 1933 in school, with committee meetings in the afternoons, boys calling on me later at home, and with my siblings planted by the radio in the evenings.

It looked, I suppose, to the outside world, as if I'd just picked right back up with my former life. My friends at school seemed relieved that I had rejoined these activities. It meant we avoided talk of "the tragedy." But on the inside, I was all knotted up with worry and heartbreak and anger and a lot of other things I couldn't explain.

I felt far away from Mamma. We'd never been extremely close. I was definitely a daddy's girl. But she'd been a fine mother, always doing just the right thing for her husband and children. Now I watched her transform before my eyes from the pretty, petite blond wife into a brittle-looking older woman, her face drawn and determined, her eyes empty of their normal sparkle.

At least Patty Robinson and Josie Chandler and Ellen McFadden still came over and sat with Mamma. I didn't hear Mamma's laughter, light and musical, but they were there with her, and that to me was true friendship—sweet and solid and present.

We never talked about Daddy when Mamma was around, but on those spring nights after Mamma had tucked Irvin in, I'd go into his room, where he was cuddled up in the bed and surrounded by a hoard of stuffed animals that I think he felt protected him from all that was terrible in his life. I wanted him to keep hugging those animals tight, no matter that he was almost eleven years old and most of his friends had long ago traded their stuffed animals for baseball cards.

"Perri," he said almost every night, "I miss Daddy."

"So do I," I'd whisper through the catch in my throat.

But one night his questions continued. "D'ya think Daddy's in heaven?"

"Of course he's in heaven, Irv. Up there with Granddaddy and the angels."

"Pete said he might not be. Said that if someone took his own life, well, that was the worst sin in the world, and he'd go straight to hell." Irvin fought back tears, but they trickled down anyway over his profusion of freckles.

I grabbed him in a tight hug. "Oh, Irvin. Pete doesn't know anything at all! Don't you dare listen to him." I held him for a long time like that, feeling his body heaving up and down. At last I gave Irvin a kiss on the head, tucked his covers tight around him, piled his stuffed animals on each side, and left the room.

I went to check on Barbara, who was painting her fingernails while she looked at a comic book. As usual, she paid me little attention. Her thirteen-year-old scowl worried me though. She surely was hurting behind her façade. I whispered "Good night, Sis," and she grunted something unintelligible back to me.

I trudged to my room, haunted by Irvin's question, a question for which I had absolutely no answer. Until Daddy's death, I had hardly given a thought to the hereafter. My feet were firmly planted on the earth. Part of me wished I'd listened more carefully to what the preacher at church said about heaven, and part of me was terrified to know what he thought. I figured I could ask Dobbs Irvin's question about heaven, but I had no desire to hear her answer either.

Dobbs

I don't know how Perri managed it, but she got me invited to Peggy Pender's spend-the-night party, in spite of the fact I could tell that Peggy didn't particularly like me. Hosea drove me to the Pender home in the Pierce Arrow. Peggy's family lived outside of the community known as Buckhead, on Powers Ferry Road, in a sprawling white brick home with lovely oak and hickory trees in the front yard as well as a few dogwoods that had already lost their petals. Across the street from Peggy's house were acres and acres of farmland.

Before I got out of the car, Hosea said to me, "That there's where my Anna is." He nodded to where colored men and women were out working the cornfields.

"There? That's where the Alms Houses are?"

"Further ova' there is where she lives, but she works out in the fields most days. Raises all kinds of vegetables, not just corn." He took a deep breath. "I'm goin' to see my Anna this afternoon on account of being right here across the street."

"It's horrible about your wife. Do you know why anyone would frame her for stealing? Does she have enemies?"

Hosea shook his head slowly, and I was sorry I'd asked, because his shoulders slumped just the slightest bit and his usually jovial appearance became as dark as his eyes. "I kain't say she has enemies; guess our main enemy is just the color of our skin." He said it without resentment, more resigned than angry. "Have a good time with your friends, Miz Mary Dobbs. I'll be here tomorrow to pick you up."

I nodded, and as he drove away, I said again to myself, or maybe to God, *I want to help Hosea and Parthenia prove that Anna is innocent. Somehow I've got to help.*

———

"Who's got a joke?" Peggy asked the six other girls sitting in the spacious guest bedroom at her house. It was after dark, and we'd eaten a delicious meal and painted our nails, and several girls were experimenting with different ways to curl their hair.

Stocky Brat immediately launched into one. "A frat boy is talking to his girl. 'Honey, do you know the difference between a taxi and a street-car?' 'No,' she says. The frat guy says, 'Good. We'll take the streetcar.'"

The girls giggled, and Lisa Young said, "We can use that one! Not bad, Brat." Lisa was a tiny little thing with dark brown hair and big eyes and, so Perri had told me, was responsible for finding jokes and ads for *Facts and Fancies*. She scribbled Brat's joke down on a piece of paper and then stuck her pencil behind her left ear.

"Oh, I have one!" Macon Ferguson said. She was the tallest girl in the junior class and had short red hair and was always talking with her hands. "Teacher—'Peggy, if a number of cattle is called a herd, and a number of sheep a flock, what would a number of camels be called?' Peggy—'A carton.'" Macon winked at Peggy and pretended to be smoking a cigarette, and the girls giggled again.

"Does anyone have a ghost story to tell?" Brat asked.

"Oh, I've heard that Mary Dobbs tells the best stories," Mae Pearl said, smiling sweetly and glancing first at Perri and then at me. "Won't you tell us one?"

"Yeah, go ahead," Perri encouraged. "All of her stories are true," she added, turning to the other girls, as if to convince them that I was somehow legitimate.

"But they aren't ghost stories," I said.

"That doesn't matter. Just tell us something. Unless you'd rather hear another one of my jokes," Brat said.

There was a chorus of "No thanks, Brat!" and they all turned to look at me.

We sat there on the comfortable old bed—big enough for a tribe to sleep in—with all the overstuffed pillows and two quilted comforters wrapped around us. The windows had blown wide open, and the sweet scent of honeysuckle wafted into the room. I almost wanted to climb out the window and pick myself a long white and golden cord of the plant, but I refrained. I needed to be on my best behavior. I searched my mind and landed on the perfect story.

"One summer about three years ago, Father and Mother took us to a little town in Oklahoma. In that town the people were so poor that they'd been eating their pets for two months."

Mae Pearl let out a squeal, Macon said, "How disgusting!" and Peggy just raised her eyebrows and gave me a doubting look.

"Every person had to contribute a dog or cat to the cause of survival, and they all did, because they'd read in the Bible about people sacrificing their kids, and they sure didn't want to have to do that.

"My father, Reverend Billy, had gotten wind of the horrors going on among those desperate people in that little town, and he was preaching to them about grace and God providing and trying to comfort them in his way when this old, old woman, all wrinkles and loose skin, walked straight up the aisle toward the pulpit, wobbling along like she might just fall flat on her face before she got there. She was holding on to a leash with this big ol' mangy dog beside her—the ugliest dog I'd ever seen, all yellowish brown with his long hair missing in spots and so dirty and skinny you saw his ribs through his long hair—and he couldn't walk any better than the old woman.

"Daddy was still preaching but having a hard time of it on account that no one was really listening to him but everyone's eyes were completely glued on that old woman. When she got to the front, right by the stage, she stopped and started shaking so much that I was sure she'd topple over. Then when she regained her balance, she bent over, just shaking and trembling, and reached her withered hands down onto that dog and gave a loud grunt that every one of us could hear—there were only about fifty people at the meeting that night—and she lifted that big ol' mangy-looking dog up in her arms and started hollering at my father, saying, 'If God provides, why do we have to eat my dog tonight? You tell me what kind of God provides that way, Mister Preacher-man! You tell me!' And she cried and wailed for a while, and then murmured, 'He's all I have, my only friend, and now we have to eat him.'

"The people were completely speechless, and I wanted to go puke right there. But Mother always knew what to do, and she rushed up to the old woman and took the dog from her arms and gently placed it down on the ground—and that dog must've been half dead already because he didn't move—and Mother said, 'You will not be eating this animal for supper! You, and anyone else who is hungry, will be eating at our tent tonight.'

"And you could tell that some of those people in the crowd were the ones telling the old woman that they had to eat her dog. I promise those people were the saddest-looking bunch, all hollow-eyed and so skinny you thought they just might be dressed-up skeletons.

"Well, Father just looked over at Mother from the pulpit like she was as loony as the old woman, because he knew we didn't have a scrap of food in our tent, and we were half starved ourselves. But Mother smiled and said, 'Loaves and fishes, Reverend. Loaves and fishes.'"

I paused for a second and let the silence speak for itself, and the girls—every one of them, Mae Pearl and Peggy and Brat and Macon and Lisa and even Perri—looked completely mesmerized, as if they'd never before in their lives heard a good story being told at a girls' spend-the-night party. I stood up and said, "I'll be right back. I've got to go to the powder room."

When I came back in the bedroom, those girls hadn't budged.

Brat begged, "So what happened, Mary Dobbs? What happened to the old woman and her dog and your mother? Did she have food in your tent?"

I smiled and shrugged. "Just what Mother said. 'Loaves and fishes.'"

They looked at me, annoyed. Peggy said, "Look, Mary Dobbs, we get the biblical symbolism. But what we want to know is how *your* story turns out. How *your* mother got loaves and fishes."

Satisfied with their interest, I continued. "Well, after the meeting probably fifteen or twenty of the hungriest-looking people you can imagine crowded around Mother. She was trying to soothe them with her words, and Frances and Coobie and I were whispering behind our hands about what was going to happen.

"And then this lady—a real lady, she could have been one of your mothers, all dressed up fancy with her pretty suit and her hat and her gloves—came up to Mother. She was wiping her face with a handkerchief, and you could tell she felt pretty emotional about something.

"She said, loud enough for everyone to hear, 'Mrs. Dillard, I'd like to invite all these people to my house. I can drive some in my car, and whoever else has cars can bring the others, and we'll have a fine dinner for all of you who want some good country cooking! It would be a privilege to have y'all at my house.'

"Well, Mother swooned a little, caught herself, and said, 'You don't have to do that, ma'am.'

"And the woman said, 'Yes. Yes, I do. I haven't heard a real sermon in a long time, and I haven't wanted to listen to the Good Lord for a longer time—just wanted to protect my family and my things—and all the while He's been asking me to feed the poor that are right here in my backyard.'

"And just like that, we all piled into the different cars, and we drove out to her big ol' plantation house, and everyone pitched in to help her servants, and before you knew it, there was a pig roasting and all kinds of vegetables and corn bread dripping with butter and honey and bubbling peach cobblers served with fresh cream. It was one of the best meals I've ever eaten in my whole entire life! The evening wore on and on, and when we left, everyone was full and laughing and happy."

"Loaves and fishes, indeed!" Perri exclaimed, delighted.

"Is it true? A true story?" Macon asked.

"I promise it is. You can ask my little sister Coobie when she comes to visit. Coobie always loves to catch me when I exaggerate. Ask her.

"And the best part of the story is that that lady has just kept right on feeding the hungry neighbors now for about two years. Every time Daddy goes back to do his revival, she's there, all dressed up, and the old wrinkled lady is there, but she has a little sparkle in her eyes now, and the mangy dog is still the ugliest dog you've ever seen, but he isn't nearly as skinny."

The girls got off the bed, some stretching and yawning. Brat threw a pillow at Perri, and Mae Pearl went to the powder room to take off her makeup and get into her nightgown, and each of them smiled at me and said stuff like, "That was some story, Mary Dobbs." But once again, I had the distinct feeling that I didn't belong.

The next morning after we'd eaten pancakes smothered in real maple syrup and fresh blueberries, I stepped outside to look past the cornfields to the Alms Houses. I crossed the wide road and walked to the field where the Negro men and women were working away. I watched one woman, her hair pulled back in a dark blue scarf, lift the hoe over her shoulder and then swing it down to the ground, over and over, a motion that could have lulled me to sleep with its repetitiveness.

Mother visited women prisoners in Chicago. She told me the darkest stories about all kinds of people, colored and white, but mostly so, so poor. One day I asked, "Mother, why isn't God providing for these people," and she replied, "Honey, it is not up to us to tell God how to provide. The Good Book says to care for the widows and orphans and to visit the prisoner and bring hope to the captives. That's what we're here to do."

Standing there, my belly filled with pancakes, I prayed out loud, "God, here are the poor and the prisoners. I'd like to help, if you have an idea. I'm willing."

When I went back across the street, Peggy and Macon and Brat were out in the front yard. "Wherever have you been?" Macon asked me.

"Just looking at the prisoners out working in the fields. Mrs. Chandler's servant, Anna, is there, and I can't imagine how hard it must be for her."

Peggy lifted her eyebrows, as was her habit, and said, "I imagine it is hard for her, and that's all well and right. She deserves what she got. She stole from the Chandlers, and after they'd been so good to her. I think that Mrs. Chandler should send them away, all of them!"

I started to disagree, but then I considered the girls' faces, and I knew it wasn't worth it. And I knew something else. I wasn't ever going to fit in with them.

———

One day Parthenia and I were in the kitchen canning cherries— there were thousands of them in the Chandlers' orchard—and 'sweating up a storm,' as Parthenia put it, when we heard the front door open and then slam closed.

"Mother! Mother, where are you?" came a shrill, commanding voice.

Parthenia almost dropped the jar she was holding. Her eyes got big, and she whispered, "Uh-oh. We's in for trouble now." She went all rigid in her body. "It's Miz Becca come by."

Becca pranced into the kitchen, carrying her head high. She was tall and slim with the perfect figure to enhance all those gorgeous gowns in her closet. She had lost none of it by having babies—two of them, I'd heard. Her reddish blond hair was coiffed under a fancy hat with a peacock feather sticking out, and she fanned herself as she hurried into the kitchen.

She stared harshly at Parthenia and asked, "Where's Mother?"

"How do you do, Miz Becca?" Parthenia said with a slight curtsy. "Yore mama ain't here right now. Kin I hep you?"

Becca seemed to notice me as an afterthought. I stood up and smiled and said, "Hello, Becca, it's nice to see you again. Goodness, it's been years. You remember me, don't you? I'm Mary Dobbs."

Becca narrowed her eyes, frowned momentarily, and then her face relaxed. "Well, of course I remember you. Mother said you were here, studying at Washington Seminary. It's nice to see you."

She turned toward Parthenia again, and her voice became icy. "Do you have any idea when Mother will be back?"

"Shouldn't be long now, Miz Becca."

"Very well. I'll just be about my business then." She went down the hall, and we heard her high heels clacking up the stairway.

"She ain't in a good mood today. Somethin's eatin' at her," Parthenia whispered. "I gotta be awful careful when she's in one of her moods. She'd just as soon have me sent to the Alms Houses to work on the prison farm too, if she could. She's just an ornery and mean person, is all."

Ten minutes later, Becca rushed back downstairs. Fortunately Aunt Josie arrived at the same time. I tried to keep Parthenia busy with the canning, but we both heard Becca's agitated voice as she talked to Aunt Josie in the foyer.

"It's just what I was afraid of, Mother! More things have been stolen. Grandmother's pearls and her emerald-and-diamond ring and the ruby-and-diamond heart necklace. Priceless jewelry! Gone!"

"Oh my! Are you sure, dear? Positive?"

"I can't think of anywhere else they would be. I was planning to wear Grandmother's pearls to the dinner and dance last night, and I couldn't find them at home, nor the ring and necklace. I hoped I'd find them in the safe. But they aren't here." Becca's voice rose another decibel.

"Dear me. I certainly hate to hear it."

"How could Anna do it? I should have suspected something, the way she talked about taking Cornelius to see some speech specialist in New Orleans. I'll bet you anything she's pawned it all off and hidden the money somewhere, and we'll never find it! I'm not gonna let her get away with this!"

"Becca. Please calm down. You'll frighten the child."

There was a moment of silence, and then Becca asked, "What is it, Mother?"

Aunt Josie lowered her voice so that I had to strain to hear her next words. "Your father said there'd been a hanging down in Columbus last week. A colored woman accused of stealing—no proof either. But they strung her up in a tree right on the property. Can you imagine the horror? So please keep quiet about all this, Becca, you hear? I'll talk to your father about it."

Evidently Aunt Josie ushered Becca outside, because we heard no more of the conversation. Parthenia grabbed onto me and whimpered, "Are they gonna hang Mama?"

"*Shh*. No. Of course not."

"She didn't do it."

I knelt down in front of her and looked her straight in the eyes. "Do you know who did?"

Her little face got tense, and she shook her head back and forth. "I don't know, Miz Mary Dobbs. I just knowed it wasn't Mama."

I was convinced that Parthenia knew a lot more than she was telling me, but I couldn't force her to talk, not with her trembling and looking just about as pitiful and sad as that poor old lady had on the day she thought she was going to have to eat her dog.

I was out in the darkroom that evening when Cornelius came into the barn. I heard his heavy footsteps and the squeak of the wheelbarrow as he pushed it down the hallway and stopped in front of Dynamite's stall. The mare was out in the pasture, and Cornelius began cleaning her stall with a pitchfork. I heard him grunt and breathe, grunt and breathe. Usually gentle, his movements seemed rushed and angry.

A minute later, Parthenia came into the barn, calling out, "Cornie! Cornie, where are you?"

She found him in Dynamite's stall. "Don't you pay no neva' mind to what Miz Becca says! It ain't yore fault 'bout Mama, and you knowed it. She'd neva' steal nothin'—no matter how much she wants you to learn to talk."

Cornelius gave a grunt, and I heard again the scrape of the pitchfork through the shavings.

Then Parthenia whispered to her brother, "I'm sorry I told you 'bout it. It's jus' that I's scared. That's all. I's plumb scared."

Evidently Cornelius set down the pitchfork, because I didn't hear much movement. When I left the darkroom a little while later, tiptoeing away so as not to be noticed, I saw Cornelius Jeffries sitting in the shavings with Parthenia snuggled in his arms. She was sniffing, and he was just rocking her back and forth and making a deep, guttural sound in his throat that I imagined was his way of singing a lullaby.

CHAPTER
8

Perri

I guess Dobbs had been praying about God providing for my family—or at least for me—because one day Mrs. Carnes gave me two developing trays and an enlarger, things she said that Washington Seminary was replacing with newer models. And if that wasn't good enough, a few days later when Jimmy took me over to the Chandlers', I had another surprise.

Red and Dynamite nickered at us as Dobbs and I walked into the barn. I stroked their muzzles and went into the darkroom. When I lit the kerosene lamp, I gasped. The whole room was furnished! The developing trays were sitting on low shelves, the enlarger was beside them, and a light box and a vat were on the other side of the room, along with the basin for dipping the negatives and a bright light and a table. And stacked on a shelf was a whole row of photographic rolled film. I burst into tears as I touched every piece of equipment.

"Isn't it fine?" Dobbs said. "Aunt Josie had Hosea go and get the rest of the supplies. She said it wasn't handing out charity to furnish this room since it was on her property, and she said to tell you she didn't want to hear one word of argument about it."

Mrs. Chandler knew me well. Just like my father, I was stubborn enough to refuse charity. We were self-made people, having worked long and hard to carve out our place in society. But I smiled at Dobbs and simply said, "Thank you for this—I know it was your idea. And now I can take pictures. Loads of pictures."

In her intuitive way, Dobbs must have sensed I wanted to be alone in the darkroom and went back to the house. I picked up my Eastman

Kodak camera, which I had brought from my house, and thought of Daddy. My education about work had begun as a small child, before Barbara and Irvin were born. Often at the end of a long day, he invited me into his office, and I hopped into his lap. "You work too hard," I'd say, mimicking Mamma.

"Hard work has gotten us ahead in life, Perri-girl." Here he produced a penny and said, "Never turn your nose up at a penny—it's our future. Your grandfather didn't have a penny to his name when he was a boy, but he put himself through medical school and became a well-respected physician. And he taught himself how to build things too. When he wasn't with patients, he was building this house for your grandmother, and I was right there beside him, laying bricks and mixing mortar. He was a fine, hardworking man."

"But I don't want you to work that hard, Daddy. Grandpa wore his body out and died at fifty-three." Another tidbit I'd overheard from Mamma.

"I know it, Perri-girl, but I'm different. After a long day at the bank, I come home at night to a good meal and a wonderful wife, and if I'm lucky, after supper I get to have an angel sitting in my lap." Then he'd squeeze me tight. "You can't be tired for long when an angel sits in your lap."

I remembered those long-ago family days before my siblings arrived, watching my father change into overalls after work and go to the barn or to the garage and tinker. He had a habit of making the practical things of life understandable to a child. So I found myself studying the way he wrote figures on the lavishly lined accounting paper and watching as he repaired the faucet or put oil in the Buick.

In everything he did, his work was meticulous, detailed, perfect— whether at the bank or at home. The physical work, the sawing and hammering and digging, seemed to drive away his dark moods, giving him something else to concentrate on. "You need balance in life, Perri," he used to tell me. "When things get a bit difficult, you gotta have a way to stop thinking about the hard things for a while."

When had it all begun to crush him?

Mr. Robinson had given us more bad news recently, all the while fiddling with his glasses. Daddy's insurance policy and stocks were worthless, the savings account nonexistent, and we still owed a sizeable note on the house. I found it hard to believe how terrible our predicament really was, for Daddy was the wisest, most wary of bankers. The stocks had vanished in the crash, but what had happened to all the money he had so carefully saved?

With my Rainbow Hawk-Eye camera sitting in my lap and the smell of fresh hay and shavings wafting in from Dynamite's stall, I closed my eyes and thought of "White Angel Breadline" and how Dorothea Lange had captured the look of despair on that man's face. I wondered if some day I would look through my viewfinder and see straight to the moment when a person stopped believing in all the good things life could bring. I owed it to my father to try.

———

Only two days later, after Barbara and Irvin were in bed, Mamma came into my room, where I was studying history and writing some copy for *Facts and Fancies*. She brushed her lips across the top of my head and sat in my armchair. I'd never seen her look quite so thin. Haggard. I felt a tiny pinprick of fear. What if Mamma came down with pneumonia like Macon Ferguson's mother had after she started working in the bottling factory? She'd developed a terrible chest cough and then been hospitalized and almost died. By the time she recovered, her job had long since been filled by someone else.

"Perri." She took my hand, and hers was bony and cold, so cold. "I've been talking with Bill—with Mr. Robinson—for the past week, and he and I have had to make a hard decision."

I immediately wanted to shout, *How dare you make a decision without me? I'm the one who knows what's going on.* But Mamma just continued.

"We're going to have to sell the house."

"No!"

"There's no other way. We'll find something smaller. If we sell the house, you and Barbara can keep going to Washington Seminary and we can keep the car and Dellareen and Jimmy can keep coming. It'll work out okay."

"How in the world would you find someone to buy this house in the middle of the Depression?"

"The bank will buy it from us. Mr. Robinson has worked it out—a very fair deal, Perri. Much more than fair. Extravagantly kind."

"Oh, Mamma. We can't sell our home. We just can't."

"I know how much it means to you, and does to me as well." She sniffed and turned her head away, and I noticed how her dark blond hair was filled with gray. "Sometimes you just don't have a choice."

I didn't want to cry. I needed to be strong for Mamma. But I felt something drain out of me. It struck me that if I could have taken a photograph of myself at that precise moment, I would have represented just what I wanted to capture: the moment when a soul stopped believing in all the good things life could bring.

After Mamma left my bedroom, I stood in front of the four framed photographs of the house. Dobbs had called them artistic and told me I had talent. I looked at them with love. Although smaller than the Chandler residence, our house was every bit as beautiful, in many people's opinion. In fact, often someone would turn up at the house, either walking or driving up the long driveway, just to get a peek at our home. The grounds were landscaped with what Daddy had called "Jimmy's genius—just making people want to stop and stare and then walk right up the front steps and have a seat on the porch." I heard Daddy saying that in my mind, and I began to cry, standing in front of my photographs.

Then I imagined Daddy working beside his father, talking of medicine and construction. Together the two of them, along with the finest professionals, designed and built our house. Later, after my grandfather died and my grandmother moved to an apartment, Daddy and

Mamma moved into the house. Daddy tinkered after work, adding a back porch, building the barn on the property, which he filled with five fine Thoroughbreds, and constructing a tool shed where he stored his equipment. I remembered what his friends started calling him when I was a child—*"the banker with a builder's hands."*

If we sold the house, we'd be selling part of Daddy.

Late that night, I got the financial books from downstairs, spread them on my desk, and scrutinized Daddy's small handwriting. I had looked at the numbers many times before, but I had never paid attention to one item. Jimmy and Dellareen's salary. There it was, on the monthly budget page. They earned eleven dollars a week.

Daddy had taught me how to save money, and when I was a little girl, he liked to remind me of something Benjamin Franklin had said—"A penny saved is a penny earned." He had even given me what he called a Penny Pinching Jar to help me save pennies, which I had faithfully done for years.

As I thought about that, I got on my knees and reached under my bed. Years ago, the glass jar had overflowed with pennies, and I'd replaced it with a deep round tin the size of a hatbox, which at the time I felt I'd never fill. But as I pulled it out from under the bed, I smiled to myself. It was so heavy I could barely move it.

I rolled the big tin on its side, and when I removed the top, copper pennies spilled onto the floor, making the sound of crashing thunder. Several spun under the bed, and one twirled all the way across my room and came to a stop only an inch in front of the heat vent. I quickly rescued it from disappearing into the grate. Heart pounding, I waited to see if the noise had awakened my mother and siblings. When no sounds came from across the hall or downstairs, I breathed a sigh of relief and methodically began counting the pennies—some shiny light copper, others badgered and worn and dull, a few covered in a greenish mold—putting them in piles of a hundred.

Over the years I'd envisioned many different things this money would buy—from a palomino pony when I was nine, to the fanciest Kodak camera last year. But I'd always convinced myself to save the money instead. Now I was thankful.

When I finished counting, I burst into tears. There were 2531 pennies in the tin. That wouldn't even pay Jimmy and Dellareen for a month! All those years of saving pennies and what good would it do?

I sank onto the velvet-covered bench in front of my vanity chest and stared into the gilded oval mirror. My face was flushed from crying. Through clenched teeth I said, "We're going to survive. Daddy bred into me the instinct of survival." Then I thought of Dobbs's farfetched stories of starving people eating their domestic pets. "No," I seethed. "We'll do more than survive. I am going to figure out a way for the Singleton family of Atlanta, Georgia, to retain every bit of the position and respect we deserve."

Then I got up, went to my bed, collapsed on the yellow comforter, and cried again.

We never talked of my family's financial problems at school, although Mae Pearl and Brat and Peggy had probably guessed how bad things were. For heaven's sake, they had all seen horrible financial times. But no one ever breathed a word about her family's struggles. I thought of telling Dobbs but then decided that, although she might be able to sympathize, she'd never be able to understand all that I had lost.

I acted as if I were handling my circumstances well on the occasions Spalding came over to the house, and I made sure that Dellareen served his favorite cake. But I always had a knot in the pit of my stomach, and I wondered if Spalding Smith would still think I was wonderfully fun and wild and pretty if he knew that my family barely had a cent to its name.

Dobbs

One Sunday I went to church with Perri—her family attended St. Luke's, and the Chandlers went to St. Philip's—and went back to her house for Sunday lunch. Sure enough her mother did fix a delicious pot roast, and as I partook of the food, savoring every bite of the roast and the mashed potatoes with gravy and the green beans and the homemade biscuits, I thought about what my family was eating—or not eating, perhaps. I concluded that the Singletons might *feel* poor, but they were actually very well-off. They were rich. They lived in a gorgeous house and had two full-time servants and a stable full of horses. Oh, it was like a museum at their place, and I thought how Mother would ooh and ahh over the antique furniture and the exquisite material on the sofa and armchairs. As I ate that lunch and watched Perri teasing Irvin, and Barbara frowning and just picking at her mashed potatoes smothered in gravy, I imagined my family being rich, and for just a flickering moment, I liked it.

In the afternoon, around two, the boys started stopping by the Singleton residence. Perri begged me to come down and join her, but I refused and spent the afternoon reading and looking out her bedroom window at the scene below. I was incredulous. Sure enough, five young men stood on the front porch, dressed in their Sunday suits, laughing and talking to Perri, who sat on the cushioned bench, wearing a pretty teal dress that set off her eyes. Her cheeks were ablaze with those two dark pink spots, and she nodded and talked, looking like the picture of happiness and health and confidence when I knew inside she was always calculating her family's fragile position in Atlanta society.

When the last boy left, Perri came inside and hurried up to her room. "Dobbs Dillard! If you aren't the rudest thing!" Her eyes flashed, and she had her hands on her hips. "You could have at least had the decency to come down and meet the boys. Heavens, you liked to embarrass me to death!"

"Oh, Perri! You're so smooth and at ease. What do I have to say to all those boys? I told you I have Hank, and I'm just not interested in meeting other young men. Is that so awful?"

Perri gave a sigh and shrugged. "No, I don't suppose so. I just want you to be happy here in Atlanta."

"I'm happy, Perri. I have a roof over my head and a wonderful room to sleep in and kind relatives and I go to a fine school and I have clothes and food and a dear, dear friend with whom to share adventures. I don't need anything else."

Perri seemed to acquiesce and was about to say something when Mrs. Singleton called up from below, "Perri! Spalding Smith has just arrived."

Perri's cheeks turned perfect pink again, and she grabbed my hands. "Please come down and meet Spalding. It'd mean the world to me. Afterwards, we're going for a drive, and he can take you back to the Chandlers'."

For Perri's sake, I agreed.

Spalding Smith was wearing Madras pants, white dress shoes, and a blue blazer. He handed Perri a huge bouquet of flowers, which must have cost a fortune, pecked her on the cheek, and turned to meet me.

Perri said, "This is Mary Dobbs Dillard, from Chicago. She's Robert and Josephine Chandler's niece."

"How fine to meet you, Mary Dobbs." He took my hand lightly in his and squeezed it as he met my eyes. He certainly was good-looking. Nothing I could contest about that. His black hair was slicked back from his forehead handsomely and parted on the side, and he had dimples that creased down his strong, sturdy face when he smiled and perfectly curved black eyebrows that he seemed to use to the best advantage, raising them in a way that took me aback. Right away, I felt reservations about Spalding Smith. Something struck me as wrong. He seemed too confident or too smooth or too certain of himself and his appeal to girls. It leaped out at me, and I wondered how Perri missed it.

After that initial shock, the way he took my hands and gazed at me as if I were the girl he was dating, I realized what upset me the most. His eyes. I didn't trust his eyes. They were luscious dark brown— "gorgeous," the Washington Seminary girls would proclaim—with a hint of seduction in them. His eyes grabbed you and drew you in. But something important was missing in them.

Kindness. One look into Hank's eyes and I'd melted with the kindness there. Kind eyes. Eyes I could trust.

Right away, I didn't think I could trust Spalding Smith. Unfortunately, I could tell that Perri had already fallen for him real hard.

I couldn't stop thinking about Spalding's eyes contrasted with Hank's, and later that evening as I strolled down toward the Chandlers' lake, a memory came to me.

It was late at night after a revival meeting, and Hank was walking Coobie, Frances, and me back to our apartment. A man with a terribly scarred face started following us, calling out, "Hey, preacher man! I saw you up there talking about God. What do you have for me?" His voice was eerily high-pitched, and his eyes had a crazy gaze to them.

Coobie began to cry.

And right there in the street, Hank knelt down, looked Coobie in the eyes, and said, "You stay with your sisters. I'm gonna take care of everything." Coobie was almost hysterical, but Hank put his hand on her shoulder and said, "Trust me, Coobie."

She still hid behind Frances and me, but she stopped crying, just peeking out at Hank, who walked over to the crazy man and started talking to him as if he were his next-door neighbor.

"Tell me what you need, sir."

Startled, the man stuttered, "I-I-I jus' need some money for food, jus' a little food."

Hank handed him a dollar bill—I think it was the last cent he had—and said, "You buy yourself something to eat, you hear? And tomorrow night, you come to the revival and I'll bring you something more."

I was amazed when the man showed up the next night, and when Hank handed him a bag of food, the man once again looked startled. Then tears sprang to his eyes, and he whispered, "You're the first person who's kept his word to me in a long, long time."

Remembering that incident made me miss Hank all the more.

CHAPTER
9

Perri

Late on Sunday night, I searched through my closet three times before admitting the truth. I had nothing to wear to the SAE formal. "Daddy," I whispered, "what would you say if you knew I didn't have the money to buy a dress for the fraternity party?"

I shut my eyes to squeeze out that awful memory that slipped in when least expected—Daddy's legs dangling in front of me. With a sob, I went to my vanity and picked up a small photograph of my parents from their wedding day. I brushed my hand across the glass, wanting to get beyond it to touch the handsome face of my father. "If you were still here, Daddy, it wouldn't matter that we had to move. We'd do it all together. We'd sell the horses and pack up our things in boxes, and we'd find another place and it would be okay. It really would." I set the frame down, clenched my fists and tried to find something to do with my anger.

"But you're not here! You . . . killed yourself!" I strangled on the words, tears sliding down my cheeks, a feeling of profound helplessness engulfing me. "We'll be moving out of our home soon. I told Mamma I'd break the news to Barbara and Irvin, but I don't know how I'm gonna do it, Daddy. I really don't. You should see how scared Irvin is already—scared and sad. And Barbara is just all shut up in herself. And Mamma. Oh, Daddy, I can't even reach Mamma."

There was a sudden release in saying those things out loud, saying the truth. Even if my father could not hear my words from wherever he was, I *imagined* he could hear me, and so I ended with a pitiful admission. "And all I can think about is finding a dress. What does a silly dress matter with everything else that's going on? But Daddy, it *does* matter, and it has to be the perfect dress. I need to wear a shimmering gown and be beautiful and fun if I want to impress Spalding Smith and his fraternity. And I do, Daddy. I know you'll think I'm crazy. I've never settled on just one boy. But I need to now, for the family. He's a good one to settle on, Daddy. He has enough money for us all."

I washed my face, changed into my pajamas, crawled into bed, and fell into a dreamless sleep.

———

The next morning, my mood had lifted, but I could not concentrate at all during history class. I scribbled drawings of stick-figure ladies in long gowns on my notepad instead of paying attention to Miss Spencer's lecture on the election of a new ruler in Germany whom I had never heard of, a man named Hitler. Dobbs, always frantically taking notes, glanced over at me and whispered, "What in the world is the matter, Perri?"

"I don't have a gown for the formal. No money, and I can't show up in any of my old things."

Miss Spencer made a clucking sound in her throat that sat us both up straight. But after class, Dobbs took me by the elbow and said, "I have an idea, but I need to check on something. I'll talk to you tomorrow."

The next day, before English, Dobbs skipped up to me and pronounced, "If you can't buy a gown, then make one!" She said it as if she had told me to go outside and pick a dandelion—of which there were hundreds in our backyard.

"I haven't the faintest idea of how to sew."

"Hmm, well, that could be a problem." But she was fairly beaming. "But don't worry. I told you I had an idea."

After school, instead of Jimmy driving me home, Dobbs whisked me to where Hosea was waiting with the Pierce Arrow, and in no time she and I were standing in Becca Chandler's bedroom, peering into a spacious closet. On one side of the closet hung row after row of evening gowns.

"My heavens, there are dozens of dresses in here!" I reached out and touched the silky material on a sparkling cherry red gown. "It's gorgeous!"

"Aunt Josie said they were all for Becca's debut summer. She had forty-seven parties to attend, and of course, she refused to show up in the same frock for any of them." Understandably, Dobbs informed me of this with indignation in her voice.

"Well, it's an unwritten rule of etiquette for debut parties—you never wear the same thing twice. I've heard Becca was quite the prima donna. She had every boy swooning for miles and miles, and her dance card filled weeks in advance."

"How did you hear that?"

- "Mae Pearl and Peggy and Lisa all have older sisters who made their debuts with Becca. It's common knowledge among our group."

Dobbs gave me one of her startled-but-in-control looks. "Anyway, I told Aunt Josie about your predicament, and she said you could have your pick."

"Oh, I couldn't."

"For heaven's sake, Perri. She said she'd be happy for someone else to use them. Each of them was only worn once."

"But someone might recognize them as Becca's."

"You're a fine one to talk. Haven't you heard the expression 'beggars can't be choosers'?"

I scowled at her.

Dobbs rolled her eyes. "Perri, Becca is twenty-eight years old—that's nearly a decade since she made her debut. Surely no one has *that* good of a memory."

"Oh, you'd be surprised. And anyway, the styles have completely changed."

"You're being snooty and impossible, and it doesn't become you at all!"

I almost made a retort, but then I laughed. She was right.

Dobbs insisted I try on every one of those dresses, and it was fun, I must admit, lifting my spirits a little more each time I stepped from the dressing room into Becca's bedroom and struck a model's pose.

Dobbs surveyed me carefully, giving her opinion—"too short," "a bit out of style," "too low cut"—until at last she proclaimed one "exquisite" and "the perfect color of blue" and "finely designed."

But what did Dobbs know of style?

"No," I argued. "It's too long, and I don't fill out the top well enough."

Ignoring my protests, Dobbs produced a tape measure and a pin cushion and went about measuring and pinning the dress as if she were a professional seamstress. "Yes, I can make this work. It will be gorgeous on you."

"What in the world are you talking about this time, Dobbs?"

"My mother is an expert seamstress, and I grew up watching her alter the ball gowns of rich ladies. And Mother taught me a few things about alterations along the way. I believe I can make this into something absolutely gorgeous for you."

And she did. Dobbs Dillard never ceased to surprise me.

———

It turned out that Spalding and I were very congenial. He pronounced me the belle of the ball and whispered that every eye was on me when I walked into the ballroom at the Georgian Terrace in my sapphire blue off-the-shoulder gown.

I took the compliment like a strong cocktail until I felt dizzy from all the attention. Loads of boys asked to dance with me, and then, every once in a while, Spalding came over and cut in and took me into his arms, and I thought I was floating, my feet not touching the ground.

My, he could dance! I was thankful for all the times Mae Pearl had put a record on the Victrola or found music on the radio and taken my hands and taught me the latest dance steps. She danced classical ballet, but she had an amazing sense of rhythm for popular dancing, which she enjoyed teaching others.

Spalding noticed. "You're a swell dancer, Perri. Where'd you learn?" He placed his hand in the small of my back and drew me so close it took my breath away. "Other boys? All your other beaus?"

I laughed giddily and proclaimed, just as if I were tipsy from drink instead of compliments, "Oh no, not at all. Mae Pearl McFadden showed me the steps."

"Mae Pearl. Well, isn't that something."

We danced until late in the night, and I forgot all of my family's troubles as I let Spalding spin me round and round to the sound of the band, his eyes occasionally catching mine with a dark look of fire in them.

———

May Day—the May Fete as we called it—came and went with its usual grandeur and flourish. The event was held in the spacious yard behind Washington Seminary, and family members and boys from nearby colleges and many important people in Atlanta attended. Mae Pearl danced as a fairy princess, and ten of us juniors were on the Princess Court.

Dobbs, ever true to herself, did not participate in the events but sat beside her uncle and aunt, her black hair caught up in long sweeping braids and pinned up with a beautiful golden clip given to her by her aunt. She wore a lovely pale pink dress that was covered in sheer lace and fell to her ankles. I recognized it as one of Becca's debut gowns, no doubt altered to fit Dobbs.

"You were marvelous," she told me after the finale, grabbing my hands and squeezing them as only she could. Bless her, Dobbs was the picture of beauty and enthusiasm.

"I seem to recognize your gown," I said, with a wink.

"Yes, what do you think?" She twirled once and then again, and we began giggling like little girls.

Spalding approached us, holding two glass cups filled with punch. "Whoa there, girls! It looks like you've spiked the punch in spite of Prohibition."

Dobbs gave him a smoldering look and said, "How dare you accuse us of taking strong drink! Can't you tell we are simply inebriated with life?"

Spalding blushed slightly, gave a chuckle, and handed a cup to each of us.

"No thank you, Spalding," Dobbs said with a slight curtsy. She gave me a squeeze and said, "Talk to you later."

Spalding watched her leave, his eyes following her with a look of suspicion and disapproval and distrust, all melded into one. "She's a very strange girl, isn't she?"

"She is the oddest girl I have ever met, and I love her like a sister, more than a sister. I feel closer to Mary Dobbs than to any other person on this earth." I think I said this as a warning to Spalding, lest he burst our bubble of congeniality with criticism of my dearest friend.

"You must feel lucky to have a friend like that," he commented, but almost as an aside, almost as if he had to find something to fill up the silence that spilled between us.

I laughed lightly, sipped my punch, and said, "I do. I really do."

When he took me by the elbow and guided me smoothly to the tables set out with tea cakes and finger sandwiches, I went blithely on my way with the absolute assurance that Spalding Smith played perfectly into my plan of survival.

Dobbs

I had never imagined that my sewing skills would come in handy in Atlanta. What fun I had looking through Becca Chandler's closetful of gorgeous gowns and picking one out for Perri's formal. Seeing my success, Aunt Josie encouraged me to pick another gown for my dress at the May Fete. I spent all of the Saturday before the fete altering a beautiful light pink tea dress—I had to take in four inches in the bust—and I wore it happily to the May Fete. But clothes can't make a person fit in.

It was a lovely day, and the Washington Seminary girls were worked up and giddy from preparations and little sleep and the success of the day. After the performances, Spalding Smith stole Perri away. I could not bear to be in his presence so I went and stood with sweet Mae Pearl and boyish Brat and snobby Peggy and tiny Lisa. Tall skinny Macon slinked over to us and said, "What are y'all doing here, Pinks? I'm going to find me a Gel!" She gave a wink and hurried off.

"A Gel?" I said.

The girls laughed, and Mae Pearl explained, "The older girls at Washington Seminary are called the Pinks and the boys who come to court us, well, they're called the Gels. And there are a lot of Gels here today!"

I nodded as if that made perfect sense and listened to them talk about the upcoming Kentucky Derby and the new luncheon special at the Piedmont Driving Club and about a movie called *King Kong* that was sweeping through America as the new rage.

At the mention of *King Kong,* Mae Pearl squealed, and little Lisa grabbed her gloved hands and said, "It's the most splendid movie in the world, isn't it?" They headed to the refreshment table, jabbering about a giant ape that stood on top of the Empire State Building, swatting at attacking planes, and something about how the actress Fay Wray fell in love with the ape, of all things!

Brat tugged on her skirt and said, "I'm not going to talk to any Gels. All I want to do is to get this thing off and put on my tennis outfit. I'm leaving." I had to smile at Brat, with her short brown hair and stocky frame. Somehow, a long white "fairy" gown didn't suit her very well.

That left me standing with Peggy, who looked more sophisticated than ever in a slim-fitting off-white tea dress and a stylish matching hat. Her soft brown hair curled slightly and she narrowed her brown eyes, big as a doe's. She took me by the elbow and led me toward a little bench at the back of the Washington Seminary property.

She let go of my elbow and put her hands on her hips. Leaning toward me with her mouth fixed in a pout and her brow furled, she whispered furiously, "You are too much—coming down here from Chicago and trying to steal Perri away from all of her lifelong friends, the people who care about her. Do you know who Perri Singleton is? The girl with a thousand dates! A thousand dates last year, the most popular girl in Atlanta! I don't see why in the world she wants to spend time with the likes of you! So quit trying to weasel your way into this social circle. You don't fit, and you know it."

I was too stunned to say anything. I gave a feeble attempt at a sentence. "I never—" But Peggy cut me off.

"Don't you try to defend yourself, Mary Dobbs. I know how my friend was before you came, and I know how she is now. You and your big mouth are going to throw her into something deep and dark like her father! I won't have it!" Peggy poked a white-gloved finger at me. "Leave her alone! Do you hear me? Leave her alone."

I didn't have a chance to reply because she turned on her heels and walked back to the crowds of happy people standing around with glasses of punch in their hands. Shaking all over, I stepped behind the bench into the bushes of flowering azaleas and tried to sort out my thoughts.

I had barely composed myself when a young man came to the bench and sat down, alone. I was half hidden in the bushes and didn't want to frighten him by stepping out, so I coughed twice, loudly, came out, and gave him a timid smile.

"Hiding from someone?" he asked.

"No, just admiring the beauty of this place," I said, looking for another spot to escape to. I longed to go home, but Uncle Robert had driven us to the Fete, and he and my aunt were happily chattering with friends, seeming not in the least bit interested in leaving.

"I won't bite." The boy had said something else, but I missed it. I turned and saw he was patting at the bench. "Have a seat. I won't bite."

"Oh." I felt my face flush. "I . . . I was just . . ."

"Leaving? I'm Andrew Morrison." I sat down beside him. He had blond curly hair and dark blue eyes and was wearing a smart-looking suit. He smiled again. "I go to Tech and enjoyed the May Fete very much."

"I've heard nice things about Georgia Tech," I said, still in a daze from Peggy's stinging comments. "A fine school."

"And your name?"

Embarrassed, I blushed again. "Forgive me. I'm Mary Dobbs Dillard. I recently came down to Atlanta from Chicago."

"Splendid. And do you like our fair city?"

We engaged in small talk for probably ten minutes. At first I could barely concentrate on what he was saying, but slowly I relaxed and listened as he talked about being a mechanical engineer and hoping to use his skills to help some of the needy in Atlanta. And then he blushed and said, "I've talked too much about myself. Tell me about you."

I looked into his dark blue eyes and said, "I really need to go, but it was nice to meet you, Andrew."

He chuckled. "Likewise, Mary Dobbs. Perhaps we'll see each other again."

"Perhaps." I nodded and hurried away to where Uncle Robert and Aunt Josie were standing, puncturing meatballs with their brightly colored toothpicks and popping them into their mouths and laughing as if they hadn't a care in the world.

Perri

That evening, all worked up over the great success of the May Fete and my date with Spalding, I asked Mamma if I could go spend the night with Dobbs, who had disappeared at some point after the Fete.

Mamma agreed, in happy spirits because the folks at the license department had let her off to see me in the May Day festivities. She drove the Buick with me beside her while Barbara and Irvin sang at the top of their lungs the theme song from the Fete, a song that Gloria

Swanson made famous in a musical from the twenties. I felt such a relief to see them laughing and happy when only two days ago I'd told them about us having to sell the house and they had both cried for hours.

Mamma let me off at the Chandlers' driveway. Bypassing the house, I hurried to the barn and into the darkroom and grabbed my camera. I didn't know what I would photograph, only that a new feeling of creativity was rushing through me, and I wanted—I needed—to profit from it immediately. I thought of the photo of the starry night so beautifully rendered in *Patches from the Sky*. Alas, the spring evening was far from pitch-dark, and stars would not come out for hours. So I hurried to the house, ran through the back door into the kitchen, and greeted Parthenia, who was crying rather dramatically as she peeled onions.

I climbed the stairs to Dobbs's room, impatient to talk to her about my date with Spalding and ask her advice about what to photograph. I found her lying perfectly still on her bed, staring up at the canopy. She was still wearing the soft pink tea dress, but she'd taken out her braids so that her black hair fell over her shoulders and off the side of the bed. Stretched out and recovering from the excitement of the day, she looked to me like a winsome starlet or a foreign princess. Before she even knew I was there, I had taken the photo.

She heard the noise of the shutter clicking and turned to the doorway. "What are you doing, Perri?"

"Taking pictures. I couldn't wait. Wasn't it all divine—the whole day? I feel so inspired; I can't begin to describe it."

For once, Dobbs did not share my enthusiasm. She sat up and tossed loose strands of her hair over her shoulder and whispered, as if she were choking back tears, "I had no idea."

"No idea about what?"

"That I was making your grieving harder by taking too much of your time."

I gave her an odd look, my mind a thousand miles away. "Are you crazy? What are you talking about? You've saved my life, Dobbs Dillard."

"That's not how your friends see it. Especially Peggy."

"Of course not," I acquiesced. "But they're jealous. And what can I say to them? I like you better? They'll come around." I sat on the bed, set the camera carefully beside me, and ran my hands along my white dress. "You've done a marvelous job with our gowns."

She barely acknowledged the compliment.

"Oh, heavens. Forget about Peggy." Then I grabbed the camera and went to the far side of the room. "Look this way. I'm going to take your picture."

She smiled a little then and rolled her eyes at me. I snapped the picture of quintessential Dobbs, with her black hair falling to her waist, a quick smile on her lovely olive-skinned face. Then she frowned. "Is it true what Peggy said? That you had a thousand dates in one year? A *thousand*?"

I felt my face go red with embarrassment. "Peggy said that?"

"Yes, she did. She said you were the most popular girl in Atlanta."

"Well, she's wrong. It's just silly stuff. Stupid. We used to record in our diaries all the boys who came over to our homes, and last year she decided to count them."

"So it's true? You had a thousand dates in one year? That's extraordinary."

"I told you—it's just silliness. You know, pop-calling—just boys coming over to the house. Loads of girls had guys visiting all the time. The only reason those boys came over was because Dellareen baked the best brownies in the world."

"I'm sure that's the only reason."

"Anyway, it doesn't matter a bit now, because I'll have no more dates after we move."

That's when I finally spilled out the truth to Dobbs—that we were going to have to sell the house. She listened to me but, thank goodness, didn't give me any shallow platitudes about God providing.

She just said, "I'm really sorry, Perri. It's another excruciatingly hard thing, with all you've been through." Then we both lay across her bed and she began to recite something from memory about God's compassions not failing and being new every morning. I recognized it as Scripture.

She recited it softly, but with intensity, and I didn't know why, but afterwards I felt neither sad nor angry nor giddy. I felt a type of gentle cloth float down and cuddle me within its folds.

Dobbs

I'd never expected to fit in at Washington Seminary, but it got worse after my confrontation with Peggy. Maybe she'd told the rest of the girls, because suddenly Perri's friends, Macon and Brat and Lisa—and Peggy, of course—were at times downright rude to me. They didn't smile at me in the halls, and even though we sat together at lunch, they carried on conversations that seemed expressly meant to exclude me. Only Mae Pearl continued to treat me kindly, and for all the ways her sugary sweetness grated on me, I still was thankful for her.

The talk at Washington Seminary for the first half of the month of May volleyed between the huge success of the May Fete and the "big swoon" over the Kentucky Derby. That's how the girls described it, and they jabbered on and on, not about the horses, but the jockeys!

I nodded politely and had a smile planted on my mouth, but in my mind, we were crowded around the little radio in the apartment in Chicago—Father, Mother, Frances, Coobie, and myself—listening enraptured to the Kentucky Derby. Father loved horses and, although he strongly disagreed with gambling, he enjoyed a good horse race. I had grown up listening to the frantic shouting of the announcers as they made the race come alive with mere words. Another pang of homesickness swept over me.

I had hoped after spending two months in Atlanta, I'd begin to feel at home, but in reality, I found myself counting the days till the end of the school year. Sixteen. Soon Hank would come and bring my sisters for a visit, and then we'd ride home on the train to my town. I longed for a walk beside Lake Michigan with the blustery wind blowing my hair all in knots while Coobie chased a kite and Frances tossed dry bread crumbs to the ducks.

————

On the second Saturday in May, I found Parthenia in the kitchen making sandwiches and sniffing away, occasionally wiping her nose and eyes on her sleeve.

"Whatever is the matter?" I asked.

She looked up, surprised, then seeing it was I, she said, "They's done found something else that's gone missin', ova at Miz Becca's house, and she sez it's Mama done stole it too, jus' like she stole the knives from Miz Chandler and Miz Becca's fancy jewelry."

"Oh no! I'm so sorry." I tried to give Parthenia a hug, but she turned away. "What did Becca say was missing?"

"Her heirloom earrings from her great-grandmother, and two pieces of her fine silver. Miz Becca sez it was the day before the Valentine's Party when Mama was there that she stole those things and that she sold 'em to the pawn shop, and so we ain't neva' gonna find everything that's gone missin'. Miz Becca sez Mama pawned off those fancy knives too, and that she's hiding the money somewhere so's she and Papa kin take Cornelius to a special doctor so he kin learn to talk. But it ain't true! I knowed it ain't true! She didn't steal those knives, and I don't believe she stole nuthin' else either." She started to cry, and eventually she let me wrap my arms around her.

"Mama wouldn't neva' go an' steal from the Chandlers, and I don't know why Miz Becca hates her so much to say such things. Now she ain't neva' gonna git out of that there Alms House."

"We have to keep praying about this, Parthenia. The Lord knows where all the missing silver is. It's not hard for Him to help us find it when it's His time. So we have to pray that He shows us. Okay?"

Parthenia backed out of my embrace, braced her small hands on the counter. "You bin talkin' to my mama?"

"No, of course not. I've never met your mother, Parthenia."

"Well, she sez the same things as you do. Last time we wuz there, Mama took me on her knee and she said, 'Parthie, I know I didn't steal nothin' and so I'm thinkin' the Lawd must need me here at this Alms House for some reason, and so I jus' pray He'll let me accomplish what He has set out for me.'

"*Hmpff!* I ain't one bit sure the Good Lawd knows what He's doing; I think mebbe He's jus takin' a long nap." She spread mayonnaise on slices of bread, all the while looking at me. "I's sorry to say it, Miz Mary Dobbs, but that's what I think."

Fortunately Mae Pearl and Perri showed up for lunch, and while Parthenia fixed the sandwiches for us, Perri started taking photos of her. The little girl glowed with pleasure and posed for several more photos, and I think she forgot about her mother's predicament for just a little while.

I didn't try to get any other information from Parthenia that day, but I felt afraid for Anna. Three accusations of stealing could mean a lot worse than time at the prison farm. As Aunt Josie had said, coloreds had been hanged for less than that.

"Tell us another story," Mae Pearl begged me, as she and Perri and I walked from the kitchen down to the Chandlers' lake.

"Why do you want to hear another story?" My mind was still on the story Parthenia had just told me.

"I don't know. It's just that they are . . . inspiring."

I glanced at Perri, who shrugged, and so I launched into another tale from my repertoire. "When the cotton prices fell in 1931, Father drove us over to Arkansas and spent a few weeks there preaching to the poor people who'd lost just about everything in a day. No money. No crops. On the first night of the revival in one little town there in Arkansas, a woman brought her sick son on stage. The lady looked about twenty and all skinny, and the little boy, maybe three or four, but hollow-eyed and yellow-skinned. The mother was crying for Father to save her little boy and pronounce healing.

"Father took one look at the boy and bowed his head and prayed, entrusting the boy to Jesus. Then Father took him in his arms and said, 'He needs to go to the hospital, ma'am. My wife will take you in the car.' But before he could even say another word, the little boy died, right there in Father's arms."

"Oh, Mary Dobbs! You have the saddest stories!" This from Mae Pearl.

"*Shh,*" Perri hissed. "You're the one who asked for it."

"The woman was wailing, and I thought the people in the tent were going to rush on stage and pull Father apart. But Mother helped the woman off stage and held that dead little boy in her arms, and Father just stayed on his knees before the people, praying and crying and talking about how God was near to the brokenhearted and in this life we will have suffering and how Jesus suffered.

"And people started coming forward, right down that sawdust trail, begging for salvation. Coobie and Frances and I just sat on the front row and watched—Mother had left with the woman. And I don't know how many people came down that night, but Coobie said it was over a hundred."

Perri and Mae Pearl just stared at me, not quite sure of what to say, and so finally I broke the awkward silence with, "Time to eat!"

Perri and Mae Pearl and I unpacked the sandwiches and ate them under one of the big hickory trees along the shore. We stretched out our bare legs on the blanket and let the sun warm our faces. The sandwiches had that early summer flavor, fresh and pungent, and we sipped freshly made lemonade and nibbled on lemon squares. Mae Pearl and Perri talked about tea parties and Phi Pis and boys from Georgia Tech, but I kept seeing Father there in that tent in Arkansas, down on his knees, praying and crying, and me sitting there knowing that my father was in a holy moment with the Lord.

———

The more I got to know my surroundings and the more I got to know Uncle Robert and Aunt Josie, the more I wondered why my father had left all of this. There are things that families do not talk about, and Father's decision to leave Atlanta was one of those in our family. I had no idea when he had packed up his belongings and moved to Chicago, or what the circumstances were.

"Your father left another life, an easier life," Mother had told us years ago, "to follow God's call on him."

Two men who had graduated from Moody the same year as Father had become very famous evangelists, traveling throughout the country and even overseas to hold revivals. Walking down the streets of Chicago each June, I saw their pictures plastered on every billboard in sight. Their tent meetings were usually packed out with hundreds, even thousands, of attendees.

But it hadn't worked like that for Father. He had the charismatic personality, the booming voice, and the theatrical movements that made a good evangelist. He certainly had the faith and the knowledge of the Bible. But for all the years I'd attended his tent meetings and sat in the pew at the little city church he pastored, it seemed Father did indeed attract the down-and-outers. Even though we saw God show up time and again, I often wondered what it did to a man's pride to walk by those posters and not be a part of that great movement of God. I was pretty sure that both of those men kept their families well fed, all the while remaining true to the Gospel and reaching out to the rich and the poor alike.

One night, cuddled in bed together, Frances, Coobie, and I had looked at my parents' wedding photo. "Mother was so beautiful," Coobie whispered. "She looked like a princess."

Then, out of the blue, Frances asked, "Do you think Father decided on being poor? Did God tell him we should be poor and that's why he left his nice house in Atlanta?"

I didn't know what to say. I always supposed that Father left Atlanta because he felt a strong call of God to attend Bible school and be a preacher. Since almost every one of Daddy's sermons included something about the sin of loving money, women, and strong drink, all lumped together, I figured maybe the whole Dillard clan in Atlanta, wealthy by anyone's standards, had gotten tired of his moralizing and shooed him off, and that was why he had become estranged from his family.

But now I was not sure about my assumption. Uncle Robert and Aunt Josie did not strike me as frivolous people. Yes, they lived in luxury, but they were extremely generous with their time and money, and Aunt Josie seemed truly to love my father and our family. She spoke of Father with a little catch in her throat and worry lines on her brow. Somewhere along his life story, Father had decided he didn't need his parents or a big sister, and after getting to know my aunt and uncle, I couldn't imagine why.

I had a vivid memory of my family getting ready for one of Father's week-long revival meetings. The old Hudson was packed to the brim with our luggage and affairs, and we were about to start our drive down to Arkansas. But before we left, Father received a telegram from Aunt Josie explaining that his mother had died. I remembered him staring at the telegram, his round, boyish face ash white, a look of defeat in his eyes.

Then, calmly, he had folded the telegram and handed it to Mother. "I can't go to the funeral. You can see that, Ginnie. The revivals start tomorrow night. Five days straight. Atlanta is in the complete opposite direction."

In tears, Mother begged him to postpone the services and attend my grandmother's funeral. "Heavens, Billy, the people in Arkansas will understand. Sometimes you must put your family first."

So instead of heading to Arkansas, we drove down to Atlanta. I was six or seven at the time, and all I remember were the crowds of people at the funeral and us sitting up front with Aunt Josie and Uncle Robert and my grandfather, and me feeling sad for the death of a woman I hardly knew. And I remember Father's tear-stained face when they lowered the casket into the ground.

———

I was looking at the photo albums I'd found in Becca's closet on a Sunday afternoon two weeks before Hank and my sisters were to arrive. Uncle Robert was out playing golf at the club, and Aunt Josie was sitting on the couch across from me, knitting.

"Why is my father not in these pictures? Christmas and Thanksgiving from 1907 on, he seems absent. He wasn't old enough to be at college, was he?" It was an innocuous question, but the answer Aunt Josie gave was not.

She glanced up from her knitting and said, "You know, those were during his wild years."

Her remark caught me off guard. Then I remembered vaguely hearing reference to those years—always from the pulpit, always my father's voice choked with emotion, pleading with parishioners to turn their backs on sin and run, run, run. But I never knew what had happened in my father's past. It was another secret, something he carefully guarded.

Aunt Josie must have seen the look on my face. She stitched for a moment in silence and seemed to be contemplating something complicated with each stitch. Finally she said, "Your father was the most impulsive boy, with the biggest ideas, ideas to change the world and the personality to make it happen—not unlike you, Dobbs." She gave me a sympathetic smile.

"But in his teen years, he became like a wild stallion. He left home several times and was found squandering money, hanging out with women of ill repute." She glanced at me, put in another stitch, and set down the needles. "Dear me, it is not my place to be telling you these things."

"Please tell me, Aunt Josie. I need to know. I think it's important."

She let out one of her deep sighs and continued. "Our dear parents, God rest their souls, grieved and mourned and worried themselves sick—literally—over William. When he 'got religion' at some revival meeting when he was around eighteen or nineteen, no one was more surprised than he himself. He announced to us that God had called him to be a preacher. Mother was overjoyed, Papa cautiously optimistic; after all the pain his son had taken him through, Papa didn't mind the idea of his son becoming a preacher.

"Things were good in the family for some months after that, maybe even a year. Lots of warmth and laughter and respect. A type of restoration for us all, Mary Dobbs. Your father begged us to call him Billy—he wanted nothing to do with his former self. I think he saw himself as another apostle Paul—his conversion had been that dramatic." She smiled and looked my way. "Of course, most everything for Billy was dramatic.

"It was a sweet time in the family. Billy planned to attend Moody—tuition was free and he felt he owed it to the whole family to make up for his wild past. Papa gave him a small stipend for room and board. When he left on the train, we all embraced and he had tears in his eyes. He told each of us how much he loved us." Aunt Josie looked away and cleared her throat. "But we didn't see him much after that. We all attended his wedding, of course, in Chicago, and loved your mother right away.

"After the wedding, your father rarely came back to Atlanta, seemed like he didn't want to have anything to do with his family. It ripped Mother's and Papa's hearts in two again. Something changed, Dobbs, and we couldn't get him back."

Now Aunt Josie definitely looked vulnerable. "You hardly got to know your grandparents, Mary Dobbs, and they were such lovely people. Fine Christian people. I never could understand Billy's reasoning—I guess he thought being back in his old surroundings might drag him back into his former ways. I don't know. I've wondered and wondered about it.

"Papa begged Billy to take some money back in the early twenties, when things were so tight for your family, but Billy refused. Your grandparents wanted you and your mother to visit, they wanted to help, but Billy could not accept it. And then Mother died and Papa followed soon after."

She put down the needles and gave a long, slow sigh. "I love your father; he has a good heart and all the enthusiasm in the world. I just wish he could accept us as we are."

Her story haunted me for days afterward. How could my father, the epitome of a Christian man, refuse to accept his own flesh and blood, who loved him dearly? And right on the heels of that question was the one that Perri had asked. What had happened to all the money Father surely inherited after my grandparents' deaths? Did he refuse that too?

I admired my father; I'd watched him suffer and stand firm in his convictions. I wanted to brush away that tickling suspicion in the back of my mind, but I found the itch just out of reach, like so many other things in my life.

That night, as was my habit, I read from my Bible. The photo of Jackie Brown with me and my sisters stared out at me from the psalms. Jackie Brown. She had died when I was fourteen, and no amount of Father's prayers or Mother's visits to the hospital had helped at all.

Jackie's death affected me a lot more than those of my grandparents.

I could still hear the horrible wailing of Jackie's mother, Irene, and of her accusations. *"What kind of preacher prays for the sick and they die!"* But even at fourteen I knew . . . *It wasn't Father's fault. It was God's.* Humans had access to supernatural power through God's Spirit. But God was the one who decided.

I should not have kept that photo of Jackie in my Bible. It rubbed salt in the wound, again and again. It whispered to me an accusation against God Almighty. That scared me more than my perplexities about my father and his spending habits. After all, Father was merely human and thus prone to mistakes. But everything I had ever been taught about God, and what I believed down in my heart, was of His goodness and mercy and justice and loving-kindness.

Jackie Brown was the fault line in my theology. Perhaps I was naïve. All I knew was that God didn't always provide in the way we expected, and who in the world was I to tell Perri Singleton that He did?

Perri

The last half of May proved to be sweltering, and we suffered inside the high-ceilinged rooms at Washington Seminary, fanning ourselves and dreaming of swimming at the Capitol City Country Club. Mae Pearl swore she was going to faint, and poor Dobbs pulled her hair into a ponytail and got to twirling it up in a bun because of the heat. She looked even more out of style, but no less pretty. We struggled to concentrate on our lessons, and most of us had knots in our stomachs, knowing that exams were just around the corner.

Every year when the Georgia heat started its slow and lazy creeping up to Atlanta and the peaches on the trees in our orchard got rosy cheeks, Dellareen would make her famous homemade peach ice cream. It was the most delicious and refreshing food I had ever put in my mouth. Barbara and Irvin and I loved to stand out on the porch with her as she put the fresh peaches and cream in the small inner bowl of the ice cream machine. Irvin filled the outer bowl with salt and ice, and then we kids would swap off emptying the melted salt water in the outer bowl while Dellareen kept turning the crank, around and around as the mixture slowly became ice cream. We always made at least two batches, because the moment Dellareen let go of the handle, signifying the ice cream was ready, Irvin reached in and gobbled up handfuls of the delicacy. So of course, Barbara and I clamored to get our share too.

One Thursday afternoon, we got home from school to find Dellareen, her face shiny with perspiration, humming some song as she prepared the ice cream. We rushed up the steps to the porch just as Jimmy came from the barn, where he had been tending to the horses.

He slapped Dellareen on the bottom and said, "Lemme take over, woman." Then he winked at us and we laughed. We enjoyed watching what Barbara dubbed "the strange, ongoing courtship of Jimmy and Dellareen." They teased and hollered throughout every day, but anyone could tell that they were absolutely crazy for each other.

"We come together like a pair o' shoes. Kain't have one without the otha'," Jimmy was fond of saying. Oh, how I didn't want that to change! I hoped we could keep them on.

Once the ice cream was made, Barbara and Irvin delved in, ladling huge scoops into their bowls. Dellareen scraped out the rest into a big bowl, handed it to me, and started making her second batch. I went in the house and chipped off a big block of ice from the icebox, got a milk bucket, and packed it with peach ice cream for Jimmy and Dellareen to take home to their five children.

After Jimmy and Dellareen left, Spalding and three other boys from Georgia Tech came over to visit. For the afternoon, I forgot about selling the house and how my friends had turned against Dobbs, and worrying for Jimmy and Dellareen. Instead, I listened to the boys talk about one of them getting hired by Coca-Cola, a big thing during the Depression, and another planning on getting a summer job at the Chicago World's Fair before he started his senior year at Tech.

"Would y'all like some homemade peach ice cream?" I asked, and of course they all said yes. I fairly skipped inside, so happy with the way Spalding was paying such close attention to me.

Those boys devoured the ice cream in no time flat, and before long the other three stood to leave.

Spalding called out, "See ya later, guys," and came and sat next to me on the cushioned bench. "What a nice evening. Would you like to take a ride with me, Perri?"

"Sure!" I said, knowing full well I had a stack of school books I needed to review before exams started the following Monday. But off we went in his fancy car, and I don't remember a thing we talked about, but I do remember the way he looked at me before he told me good-night, and I thought I might melt, like homemade peach ice cream on a humid Georgia night.

————

The next evening, Mrs. Chandler took Mamma and me and Dobbs to the opera, a special production of *Madame Butterfly*. I was beside myself—it had been months since I'd gone to the opera—but Dobbs was even more excited. We wore our long dresses from the May Fete, and I could tell Dobbs was starstruck. Maybe she couldn't attend parties or movies, but her father had never forbidden her to go to the opera, and when we got to the theater, she was like a kid at Rhodes Bakery, inhaling the experience.

The opera was held in the Fox Theatre, my absolute favorite place to go to the movies. "It's like a castle or a Byzantine temple," Dobbs said, breathless. Dobbs was staring up at the intricate gold painting on the foyer ceiling. Then she gasped, "Look at the gorgeous gowns those women are wearing. And their hats!" She twirled around right there in the foyer, and her pink tea dress billowed out around her legs.

We all found our seats, and when the lights went out, Dobbs grabbed my hand and exclaimed, "Oh, Perri! Have you ever seen anything like it? It's a literal *Patches from the Sky*!"

High up above us, the ceiling was painted ultramarine blue so that it really looked like the sky. Thanks to some kind of technological magic, fluffy white clouds floated in the blue, and a sun rose on the east side of the theater and slowly traveled across the blue to set on the west side. As it did, hundreds of sparkling dots shone above us, just like real twinkling stars.

" 'The night has a thousand stars,' " Dobbs whispered to me and squeezed my hand.

Then the opera began, and Dobbs was completely mesmerized by the music and the costumes. She dabbed her eyes throughout the whole thing, whispering "Magnificent!" whenever the audience broke into applause.

135

During intermission, I took Dobbs down the red-carpeted winding staircase to the bottom floor, where the fancy powder rooms were located. We had just come back upstairs when someone said, "Mary Dobbs? Mary Dobbs Dillard?"

We both turned around to see a handsome young man with curly blond hair smiling at her.

"It's Andrew. Andrew Morrison. I met you at the May Day celebration."

Dobbs's cheeks went crimson, and she seemed completely at a loss for words, so I stepped in to help. "Hello, Andrew. I'm Perri Singleton. I've seen you down at the SAE house."

"Perri! Yes, of course." He cleared his throat, and his face was beet red too. "Good to see you both."

Dobbs finally found her voice. "Yes, nice to see you again, Andrew."

Right then the lights flickered off and on as a signal for us to find our seats, and Andrew left us.

As soon as we took our seats, Dobbs said, "I've got Hank. So don't say a thing."

I laughed and nudged her in the ribs.

She giggled, too, and whispered, "He is kinda cute, isn't he?"

Then the curtains came up and the opera started again.

I had been to the Fox many times before, but that night, dressed finely, sitting by my dearest friend, and with memories of the beautifully photographed night sky in that little book, I really did feel I could float to heaven and that things were going to be all right. I didn't think about the house, not when I was at the opera with thousands of stars twinkling above. Life seemed, for that short time, perfectly normal, with all kinds of wonderful possibilities ahead.

If only, oh, if only, it could have stayed that way.

We were just leaving the Fox Theatre and crossing the street when I heard a familiar "Yoo-hoo!" Macon and Lisa rushed up to me, all smiles. Macon started talking with her hands, proclaiming, "Wasn't it just absolutely grand! Oh, the diva could sing!" Then they caught sight of Dobbs, walking just ahead of me with Aunt Josie.

"What in the world is *she* doing at the opera?" Macon whispered, a little too loudly.

"Her aunt invited us all," I said, slowing my pace to give room between Dobbs and us. "It was Mary Dobbs's first time at the opera, and she loved it."

"Well, at least she didn't stand up in the middle of it and start preaching about the poor and needy!" Lisa said with a laugh.

Anger flashed through me, and I wanted to defend Dobbs. But I didn't. I just said, "We're getting a drink at the Georgian Terrace, so I'd better run along!" and waved good-bye to Lisa and Macon. As I caught up with Mrs. Chandler and Mamma and Dobbs, I suddenly felt like a traitor.

———

Saturday night, I spent an hour flipping through our school annual—we finally got it—and I must say I felt so proud to see ten of my photographs in there. My favorite one was on the Class Memories page. I'd taken a picture of Mae Pearl and Peggy, all dressed up at the Christmas tea that benefited the children's hospital. Each was leaning over on either side of a little girl in a wheelchair, and they were kissing her on the cheek. The expression of pure delight on the little girl's face definitely depicted what Dobbs called "reality," and again, I got a warm feeling of pleasure. With my new darkroom and all the materials, there was no telling what type of photos I could provide for next year's *Facts and Fancies.*

I was cuddled up on the couch in the living room with *Facts and Fancies* lying over my chest and the *Saturday Evening Post* lying at my feet. Irvin and Barbara were playing a game of checkers, and neither one was whining, which was a miracle. Mamma was sitting out on the back porch, smoking a cigarette and sipping on lemonade as she talked with Mrs. Chandler and Mrs. Ferguson, who had both stopped by after dinner for a chat. The sun had set, so the air had lost some of its heavy humidity, and the window in the living room was open so that we could hear the crickets "going to town," as Dellareen said, and again, life felt calm and normal.

If I closed my eyes, it was easy to pretend that Daddy was just down the hall in his study, puffing on his pipe. I almost believed that at any minute he'd step into the living room and go stand over the checkers game. Then, talking in the funny way he did when he was holding the pipe between his teeth, he'd give little hints to Irvin about what piece to move, and Barbara would get exasperated and call out, "Daddy, that's cheating!"

The memories were so sharp, like a perfect snapshot from my camera, that I felt my heart accelerate and then plummet as I realized my reverie. Daddy wasn't in our living room, and soon we would not be sitting in this house, in this room, comfortable with its memories. Soon the rooms would be bare and our life would be packed up in cartons.

I felt tiny pinpricks of tears in my eyes and got up quickly from my chair and went down the hall to the powder room. A light was coming from Daddy's office. I walked in and was surprised to see Mamma at Daddy's desk. I had not heard her friends leave nor seen her come back in the house.

She had her head down, and she was sobbing.

She looked up—"I'm sorry, Perri"—and swiped at her tears, but they just kept running down her face, and she looked more haggard and desperate than ever. "I can't do it! I can't pack up his things. I . . . I thought he was doing better."

She was clutching a professional photo of the five of us.

"I thought he had turned the corner. Everything seemed so black, but then for a few days there, he was better."

I pried her hands open and took the framed photo from her. Setting it back on the desk, I reached out to Mamma and hugged her. I wanted with everything in me to keep being strong, but I found tears spilling out of my eyes too.

I don't know how long we sat there, but finally I said, "Mamma, don't stay in here. You don't have to pack all this up. Someone else will do it, but not you."

She followed me up the stairs like a frail old lady, and as she climbed the steps, I thought, *Thank heavens Barbara and Irvin are still sitting in the den playing their slow game of checkers, oblivious to the fact that their mother is falling apart with grief.*

———

On Sunday afternoon, I had a date with Spalding. I wore a pretty frock that Dobbs had plucked from Becca's closet, and I felt fashionable and almost sophisticated. He looked at me in that way he had—careful appraisal and then approval—and whisked me off to see the Joan Crawford movie *Today We Live*. Twice during the movie, Spalding took my hand in his, especially when I cried at the end. Then, ever the gentleman, he gave me his handkerchief to wipe my eyes and insisted I keep it to remember him by when he wasn't around. I thought that was such a romantic thing to say and put it in my purse.

On the way back from the movies, I asked Spalding to let me off at the Chandler residence.

"Whatever for?" he asked.

"Oh, I've just got a few things to do with Mary Dobbs. You know, exams are coming up."

He frowned, looked for just an instant irritated, recovered, and said, "Okay. As you wish, my dear." And he winked at me.

I just beamed at him on the drive, ignoring every thought except that I was out with one of the wealthiest young men in Atlanta.

When we stopped in front of the Chandler property, he came to my side of the car and opened the door. As I got out, he took my hand and pulled me to himself. I smelled his aftershave, a whiff of something strong and masculine, and I thought he truly was going to kiss me. I almost closed my eyes, trying to prepare myself for the moment. Instead, he tightened his hold around my waist and said, "Remember,

I've got dibs on you now." He pressed his lips to my cheek and let me go. I waved good-bye to him with a giddy feeling in my stomach and stumbled toward the Chandlers' house, once again inebriated on nothing but his all-out good looks and strange kind of charm.

We developed my first roll of film that night, Dobbs and I, with Parthenia perched beside us, oohing and ahhing with every step in the process—especially when I turned on the red light and opened the camera to remove the film. She watched anxiously as the film was submerged into the vat that held the chemical solution.

For two hours we worked printing pictures. My favorites were of Dobbs on her bed, but Parthenia pronounced the ones of herself "the most gorgeous things I ever done seen" and she "hoped to high heavens" she could take one to her mama at the Alms House next week.

We finally shooed Parthenia off to bed, and breathlessly I told Dobbs all about the Joan Crawford movie and how Spalding had kissed me on the cheek and offered me his handkerchief. "It was all so very romantic!" Then I had an idea. "Dobbs, do you think that you and Hank would go on a date with Spalding and me while Hank is here?"

"You really like him, don't you."

"Oh yes. He's such a gentleman and most dashingly good-looking, and I think he's taken a fancy to me for some odd reason."

Dobbs looked unconvinced. "Perri, you're so pretty and feminine, and oodles of guys fancy you."

"But he's practically a college graduate. Why think of it! He might some day consider marriage, and it could be sooner than later, and if we married, well, for goodness' sakes, he's so rich I know we'd be just fine. Can't you just see it?"

Her face, so lovely, so often filled with enthusiasm, fell, and she grabbed my hands. "Anne Perrin Singleton. You take your time. You don't have to marry a rich guy to save your family. I tell you—the Lord's going to provide. He will. I just know it." Then, probably seeing the disappointment on my face, she added, "But of course Hank and I would be happy to go on a double date with you and Spalding. That would be our pleasure."

Before I turned out the light in the barn, I glanced back at the photos hanging on the line, a row of shiny black-and-white rectangles. A stream of light caught on the one of Dobbs stretched out on the bed, and I secretly congratulated myself for having taken such a fine photo.

Dobbs came beside me and pointed to a photo of Dellareen and the ice cream maker in front of my house. She said matter-of-factly, "Taking photos is your future, Perri Singleton. I guarantee it."

I switched off the light, and Dobbs locked the door to the dark-room, and we gave a carrot to Dynamite, who nickered to us softly as we stepped into the hallway of the barn. "Thanks, Dobbs, for the vote of confidence." I felt again as light as the breeze, swept along with happy thoughts. A photographer! My future! But just in case Dobbs was mistaken, I had another key to the future: Spalding Smith.

Dobbs

The letter from Mother arrived during exams.

> Dearest Mary Dobbs,
>
> Father has heard of the tragedy that has descended on the poor people in Oklahoma and Texas—they are calling it the Black Blizzard of dust. Crops ruined, people homeless—as if their lives were not already so horrible. We will be traveling there to hold tent meetings this summer. As such, we have discussed the possibility of Frances and Coobie staying in Atlanta with you at the Chandlers'. We feel this is God's provision and protection, especially with Coobie's chronic bronchitis—which hasn't been acting up lately, thank the Good Lord. But surely all that dust would be dangerous for her.
>
> Your sisters will come to Atlanta with Hank next week and stay with you throughout the summer. Your father has spoken with Aunt Josie and she is quite satisfied with the idea. I hope you are not too disappointed. I know you were looking forward to coming back to Chicago this summer.
>
> I am so anxious to see you when your father and I come down for the revival. Only a few weeks away.
>
> > Oodles of love,
> > Mother

On the last Saturday in May, while all the other Washington Seminary girls were rejoicing at the end of exams and hurrying to one or another country club for a swim, I prepared myself to meet Hank and Coobie and Frances. I chose the second of the two dresses Aunt Josie had bought me, a pretty soft yellow with a white lace collar and white leather belt. I spent too much time fiddling with my hair, finally deciding to wear it down long, the way Hank liked.

I wanted to be alone when I picked them up at Terminal Station, but I did not feel comfortable driving a car, not to mention that Aunt Josie didn't volunteer to let me use theirs. Hosea was ready to take me, but Perri finally convinced everyone that she could drive us. She knew how—most everyone did by the time they turned fifteen—but she was a bit skittish behind the wheel.

"You're a pack of nerves, girl," I said. She laughed, putting along toward the train station, hands gripping the steering wheel as if it might fly away if she didn't. I actually thought she looked more nervous than I probably did.

Perri killed the engine twice, and we ended up being a few minutes late. She let me out at the entrance to Terminal Station while she parked the car. I got to the platform out of breath and stood on my tiptoes to see over several men who were in front of me. I finally spotted them. Hank was walking toward me with Coobie perched on his back and a suitcase in each arm. Frances was talking animatedly to Hank, but he was looking straight ahead, neck craned and eyes shining.

Coobie saw me first. "Dobbsy! Dobbsy!" she called out, all exuberance, her pale face, framed by an abundance of black curls, lighting up with a smile. She slid off of Hank's back and galloped over to me, dodging in and out of the crowd. Nothing planned or primped about Coobie.

I ran to her, picked her up, and swung her around. "Coobs! It's so great to see you." When Hank and Frances arrived, I hugged Frances first, and she said, "Hi, Sis," sounding a bit aloof. She'd pulled her dark brown hair back with a headband, and she was wearing a pale blue dress I'd outgrown that fit her nicely and showed off her developing chest.

Then I turned to Hank, my heart hammering away, and I had no idea what to say. He towered over me, his sandy hair a little ruffled from Coobie's holding to it. He was wearing the gray suit he had for revival meetings, and I thought he looked marvelously handsome. His face broke into a wide grin. "Dobbs!"

He set down the suitcases, then picked me up and twirled me around, and I knew it was all okay. He still felt the same way. We stood there looking into each other's eyes and grinning a bit foolishly. Then Perri hurried through the crowd, lifted her eyebrows, and I saw the perfect little red spots on each cheek. I went over to her and said, "Perri, I want you to meet my sisters, Frances and Coobie, and my friend, Hank."

Right away, Coobie gave Perri one of her impromptu hugs, saying, "We've heard all about you and have been praying for you and your family, and Dobbsy is right—you're downright beautiful."

Perri's spots darkened, but her green eyes sparkled with the compliment.

Frances said, "Yes, it's very nice to meet you," and Hank said, "Thanks for taking such good care of our sweet Dobbs."

At that moment, standing there with my best friend and my boyfriend and my two sisters, life seemed absolutely perfect. I twirled around and gave a laugh. "I am so incredibly happy to have you all here. I think I'm the happiest girl in the world!"

Everyone laughed, and Coobie took Perri's hand and then Frances's, and they started walking ahead of Hank and me. Looking back over her shoulder, Coobie said, "You can kiss her if you want, Hank. I don't think Father would disapprove after all you two discussed."

Poor Hank blushed from his hairline down to his neck. He didn't kiss me, but he reached out and rubbed Coobie hard on the head and then picked up the suitcases, and I stayed ever so close to him as we walked out of Terminal Station.

Perri let us off at the Chandlers'. Coobie and Frances hopped out of the car and just stood and stared at the house. "Oh my, oh my, oh my," Frances whispered. "This is some place!"

Coobie balled her fists together, closed her eyes, and scrunched up her face. Then she opened her eyes again and began jumping up and down, so that her black curls jiggled softly. "It's real! It's a fairy castle and it's real! Just like in the pictures Mother showed us."

Hank busied himself with the luggage, and Perri pulled me aside. "I can't stay, Dobbs. The vans are arriving at one to pick up the horses."

"You going to be okay?" I asked her.

"I'll be fine. You enjoy Hank. Don't think about another thing, okay?" As she got back in the Buick, she looked at me, her eyes shining, her cheeks red, and she said, "Oh, Dobbs, he *is* swell. One look at him, and you can tell he's just crazy for you. And he's so good-looking, but more than that . . . He's, he's just *good*. Yeah, that's it. He oozes goodness. I'm so happy for you." Then she started the engine and putted along, leaning forward, in deep concentration.

Aunt Josie came out the side door and greeted us warmly, letting Coobie envelop her in a spontaneous hug. "Mighty nice to have y'all here," she said, looking like a robust mother hen, clucking at her chicks. She showed Coobie and Frances up to Becca's room, where they would be staying. The room had two single beds in it, and when she opened the closet for Hank to set down the suitcases, my sisters ran inside and stared in wonder at the beautiful dresses and gowns, giggling and pushing each other, with Coobie whispering way too loudly, "This closet's bigger than our bedroom!"

"Anyone hungry?" Aunt Josie asked, after she'd installed Hank in the downstairs guest bedroom.

Coobie chimed in, "I'm practically starving," and Frances elbowed her in the side and whispered, "Don't be so rude!"

Parthenia served us lunch, and when she saw Coobie, she asked me, "Is this yore little sista' who's seven and two-thirds?"

I laughed and gave Coobie a wink. "This is she."

Coobie narrowed her dark eyes and said, "Who are you?"

"I'm Parthenia Jeffries"—she gave a little curtsy—"and I used ta be eight and three-quarters, but my birthday is coming up real soon, so then I'll be flat-out nine."

Hank laughed out loud, which made Parthenia smile.

Coobie frowned, then remembered her manners. "Nice to meet you, Parthenia." I could tell she was concentrating on something, and finally she said, rather brightly, "Well, I'm not seven and two-thirds anymore, 'cause my birthday is coming up soon too, and then I'll be flat-out eight!"

Aunt Josie cleared her throat, and Parthenia scooted back to the kitchen to bring out the hot rolls, but later, after she had cleaned up from lunch, she came up to Coobie and asked, "You wanna see the bracelet my mama gave me for my last birthday?"

Coobie nodded, so Parthenia took her hand and off they went. Coobie didn't even bother to ask permission to be excused from the table, which didn't surprise me one bit.

Frances just rolled her eyes and said, "She's the rudest kid in the world."

Aunt Josie busied herself with something, and Frances pronounced herself exhausted by the two-day-long train ride and went upstairs to lie down. I could have kissed them both for leaving me time alone with Hank.

Hank changed into a white T-shirt and his work overalls, and we walked out to the back of the property, hand in hand. I showed him the barn and the darkroom and the servants' quarters, where Parthenia and Coobie were playing. Continuing down the hill, we came to the lake. It sparkled a lovely blue green in the May sun, and the scents of roses and honeysuckle, jasmine and peaches, all mixed together gave off an almost exotic aroma, but as we sat side by side on a stone bench, our shoulders touching, I think we were mainly just breathing in the fragrance of each other.

"I've missed you something awful," I said at last.

"Me too, Dobbs. I go to work every day with a lump in my throat, and it doesn't go away 'til I get home and find a letter from you."

We sat there for the longest time, not needing to say a word.

Perri was right about Hank. He had a simple goodness about him, a lack of pretension. Kindness and goodness mixed together and topped off with physical strength and fortitude. He had strong, sturdy shoulders, and on them I thought he could carry the burdens of the world. He'd carried enough as a child and teen—his father's death when he was ten, starting work at the steel factory when he was twelve to help his mother pay the bills for the family. He finished high school while holding down two jobs, and I don't think he ever complained. He carried things inside, silently, but I knew the strength came from a rock-solid faith in almighty God, and his faith encouraged mine. For as spontaneous and vivacious as I was, Hank had a special calmness in his soul that seemed to me unshakable. I think Father appreciated this quality too, knowing that, with his own fiery temperament, he could use a co-laborer who breathed stability.

"You've gone and gotten all sophisticated on me, Dobbs," Hank said, interrupting my thoughts. "That's a real pretty dress."

"I didn't mean to. Aunt Josie bought this dress for me. Do you mind terribly?"

"Not a bit. You look splendid, more beautiful than ever. I hope there aren't too many boys fighting for your attention."

"Oh, not a one. I don't even see boys. I told Perri I wasn't interested in parties and boys coming over—that's what they do down here—boys just come over any ol' time of the day or night and sit on a girl's porch and talk and talk. But I told her I have you, and so the boys leave me alone."

We sat there in silence. A small fish, perhaps a bass, soared out of the lake and twisted back in, causing a long ripple. I watched the water moving gently.

Finally, almost meekly, Hank said, "There's something I need to tell you, and I guess now's about as good a time as any." He pushed a hand through his hair and looked straight at me. "I've lost my job. They closed the steel mill last week—incorporating it into the U.S. Steel down in Gary, Indiana. Three hundred of us were laid off, and most of those men with families to feed. We're hoping some jobs will open in the other mills around Lake Michigan. And there's a possibility I may get a job at the World's Fair this summer."

We were sitting all cuddled together, the lake shining in front of us, and Hank had put his arm around me. I wanted to forget everything except the ecstasy of being with him. But his words "lost my job" had stopped me short, and I couldn't think of anything to say.

"It's okay, Dobbs." He looked me in the eyes, and his were that blue violet, bright but calm. "The Lord will provide. I know He will; you know it too. He always does. I'll get a job and you'll finish your high school down here, and then we can think about a future. Your father is mighty happy to know of my intentions, and nothing in the whole world could make me change my mind. Don't you worry about anything."

I nodded, but I was thinking how Father had always said that the Chicago steel mills would never close.

"I'm afraid of being poor," I whispered, clasping his hands.

And then it all tumbled out about the people in Atlanta thinking they were poor when they had so much and the way I didn't fit in at Washington Seminary and about Peggy's meanness and how I felt more and more ostracized from the girls. I told him about Father's wild years and wondering why we had no money. I even mentioned my reservations about Spalding Smith. On and on I talked about my life for the past two-and-a-half months.

Hank knew how to listen, not just with his eyes, which followed me intently, but his body posture, leaning forward, interested. I felt a huge relief at having told him everything, more than I had ever said in my letters, and peacefulness settled on me, sitting beside him with his arm draped over my shoulder. I wished we could have sat there forever.

At length he stood up, offered me his hand, and pulled me up beside him. "You've got the rest of the afternoon to show me around."

"That, Hank, will be my great pleasure. Mighty fine. Splendid indeed. Swell."

He cocked his head and grinned down at me. "You're talking differently, and you've picked up a Southern accent."

I wondered for the briefest second if I hadn't picked up a lot more than that.

Perri

For two months, Mr. Robinson had been trying to find buyers for our horses. At last, he did. I hadn't spent a single minute in the barn after Daddy's death, but the day the horse vans arrived in front of the house, I got a horrible stomachache and knew I had to see the horses one more time. Mr. Robinson said we'd gotten a good bit of money for the Thoroughbreds, and they were all going to a fashionable stable in Virginia, to a family that, I supposed, wasn't counting their pennies as we were.

It was the next step in the unwinding of my life. I was amazed at how I had been able to smile on the outside and even bat my eyes at Spalding and the other boys, could chatter with Peggy and Brat as if my life were just humming along, when in reality, it was imploding, crashing in on me.

I went into the barn, and the memories from that horrid day assaulted me—the strand of hay on the floor, the way the horses were stamping and fretting, Daddy's shoe. With tears sliding down my face, I went over to Daddy's gelding, Windchaser. He poked his fine head out of the stall, ears pricked forward, and greeted me as if I hadn't seen him in three days instead of three months. "Bye, Chase," I whispered, and ran my hand over his muzzle and then along his wide, flat forehead.

Jimmy and Ben—they had come on Saturday specially to help with the moving—entered the barn and led the horses out, first the chestnut gelding and then the gray pony that I used to ride as a child. My bay mare, Shadowbox, threw her head impatiently in the air, and I went to her then, my throat catching horribly, and hugged her around the neck, trying my hardest to pretend I wasn't saying good-bye to her, saying good-bye to all those Saturdays of fox hunting with Daddy—him riding dark, dappled Windchaser, and me following on Shadowbox. The scene of my first fox hunt flashed before me.

The crisp October air stinging my face, I was galloping across an empty field behind Daddy, who was wearing his scarlet coat, with the sound of the hounds' frantic baying before us. At twelve, I was thrilled to be out on a real hunt with Daddy. The hoofbeats of two dozen horses thundered along while the hounds screamed their bloodthirsty cry. At the end of the field, we crashed through the woods, lying flat on our horses' necks as we dodged brittle limbs. At last, we came to the clearing where the hounds had trapped the poor fox inside a hollowed-out log. When it came time for the killing, I closed my eyes and squealed.

"Got to get used to it, Perri," Daddy said. "It's part of the thrill of the hunt." But I never did. I hated the killing, but my love for my father, my desire to be with him, propelled me along on those Saturdays. I became a fine equestrian for him and him only.

Now I was saying good-bye to a part of Daddy and an era of my childhood and adolescence that I could never reclaim.

We had decided to sell all the accessories with the horses—the tack and blankets and lead shanks, the buckets and brushes and hoofpicks, even the bales of fresh hay that made me sneeze and the bins filled with oats. All of it was being packed into the horse vans to travel to Virginia. I lifted the wooden cover off the deep bin where we stored the oats and thrust my hands into them. In sharp contrast to my tin of pennies, the oats had the comfortable feeling of sticky honey and hard kernels, and they smelled sweet and musty. I got an aching in my chest.

"Good-bye," I whispered as I stood in the very room where Daddy had taken his life.

I turned to where my saddle hung on a wooden rack. I pressed my nose to the pommel, closing my eyes and relishing the smell of the leather. I ran my hand over the seat, brushing off a layer of dust that had accumulated from months of unuse. I ran my hand down one stirrup leather, noticing how many of the holes looked worn, a testimony to my lengthening legs over the years, and then held on to the cool metal stirrup. *"Heels down, Perri! Keep your heels down,"* I could hear Daddy admonishing.

I lifted my saddle from the rack, to carry it out to the van, and as I did, a white envelope floated in slow motion to the floor. I watched it, entranced, set the saddle back on the rack, and leaned down to retrieve the envelope.

Perri was written across the envelope in my father's stilted cursive.

I dropped the letter with a gasp, as if it had burned me, and stared at it lying overturned on the dusty floor beside strands of hay. It had fallen in a corner and lay trapped within a few spider webs.

Catching my breath, I picked it up again, my hands shaking, and fiddled with the envelope's flap. I steadied myself by holding on to the saddle rack with one hand and, with the other, dislodged the single sheet of Daddy's monogrammed stationery.

> *My dearest Perri,*
> *I am so sorry, so sorry.*
> *I promise I didn't do it!*
> *I love you, Daddy*

Then something was scratched out, and underneath his name he had scribbled, so that it was almost illegible—*Don't give up.*

I began heaving and holding my stomach as I leaned over, trying to catch my breath. Then I sank to the ground and balled up the letter in my hands, the letter that had been waiting for me all these months. I imagined Daddy slipping it under my saddle only moments before he slipped the noose of the lead shank around his neck. Why? As a proof of what? Despair and love? Perhaps he had expected me to go out and ride Shadowbox a few days after his death and find the letter. Surely he hadn't planned for me to stay away for a long time and stumble upon it almost by chance, so that the scab on the wound was knocked off and I started bleeding all over again.

"Oh, Daddy, why? Why did I leave you that day? I saw the pain in your eyes, and the fear. Why did I think Mr. Roosevelt's speech would make everything better? You had decided long before what your course of action would be, but why, Daddy, why?"

I unfolded the crumpled note and forced myself to read it again. *I didn't do it.*

"What do you mean, Daddy?" I said out loud. "You did it! You did! You killed yourself."

I stayed in the barn, sobbing, for probably ten minutes, until Ben and Jimmy came in to get the last of the tack and found me there. I'd stuffed the letter into my pocket, so all they saw was me lying on the floor in tears. Skinny Jimmy, bless his heart, tenderly picked me up and carried me to the house, just as he'd done on that fateful day in March.

I lay out on the porch and wept.

Mamma was at a Junior League event, raising money for a charity—we'd planned it that way so she didn't have to witness the horses leaving—and Barbara and Irvin were at friends' houses. Jimmy ran and got Dellareen, and when she found me, she kept saying, "Chile, chile. You don't need to be the strong one, Miz Perri. Don't go breakin' yore heart in two all ova' again. Stay here now." She brought me peach ice cream and a Coca-Cola and left me alone on the porch while the ice cream turned liquid and the Coke lost its dark caramel color as the ice melted in the glass.

I didn't want to be alone. I wanted to drive over to the Chandlers' and spill out everything in my heart to Dobbs. But there was no way I would spoil her one weekend with Hank, and so I just lay on the bench, fanning myself and staring into nowhere.

I watched Ben and Jimmy load up the horses and could tell they were torn up about seeing them go. I cried all over again when Shadowbox walked up the ramp and disappeared into the van. I suddenly got ferocious cramps, much worse than with my period, and thought I would vomit, but I didn't. I just lay there and watched another part of my life come to an end.

Spalding came by in the afternoon. I honestly didn't remember if he had asked me on a date or if he was just pop-calling, but he found me unmoved from that spot on the porch, my face and hair a mess and my light blue dress still covered in shavings and hay. He was wearing a smart-looking golf outfit—a crisp polo shirt and blue and green plaid knickers and high socks and white golf shoes. He looked like an ad I'd seen in the *Atlanta Journal* of a young man leaning on a golf club. In spite of myself, my heart skipped a beat. Heavens, he was handsome.

"What on earth is the matter, Perri?" he asked, sitting down beside me.

I swiped at my tears, too despairing to even care about my appearance. "A horrible thing. Oh, the worst." And because I had no one else to share with, I poured out all I was feeling to Spalding. "We sold the horses today, moved everything out of the barn, and I took my saddle and there was an envelope with a letter in it, left by Daddy on that day, that horrible day, and it was for me, and he said he was sorry and that he didn't do it, and I don't know what he meant by that. Oh, if only, if only I had known and I could have stopped him." I started sobbing all over again.

Of course Spalding took me in his arms, just engulfed me with his whole body, saying things like, "I'm so sorry, Perri. How very disturbing that must have been," and "Stop crying now; it can't help," and "Here, dry your eyes, my dear."

And then he did what I had always detested in men in the movies. As soon as the damsel in distress started crying, the hero, or villain, as the case might be, would swallow up the fragile lady in his arms and try to soothe her pain. Right at her weakest moment, he'd bend his suave and handsome face toward her, look her straight in the eyes, and kiss her on the lips. And she, all worn out from sorrow, would accept the kiss without protest. I always boiled with anger in those scenes and murmured to myself, "He's just taking complete advantage of her, the rotten cad!"

But in that moment I was the damsel in distress, and when Spalding pressed his lips to mine, I first felt shock, then foreboding and then a tinge of pleasure, and I held on to him more tightly because I did not know what else to do, and I needed to be held. He kissed me more forcefully. When he finally stopped, I felt limp in his arms. He smiled his seductive smile and whispered, "There now. Do you feel better?"

I nodded yes, but I wanted to shout, *No! No! That's not what I need. You don't understand at all!* But he, of course, did not see this, and his eyes were burning again with desire, a desire so fierce I felt momentarily afraid.

I took a deep breath, backed out of his arms, and said, "Thank you for caring, Spalding. Please forgive me, but I am all worn out, and I haven't got the strength for anything now."

He kissed me again—all of this right on our front porch, where Dellareen could have seen it. Maybe she did. Jimmy and Ben were still gone with the van. He finally left me there, looked back at me, and said, "You sure you don't want to go for a ride in the country?"

When I shook my head, his face clouded with disappointment, and I felt a tinge of guilt.

"I'll come by tomorrow. Rest, my dear. Rest, and don't think another minute about the letter."

I stumbled upstairs to my bedroom, fell on the bed, and cried again. I curled up in a ball, covered my face with my hands, and succumbed to one crushing sentiment—feelings of guilt over Daddy's death and about Spalding's kisses, for I had enjoyed them in spite of the initial repulsion.

When Dellareen called up to me and I didn't answer, she climbed the steps, saying, "I'm going on and catchin' the streetcar, Miz Perri." Then she stepped into my room and saw me there and came over and took me in her arms and rocked me back and forth. She stayed with me until Mamma got back from the Junior League event, brushing her hand through my hair and whispering over and over, "Chile, chile. Honey chile, I want you to remember somethin', you hear me? Your daddy loved you so much, and he was a fine, fine man. He was. You remember."

I thought that even though she didn't know a thing about Daddy's letter, she was giving me exactly what I needed—human warmth and touch with no expectation in return. She had consoled me for seventeen years, and she did it once again, and I fell asleep right there on my bed with Dellareen's thin dark arms around me.

CHAPTER
13

Dobbs

We had a delicious dinner on Saturday evening, a big pot roast with rice and gravy and homemade biscuits and butter and honey and several types of vegetables. I watched my sisters' eyes grow round with pleasure as they ate. Frances waited politely to be offered seconds, but Coobie kept reaching for hot biscuits and gobbled down her food so quickly that I was sure she would have a stomachache. It hurt me to watch them eat, seeing their thin, pale faces erupt in pleasure with the bounty before them. I was so thankful that Mother and Father had decided to send them down to Atlanta for the summer.

Uncle Robert, usually silent and serious, had taken a quick liking to Hank, and they carried on their own private conversation about FDR's second Fireside Chat and what people were calling the New Deal and the president's first months in office. I think Uncle Robert was delighted to have another man around the house. They talked nonstop throughout the meal, and Hank seemed as at ease with my uncle as he was with my father. As I watched Hank with Uncle Robert, I realized how proud I was of my boyfriend, and I wanted with all my heart to be worthy of his love.

But I realized something else. I liked the sight of my sisters all full on good food and laughing and happy in the midst of plenty. I liked wearing a pretty dress and having a room to myself and going to a fine private school. I liked the feeling of comfort. Perhaps I would never fit in with the Atlanta girls, but it sent a chill up my spine to think that I hoped Hank would find a job soon—a good job, a job that meant we wouldn't be eating rice and potatoes for the rest of our lives.

———

Sunday morning, before church, Aunt Josie got the notion to have Hank try on several of Uncle Robert's old suits. "Things he outgrew in the gut long ago," she stated bluntly. By the time we left for church, Hank looked almost, but not quite, comfortable in a suit that Aunt Josie had fished out of the attic and pronounced just his size. It was a dark gray pinstripe that he wore with a blue tie, also Uncle Robert's. The tie almost matched the color of his eyes, and he did indeed look sophisticated. I wore the bright pink dress that Aunt Josie had bought me, and I wished that Perri would appear and snap our picture together, because that Sunday I felt on top of the world and as beautiful and stylish as anyone in all of Atlanta with Hank beside me.

After church at St. Philip's, Uncle Robert took us to the country club. Coobie was beside herself with excitement as we drove out there, all smushed together in the Pierce Arrow. Even Frances could not stop smiling as she fiddled with her white gloves and kept tugging at the blue dress, which was too short for her. I suspected that Aunt Josie was noticing every movement and formulating a plan to provide dresses for my sisters.

At the club there was an enormous buffet, a smorgasbord of choices that seemed decadent for the middle of the Depression, but we helped ourselves without guilt. Frances and Hank and Coobie and I all had fried chicken—a southern specialty that we Dillards had rarely tasted. Coobie ate three pieces, a thigh and two legs, and she had two helpings of mashed potatoes with gravy and lots of green beans and corn casserole, and then, for dessert, she loaded up her plate with apple pie and plopped a scoop of vanilla ice cream on top—and she ate all of that too. A little color had come to her face, but her off-white dress, another old hand-me-down, still hung pitifully on her, and in my mind, I was saying, *Eat your fill, Coobie. Eat and eat and eat.*

Hank ate his fill, too, slowly and deliberately, enjoying every bite, occasionally wiping the starched white napkin across his mouth and saying things like "This is absolutely delicious."

I could tell my aunt and uncle approved of Hank, even if he had the slightest bit of a lost look at the club. I was pretty sure Hank had never been to a restaurant before, much less a country club.

"I'm going to take Frances and Coobie to the swimming pool," Aunt Josie announced. When Coobie protested that she didn't have any swimming bloomers, Aunt Josie smiled and said, "We'll fix that." I accompanied them to the ladies' lounge, and somehow my aunt came up with a blue-and-white-striped swimsuit for Coobie and a red-belted maillot with boy-cut legs for Frances. Coobie had the hardest time tucking her black curls under the bathing cap, and she squealed when Frances accidentally yanked her hair. They were beyond happy as they left the lounge, trotting obediently after Aunt Josie out to a large rectangular swimming pool, the water shimmering in the sun.

Uncle Robert encouraged Hank and me to go for a stroll around the grounds while he smoked a cigar in the men's lounge, and we needed no extra prodding.

The club spread out over acres and acres of land in northwest Atlanta, some of the prettiest land I'd ever seen. The buildings were sandstone and cobbles. Walking toward the golf course with Hank, I said, "I'm so proud of you for coming down here and fitting in with Uncle Robert. Oh, Hank, I know it isn't easy, but you've been splendid. And now that you've gotten a taste of all this, tell me what you think."

"I think it is completely scrumptious," he said, pulling me close to him, his arm around my shoulder. We walked for a while in silence, and then his arm came off my shoulder and he took my hand in his and my heart started thumping in a way that I could feel it.

At length, I asked something that I'd wanted to discuss with Hank but never dared mention in all my letters to him. "Do you think it's wrong to go to movies, Hank? Everyone here loves them. And parties? Are parties wrong? There's no liquor at them, I'm sure, with Prohibition. Just dancing. Is all dancing wrong? And what about social clubs?

It's like you need to be part of these things if you're going to belong to this society. At first I thought it was all wrong, and all I could hear in my head was Father talking about it, but now I'm not so sure. What do you think?"

Hank had a way of taking his time before answering a question—said he liked to turn things over in his mind. So I waited while we walked down a path that led beside the golf course and then into a wooded area that opened into a perfect little garden, complete with a natural spring trickling into a pond of goldfish.

"I actually kind of like dancing," Hank said with a big smile, and he took my hand and twirled me around him and then slowly pulled me close to himself.

He pecked me on the cheek. "Think of square dancing. Nobody I know has a problem with square dancing. Not even your father, I believe." Then he crisscrossed our hands, promenaded me home, and gave a quick little bow, and I curtsied and giggled again. A golf ball swished somewhere overhead, and Hank pulled me along, back through the woods and onto a path that led around the lake.

"I don't blame people for wanting a little fun, Hank. I really don't. Why, the radio and Hollywood and musicals and parties are just a way to escape the trying times for a few hours. Is that so bad?"

At last Hank seemed to seriously consider my questions. "Your father preaches against anything that takes the place of God in a person's heart. He says America is always trying to find something bigger and better to fill up our hearts, but most of us can't figure out what we really need."

I nodded. Father's words were all too familiar.

"Movies are just one way to fill ourselves up for about a nickel. Could be the radio, or the dance hall, or a social club. But it could be books and learning for learning's sake or charity work or anything, no matter how worthy, that takes up too much room in our hearts." He blushed and added, "At least that's what I've always felt the Scriptures were saying."

"Exactly! 'Where your treasure is, there will your heart be also,' "
I quoted the familiar verse.

"I think it's up to each of us to decide, before the Lord, what is
right for us in entertainment. Ultimately, it just comes down to your
heart, Mary Dobbs."

I knew my heart. My heart wanted to do whatever Hank said and
follow him anywhere. I wanted to throw myself into his strong arms
and stay there forever because I felt sure that with him I'd always be
making the right decisions, those that honored God.

Maybe he sensed what I was feeling, because he came close again
and gave me another twirl and then just held me tight, our arms crossed
in front of us, and he whispered, "Dancing is just fine as long as you
do it always and only with me."

"Only with you," I happily agreed.

Then he found a bench along the path. We sat down, and he said,
"I mean it, Dobbs. The Lord will take care of us together. I don't want
you to worry about that, okay?"

"Okay."

And for just a few seconds, he kissed me softly on the mouth,
and I took a long breath of the hot summer air and gulped in his love.

I had not seen Perri all weekend, and when she called and reminded
me that we'd promised to go on a double date with Spalding and her,
I didn't dare refuse, especially since she sounded almost desperate.

"All right, but you know Hank and I don't have a cent between
us. Let's make a picnic supper and just drive somewhere—it's such a
beautiful afternoon. Will that work?"

"Of course! That's a fine idea." Then she added, "I need to talk to
you something awful—not with the boys around, of course. But maybe
later tonight, after you take Hank to the station."

So Hank and I got together a picnic, and Spalding and Perri showed
up at four in his sporty red Ford Roadster convertible. Spalding was
wearing his typical attire—plaid pants, with a dark blue polo shirt that

lit up his eyes. He had on his white leather tasseled shoes, and every black hair on his head was in place. Perri looked pretty in a light-green tea dress. I had begged Hank to keep on his suit slacks and Uncle Robert had lent him a polo shirt, and I was still wearing the pink frock, so we at least looked on the same social level as Spalding and Perri, which for some reason mattered to me that afternoon.

"Nice to meet you, Hank," Spalding said, offering a confident smile and a firm handshake. "Glad you could come down from Chicago for the weekend."

I had hoped that the two of them would engage in easy conversation, as Hank had with Uncle Robert, but almost at once I felt a tension between them.

We ended up driving way out to a place called Stone Mountain for the picnic. It took nearly an hour to get there, and with the top down in Spalding's convertible, I was more than content to sit beside Hank in the back after pulling my hair into a quick braid so that the wind wouldn't whip it into a tangled mass.

"My family has always liked to come out here," Spalding told us as he pulled off the road. "It's a swell place for a picnic . . . and other things too." He turned in his seat and winked at Hank.

We got out of the car, and Spalding directed us to a path. It wasn't long before we turned a corner and there before us appeared an enormous monolith, a completely treeless hunk of rock, sitting like some gigantic round-topped spaceship in the midst of fields and woods. "Heavens!" I said. "It's huge!"

Spalding looked pleased with my reaction. "That, my friends, is Stone Mountain, the biggest piece of granite in the world, or so they say."

The immensity of the mass of granite took my breath away. It seemed to belong to another world.

"And as you can see, they're busy carving a sculpture into that stone. Or, should I say, *were* busy carving it."

Indeed, a large unfinished sculpture of two men's heads and the outline of a horse were roughly carved into the side of the granite that faced us.

"Is that supposed to be Jefferson Davis and Robert E. Lee?" Hank asked.

"Exactly," Spalding said. "Our Confederate heroes. It's probably never going to be finished, though. The first sculptor, who designed and began the work in 1923, threw a temper tantrum a few years later, destroying all his sketches.

"Another sculptor took over and got as far as you see today. He managed to blast off Davis and Lee and the outline of Lee's horse, Traveler, but didn't finish before the owners reclaimed the mountain. So the sculpture has stood there in its unfinished glory for five years."

"That's too bad, but it is a wonder, isn't it?" Perri said. She had brought her camera, which pleased me immensely, and she snapped a photo.

The area was crowded with people milling around, sitting at picnic tables, buying soft drinks at little kiosks. There were even trolleys taking tourists around the base of the mountain.

"There's a path that winds around to the top, if you'd like to climb up," Spalding said.

"Oh yes, let's!" I cried, and so we followed Spalding as he narrated the history of the mountain. "Used to be a tower on the top, a lookout of sorts, with a restaurant and club, back in the 1850s . . ."

We climbed slowly, feeling wilted by the afternoon heat. None of us were really wearing the appropriate clothes. Spalding started humming a song that Perri explained was the fight song of Georgia Tech, and then he asked Hank, "Where'd you go to college?"

Hank rubbed his head and looked for a second like a real hillbilly. "I didn't get any higher education right away. Needed to keep working to help the family. But I'm taking night classes at Moody Bible Institute now."

"His father died when he was ten," I volunteered, trying to steer Spalding away from potentially hurtful questions.

Spalding slapped Hank on the back and asked, "Do you mind if I call you Henry? Kinda like the sound of it."

Hank scowled momentarily, but Spalding paid no attention and continued, "And where is your work, Henry?"

"I've been at the steel mill for years, but they just closed it down."

"So you're out of work like the rest of the country. That's too bad." But Spalding didn't sound one bit concerned. "I think my dear mother would like for me to go to work for once in my life, but I've still got the studies to fall back on if anyone prods me too hard. Studies and, of course, the football team. And girls. Always girls." Then he realized what he'd said and corrected, "Well, one girl now. I've found my girl."

Perri gave an awkward little giggle, but her forehead was creased, and she fanned herself with her hand.

"I've got plans to own the biggest empire in America, bigger than Coca-Cola and Rich's Department Store combined. Bigger than U.S. Steel." He lifted his thick black eyebrows and smiled at Hank. "By the time I finish with Atlanta, people will know I've been here."

We were halfway up the mountain when Perri, who had been hanging on to Spalding's every word, said, "Is this not the most incredible view ever? Oh, Dobbs! Look at it! I have to get a few shots of this. I simply have to. Boys, y'all go on ahead. We'll be along shortly." She linked her arm through mine and said, "It's just ferociously hot, isn't it?"

I nodded.

Spalding kept climbing, saying, "Henry and I will find a suitable spot for a picnic. Join us when you can." Hank followed halfheartedly.

I thought that maybe Perri would share whatever was troubling her, but she didn't. She just walked from one spot to another, snapping pictures and seeming so completely satisfied. I wanted to be happy for her, and content, but I could not ignore my mounting dislike for Spalding.

When we rejoined the boys, Hank took my hand protectively, and I sat down on the blanket beside him. Perri flitted beside Spalding and said, "This is just such a splendid idea, Spalding. I've always wanted to climb to the top of Stone Mountain, and here I'm getting to do it with you."

I cringed slightly, unused to the silliness that had crept into Perri's voice. Perri was a practical girl who enjoyed having fun, but never would I have expected her to use the ridiculous candy sweetness that some girls adopted around a boy they liked. And yet, now she was fairly oozing the sticky stuff.

As we ate our pimento-cheese sandwiches and potato salad, Spalding launched into a story about how his father got started with Coca-Cola way back when, and how he had made a fortune there and had also been involved in several wise investments. Then, with barely a breath, he switched to the Georgia Tech football players. And on and on he talked with a convincing charm, a complete self-absorption that was nonetheless intoxicating to listen to because Spalding seemed absolutely convinced what he was saying was of utmost importance.

Perri occasionally interjected some inane comment such as, "Oh my! How absolutely fascinating!" or "Well, that is just the most interesting thing I've ever heard, Spalding!" and I tried my best not to roll my eyes.

What I read on Hank's face was a mixture of anger and annoyance and, finally, intimidation. And little by little, it seemed to me that Hank disappeared until, at length, I could not find him. Of course he was still there sitting beside me, but he never made the slightest sound, and after a while he didn't even look at Spalding. Perri occasionally smiled at me sweetly, and I could tell she wanted Spalding to hush up a little, but he paid no attention to anyone except himself.

I had never seen Hank act intimidated before. He always seemed genuine and at ease. I guess that Spalding's pompous self-absorption sucked the life from Hank, and he remained virtually silent on the rest of the date. I felt mortified and then embarrassed and then apologetic, and then I volleyed back and forth until finally, thank heavens, it was over.

Spalding let us off at the Chandlers' and called after us. "Nice to meet you, Henry. Good to see you again, Mary Dobbs," and he drove off with poor Perri beside him looking after me with an expression of frozen superficiality on her face.

Every emotion tumbled out as Hank and I walked across the vast lawn to the Chandlers' main house. "That was one of the worst picnics of my life. Spalding is horrid, but I was embarrassed too, Hank. Couldn't you think of anything to say, the whole entire time?"

Hank stopped and looked straight at me. "What did you want me to say, Dobbs? He is the most self-important person I've ever met."

"I know, but you could have said something. Instead you just sat there and looked, I don't know, you looked . . ."

"Stupid?"

"Yes, stupid. No, I don't mean that, but still, it was so terribly awkward."

"I'm sorry to have embarrassed you, Mary Dobbs." The formality that crept into his voice took my breath away. We reached the house. "I'll get my things together. Hosea is taking me to the train station."

I hurried after him. "I don't care one bit for Spalding either—you know that! I think he's very stuck on himself, and . . . and . . . he scares me. But it's just that you disappeared; you became invisible, and I needed you to say something."

Hank walked down the left hallway toward his room, not looking back at me.

"You're usually so strong and wise. But today you were different, and I didn't know what to do."

He began undoing his tie, went to his room, opened the drawer with his clothes in it, and put them into his small suitcase. He looked so handsome and so uncomfortable in his suit pants, the ones he had worn, in spite of the humidity, simply because I asked him to. "Do you mind? I'm going to change."

He closed the door but kept talking to me on the other side. "When someone needs to hear himself talk as much as that guy did, then I'll just oblige him. He took the Lord's name in vain twice when we were setting up the picnic, and when I asked him to please refrain, you know what he said?"

Hank opened the door and stared at me, eyes flashing. He was bare-chested, and I gave a little gasp, but he didn't even notice. "He said, 'Henry, I'm surprised you want to be a preacherboy with the way the Good Lord's been looking after His people in America. It's enough to drain the faith out of you, I would think.' And then he cursed again." Hank pulled on a white T-shirt, buckled his overalls, picked up his Bible, placed it in the case, and closed the lid.

He looked at me, and his face softened. "I'm sorry, Dobbs. Forgive me. What could I say? I had no idea what he was talking about most of the time. I did feel totally brainless. I'll give that to the guy. He has a way of overpowering you with his words."

"But you could have tried!" Immediately I wished I could have taken those words back.

Hank started down the hall, suitcase in hand. "I'm leaving here in about thirty minutes, so hopefully you won't have to go through another—" he thought for a moment, then quoted me—" 'terribly awkward' time like that ever again."

"No, Hank! Heavens, I've never seen you like this. First intimidated and now mad." We'd never had a fight before, and I felt panicky and afraid.

He kept walking. "Dobbs, it doesn't matter. I'm taking the train to meet your parents in Tennessee for two weeks of revivals there, and then the three of us will come back here for one week of revivals. But after that, I'll probably never set foot in Atlanta, and I doubt I'll ever see Spalding Smith again. I will pray for his soul, though. And I'll pray for your friend Perri, because if she is willing to fall for someone like him, I feel sorry for her. She has a lot less brainpower than I do."

I should have agreed with him. I *did* agree. But keeping my mouth shut had never been high on my list of priorities. I felt angry, too, and said, "Please refrain from insulting my friends, Henry Wilson."

He set the suitcase down in the foyer—thank goodness no one else was around—cocked his head, and gave me a sad smile. "You're gonna call me Henry too? This certainly isn't how I wanted our weekend to end." He reached over gently and took my face in his big rough hands. "I'm sorry, Mary Dobbs, if I've embarrassed you. It was never my intention. You know I'm not very good at pretending to be someone I'm not."

It was one of the things I loved most about him. I grabbed him around the waist and held him tight and said, "I'm sorry too, Hank." And perhaps it was just my overactive imagination, but he didn't seem to be holding me nearly as tightly as he had at the club, and he let go quickly.

In that instant, I wanted to pack up Frances and Coobie and myself and hurry back to Chicago with Hank beside me. But my parents needed us to remain in Atlanta while they held revivals and then set off to save the people destroyed by a blizzard of dust. So we stayed.

Hosea brought the Pierce Arrow around front, and Frances and Coobie and Parthenia begged to ride with Hosea to the train station, and so it turned out that there wasn't much room for me in the car. "You've been with him all weekend, Dobbsy," Coobie complained. "Please let us tell him good-bye."

Hank took my hand and said, "I'll see you in a couple of weeks."

I wanted to tell him how much I loved him and how I would be praying for his job and a thousand other things, but instead I stood under the covered entrance and watched the car drive away. Hank turned once and waved, and I waved back. Then I went to my room and cried my heart out, with the sound of the crickets chirping madly just outside my window.

Although I had absolutely no desire to do it, late that evening, I asked Hosea to drive me over to the Singletons', as I had promised Perri. I found her in her pajamas, looking through the latest pile of photographs she had developed in the darkroom.

"Well, our double date was a complete disaster, wasn't it?" I said with a dry chuckle. I hoped she'd admit it too.

Instead, she said, "Yes, it's too bad that our boys aren't very congenial.

They're so different, is all, coming from such different backgrounds. But I'm sure they'll get along in the long run." She gave me a sweet smile, but I felt cold inside, and a tiny bit of awkwardness slipped between us. "Poor Spalding has his hands full with school and deciding about the family business. It's a lot on him. I just don't think Hank could understand."

A chill ran up my spine. How could Perri defend Spalding Smith? Did she really feel something for him? I had secretly hoped that her "bad news" would be the fact that she'd realized what a louse he was. Obviously I had been mistaken, and even though we were sitting only a foot apart in her room, I suddenly felt very far away from her.

Perri didn't seem to notice. She showed me the photographs—some were splendid—and then told me the story of finding her father's letter underneath the saddle. "It was absolutely horrid and I cried half the day, but I was determined not to bother you and Hank."

"I'm sorry I wasn't here. You could have called me, Perri. You can call me anytime. Hank would have understood."

She shrugged. "No, no. And in the end it worked out fine because Spalding came over, without me asking—just like he knew. He was a real gentleman and listened and understood and comforted me. And it worked out okay. Fine, really. Just fine."

But the tone in her voice was off, falsely light, almost superficial, and even though I stayed for another hour, I felt like I was losing Perri, as if she was retreating into a hidden place, a hard place where she was going to protect everything that mattered to her, and suddenly, I wasn't invited to enter.

CHAPTER
14

Perri

Memories come in strange snippets, parts of days of our lives that are mundane, but for some reason, our mind recalls them. I kept Daddy's note to me between the pages of *Patches from the Sky*, but I took it out one afternoon and stared at his hurried handwriting, and that's when the memory came.

It must have been a year earlier at least. It was summer, and the Chandlers, McFaddens, and Robinsons were at our house. It was late, past midnight, but I tossed and turned in my bed, sticking to my sheets in Georgia's humidity. I got up and headed downstairs for a drink of water. I guess the ladies were still outside, but as I came back from the kitchen, I heard angry voices. First my father's, "Bill, there is nothing I can do about it now! How did this happen?" And Mr. Robinson's reply, "You've got to find a way, Holden, don't you see? You could get in big trouble for this."

I went upstairs and promptly forgot what I'd heard. But now, looking at Daddy's note, I wondered what Mr. Robinson meant about getting into trouble, and then I wondered why my father scribbled me a note, only moments before he took his life: *I promise I didn't do it.* I had no idea what he was trying to tell me, and I was pretty sure I would never find out.

———

I have wondered, when two people grow as close as Dobbs and I did in such a quick and dramatic manner, if that makes it easier for the bonds to break later. I thought our friendship was rock solid, but after the double date that Dobbs pronounced "disastrous," I had a nauseous feeling in my stomach that I was going to have to choose between Spalding and Dobbs. Already I was torn between Dobbs and the rest of my friends. Dobbs was in no way discreet, and her disapproval of Spalding was etched deeply on her face, and suddenly, I couldn't tell her everything on my heart. I hated it; it felt like a small death between us. It felt like yet another loss.

We still spent plenty of time together, and when Dobbs had the idea to visit the Alms Houses, I didn't dare say no, especially since Mae Pearl, who was all torn up about us selling our house, loved the idea, and it gave us a chance to be together before I moved.

So on a Sunday in early June, we packed up the picnic baskets with all kinds of goodies that we had helped Parthenia bake for Anna, and Hosea drove us out to the Alms Houses in the Chandlers' old Ford. Mae Pearl and Dobbs and I sat in the back, with Coobie and Parthenia sitting up front with Hosea, those little girls all crazy with excitement.

Barbara was not about to venture there, and she convinced Frances to stay with her at the Chandlers' to paint their nails and probably talk about some boy Barbara hoped would invite her to her first tea party.

I had heard all about the Alms Houses because of Mamma's involvement in the Junior League—they often made things for the residents—and also because for years and years a wonderful man and close friend of Daddy's, Dr. R. L. Hope, was in charge of the houses. Dr. Hope had retired a few years earlier on account of his heart, but we children knew of him because they'd built a school and named it after him right smack on the property where the old Alms Houses used to be, on the corner of Piedmont and Peachtree roads.

But even though Peggy lived just across the street from what Daddy called the "new" Alms Houses—they'd been in that location for years by then—and I went to visit her regularly, I'd never paid any attention to the houses themselves. Now I looked at them and thought they were lovely—not at all what I had expected. The redbrick Alms House, where the white folks stayed, was built in a horseshoe shape with a courtyard in between the two wings. The building had white columns, not unlike Washington Seminary's, out front. It was a big, imposing building but welcoming in its way, with a long banistered porch that flanked all the resident rooms. Behind the house rose a very steep wooded hill, and forest surrounded the other sides, except to the east, where a broad undulating field lay.

I followed Parthenia and Dobbs and Mae Pearl to where the Black Alms House was located not far away. This building was white brick and smaller, with a porch out front and beautiful tall hickory and oak trees shading it on every side. Both houses were immaculately kept and comfortable seeming, which surprised and pleased me.

One of the residents sitting out front of the Black Alms House seemed a little off in the head—holding herself in that awkward way of the mentally unstable with hollow-looking eyes and drooling lips—but that didn't bother Mae Pearl, who leaned over and said, "Howdy, ma'am," in her sweet voice.

The woman stared at her like she had just received an angel in her midst, and a feeble smile spread across her lips.

"Bless you, chile," whispered an old toothless colored man who was sitting in a rocker on the other side of the front porch. Mae Pearl immediately knelt down beside him and placed her soft white hand right over his old black hand with its chipped fingernails and splotches of pale scarred skin.

And I saw it then—my first real inspiration, the first time I could literally see something deep and important that needed to be translated into a photo. Their hands. A simple gesture of the one hand covering another. I got tears in my eyes. I knelt down nearby, almost like I'd kneel in church, and it even felt like a holy moment. I put my eye to the viewfinder of the Eastman Kodak and I stared at those hands, breathing so slowly, afraid I wasn't worthy of the photo. Then I pressed the shutter, and it was recorded; a chill of excitement zipped down my back.

I walked out into the yard in front of the Black Alms House and waited and waited, propping myself against a tree so Mae Pearl and the old man couldn't even see me, not that they were paying any attention. The afternoon sun kept shifting through the leaves, and shadows played across Mae Pearl's face. She wore an expression of such natural purity. I snapped the photo. Then the old man started telling her something—the story of his life, perhaps—and Mae Pearl leaned in closer to him, instinctively, and I captured that too, the perfect contrast of light and dark in the faces of the two of them as they were engaged in conversation.

A moment later, Mae Pearl threw her head back, and smooth, musical laughter escaped from her mouth, and the man's skinny shoulders started moving up and down in a jolly way and a twinkle of light came into his tired old eyes, and I caught that too.

Later, all filled up with enthusiasm, I went through the building to the back, where the prison quarters were, behind the regular rooms for the poor people, and I found Dobbs and Coobie and Parthenia there with Hosea and Anna. Parthenia was rattling on about one of Dobbs's strange stories when she saw me approaching. "And this here is her friend, Miz Perri Singleton, and you know about her troubles too."

For some reason, I felt as if I were warming up inside, as if I were sipping on a never-ending cup of Dellareen's hot spiced tea, the kind she made with lemon and honey and cloves and mint and gave us in the winter when one of us kids had a cold. I wondered at the irony, how I felt the same pure comfort that afternoon, warmed and filled up and comfortable, in a place for castoffs and elderly and prisoners.

Dobbs began talking animatedly about the theft that had put Anna in the Alms House, so I just faded into the background and listened.

". . . And you see, I've been thinking about your situation, Anna. I'm just begging Aunt Josie to do something." Dobbs's expression was intense. It appeared she planned to right the wrong—and soon.

Anna's eyes got all dark and scared, and she said, "Don't you be botherin' Miz Chandler with my case. She's tried and tried, and I tell you what—I've learned if you push and push and the door won't open, then mebbe it's the Good Lawd keeping it closed and we should just stop trying. One day or another they'll clear it all up, and until then, well, I got my work."

"But Parthenia and Cornelius should be in school!" Dobbs blurted out. "Aunt Josie knows that!"

"Miz Chandler's given my family a place to live and all the food they can eat and a way for them to come an' visit me, and for right now, that has to be enough. You understand, Miz Mary Dobbs? Please don't make no trouble for my family. Parthie's got a big mouth, and she might complain a bit, but she don't mind the work, and she'll catch up on her schoolin' when times git better."

I listened to Anna's words, but what I was really concentrating on was her expression. I had seen her before during parties at the Chandlers', but that day I really *saw* her. She was small in stature, much smaller than Dellareen, but whereas Dellareen was tall and thin as a reed, she was wide around the girth. Anna had a dark blue bandanna tied around her hair and two deep crevasses ran under her eyes, as if maybe she never got any sleep. But she looked sturdy and determined, and something else took me completely off guard. I'd expected a surly woman with a lot of bitterness holed up inside, but what was leaking out of Anna was something wary and tough and peaceful, all mixed together.

Then I knew what it was, and I felt a kinship with her. I understood her in one thoughtful study of her face. She had the same grit in her as I did, that deep protectiveness, that stubborn refusal to give in. She was going to protect her family—no matter if she was locked up on a prison farm; she was going to take care of the ones she loved. I didn't know how she'd do it, but she did.

I felt bound to her in that moment.

Parthenia saw my camera and begged, "Miz Perri, will ya pleeee-ze take a picture of me and my mama," and I happily consented. That sassy little maid curled up in her mama's big lap, just like a child should, and for that afternoon, Parthenia was no longer the fill-in servant in a family turned upside down—she was just a kid.

Then I took a few photographs of Coobie, who, for all the times

Dobbs had described her as mischievous, was actually very docile that afternoon. I got three fabulous shots of her leaning on Dobbs's shoulder, her soft black curls mingling with Dobbs's long wavy black hair.

At length, I left all of them and went walking around the property, taking photos of the fields of corn and wheat, of an old woman with her gnarled hands all drawn up around her and trying to bring a biscuit to her mouth, of three men playing a card game in the shade. Every time I snapped the shutter, I felt warm all over, endless sips of Dellareen's tea. Indeed for the rest of the afternoon, I felt content and free and wonderfully absorbed, away from my family's troubles, looking at another side of life, at people who truly had nothing but had found a home of sorts.

I had brought four rolls of film with me, and after using up every last one, I decided that Dobbs was right. *This* was what I was meant to do—look through my camera and see something that mattered, something simple and important, and put it in a photo so that others could understand. I felt a thrill and congeniality with my heroine, the photographer Dorothea Lange. Like her, I was discovering my passion, my calling, and I wanted to stay out in the fields forever, looking through that lens at a different world.

I had taken to keeping the little volume *Patches from the Sky* by my bed and reading a poem or Scripture verse each night. The first time I held the volume at Daddy's funeral, I had been reassured, at least momentarily, that life could go on. Dobbs said that Hank's grandmother had called it a pathway through grief; I had a feeling the book was leading me on another pathway, too—a pathway toward the Bible and faith.

On the night after that glowing afternoon at the Alms Houses, I held the book and closed my eyes and thought of the way Mae Pearl's sadness and worry at my moving had just gotten erased away as she sat on the porch and listened to a destitute old man. The touch of human kindness had been a balm between them. I hope I had gotten it right in my photo.

I turned several pages in the book to an excerpt I had read a few nights before from Shakespeare's *The Merchant of Venice*.

> *The quality of mercy is not strained;*
> *It droppeth as the gentle rain from heaven*
> *Upon the place beneath: it is twice blest;*
> *It blesses him that gives and him that takes . . .*

I kept repeating that last phrase in my mind, again and again, and I nodded. Yes, mercy. Yes, it blessed him who gave and him who received. Once it was developed, I would slip the picture of Mae Pearl's hand covering the old man's in between this page in the book. That would be my first perfect illustration of reality. I knew there would be others.

————

But another reality forced itself upon me the next day. School was out, so I had no excuse not to join Mamma in packing up the house. Summer in Atlanta usually meant attending fancy tea parties, swimming, playing tennis at the club, horseback riding, and shopping for dresses. But what it meant for me in the summer of 1933 was facing the inevitable—we were moving out of our home.

The bank was providing professional movers to pack up the furniture and paintings and appliances and such, but Mamma expected Barbara, Irvin, and me to sort through our belongings and choose what to take with us and what to throw out or give away. Poor Irvin was completely lost as to where to start. I went into his room and found him lying on his bed, staring at the ceiling, throwing a baseball in the air and catching it.

He turned his freckled face to me and asked, "Do ya think I have to give away my stuffed animals, Perri?"

I hurried to the bed, sat down, and grabbed the baseball from him. "Of course not, Irvin McDowell Singleton. You will keep every single thing that means something to you. I'll pack up the clothes that you've outgrown and put them in the stack of things we're taking to the Alms Houses."

So I stayed with him all that morning. Every once in a while, I'd stop packing long enough to really look at my brother. He seemed so small and fragile, his short brown hair tucked under a baseball cap and all his stuffed animals lined up on his bed like silent friends who were encouraging him on in his dismal task.

"You okay, buddy?" I asked at one point.

He didn't look up at me but shrugged, and in that gesture I saw a mound of sadness as big and impenetrable as Stone Mountain, and I didn't know how to get my little brother back to a time when he laughed easily and whistled as he tossed his baseball.

That afternoon, Dobbs came over to help me pack up my room. I placed my photo albums in a cardboard carton and then went back in my closet to where my dresses hung. I touched my favorite, a dark green tea dress, fitted at the waist, with a full skirt. I put the fabric to my face and relished the feel of the smooth, cool silk. Would I ever buy a dress like this again?

Dobbs started humming as she worked, and I turned around and snapped at her. "God doesn't seem to be providing for us at all. There are no loaves and fishes here. Just a dead father and a house for sale and my family's life unraveling!"

Dobbs, who was carefully wrapping the four framed photos of my house in newspaper, looked truly dejected for a moment. Then, with her voice softened from her usual enthusiasm, she said, "He doesn't always provide the way we want, Perri. That's the thing. He's God and we're not. Our job is to trust Him and ask Him for things and let Him decide the best way to do it."

"The best way!" I looked around to make sure Barbara and Irvin weren't within hearing distance and said in a fierce whisper, "You think the best way is Daddy dying and Mamma going to work and us selling the only house we've ever known and everyone shaking their heads and whispering about the poor Singletons falling on hard times? You think that's best?"

Dobbs's face got a bit red, and then she looked flustered. She was hesitating, trying to decide what to say, but when she decided, she spoke with a clarity that stung. "It doesn't matter one iota what I think. Or what you think, Anne Perrin Singleton. It's God's problem, and He has a right to solve it the way He sees fit!"

She was wearing her potato-sack dress, which made her look almost disheveled as she wrapped the photos. She threw her hair over her shoulders and her eyes were shining—not in that happy, enthusiastic way I was used to, but in a passionate way that must have been like her father's when he was fired up and preaching. "You know, Perri, I'd much rather have lived like you have here in the lap of luxury and never thought once about where the next meal was coming from or if we'd have shoes in winter or a roof over our heads. If you'd asked me, I'd have told the Good Lord that I didn't much appreciate being hungry and having my stomach growling all through my classes at school.

"But it's like Father says; the Depression is a wake-up call, forcing us back to trusting in God instead of trusting only in ourselves. He says we have to work hard and pray hard and trust hard."

I didn't believe her about God providing, but her outburst showed me something that caught me off guard and made me embarrassed. I'd noticed it first when she'd shown up at Daddy's funeral and handed me *Patches from the Sky.* Mary Dobbs Dillard knew all about suffering and courage. I could never quite figure out what to do with her fantastical tales, but that day I saw the hurt and the frustration and the suffering on her face, and I felt uncovered. How could I harden myself from Dobbs as if she knew nothing of pain? What right did I have to accuse her or her God?

"I'm sorry, Dobbs," I mumbled, and saying those two words did not come one bit naturally to me. "I'm sure you look at my life and think I am insanely superficial. I'm sorry for all you've been through, and I'm glad you're here now with Frances and Coobie."

"I'm sorry too, Perri." When Dobbs said those words, they were sincere, bubbling up from the depths of faith, and a genuine sorrow accompanied them. She hugged me and said, "I would never mean to hurt you. I know you're going through awful things. Sometimes in the Bible someone is too tired and sad and hurt to pray, and so others come alongside and do it for them. That's what I've been doing for you, and I'll just keep on doing it." She hesitated and then added, "I'm praying that one day God will provide something for you, you alone, Perri Singleton, in a way that you won't be able to doubt it is from Him."

I frowned at her and conceded, "You can pray however you want, Dobbs."

She brightened. "And if you don't mind, I'll keep coming over here and helping you pack up things; I know it will be excruciating for you, so I would like to help you carry that burden."

I didn't mind at all.

Dobbs

One day when I was helping Perri with her sorting and packing, she confided, "There's no way Mamma can go through Daddy's things right now. What would really help me the most is if you could clean out Daddy's closet. Mamma can't bear to do it, and neither can I, but it won't be so hard for you."

"Of course, Perri, but I won't know what to do with his things."

She sniffed. "Well, anything sentimental, you just put to the side. But you can pack up his clothes."

"Shall I put them in bags for the poor, for the Alms Houses?"

Perri looked at me miserably. "Yes, you can do that with his work overalls and such, but . . . but as for his business suits . . . Well, what in the world will the poor do with business suits? Take them for your father and for Hank. Preachers can always use a good suit."

So Perri directed me to her father's closet. I made different stacks of clothes—one for the nice suits and dress shirts that Mother could alter for Father and Hank and another of clothing to give away. I also made a pile of what I considered "sentimental things" or clothes and other items that seemed to have certain value—a pair of silver cuff links engraved with the initials HS, two beautiful V-neck cashmere sweaters, also monogrammed with Holden Singleton's initials, and one box that he had lovingly kept filled in neat order with cards from his wife and children. That one made me tear up.

I had just closed a shoe box with a pair of tasseled leather loafers, which I imagined would fit Father perfectly, put it in his pile, and pulled the top off the next shoe box, when I noticed something tucked away in the far corner of the closet.

I reached back and pulled out an old toolbox. I couldn't imagine why Mr. Singleton kept a toolbox hidden in the back of his closet instead of in the garage. I opened it and found a top compartment with a hammer, a wrench, several screwdrivers, and nails—all the things one would expect to find there. I lifted that compartment up and looked underneath, expecting to find more tools. If I hadn't made that one gesture, so many things would have been different. But Perri had talked so affectionately of her father, how he was a banker with a builder's hands, that I was curious to see his other tools.

I gasped.

Instead of finding tools, there was a soft cloth on which sat five pearl-handled knives.

I touched one, then drew my hand back, as if I'd cut myself. I couldn't believe what I was seeing. I carefully removed the knives, setting them beside me, and lifted up the cloth. Beneath it were the heirloom earrings, the emerald ring, the ruby-and-diamond heart, three strands of pearls, and silver candlestick holders—everything that Becca claimed had been stolen.

A wave of nausea washed over me, and I sat there for the longest time, not having the foggiest idea what to do, wondering how in the world the silver and jewelry, stolen from the Chandlers' and Becca's house had ended up in Holden Singleton's toolbox. My first reflex was that it was some silly practical joke that the Singletons had wanted to play on their best friends, the Chandlers. But surely they would have admitted it when poor Anna was thrown in jail for stealing.

Then another idea came to me. Maybe Holden Singleton had been terribly desperate for money for a good while and had been stealing from rich people in Buckhead! I imagined him sneaking the knives into his suit pockets while he laughed and joked at the Chandlers' party down by the lake, the orchestra playing and the food being passed around.

Impossible! From every description I'd gotten of Holden Singleton, I could not make that theory work. Anyway, if he had stolen them, surely he would have pawned them off immediately so that no one would ever know.

Now, I had a horrible choice. If I took these things to Mrs. Chandler, it would be proof of Anna's innocence and she would go free, but Mr. Singleton's and his family's reputation would suffer perhaps a greater blow than what the suicide had already done, and I doubted Perri would ever forgive me.

If I said nothing, Anna would keep working on that prison farm.

I heard Perri calling to me from down the hall. Heart racing, I quickly replaced the knives in the toolbox, set the top container inside, closed the lid, and slid it back in the corner of the closet, where no one was likely to find it. Once I decided what I'd do, I would come back.

But no matter how hard I thought about it, I didn't know what to do about the silver and the jewelry and the pearl-handled knives. Thank goodness Mother was coming down in just a few days. Surely she would have an idea.

Perri

Dobbs's parents and Hank came to Atlanta in mid-June to hold a youth revival in a big tent in Inman Park in downtown Atlanta. To please Dobbs, I agreed to attend the first night with Barbara and Irvin in tow. We rode the streetcar to the park, and Dobbs greeted us outside the tent, all smiles, and introduced us to her parents. Dobbs's mother had that same olive skin and what must have once been jet black hair, now tinged with gray and worn back in an attractive chignon with a scarf twirled around it. Her dress was simple and yet smart-looking, and I realized right away where Dobbs got her eye for style. Dobbs's father, who definitely had a family resemblance to Mrs. Chandler, was wearing an outdated summer suit and looking very hot. In that first meeting, the Dillards didn't strike me as destitute, but rather as good people trying hard and not having much to fall back on.

I was surprised to see the tent packed with young people—the Dillards and Hank had been putting up posters everywhere to advertise—and we squeezed into a row halfway back. Sure enough, there was sawdust on the ground. Dobbs and Frances and Coobie were sitting down front with Mrs. Dillard. Reverend Dillard welcomed the crowd and sat down, and Hank went up front and began to speak.

It was muggy and so hot under the tent. Hank was sweating profusely but didn't look like he was paying one bit of attention to the heat. His attention was on those kids, and they were riveted to his story about a foolish, wealthy young boy who squandered all he had and ended up in the ghetto, until one day he went back home to where his father had been waiting for him all along. The way Hank spoke about God was down-to-earth.

". . . And we can be like that son, taking all the good gifts God gives us and spending them in the wrong way. But eventually, we hit rock bottom, and that's when we crawl back to God, and He makes us His children, and we get to have part of His unending inheritance. More than all the Coca-Colas in the world." The kids laughed. "We get to have eternity. Don't let it pass you by. . . ."

He spoke with such conviction that I got goose pimples on my arms. I felt uneasy and reassured at the same time. I stayed put when Hank asked the youth to "walk the Sawdust Trail" if they wanted to commit their lives to Christ, but many of the kids went up to talk to Hank and Reverend Dillard. Dobbs was there, too, talking to several girls. Watching her from afar—her beautiful face radiant, enthusiasm in her eyes—I understood her a little bit better. This was her cause—the Sawdust Trail. This was what Mary Dobbs Dillard lived for.

————

The next morning, as I was eating breakfast with Irvin and Barbara, Hank and Dobbs drove up to the house in Mr. Chandler's old Ford. Dobbs burst into the kitchen and announced, "Hank has a wonderful surprise for you!" She grabbed my hand and said, "Get your purse. Barbara, Irvin, I'll bring her back in a few hours, okay?"

I left my siblings at the table, staring after me. Hank drove us down to Five Points and led us to a tiny store with a bright yellow sign hanging outside that read *Saxton's Photography*. A lanky young man with a headful of red curls came to the door as we stepped inside. I had noticed him taking photos during the revival meeting the night before.

"Perri, Dobbs, I'd like for you to meet a friend of mine, Philip Hendrick," Hank said.

"Good to meet you," we chorused.

"The pleasure's mine," Philip said.

Hank slapped him on the back. "Philip, here, is an up-and-coming photographer from Chicago—he and his brother have a kiosk at the World's Fair up there." Another boy, who had an equally unruly mop of red hair, came out of a door at the back of the shop. "Here's his brother, Luke."

Luke could not have been more than fifteen or sixteen. He greeted us and blushed so fiercely that his face matched his hair.

Philip began to explain, "We're just down in Atlanta for this week, helping out our uncle. He owns this shop, but with the economy so bad, he's had to take on another job too. He called us all in a panic and begged us to come help until he could hire someone part time. He taught us everything we know about photography, so we weren't about to turn him down. And the bonus is that I can shoot photos at the revival." Philip punched Hank playfully.

Dobbs and Philip began jabbering about Chicago and the World's Fair while I inspected a display of amazingly clear photographs of bright, modern buildings with their shadows cast on the street.

"Were these all taken at the World's Fair? Did you take them?" I asked. When he nodded a bit self-consciously, I added, "Your work is marvelous, Mr. Hendrick," and I meant it.

"Call me Philip, please. And Hank here has told me a lot about your work too. He says you've got real talent. Did you bring any photographs with you?"

Without asking my permission, Dobbs had brought a small portfolio of my photos from the darkroom. She handed the portfolio to Philip, and he studied my photos for a long time, leafing through those from the Alms Houses and the May Fete at Washington Seminary and those of Dobbs on her bed. After a while, he set down the photographs and met my eyes. His were deep green and sparkly. He smiled at me and said, "Like I said, my uncle is looking to hire a part-time photographer. We can't stay—we head back to Chicago next week. Would you be interested in the job?"

I was so surprised, I blurted out, "Working . . . as a photographer?"

Philip laughed. "Well, helping out at the store, doing all kinds of things. My uncle's begged me to find someone, and when Hank told me about you, well . . ."

I felt light-headed. "Are you serious?"

He nodded. "I trust Hank Wilson with my life. And he's right about your work. You're talented."

My heart was hammering in my chest, but I composed myself enough to say, "Oh, Philip. This is a most generous offer. Can you give me a day to talk it over with my family?"

"Certainly, Perri. Come by tomorrow. You can meet my uncle then."

We shook hands. My throat was dry, but I managed to squeak out, "Thank you so much for this opportunity."

We walked out of the shop calmly, looking like sophisticated young people, but as soon as we stepped out into the warm June air, I grabbed Dobbs by the shoulders and we started jumping up and down, and I was almost screaming as loud as she was. Hank stood to the side with a satisfied smirk on his face, shaking his head and saying, "Girls."

Then I turned to Hank and said, "I can't thank you enough. It's such an amazing coincidence and a dream come true. It's . . . it's more than I could have ever imagined."

"It's an answer to our prayers," Dobbs said.

Hank nodded and winked at her, "I told you she'd be interested." Hank also told us that eighteen months earlier, at Hank's first revival meeting in Chicago, Philip Hendrick had been the first young man to walk the Sawdust Trail.

I couldn't attend the revival that night because I had a date with Spalding at the Piedmont Driving Club. When I excitedly told him of Philip's offer, he seemed completely unimpressed, quickly changed the subject, and led me to the dance floor. Soon I forgot about the revival and photography and felt my hands growing moist as he pulled me closer and brushed his lips over my cheek.

On the way home he parked his car in a dark lot, took off his dinner jacket, loosened his tie, and wrapped his arms around me. He began to kiss me, softly at first, then almost fiercely, holding me so tight that fear sizzled through me.

I pulled back from him and whispered between his kisses, "Spalding, please, you're going too fast for me."

He paused, sat up reluctantly, eyes filled with that scary desire, and laughed, but it was a hard, calculated laugh. "Perri, my dear, you'll catch up quickly, and you'll learn to love it. All girls do."

I pushed away from him, heart beating wildly, ran my hands through my tousled hair, and said, "We need to go."

Reluctantly, he drove me to the Chandlers', where I was spending the night with Dobbs. He walked me to the door and whispered, "We have a date Thursday night too—don't forget. And wear that yellow frock. It's not bad on you."

I gave a nod and watched him leave, a ball of fear in my stomach. I suddenly felt trapped by Spalding Smith, as if he had wrapped himself around me and I couldn't break loose. Anyone would have argued that I simply should have told him to leave me alone, that I wasn't interested, but they would not have known him and the power of his presence.

I felt stuck.

Dobbs knew things before anyone gave the slightest hint, so I was beyond thankful that she had not yet returned from the revival meeting and that I had time to quiet my spirit, which was racing with hopes of photography mingled with images of Spalding's dark eyes.

When Dobbs came into her room, her face was radiant, and she twirled around and caught me and said, "It's been the most wonderful evening of my life."

Completely taken aback, I whispered, "You mean, Hank asked you to marry him?"

She looked shocked, then smiled and shook her head. "Heavens no, Perri. We can't talk marriage yet. I'm barely eighteen, and he has his studies. No, it was the youth service. Oh, Perri. There were over two hundred kids packed under that tent, all kinds of kids, some from wealthy families and others just paupers, precious hungry kids, but at that moment, they were all the same, listening to Hank's every word.

"And at the end, a whole crowd of them walked the Sawdust Trail. There was such love, such power, the Spirit's presence . . ."

Dobbs might as well have been speaking to me in Chinese. I could not comprehend what she was saying, but I saw power and goodness and love radiating from her, and I ached for it.

If the circumstances had been different, if she hadn't been in such a religious fervor, I might have admitted that she had been right about Spalding and that I was suddenly afraid of him. But pride is a horrible thing, and I withdrew into myself, determined not to show her how foolish I had been. I wanted, longed, to reach out to her and feel the electrical love in her person, a power so opposite of Spalding's, but I was too proud, too afraid, too confused.

So I listened to her talk and remembered the crowd from the night before. But as my eyes closed, what I saw was Spalding and his dark desire and the way he was going to pull me along whether I wanted to follow or not.

———

Mamma thought the job offer was a marvelous opportunity. I rode the streetcar alone to the photography store the next afternoon, clutching my Rainbow Hawk-Eye. Philip and Luke greeted me with smiles.

"Perri, let me introduce you to my uncle, Mr. Saxton."

A middle-aged man, short and stocky with an enormous black moustache that curled up on the ends, came from around the counter. "Pleased to meet you, Miss Singleton."

My eyes grew wide. "I recognize you! Why, you take the photographs for Washington Seminary! I didn't know this was your store!"

Mr. Saxton laughed heartily. "Yes, ma'am, here I am. Joe Saxton himself."

While Philip and Luke went out on a photo shoot, Mr. Saxton

showed me around the store, explaining the way he took appointments and allowing me to observe his interactions with clients.

"I've had to take on extra work, times being what they are, so I need someone to keep the store part time. I can't pay you much, but you'll get experience."

A little cash and a lot of experience sounded perfect to me.

"So are you interested in the job?"

"Yes, sir!"

Mr. Saxton hired me on the spot. He handed me a camera and said, "You'll be using this little baby when it's time for you to take the portrait shots."

I looked at the camera, speechless, and finally managed to say, "It's a Zeiss Contax 1 Rangefinder!"

He chuckled. "Good girl! You know your stuff. Yep, it's a step or two up from your Kodak Hawk-Eye."

"I'll say! It's a 35 millimeter luxury camera. I've read about them, but . . . but are you sure you want me to use it?"

"Positive. It has its glitches though—the shutter isn't the most reliable in the world—so bring your Hawk-Eye along as a backup." He spent an hour, at least, showing me how to use the Zeiss and then let me practice.

When Mr. Saxton closed the store, Philip insisted on accompanying me back to my house, and I was too surprised to turn him down. Only he didn't take me directly home. Instead we walked to Jacobs' Drugstore. He ordered us both Coke floats, and we sat at a little table talking about cameras and photography and our dreams for the future.

Later, we rode the streetcar to the stop near my house, and before he left me, he said, "I've got only a few more days down here, Perri, but if you'd like, I'll take you out on some photo shoots with Luke and me after you close Uncle Joe's store in the evenings." He grinned at me, his green eyes dancing with life.

"I . . . I don't know what . . . to say."

"Thanks'll do," Philip said, with another grin.

"Yes, of course. Thank you. Thank you so much, Philip." As I watched him ride away on the streetcar, I wondered for a brief moment if Dobbs was right—that God had provided this job for me.

Dobbs

Father and Mother didn't stay with Uncle Robert and Aunt Josie, preferring to do as they did in every other city—camp in their tent near the revival grounds. But one afternoon, Mother came out to the Chandlers', and at last I had time to talk with her, alone. We went down by the lake and sat in two chairs on the porch of the Chandlers' little summerhouse.

A weeping willow gave us shade, and Mother closed her eyes for just a moment. She inhaled the fresh air and her face relaxed. "Honeysuckle," she whispered.

"And gardenias."

"And Queen Elizabeth roses."

We laughed together, and then for an hour, I poured out my heart to her, with the lake water licking the shore. Our conversation wandered from homesickness to Hank to Washington Seminary to my questions about dances and sororities and movies. Mother had grown up in the north of Chicago, an area considered upper class. "Was it hard for you to give up all the nice things you grew up with—the parties and dances and such, Mother?"

"Of course it was hard. I loved where I was raised, and I enjoyed being part of the social fabric of our society. But I met your father at a youth revival at Moody, and I was smitten with God and with him. He was very forthright about what our life would be like. We both felt such a strong call to serve Christ, and it seemed very clear to me. I didn't think of it as a sacrifice, Mary Dobbs."

"And Grandmother and Grandfather—how did they react?"

"Like the true fine people they were. They let me choose, and they never reprimanded me about my choice."

"But they never helped us either, when times were hard. And they could have—right?"

"They helped a great deal when you all were little, Mary Dobbs, keeping you and your sisters on weekends so that I could be at Father's meetings. They fed you, bought you beautiful clothes, took us out to eat at restaurants." Her pretty eyes clouded over. "But they lost a lot in the Depression, and then Grandfather died, and Grandmother has enough to live on fairly comfortably, but she doesn't have a lot extra, and I don't want her giving it to us. The Lord always provides for us, Mary Dobbs. You know that."

"But it's so hard. And it just seems like it wouldn't have to be so hard if . . ." But I could not finish the sentence.

"If what?" Mother prodded gently.

"If Father had accepted the inheritance that was his when his parents died."

Mother's face fell. "Is that what's worrying you?"

"Yes. Aunt Josie told me—because I begged her to—about Father's wild past and then 'getting religion,' as she put it, and then basically rejecting the family and the money, and I don't understand why."

Mother said nothing for the longest time. Then, "You know how passionate your father is, Mary Dobbs. His past had been so 'filthy and wicked'—his words—that he was determined to make a radical change."

"So he gave up all the inheritance money? We could have lived more comfortably with it. Or he could have at least put it in a savings and loan for us kids!" This information came from something Perri had mentioned.

"You know, Mary Dobbs, there are consequences we live with all our lives. Your father's past left him with heavy debts, and he chose to pay them off with the inheritance."

"What debts, Mother?"

Here Mother faltered for just a moment. She opened her mouth to say something. Then tears sprang to her eyes, and she brushed her hand across her face to wipe them away.

I suddenly regretted my harsh comments.

At last she whispered, "It's the past, Mary Dobbs. If you want to know those details, you must ask him. He can decide what he wants to tell you. It's not my story to share." I was startled when tears again sprang to her eyes. "Your father is a good man. Flawed like all of us, fairly complicated, and very zealous. But I trust him. I hope you will too."

I got up and gave my mother a tight hug, but inside I felt confused. Perhaps one day, I would ask my father about the inheritance.

As Mother and I walked back toward the big house, I told her about Hosea and Cornelius and Parthenia, and about Anna at the Alms House, falsely accused of stealing.

"Everyone knows she didn't do it, Mother."

"Yes, it sounds as if she's a victim of circumstances."

"But why wouldn't Aunt Josie get her out?"

"You say she's tried."

"Yes."

Mother gave a long sigh. "There are so many things in this world that aren't fair, Mary Dobbs, things we cannot change, no matter how much we long to."

"But, Mother, perhaps I *could* change this." Quickly, almost desperately, I related the story about finding the stolen articles in Mr. Singleton's tool chest.

Mother reached over and took my hand. "You need to tell Aunt Josie, and I'll be with you when you do it."

"You will?"

"I will."

She hugged me, and I felt safe with Mother, and suddenly I didn't want my parents to leave for the dust blizzard.

———

The next afternoon, Mother came for tea with Aunt Josie and me. We sat out on the porch and ate delicious little cakes and sipped Earl

Grey tea in Aunt Josie's fine china cups. "This is such a treat, Josie," Mother said.

"We love having the girls here. Wish we could convince Billy to stay too."

Mother shrugged. "You know Billy."

"Stubborn."

Mother nodded, and they both laughed.

At last Mother said, "Josie, I believe Mary Dobbs has something she wants to tell you."

I launched into my story, explaining the whole situation about me helping Perri pack up things at her house and about cleaning out Mr. Singleton's closet and finding his tool chest there, filled with the stolen jewelry and silver. Only when I'd finished did I notice how hard my heart was beating and how sweaty my hands were.

Aunt Josie sat in silence for a long moment, her face wearing a perplexed, flustered expression. "That's quite amazing. I . . . I can hardly believe Holden would have these things!" Her face turned deep crimson and there was perspiration on her upper lip. She recovered from her shock, tilted her head, and said, "Thank you for telling me, Mary Dobbs. Yes, of course it was the right thing to do. What an odd situation, but what's there to say? Don't worry about it anymore. I'll handle it."

We finished our tea in awkward silence, and when we left the porch, I felt a brief moment of relief, but then a sense of dread.

Perri

For three marvelous days, Philip Hendrick invaded my world, treating me as his equal, a professional photographer. I discovered Philip to be a combination of perfectionist and visionary. The enthusiasm he showed for his work was contagious. "You'll be learning on the go, Perri. I hope you don't mind," he'd quip as I followed him around. Indeed he looked as if he were in perpetual motion. I briefly wondered how someone with so much energy could sit still long enough to take such astonishing photographs.

Each day I learned more about the shop, and then, with Mr. Saxton's approval, Philip and Luke and I went to the streets with tripod and cameras in hand, and took photos of the Fox Theatre and the Georgian Terrace and Oakland Cemetery and loads of other familiar places. He even photographed our home and the Chandlers' and a magnificent villa nearby called the Swan House.

On Saturday, Hank and Dobbs joined us for a picnic lunch in Piedmont Park. When Hank and Philip and Luke left to play a game of baseball with a few other boys, Dobbs said, "I believe Philip Hendrick is sweet on you."

I rolled my eyes and whispered back, "He's my boss . . . practically."

"He's not looking at you like an employee." She giggled. "And he's taken more photos of you than of all the buildings in Atlanta put together."

"Please, Dobbs, I certainly don't need Spalding to think another boy is sweet on me. He's already annoyed that I've taken the job with Mr. Saxton. And anyway, Philip is leaving in two days."

Dobbs just gave me her knowing smile.

Of course I thought about her comment and could not deny the pure bliss I'd felt being with someone who shared my passion and wanted me to succeed—and wasn't bad to look at either.

———

Philip and Luke and Hank left for Chicago the same day that Dobbs's parents drove off for the Dust Bowl in their old Hudson. Dobbs and I took the boys to the train station. I had no idea how to show Philip my gratitude, and I got choked up a little telling both brothers good-bye. I must have repeated "Thanks so much for everything" three or four times.

The two redheads grinned at us. "It was great fun!" Philip said. Then he added, "I'm really going to miss you." He was staring straight at me, his face almost as red as his hair. "Both Luke and I. We're going to miss you."

Dobbs gave me a wink, and then Hank led her off to the side as Philip and Luke hopped on the train.

I waited on the platform while Dobbs said her good-byes to Hank. I caught sight of her clinging to him, and I thought she might be crying, and then Hank leaned down and kissed her gently, and she was lost to my view in his embrace. I wanted that kind of love—sometime, somewhere—a safe, deep love I could get lost in, one that would tear at my heart whenever I had to say good-bye.

I watched them and knew that never in all of my one thousand dates had I come near to that kind of love.

Dobbs

I cried as I told Hank good-bye. The week had passed so quickly, charged with emotion from the youth responding to Christ as Hank listened until late in the night when the last one had sobbed out his story. And me there beside him, sharing with the girls.

After the meetings, he'd drive me back to the Chandlers'—he stayed in a tent by my parents'—and we'd talk of the stolen items I'd found and of my father's strange past and of Philip and Luke Hendrick and Perri. And of us.

"I think I'm afraid to leave you here in Atlanta," Hank confided in Terminal Station. "Afraid I will lose you to that society, those boys, afraid you will be disappointed in me, like you were the last time. . . ."

I put my hand over his mouth. "No, I was all wrong the last time. I don't want anybody else, Hank. Just you."

He put his arms around me and held me close, then kissed me so softly on the lips that it took my breath away. I wanted Hank. Then I thought of Mother relaxing with me down by the lake and my sisters giggling with full stomachs, and I wanted that too. I wanted us to have enough.

During the days, Perri and her mother packed up their life, but Perri spent the nights with me at the Chandlers'. One evening we were sprawled out on my bed, perspiring in the humidity. An old fan, which sat on my desk, barely helped at all. Perri's cheeks were blazing as she talked on and on about the job with Mr. Saxton.

". . . And I've already learned so much, and he wants to give me his old equipment for my darkroom. . . ."

I got off the bed and took a little flyer about the revival from out of my Bible and began fanning her with it, but it barely made a difference. Then she reached over, took my Bible, and used it to create a breeze. As she did, the photograph of my sisters and Jackie and me fell out. She reached down and picked it up.

"Who's this girl with you?" Perri asked.

My throat went dry as I stared at the picture and whispered, "Jackie."

"Jackie? Who's Jackie? A cousin?"

But I barely heard her. I thought of all my stories about God providing, and what rushed through my head again was a simple sentence. *He didn't provide that time.* I looked over at Perri, who was still holding the picture. My eyes filled with tears. "That's Jackie with us in the picture. The best friend I ever had, before you came along."

"She looks a good bit older than you."

"She was."

Perri didn't miss my verb choice. "Was? Do you mean . . . ?"

"She died. She died of this horrible illness, completely untreatable, a congenital defect." I gulped back tears. "That's why Hank gave me *Patches from the Sky.* To help me move on. To help me get past Jackie's death." A burning sensation shot through me. "But you know, Perri, you never really get over losing someone you love."

She came and sat beside me and took my hand and whispered, "I know it." She bent her head down, tracing the outline of Jackie's face with her forefinger. "Why didn't you ever tell me about her?"

I said nothing for a long time. Finally I stole a glance her way. She looked stricken. "I did tell you, Perri. I told you I understood about tragedy. But that was all I could bear to say. And it still is."

———

The next day, when I was alone in my room, I took the photograph from my Bible, held it in my hands, put it to my chest, and closed my eyes. I saw Jackie, four years my senior, bright, beautiful, and energetic, sitting right next to Mother on the sofa, a needle in her mouth, eyes flashing with pleasure. I could almost hear Mother laughing and telling me to watch out for Jackie, not to follow her into mischief.

I thought of *Patches from the Sky,* probably packed away in some box, awaiting the Singletons' move, and I thought of the poem in that little volume that had especially comforted me after Jackie's sudden passing. It was by John Donne, the seventeenth-century poet, womanizer, and repentant preacher.

" 'Death be not proud,' " I whispered through the tightness in my throat. I did not need to look at the words, for I knew them by heart.

" 'Though some have called thee mighty and dreadful, for thou art not so.' " I recited the sonnet with tears streaming down my cheeks and wondered at the truth of what I had confided to Perri. *"You never really get over losing someone you love."*

I finished the poem as a confirmation of what I believed. " 'Why swellest thou then? One short sleep past, we wake eternally, and death shall be no more; death, thou shalt die.' "

I brushed away a lone tear with a glance at the photo. Then deliberately, almost desperately, I pushed away the doubt that inched its way into my heart and whispered, *God didn't provide,* every time I thought of Jackie Brown.

———

The moment I saw Aunt Josie's face, I knew something was wrong. She found me in the garden picking tomatoes with Cornelius and Parthenia. "Mary Dobbs, may I speak to you alone, please?"

"Of course."

I followed her back to the house and into Uncle Robert's study, where she closed the door, motioned for me to sit down, and then stood by the window, not facing me. "Two days ago, I went to Dot's house to help her finish packing the last things. You know me. I don't beat around the bush. I told her about your discovery of the stolen items in Holden's toolbox, and, of course, we immediately went up to Holden's closet. As you said, his toolbox was pushed far back in the corner of the closet. However, contrary to your story, we found no stolen silver or jewels inside, only his tools, carefully arranged in both the top and bottom trays." She turned and stared straight at me.

"That's impossible! I know what I saw."

"Dot wonders if you mentioned what you found to any of the younger children. Would they have taken the items from the toolbox? Or did you tell anyone else?"

"No! No. I promise you that I only told Mother and Hank and you!"

Aunt Josie folded her arms across her chest. "Mary Dobbs, I don't

199

want to think that you made up this whole story, but I know of your particular affection for Parthenia, and for Hosea and Cornelius and Anna, too, and how you've begged me to get Anna out of the Alms House . . ."

Tears sprang to my eyes. "Aunt Josie, I would never make something like that up! Never!"

Aunt Josie shook her head. "Well, that leaves us in a strange predicament. The Singleton house has now been completely emptied, and none of the stolen goods have turned up."

I felt sick to my stomach. Aunt Josie shrugged and turned to leave the room, but in that gesture, I thought I detected doubt. She didn't believe me.

A different doubt slipped in to taunt me. I wondered if perhaps my aunt, in her effort to protect her best friend, had indeed found the stolen items and taken them back without telling anyone. Perhaps she had decided it was better for Anna to suffer than for Dot Singleton and her family to do so.

Surely not!

I suddenly felt afraid and confused. I had seen every one of the stolen items in the toolbox. I knew I had. How I wished I could get advice from Mother, but she was far away, and it would be weeks before I heard from her again. So I poured out my heart in a letter to Hank and waited to hear what he would say.

When Perri returned from work that evening, she noticed immediately that I was upset about something. She said, "I'm sorry I asked you about Jackie. I've brought back painful memories."

I let her believe it was that. I could not bear to say a word about what I had found in her father's toolbox and what Aunt Josie had told me that day. But one thing I did know. Perri would find out at some point from someone, and she would never understand. I watched her that night and felt as if I were gazing into my future, alone. Without Perri.

Perri

Mother found a house on Club Drive within walking distance of the Capitol City Country Club. The house was small, tiny compared to our old home—a one-story white-brick house with a modern kitchen, three bedrooms, a living room with a fireplace, and a backyard big enough for Irvin to practice his pitching, with the vegetable garden behind. It sat on a little hill and had several big oak trees in the front yard. It was further out than where most fashionable Atlantans lived, but Mamma said that several fine Atlanta families had recently bought property near our new home.

Spalding spent three afternoons helping us move, along with Bill and Patty Robinson, Robert and Josie Chandler, Dobbs, Mae Pearl, and her parents. Even Barbara and Irvin pitched in every day to help Mamma and me. Jimmy and Dellareen were pleased with the little house because it was much closer for them. They lived in Johnson Town, a Negro neighborhood that some wealthy businessmen had developed years earlier. There was a streetcar that went directly from Johnson Town to Club Drive.

Spalding stayed for supper the day we were finally all moved in. Barbara and Irvin hung on to him, and Mamma thanked him endlessly for all his help. Spalding grinned and looked like an innocent pup. "Actually, I believe Jimmy and Ben did most of the work, but it was my pleasure to help. Except for the piano. It must weigh a literal ton! Football training sure comes in handy when you need strength." He flexed his muscles, and Barbara giggled. I imagined she had a wild crush on him.

I acted plenty pleased with the little house, and I even laughed that night with Barbara, each in our twin beds, sheets thrown off in an attempt to catch a slight breeze. We hadn't slept in the same room in ages. I tried my best to ignore the deep-down ache of missing our real home, the one that had the imprints of the Singleton family all over it—from the white columns and the high-ceilinged rooms and my spacious closet and the stables down to the tiniest detail of the way Mamma had placed the high-backed chairs in the living room and the smell of pipe that permeated Daddy's study whenever I entered.

Dobbs would be thankful to have her family around and a place to sleep and food to eat. I will choose to be thankful too.

I *was* thankful, but I was also heartbroken, and I wondered what my friends and Mamma's friends were saying about all the sad turn of events in the Singletons' lives.

———

My job with Mr. Saxton brought in seven dollars a week, and I loved every minute of it. Mr. Saxton proved to be a wonderful boss, giving me more and more responsibility as the summer progressed. I worked alone on Tuesday and Friday afternoons and was in charge of closing and locking up the store for the evening. Then I'd walk a few blocks and ride the streetcar home. One Friday in early July, as I walked to the streetcar, I was engrossed in thoughts about Philip Hendrick, who had written me two postcards from Chicago.

I did not see the men approaching until they were right beside me.

"Well, what do we have here? A pretty little missy."

I felt immediate terror.

There were two of them, both smelling of alcohol. I looked at one and noticed, as if in slow-motion, his brown teeth, his crusty skin, and the strange, hungry look in his eyes.

He touched my shoulder, and I shuddered, shoved his hand away, bent my head down, and quickened my pace to almost a run. They laughed behind me and were by my side again. Most evenings at this time, the streets around Five Points were still crowded, but that evening, I saw no one.

"We know missy works nearby. We seen you riding the streetcar alone and figured sometime we'd get our chance, when no one was around." The man who had touched me now grabbed me by the arm.

The other, a smaller man with a black cap pulled low on his face, yanked my purse from my grasp.

"Now, where is the money missy makes at her job?"

I felt light-headed with fear. I always kept the cash in my skirt pocket—what if they were determined to find it? He began pulling items out of my purse—my wallet, my brush—while the taller man shoved me toward a side street.

In a panic, I screamed so loud and so long that, taken aback, their reaction time was compromised. The taller man shoved me to the ground and was at my throat in half a second. "Missy shouldn't have done that." He slapped his hand over my mouth.

I tried to bite him. Then I saw his knife. Dread washed through me.

"Where's the money, missy?"

From far away I thought I heard someone calling my name. Mr. Saxton! A tall figure wearing a hat approached us, and my heart sank. I didn't know the man. Was he a cohort of these men?

No. He had called my name.

Or was I hallucinating?

My assailants cursed and took off running, with my purse. I sat on the ground, heart hammering in my chest, afraid to move. When the man in the hat came near and bent down, I screamed again. He backed away, saying, "It's okay, miss. I won't hurt you. Let me help you up."

I found I could barely stand. My legs were trembling so violently that I thought for sure they would buckle under me.

"Are you hurt?" the man asked.

I shook my head.

"Can I help you get somewhere?"

I looked up at him. He was well-groomed, middle-aged, dressed in a business suit and wearing a fedora.

"Daddy!" I cried out.

He stared at me warily.

No, not my father. Just a businessman, headed home from work.

"The streetcar," I choked out, unable to pronounce another word. He walked beside me in silence.

We reached the stop. Still trembling, I whispered, "Thank you. I . . . I want to give you something for helping me." I reached in my skirt pocket and pulled out the cash. But when I looked up, he was gone. Vanished.

On the streetcar, I sat almost glued beside a young woman with a small child. It seemed to take an eternity to get home. My mouth was parched as I stumbled inside our house, bolted the lock behind me, collapsed on the floor, and sobbed.

Mamma and Mrs. Chandler and Dobbs went with me to report the mugging at the police station, and then I begged Dobbs to spend the night at our house. For the sake of Mamma and Barbara and Irvin, I tried to act as if I were fine, but I wrestled with nightmares through the night, seeing blurred faces of evil men and then Daddy's, so clear, beside me.

I awoke to find Dobbs there, kneeling beside the bed and holding a cool rag on my forehead, hers a mass of wrinkles. "It's okay, Perri. Just a bad dream." I nodded, patted her hand, and closed my eyes. But I kept seeing the men's faces and then hearing someone calling my name and feeling that Daddy was somehow right there beside me.

Dobbs

My friendship with Perri had begun through tragedy, and it seemed to solidify, once again, after the mugging incident. Upon her request, I stayed at her house for a few nights, but I immediately felt the eyes of Mrs. Singleton on me, disapproving, suspicious. And it hurt. I wanted to take her away, alone, and tell her exactly what I had found in the toolbox, but she was not interested. That was clear.

Twice, I almost told Perri about her father's toolbox, but in the end, I could not bring myself to say the words. I needed to. I did not want her to find out from another source, and yet, in my mind, it seemed too complicated, and she seemed too fragile to hear it.

It was a few days later when Perri asked me, "Dobbs, do you believe in angels?"

"Angels?"

"Yes, like a guardian angel?"

"I think so. I mean, I know Jesus talks about children having an angel watching over them."

"I think the man who saved me was an angel."

I was so shocked, I had no response.

"I know he called my name. I just know it. I heard it. And when he came close, I thought it was my father. I could have sworn it was him. But it turned out to be just a well-dressed businessman, and when I tried to offer him something, he vanished. Really. He just wasn't there anymore." She looked hopeful and fearful at the same time. "So could it have been an angel?"

I took her hand and held it and said, "Sounds like an angel to me. One way or another, God protected you."

And I think Perri agreed with me on this one incident. I really think she did.

CHAPTER
17

Dobbs

Hank wrote me at least twice a week, and every time I saw his handwriting on the envelope, my heart would twitter and I'd get a deep
longing to be in his arms, safe. To my great relief, he was hired to
work at the World's Fair, and in each letter, he told me about his job
selling Coca-Colas to tourists who came from all over the world. He
also assured me of his prayers and encouraged me to "give the enigma
of the toolbox up to God each day and night."

So I tried. Honestly I did. But before long, I'd be calculating in
my mind, and then I'd scribble my ideas down on scraps of paper. I
had accumulated quite a few scraps by the time I jotted down what I
considered the two most plausible explanations:

*~Holden Singleton had been stealing things and hiding them
for a while; he needed money; he was certainly desperate. If he
stole them and hid them, when I found them and told Aunt Josie
and she told Mrs. Singleton, then perhaps Mrs. Singleton took
them out, to clear her husband's name and either told or didn't
tell Aunt Josie.*

*~Somebody else stole them—an unknown person—and hid
them in the Singletons' house to implicate Holden or Anna or
both, and that person is still happily going about his or her business. Who could it be? Maybe mean, ornery Becca! But why?*

Every day as I looked at those scraps of paper, I admitted that I
had no clue as to what had really happened. A verse floated into my

mind. *"Trust in the Lord with all thine heart; and lean not unto thine own understanding. In all thy ways acknowledge him and he shall direct thy paths."*

Trust. I took my Bible, and, as usual, it fell open to where I had inserted the photograph. Once again I saw Jackie's face staring out at me, bringing with it that tiny whisper of doubt. I closed the Bible without reading a single verse, wondering why life's situations were so complicated and painful.

Surely God would show me something. He'd show up, as He always did. Until then, I would wait.

Perri

To get my mind off the mugging, I organized the darkroom with the new equipment from Mr. Saxton. He had given me another light box, to replace my old system, and good advice about avoiding extreme temperatures for the chemicals. He'd also told me how to help with ventilation, to keep the chemical odor down. Finally, he'd given me quite a bit of film that needed to be used soon and a stack of postcards onto which I could print photographs.

It took a lot longer to drive from our house on Club Drive to the Chandler residence on West Paces Ferry. Instead of asking Jimmy for a ride, I began driving the Buick myself, so gradually I was less nervous behind the wheel. Once at the Chandlers', Hosea and Cornelius helped me install the light box and made a deep tank that would accommodate many rolls of film. Occasionally Mrs. Chandler came out to see the darkroom's progress and didn't seem to mind allowing her servants to help me.

Cornelius came up with the idea of making a wood reel, for washing film, which turned by the force of water passing through it, like a paddle wheel.

"You're a genius!" I told him.

But when Parthenia heard me say that, she made a face and said, "He's no genius. Jus' as stubborn a boy as anyone could imagine."

Cornelius yanked on his little sister's braids, but he gave her the sweetest smile, and I could tell he was proud of his invention and proud of his kid sister.

So little by little, in the sweltering heat of July, my darkroom began to look more like a professional space, and I couldn't help wishing that Philip—and Luke—would come down to see it.

Philip sent me postcards each week, and on one he'd printed a photo of Luke and himself standing outside their kiosk at the World's Fair. Luke was holding a small hand-written sign:

25 cents!
Have your picture taken outside your favorite exhibit
and pick it up the next day

On the back of the postcard, Philip had written, *This was Luke's idea, and I tell you what, everyone wants to have their photo made!*

When I showed the postcard to Mr. Saxton, he said, "You could do the same thing, Perri. You've got the postcards. Why don't you offer to take photos of your classmates doing their favorite activity? Ten cents a photo." He chuckled. "If there's one thing I've learned in twenty years of photography, it's that Atlanta girls love to have their photographs made."

"What a swell idea, Mr. Saxton!"

He beamed at me, twirling his moustache around a finger.

———

That weekend, Dobbs helped me pass out little handmade flyers to the girls at the club, which read:

Summer Shots:
The perfect keepsake to remember
these wonderful lazy days of summer
when your head is hidden in a school book next fall.
Three poses—30 cents.
10 cents for a postcard.

Soon the word spread around, and many girls from Washington Seminary were begging their mothers for Summer Shots. Within a week, the girls from our rival school were keen on the idea too, and then the boys found out.

So I worked for Mr. Saxton during the week, and on the weekends, Dobbs and I had oodles of work too. We even got the kids in on it. Frances and Barbara trimmed the postcards while they whispered about boys. They also added little colored hearts or stars or other symbols around the edges of the cards. Frances was quite good at drawing, and Barbara was marvelous with choosing colors.

Coobie tagged along with us, brushing a girl's hair back or arranging her hands and then standing behind me as I prepared to take a photo. She'd jump up and down, curls jiggling all around her face, yelling, "Smile! Come on, now. Smile!"

After a particularly long day of taking photos and then developing them in the darkroom, I told everyone good-night and drove the Buick home alone. I crept along at first, afraid of the dark, squinting to see with the headlights, my mind reliving the mugging incident. I gripped the steering wheel, leaned forward, and peered out the windshield as if I expected a drunken tramp to jump out in front of the car. Or perhaps an angel would show up.

Cautiously, I made my way home and parked out in front of the house. It was only when I got out of the Buick and started up the flagstone sidewalk toward the front door that I realized my mistake. I had driven to my *real* home, the one I knew and loved. My instincts had simply directed me along that familiar route. In the pitch-dark, I stared at the white columns, looking pale gray in the night. The sprawling mansion was absolutely dark, lonely.

"Someday," I said out loud, addressing my old home, "someday we'll be back. I promise."

———

In early August, I drove the Buick out to the Alms Houses so that I could take the boxes of clothes and household items we had cleaned out of our old home to Mrs. Clark, the director. Mae Pearl and Dobbs came with me, as well as Coobie and Parthenia. Dobbs and the little girls immediately went to find Anna out in the fields, and Mae Pearl walked over to the Black Alms House and went up on the porch, where the same old man she'd met the last time—Mr. Ross was his name—was still seated. It struck me that perhaps he had never even moved, and that made me smile.

Mamma and Daddy had always been involved in charity work through the Rotary Club, the Garden Club, the Junior League, the church, and many other organizations, and I'd helped at the Red Cross and the Northside Nursing Home. I had never seen charity work as a sacrifice. To me, it was normal, giving our excess time and money to help those less fortunate. But as I stood in Mrs. Clark's office, boxes filled with our possessions beside me, I felt sliced open and raw. I was giving away a part of my family's past, and as I did so, I could suddenly relate to these people who had fallen on hard times. I had seen what I thought of as *shared humanness* in Mae Pearl's and Mr. Ross's hands. Now I saw a shared humanness in all that we had lost.

Later I walked around the grounds taking pictures with the Zeiss Contax Mr. Saxton had lent me, and I felt a great solace. I caught sight of Coobie and Parthenia coming from the cornfields. They started chasing butterflies, and I followed behind them. I got a marvelous candid shot of Coobie holding out her hand with a Monarch butterfly perched on it. Her face was one big exclamation point. Beside her, Parthenia was pointing and hopping around, and in the background the colored prisoners labored in the fields.

I walked out farther to where they were working, the men's bare torsos shining with sweat and the women wiping their brows with damp handkerchiefs after every lift and pitch of the hoe. For one fleeting second, I thought of Vincent Van Gogh, whom we had studied in art class, out in the fields of southern France, painting the garlic pickers under a merciless sun. I lifted my camera, put it to my eye, and focused in on one woman, who was wiping her hands on her apron as she leaned heavily on her hoe. I clicked the shutter. She saw me. Our eyes met. I gave a brief smile and waved.

Dobbs

Perri suggested that Mae Pearl and I go out to the Alms Houses with her when she took her father's clothes and other possessions to the people living there. Yet I went with a heavy heart. For a while, I had imagined Anna freed, back with her family, living on the Chandler property. Instead, she was still working as a prisoner.

I found her coming in from the fields, and as we walked back to her room together, I told her all about the latest developments with the stolen silver and jewelry.

Anna kept shaking her head back and forth. "Heap of trouble now, ain't it? Not yore fault, though, Miz Mary Dobbs. I don't know what in the world happened in that house, but I know two things for shore, so you listen to me good."

When Anna spoke, her dark eyes bore into me, making me the slightest bit uncomfortable. "First is that Miz Chandler ain't lying. If she said she didn't find those things, she's absolutely telling the truth. She won't lie to protect Miz Singleton or to protect me. I've known her since she was about yore age, and I kin tell you this: she just goes by the rules, is all. Right by the rules. She's a good woman, and that's the truth."

Every once in a while as she spoke, Anna gave a slight wince, as if a sudden pain shot through her, which I imagined it did. I studied her deep-set eyes and the circles underneath them, her thick arms all tight and muscular from lifting heavy bales of hay and swinging a hoe and who knew what else.

"The second thing is this. Mr. Singleton ain't done no stealin' either. I knowed him—a fine man, kinda high-strung and nervous, but good and honest. Miz Singleton used ta hire me to work at their beautiful house whenever they gave one of them big fancy parties. Me and Dellareen, we'd talk, and we said it a hundred times if we said it once—our bosses is honest men, both of 'em. Ain't always that way for servants, no sir-ree, but we's lucky.

"So I don't know who took them things and hid 'em there, but it waddn't Mr. Singleton. It waddn't him."

I shook my head. "But he was depressed! Desperate! People do strange things, opposite of their typical demeanor, when they're sad and afraid and desperate."

"Listen ta me, Miz Mary Dobbs. Good Lawd's providin' for me in His own way, and you ain't got no business digging inta things way past yore understandin'. Ain't yore fault ya found them things, but nuthin' you can do 'bout it now. If'n the Good Lawd wants this mystery to be solved, well, I reckon He's big enough to solve it."

I felt rebuked, and my face must have turned scarlet. Anna's words sounded a lot like things I might say about God providing. But the way she said it came from somewhere deeper in her soul.

CHAPTER
18

Dobbs

Frances and Coobie went back to Chicago in late August. I cried at the train station as I waved good-bye, wishing I could keep them in Atlanta, where they were safe and well fed. Then I thought of the envelope I had tucked into Coobie's bag with the cash I'd made helping Perri sell her Summer Shots. I hoped that with it, Mother could buy groceries that she'd turn into delicious dinners.

The day they left, Mae Pearl insisted that I meet her at the club "to get your mind off of sad matters and on to fun things," as she put it.

I found her sunning by the pool, looking fabulous in a bright blue swimming suit that set off her eyes and platinum blond hair. She had her slim legs stretched out in front of her on the lounge chair. Her friends were right—she could very well be the next Joan Crawford or Greta Garbo. Even I knew their names. Mae Pearl saw me, waved, and patted the lounge chair beside hers, and said, "I'm so glad you came. Sit down, sit down!" Her face clouded and she asked, "Oh, how are you, having said good-bye to your precious sisters?"

"It was no fun at all," I admitted.

"Well, I have just the thing to help you. I've been talking to Macon and Lisa, and they agree that you ought to go through Rush this year."

Before I could protest, she hurried on. "I know you were against sororities at first, but surely not now. Why, with your enthusiasm, I bet we could name the Alms Houses as our charity for this year. Please consider it, Mary Dobbs. The Rush parties start in two days, and they are so very delightful. To die for!"

She had caught me off guard with her suggestion. "Oh, Mae Pearl.

That's sweet of you, but I don't have a cent to my name. I can't pay sorority dues, much less anything else."

"Now, don't worry your pretty little head over that. That's not a problem."

"Mae Pearl, you know as well as I do that just about everybody around here thinks money is a problem, even if they don't admit it." I sounded more like Perri than myself.

"But, Mary Dobbs, you're the one always talking about how God provides."

I knew my eyes betrayed me. I thought she was way off Scripture, expecting God to provide money for a sorority fee, but I just couldn't bear to hurt sweet Mae Pearl, so I said, "I'll think about it."

And for some reason, I did. That whole day and the next. During the past few weeks at the club, tiny Lisa Young and Mae Pearl and I had often gotten into discussions—Peggy and Brat still refused to talk to me—and sometimes Macon would join in, too, talking excitedly with her hands and shaking her red mane. I found that those girls could talk about all kinds of things—not just movies and boys and parties but also finances and family and how to help people less fortunate. Mother had often told me, *Mary Dobbs, you will never win people to Christ by pointing out their failings. You have to learn to care about them and love them first.*"

Father said it a different way, leaning over the pulpit, his voice booming—*"Unsolicited advice is always interpreted as criticism."*

In my room that night I went over my conversations with Hank and Mother about sororities and parties and movies, and I came to the conclusion that if I wanted to help the Washington Seminary girls, I needed to be part of their group. Suddenly it was crystal clear, a very legitimate way to get to know them better so that eventually I could introduce them to Christ.

So I decided I would attend the Rush parties, which took place at different girls' homes at the beginning of September. I reasoned that if God wanted me to be a part of a sorority, He'd let me be chosen.

When I told Aunt Josie that I was "rushing," she was thrilled and assured me she would pay the dues and offered to buy me new dresses.

"Couldn't I just wear some of Becca's dresses? She has so many gorgeous ones."

My aunt winced. "Becca is being a bit difficult at the moment. She's having a hard time with this pregnancy. I think we shouldn't touch those dresses right now. Anyway, you know how I love to shop, dear. I can't solve all the world's problems, but I can buy you a few more dresses for Rush. Nothing could make me happier."

I agreed for one reason only; it would give me time alone with Aunt Josie—and I could ask her about the toolbox.

————

The next afternoon, I broached the subject. "Aunt Josie, I'm sorry to bring it up, but I have to know. Do you believe me about the things I found in Mr. Singleton's toolbox? It would kill me to think you thought I'd made it all up. I promise I found those things."

We were in Rich's, and my aunt was studying the seams on two lovely tea dresses. She went right on looking at the dresses with her back turned to me. At last she handed me a deep burgundy chiffon frock. "This one will be perfect on you, Mary Dobbs. You have such a tiny little waist and adorable figure. I never could wear anything like this, what with my big bosoms—they sprouted when I was only thirteen and there wasn't a thing in the world to do but accept it."

I couldn't help but grin at her. I took the dress and slipped into a changing room where several other dresses we'd chosen hung. My grin faded as I realized that my aunt had ignored my question.

But when I stepped out of the changing room, she had tears in her eyes. "You look absolutely stunning in that color, Mary Dobbs." Then she wiped her eyes and whispered. "I know you didn't make any of that up, Mary Dobbs. I know you found those stolen things, and you were right to tell me. Now you have to leave it alone. It's not your problem, and if you start hunting around, it will end up worse for everyone."

I twirled around, let the full skirt billow out, and said as lightly as possible, "Did you tell Mrs. Singleton about the toolbox before you went over to look at it?"

"Mary Dobbs, I'm telling you to leave it alone."

"But it's unfair to Anna! I should tell the police."

"You will only cause a great deal of trouble for yourself. Please, dear, be reasonable."

"Was it Becca? Did you tell her?"

My aunt took me by the shoulders and put her face to within a few inches of mine, so that our noses almost touched. I could smell the thick scent of her perfume. "Child, don't ask. Please drop it. I believe what you told me is true, and I know you long to make things right for Anna, but you can't. And I cannot answer your questions because I honestly don't know what happened to the stolen things."

"But you suspect something."

"Trust me, dear girl, when I say it is much more complicated than you can imagine. Please promise you won't talk of it again. Not to me or Uncle Robert or Perri or her family. Please." She looked almost desperate—not angry, just interminably sad and desperate.

I bit my lip and nodded. "I'm sorry for the trouble I've caused. I won't bring it up again."

"There now, dear girl." She smothered me against her bosom, patting me on the back.

Aunt Josie found three more absolutely exquisite dresses for me to try on, and each time I stepped out of the changing room, her face lit up in a way that made her look like a peer, not my middle-aged aunt.

I chattered with Aunt Josie about proper etiquette for the Rush parties all the way home. But in the back of my mind, I wondered why in the world I found it so hard to follow the advice of Anna and Mother and Aunt Josie and Hank. For some reason, I simply *had* to know the answer.

———

On the night of the first Rush party, Aunt Josie came into my bedroom holding a box filled with mascara and lipstick and blush.

"You'd never know it, but all my girl friends used to ask me to do their makeup."

"Oh, I believe it, Aunt Josie. Perri and I are always saying you have the best taste in clothes, and you always look so put together and sophisticated. Mother says it too."

Aunt Josie beamed at me, and then set about applying my makeup.

When she was done I was so excited I could barely zip up the burgundy dress. Aunt Josie helped me, and then she whisked me out to the Pierce Arrow and drove me to the home of Virginia Hopkins, one of the senior Phi Pis.

I walked up the long winding driveway with my mouth almost hanging open. The drive was lined with little candles on either side, and more candles adorned every window in the redbrick mansion. My hands started sweating in my white gloves, and my throat went completely dry. The air was fresh and warm. I felt I had floated up into a dream world, and I could not stop smiling.

The point of the Rush parties was for the girls already in the sorority to talk to the girls being "rushed," to see if the rushees were an appropriate fit for a particular sorority. I had heard from Mae Pearl that the sorority girls all stayed late in the night after the party and voted yes or no for each girl. It seemed like the height of elitism to me, and yet that night, I found it perfectly enchanting.

I had decided to surprise Perri and show up at that first party without telling her, imagining her delight. But when she saw me holding my crystal goblet filled with pink punch, she had a shocked look on her face, and I thought that perhaps she felt betrayed. Then she smiled and shrugged and said, "You never cease to amaze me, Mary Dobbs Dillard. Unpredictable is what you are!" She gave me a hug and whispered, "You just better be sure you pledge Phi Pi—you understand?"

The next night, and the night after that, I hurried home from school so that I could get dressed up in a pretty dress, put on some of Aunt

Josie's jewelry, and let her apply my makeup. I enjoyed every minute of the experience—the beautiful homes, delicious food, fancy dresses, and girls coming by to talk to me. Every time the occasion presented itself, which was pretty often, I got to tell them that my father was an itinerant preacher, that he held revivals, and that I helped when I could. The girls listened politely and a few even seemed interested.

Of the three sororities, I knew I would choose the Phi Pis. Fortunately, in spite of Peggy and Brat's almost certain disapproval—a *no* vote—the Phi Pis chose me too.

———

Being part of the Phi Pis changed my life at Washington Seminary that fall. Suddenly I belonged. I was no longer the long-haired preacher's kid from Chicago, but rather a Phi Pi. The younger girls looked up to the senior Phi Pis with something like awe. My sorority sisters greeted me in the hallway and invited me to eat lunch at their table. I wrote letters to Mother and Hank, thanking them for encouraging me to reconsider my rash decisions—I called them my "rush" decisions—and explaining the new friendships I was making.

Perri and I still spent two afternoons a week taking photos and several nights a week in the darkroom. Ever since she had moved to the little house on Club Drive, no boys came to her house for pop-calling. She went from the girl of a thousand dates to a lone princess.

Of course, she still had Spalding, and most weekends she attended parties with him. But I hurt for her—the way the distance of a few miles and the size of a house made all the difference in the social scene in this part of Atlanta. Dellareen still fixed marvelous cookies, but no boys showed up, and Perri and I ended up eating many of the cookies ourselves.

The sorority did a few things for charities—Perri had headed up the Red Cross Club for the past two years, and at Christmas, the girls bought gifts for families in need. It seemed they were used to philanthropy, and I hoped they would appreciate an idea that was brewing in my overactive imagination.

On a Tuesday afternoon, I got Hosea to drive me to the Alms Houses. Peggy, who all of a sudden had decided to tolerate my presence and even talk to me, walked across the street from her house to meet me in front of the White Alms House. We talked with Mrs. Clark about the needs of the Alms Houses and asked how the Phi Pis could be of help.

"The two main things these people need are warm clothes for winter and the kindness of human touch. If a few of you girls could come visit each week, why, it would mean the world. Mr. Ross looks forward to Mae Pearl's visits like you wouldn't believe."

When we left, Peggy looked at me and said, "You're the real thing, aren't you, Mary Dobbs?"

"I beg your pardon?"

"You really do care about the poor and the prisoners, and you aren't one bit afraid to get involved. I used to think you were a bunch of hot air—with your cockamamie stories—but maybe I was wrong."

All I could think to say was "Thanks, Peggy."

We presented Mrs. Clark's requests to the girls at the next sorority meeting, and they enthusiastically agreed to make regular visits to the Alms Houses. When Mae Pearl suggested we plan a Christmas party for the residents, the Phi Pi girls came up with fabulous ideas, and I thought, *You've misjudged them, Dobbs. They can teach you many things.*

In October, I started an afternoon Bible hour for the girls in the sorority. Perri was sure no one would show up, but on the first Tuesday afternoon, eleven girls were there, including Macon, Mae Pearl, Lisa, and Perri. Even Brat and Peggy arrived ten minutes late.

"I've been wrong, girls," I started out. "I came down here and judged you and your money and acted overly zealous and religious, and I'm sorry."

Every girl stared at me. No one spoke.

"Thank you for letting me be a part of this sorority, in spite of my early faux pas."

I started reading from Matthew chapter five, where Jesus was talking to His disciples in the Sermon on the Mount. The girls listened intently, and when I got to the verse, "Blessed are they that mourn: for they shall be comforted," I couldn't help but glance over at Perri, and she met my eyes and nodded the slightest bit.

As soon as I joined the Phi Pis, it was as if someone shouted through a megaphone to every boy in town that the Chandler residence was now open to receive pop-calling. Aunt Josie and Uncle Robert thought it great fun to watch their side porch crowded every afternoon with teenagers from Boys High and college guys from Emory, Oglethorpe, and Georgia Tech. At first, I was mortified and wanted to shoo them all away. Then I decided to play the pop-calling game with my rules. Parthenia helped me bake up yummy treats, and while the boys munched on brownies and coconut cookies and lemon squares, I told them all about salvation.

At Perri's insistence, I agreed to attend a Sigma Alpha Epsilon fraternity party after a Georgia Tech football game, at which I had been duly impressed by Spalding's talent as a quarterback. I followed Perri from the stadium to the SAE house—an attractive redbrick building on the Tech campus, where the boys held meetings and parties. That afternoon, loads of guys and girls were standing on the lawn in front of the house. When Andrew Morrison, the Georgia Tech boy I'd met at the May Fete and at the Fox Theatre, saw me, he approached me, smiling, and said, "Well, my date has finally arrived."

I drew back, my face hot, my eyes wide. "I . . . I didn't realize . . ." I mashed my lips together and tried again. "I didn't realize we had dates. I have a steady . . ."

He shrugged. "Yes, Hank. In Chicago. I've heard all about him. Don't you worry, Mary Dobbs. Down here, we all date loads of girls—just for fun. I wasn't about to let the Phi Pis' most beautiful rushee go to her first frat party without a date."

Andrew turned out to be a marvelous dancer. And patient. I didn't know one step, but he walked me through each dance. As I sat out once, watching dozens of couples laughing while they danced the Charleston, I wondered if I was compromising my values. But I'd talked to both Mother and Hank about these very things, and I felt it was important to be part of the gang if I was going to tell them about the Sawdust Trail. My preaching against such activities certainly hadn't won me any friends. Enjoying life while living it for God, I felt, would speak to them more loudly.

But I kept hearing in my mind a quote Father had read me years ago from a woman evangelist: "*Social dancing is the first and easiest step toward hell.*"

Perri

The boys had stopped coming to my house, and I tried to tell myself it was because Spalding and I were getting serious. But I knew it was not that. My family had moved outside the respectable limits of our society, and the boys went to other places closer in—notably to the Chandlers'.

I don't think I was jealous of Dobbs. She was just so enigmatic. She did things I didn't expect, like joining the Phi Pis and heading up a committee to help the Alms Houses and starting a Bible study for the girls. And then, she had five to ten boys sitting on her porch in the afternoons.

Oh, I saw them all when I came over after work at Mr. Saxton's to develop photos in the darkroom, the very same boys who had sat on the porch at our real home. The only difference was that Dobbs used those afternoons for her advantage. I don't think she knew much about simply relaxing and having fun. She was much too intense. So, while Andrew Morrison and loads of other boys sipped lemonade and ate tea cakes, Dobbs told them her crazy stories about God providing. She used any and every opportunity to speak about the Sawdust Trail. The boys didn't seem to mind and kept showing up day after day.

I honestly didn't have time for pop-calling between my work after school at Mr. Saxton's store, my own photography shoots, and my dates with Spalding. He took me to the Piedmont Driving Club almost every weekend for Sunday afternoon brunch and seemed pleased to show me off. We met oodles of fascinating people, and little by little, I got caught up in the glamour of dating a football player. College football was just beginning to be very popular, especially in Atlanta, with four colleges in the city. Although Tech was not having a booming football season, Spalding nonetheless got loads of attention and was often in the newspaper. Once a photographer took a picture of us together, and it appeared in the society section of the *Atlanta Journal*.

During that football season, I tried not to think of all the ways Spalding and I were different. The attention I gained from dating him filled a void left by Daddy's death and selling our house and everything else. When I was with Spalding, I felt important again, a part of my society. Best of all, Spalding was crazy about me.

On one evening after a dance, Spalding drove me back toward the house on Club Drive but stopped in the Capitol City Country Club's darkened parking lot. "You look as beautiful as ever, my dear Perri," he said. As he cut the engine, scooted closer to me, and wrapped his arms around me, I saw the desire in his eyes.

Almost as a reflex, in self-defense, I said, "Spalding, Mr. Saxton's asked me to take some photos at a fancy party held at the Brightons' home next week. They'll pay me swell money for it. The only problem is that it interferes with the SAE party."

His hand tightened against my back, and he pulled me toward him. "Is this going to happen often now, Perri?"

"Oh no. I doubt it, Spalding. Just this once."

"Just this once, then."

To appease him, I let him kiss me, and the longer he kissed me, the more I enjoyed it, so I ended up getting home way past my curfew. He walked me to the door, pulled me close to him again, and kissed me soundly. "Don't forget that you're my girl, and I expect you to be by my side." The lightness in his voice was gone, and I got that sinking feeling again. My photos were becoming popular, and I knew that this would not be the only time I'd have to turn down Spalding for a photo shoot. I wondered what else I might have to do to appease him.

———

A few days after that incident with Spalding, I received another postcard from Philip Hendrick. On the front of the card, Luke and Philip were posing beside their kiosk, each leaning on an elbow and blowing a kiss with their free hand. Luke, who often put finishing touches on by hand, had colored their hair red and their suits gray, and they looked like smart young businessmen, carefree amidst the worries of the country. Philip had written on the back of the postcard:

> *How's my up-and-coming photographer? Loved hearing about the darkroom and the photo shoots of your classmates. Tell my uncle and Mary Dobbs hi! Yours affectionately, Philip.*

I found myself smiling as I read the postcard over several times and set it on my desk with the picture of the boys' faces smiling up at me. Then I fetched a postcard onto which I had printed a photograph from the summer and quickly wrote him a note back.

> *Dear Philip, I'm getting many requests for photo shoots, and your uncle is just swell. He's telling people to hire me to be the photographer at their fancy parties. And one of my photos appeared in the* Atlanta Journal *this week. Can you believe it?*
> *This photo was taken in August when Coobie and Frances were helping us. The little colored girl is Parthenia, the one I was telling you about.*

I hesitated. How should I sign the card? *Yours affectionately?* But I wasn't *his* at all. *Sincerely?* No, that lacked all imagination. Then I found it: *Your fellow photographer friend, Perri.*

————

Dobbs and I were working in the darkroom when she said, "That's pretty keen that one of your photos made it into the *Atlanta Journal.*"

"It's very exciting. People really go for having their portraits made."

Dobbs was washing a long roll of film. "That's because people love themselves," she stated. "We love to think about ourselves, look at ourselves, pick ourselves out of a photo, comment on how we look. Down deep, we're a lot more interested in the trivial details of our lives than anything beautiful or inspiring or profound."

"Wow, Dobbs! I think you're right. I'd never thought about it that way."

"But occasionally something moves us deeply—a book we read or a play we see or a gorgeous painting or a passage of Scripture or a true-life story or a photograph, and we reach beyond our pettiness and become truly alive."

Immediately, I thought of my diaries, the ones I'd kept for the past five years. On no page had I scribbled a deep thought or a kind deed. I had simply recorded my activities: tea dances, fox hunts, movies, parties, and dates. Name after name after name, event after event—an endless list of things that filled up my very superficial life. If someone stumbled on them, what would they learn about me? Nothing about my heart and soul, just mindless social activities that had seemed ever so important at the time.

Back at home later that evening, I got out my diary from 1932, that infamous recording of my one thousand dates, and I flipped through the pages, randomly reading my entries. A few minutes later, I closed the diary, disgusted at my superficiality. Yet I *longed* to have it back. I still participated in many of the same activities, but my heart was often heavy. I longed to recapture that blissful feeling of not having a care in the world. Sometimes I thought I would do anything to retrieve it.

Patches from the Sky lay on my bedside table. I opened it and turned to the last page, where I knew I would find a photo of the sky with billowing clouds. The photographer had caught the sunbeams at just the right angle so that it truly looked as if almighty God was sending a message down from heaven. On the opposite page was a short passage of Scripture: *"These things I have spoken unto you, that in me ye might have peace. In the world ye shall have tribulation: but be of good cheer; I have overcome the world."*

Which thing did I really want—my social life or something mysterious and beyond imagination, something that Dobbs called faith.

"I want peace."

Dobbs

One Saturday evening in the middle of the fall, the senior Phi Pis decided to go to the opening night of a new movie at the Buckhead Theatre. Clark Gable and Joan Crawford were playing in *The Dancing Lady*. The Bible study was going well, as was the project for the Alms Houses, so I thought the least I could do was attend a movie with everyone. Spalding was with Perri, Mae Pearl was ecstatic, having nabbed a cute boy named Sam Durand, and Macon was with a fellow named Jack Brooks. Andrew Morrison had asked me to be his date, and I'd agreed.

When he picked me up at the Chandlers', he had a huge bouquet of roses for me. Aunt Josie bustled about finding a vase, and all I could say was "These are so beautiful, Andrew. How extremely thoughtful of you."

"You look lovely, Mary Dobbs," he said, offering me his arm and walking me out to the car. We drove to the Buckhead Theatre, where we met the rest of the gang—about twenty of us in all. I took a deep breath and could not help grinning as I held on to Andrew Morrison's arm and went inside the theater. I felt almost as buoyant and invigorated as when we had gone to the opera at the Fox.

From the moment the big lion opened his mouth and roared while *Metro-Goldwin-Mayer* played across the screen, I was entranced. And then ashamed. The movie began with a scene in a burlesque theater, where long-legged and scantily dressed dancers were doing a striptease. Poor Father would have fainted if he saw me in a theater watching *this* at my first movie ever.

I decided that night that Hollywood's brand of heaven on earth was a deliberate and enormously successful effort to provide Americans with escape. We paid twenty-five cents a ticket to see gorgeous Joan Crawford dancing all over the place with her perfectly shaped legs—although no more perfectly shaped than Mae Pearl's, in my opinion—and making eyes at Clark Gable.

After my initial shock and embarrassment, I found myself completely absorbed in the story, the dancing, and the songs.

Afterwards, we all walked across the street to Jacobs' Drugstore and sat on the swiveling stools by the soda fountain. I twirled around and around on my chair, until I realized the rest of the crowd was staring at me. "This is the keenest place!" I offered.

Andrew asked, "You mean you've never been to Jacobs' Drugstore?"

"No."

"Your first movie and your first visit to Jacobs'."

"Yes."

"It's an incredibly famous place. This is where the first Coca-Cola was served," Mae Pearl informed me. She prattled along, giving the history of the soft drink while the man behind the counter fixed each of us a different concoction from the soda fountain—drinks piled high with whipped cream or vanilla ice cream, always with a bright red cherry on top.

For the first time ever, I knew what the girls were talking about when they gushed over Joan Crawford and giggled at the way Clark Gable made their hearts beat faster. I liked being part of the group. For that night, I really did.

Perri

Dobbs liked the parties. They suited her well, with her warm, effervescent personality. The boys flocked to her, and she could have been reciting definitions from Webster's Dictionary, for all they cared. They just wanted to be around this strange and beautiful young woman. So she quoted Scripture to them, and it didn't matter. They were entranced. Especially Andrew Morrison.

But she remained true to her beliefs. After joining us to see *The*

Dancing Lady, she proclaimed she would not attend another film without first reading the reviews. And as often as she accepted a date, she turned another one down. She only conformed to society life on her terms.

In late November, I walked into the spacious ballroom of the Georgian Terrace on Spalding's arm for the Senior Cotillion Dance. I looked across the room, expecting to see Dobbs with Andrew, but she was not there. A slight irritation coursed through me, and I wondered if she had stood up poor Andrew, who clearly had fallen under her spell.

The other girls in the ballroom looked marvelous in their long, slinky gowns. I paraded around the room, greeting each girl I knew with a kiss on the cheek, in vogue ever since the French movie *Fanny* had been a big hit.

I spotted a new girl over by the bar, her back to me. She was wearing a bright teal evening gown, low-cut down the back, and it was literally shimmering, clinging to her lovely figure. A crowd of boys were around her, laughing. I saw Andrew there among them and walked over to ask him what in the world had happened to Dobbs.

And then I let out a gasp. It *was* Dobbs standing in front of those boys in her teal gown. Her beautiful black hair was cut in the sassiest, latest style. Her eyes were outlined in black and her mouth painted a very bright pink. Everything about her was glowing, and at that moment she looked like a movie star.

"Mary Dobbs Dillard! What in the world happened to your hair!"

She left the group of boys and slinked over to me and teased, "Well, you look lovely too, Miss Anne Perrin Singleton. And your gown is so becoming on you."

"I'm sorry for the outburst. I'm just so shocked. Your hair! Your beautiful hair!"

"Well, do you like it? Yes, my long hair is gone, but what do you think about my new hairdo? Say something, Perri."

"You're breathtakingly gorgeous. You are very, very dangerous, Dobbs Dillard, and you better be careful."

She laughed. "I've told Hank every last thing, and he isn't worried.

He says he can't wait to see how it looks when I go up to Chicago for the Christmas holidays. Anyway, I did it for my family. Mae Pearl had the idea. She said she'd heard that the beauty salon cut long hair off for wigs and paid you handsomely for it. So I went in, and the stylist was 'intoxicated' by my 'amazingly perfect locks.' I didn't have to pay a thing for the haircut and style. Instead, they paid me fifteen dollars! Can you imagine that! Fifteen dollars that I sent up to Chicago before it could even get warm in my hands. It'll buy groceries for my family for another two months."

Dobbs was thrilled with it all, but for some strange reason, I had this horrible feeling of dread. She had joined a sorority, went to the movies almost every week, was at a cotillion dance looking very sensual, and now had cut her hair. I felt like I was the devil incarnate, dragging an innocent soul down a long, dirty lane into sin.

———

On a Saturday in early December, I went to the club with my girl friends for lunch. The main ballroom had an enormous Christmas tree in it, and I took several splendid photos of the tree with its blazing candles and glittering ornaments. We finished our meal by discussing the Christmas tea and how much it would mean to the residents of the Alms Houses. The waiter came with the bill, and we each gave him our club number so the club could charge our meal to our family account. When the waiter brought back the cards to sign, he looked at me and said a bit apologetically, "Miss Singleton, Mr. Jones would like to speak with you."

I felt those spots on my cheeks appear, giggled a little self-consciously at my friends, and followed the waiter out of the restaurant area and down the hall to Mr. Jones's office. He was the manager of the club.

"Hello, Miss Singleton," Mr. Jones said. He was a formidable man in his forties, handsome, broad shouldered, his hair jet black. "Please have a seat. This will only take a second. You see, we have not received your family's dues for the month. I'm afraid that your mother has chosen not to renew your club membership."

I stared at him completely speechless. Finally, I found my voice. "We're not club members anymore?"

"I'm afraid not."

I bit my lip to keep tears from pouring out of my eyes. "I'm ever so sorry. I didn't . . . My mother didn't . . ." I reached for my purse. "I can pay you cash."

He smiled patronizingly. "No, this lunch is on the club. Don't you worry about a thing. And I'm sure that times will get better, Miss Singleton."

"Thank you," I mumbled.

Somehow I got out of the plush chair and ran down the hallway to the women's lounge. I burst into tears, staring at myself in the gilded mirror. The walls were covered in expensive wallpaper, and mono-grammed little white hand towels sat beside the marble sinks. Every inch of the club spoke of comfort and grace and money.

My family didn't belong to our club anymore! I lived just down the street, and I didn't belong. It was one more thing that I had lost and would have to get back.

I sat on a pink satin stool in the lounge for a long time. Finally Mae Pearl came and found me. "I can't go back out there," I cried. "I have a horrible stomachache. I'm afraid I'm coming down with something."

"Oh, Perri. I'm terribly sorry. Do you want me to walk you home?"

"No, no. It's okay. It always passes after a little while. Go on with the others."

"If you're sure."

"Positive."

As I watched her leave, I told myself I hadn't lied to Mae Pearl. I *had* come down with something. A horrible case of shame.

I walked home from the club, fury pulsing in my temples. I lit into Mamma as soon as I walked into the house. "Why didn't you tell me you'd canceled our membership to the club? I've never been so humiliated in my life!"

Mamma looked up at me, and immediately I regretted my outburst. "Perri dear, I'm so sorry. I honestly just forgot to tell you." She let out a forlorn sigh. "Bill Robinson gave me some more bad news a few weeks ago."

My throat went dry, and I mumbled, "I am so tired of Mr. Robinson giving us bad news."

Mamma nodded. "Yes. Me too. It seems we have other outstanding debts that must be paid. I didn't want to sell the car. We need it. And I wanted you and Barbara to continue at Washington Seminary. I decided to withdraw our membership for this year. It will save us quite a bit, and hopefully I can get this new debt paid off."

"What new debt is Mr. Robinson talking about? We've been over Daddy's books dozens of times! He's wrong."

"He showed me things. Apparently, your father had been gambling." She said this in a choked voice. She looked so fragile and miserable that I took her in my arms.

"Oh, Mamma. I'm so sorry."

"I would have told you right away, but you were so busy with the photography, and I didn't want to distract you. You're doing good work, Perri, and helping us get by."

As I left the dining room, I clutched my throat. It felt as if I were slowly being choked to death. I realized that I could never get everything back that we'd lost. I was trying my best, but no matter how much I did, there was a horrible noose around my neck, just like there had been for Daddy.

Alone in my room, I took out *Patches from the Sky* and turned to the page where I had stored Daddy's note to me. I thought of him, desperate and gambling away money we didn't have. It didn't make one bit of sense. I collapsed on the floor, my back against the bed, and closed my eyes . . . remembering . . .

It was a late summer afternoon in August 1932. Daddy had

just gotten home from the office. I hurried downstairs to see him and found him in his study, his head resting in his hands, elbows on the desk.

"What's the matter, Daddy? A hard day at work?"

He looked up at me, ran his hands through his black hair, and said, "Yes, sweetie. Very hard." Then, "I had to let three of our employees go today." He began massaging his temples. "Three good men with families, little kids to feed. Goodness, Perri, I wish I could give them something. Help them in some way." His face was pale, and I thought he actually might have been crying.

I could not imagine my father, who loved his job and his employees and his family, gambling our money away in a fit of despair. That was not how Daddy acted in the midst of his morose moods. Mr. Robinson knew Daddy perfectly well. Surely there was another explanation. I needed to talk to him. Alone.

———

Mr. and Mrs. Robinson lived in a fashionable house right on Peachtree Street. On Sunday afternoon, I told Mamma I was going out and drove to the Robinsons' house and rang the doorbell. Mrs. Robinson answered. "Perri dear! How lovely to see you. Is your mother with you? Barbara and Irvin?"

I shook my head, and she noticed I wasn't smiling.

"Is something wrong, dear?"

I felt my eyes tearing up, but I said quickly, "No, nothing new. But . . . but I was wondering if I could talk to Mr. Robinson about . . ." I swallowed twice. "About Daddy."

"Oh, goodness, my dear. Of course. Have a seat there in the living room, and I'll go get him."

She disappeared down a hall.

Mr. Robinson came into the living room, greeted me as he always did, looking almost timid behind his thick glasses, and took a seat across from me. "Perri, Patty said you wanted to talk to me?"

I had to say it quickly. "Yes. About Daddy. Without Mamma here."

"I understand."

"It's just that, well, you knew Daddy so well, and Mamma said you found more outstanding debts. That he'd been gambling before . . ." I cleared my throat, closed my eyes, and whispered, "Before he died."

"Perri dear, I didn't know Dot had told you."

"She only just did, and I can't believe it. You knew him. He'd never spend money he didn't have. What could it have been?"

Mr. Robinson removed his glasses, ran his fingers around his eyes, and glanced down at his hands. He looked more timid and uncomfortable than ever. "Perri, of course your father would never do those kinds of things."

I felt a huge surge of relief.

Then he added, "Under normal circumstances." A sigh. "But things hadn't been normal for a long time, and your dear father, well, I believe he was trying everything he could think of to keep you all solvent. He worried himself crazy over it. Sometimes, in desperate times, people do desperate things."

"Like gambling to try to get money back?"

Mr. Robinson nodded. "Yes, among other things."

I could not look at him when I asked my last question. "You think he gambled our money away and then felt so bad about it that he . . ."

"Perri, your father was a wonderful man. You remember that. Don't think about the rest."

I left their home barely able to make my legs move forward, wishing in that moment that I could disappear. I drove to Oakland Cemetery and stood by Daddy's grave until the sky turned gray and then dark, until the statues and gravestones surrounding me looked like ghosts in the dusky light. The only words I spoke out loud, over and over, were, "Daddy, why did you say you didn't do it? What didn't you do?"

Dobbs

Perri was absolutely devoted to her photography work, and she missed several dances with Spalding. One evening, she was only halfway through the washing process, and we were supposed to be at a party at the SAE house. "You go on, Dobbs. I'll finish up here. I've already told Spalding I can't make it."

"I'm happy to stay with you. You know the parties don't mean much to me."

But she insisted, and I had the feeling she just needed to be alone.

Andrew Morrison was my date at the dance, and the evening sped by with other boys cutting in on me time and again, twirling me around to the music so lively and happy. Several commented on my short hair and said I looked stunning. I kept thinking of Hank, remembering what he'd said— *"Dancing is just fine as long as you do it always and only with me."*

I kept looking for Spalding, but he didn't show up during the whole party. I figured he was pretty miffed at Perri. Near the end of the evening, I went to find the toilets, which were behind the bar area. Coming back out, I walked through a storage room piled high with old files and several dilapidated pieces of furniture. One of the frat guys was lying on an old sofa, his arms wrapped around a girl with blond hair. I tiptoed past, feeling embarrassed, even though they were so involved in their actions they surely didn't notice me.

Then I saw it. The Madras pants and the white leather shoes. Spalding! I tried not to gasp and hurried to the door, but as I turned the handle, the door squeaked, and he looked up and saw me.

I had to tell Perri.

CHAPTER
20

Perri

I could not bear to tell any of my friends that we were no longer members of the club. Fortunately, since Spalding often took me to the Piedmont Driving Club on the weekends, I had a perfect excuse for why I wasn't at our club. Every Phi Pi, except Dobbs, envied me for having nabbed a college football star, anyway.

On a chilly Saturday night ten days before Christmas, Spalding drove to our favorite "parking spot," as he called it. We made up for the times I missed a party because of a photo shoot by going parking. Part of me was ashamed of the things we did in his car and part of me enjoyed it. But the part that felt ashamed could not win over the other shame I was carrying, of all that my family had lost.

On that night, Spalding had a little wrapped gift for me.

"What is it?"

"An early Christmas gift. Go ahead and open it."

Inside the little box, I found his SAE pin. "Are you serious? You're giving me your pin?"

He nodded.

"Oh, Spalding. How wonderful." I was at an absolute loss for words. Being pinned was a serious affair, meaning that girl was taken. Often a proposal for marriage followed after.

"I thought you'd be pleased," he said, gently pushing my hair back out of my face so that he could kiss me again. "You know what this means, don't you?"

I nodded.

"It means you're mine. All mine." He said it with a smile on his face and desire in his eyes. He took me in his arms again, and I honestly could not tell if my heart was beating in its rapid, fluttery way because I was terribly excited or terribly afraid.

———

The next day after church, I drove the Buick to the Chandlers' and found Dobbs up in her room, sitting at her desk.

"I'm pinned to Spalding, Dobbs! Isn't it wonderful? Why, that means we're practically engaged."

Although I wanted Dobbs's approval, I wasn't surprised by her reaction. "Oh no, Perri. It's too quick. You're too young. There are loads of other swell boys out there. Like Philip. I think it's a big mistake."

I plopped down on her bed and stared straight at her. "I knew you'd say that! I just knew it."

"I can't pretend that I think he's the right guy for you. You know I'm no good at pretending."

Irritated, I raised my voice. "You always think you have the right answers—for yourself and everyone else. I don't have time to wait on your God to somehow miraculously provide for my family. It's not going to happen!" I fingered the SAE pin. "Spalding will provide for us all! He'll do just fine."

"But you don't love him."

I ignored the fluttering in my chest, cocked my head, and said, "What in the world does love have to do with it? We're congenial; he's rich; we make a handsome couple. We'll be well thought of in all of Atlanta."

Dobbs's face fell. She didn't say a word but turned her head down.

"Dobbs, I'm out to save my family. However I can." When Dobbs didn't answer me, I asked, "You think I'm crazy, don't you."

"No. Not at all." She lifted her head and met my eyes. Hers were filled with a mixture of hurt and love. "I think it is a very noble cause, and I wish you well. But not with Spalding. That can't be the best way."

"What in the world do you really know about Spalding and me?

You made up your mind the first time you met him that you didn't like him. Why do you always have to be such a stick-in-the-mud?"

Dobbs frowned. "I just think that marrying a guy for his money is dangerous. You should aim for something higher."

"Oh, like what? Religion? I've told you what I'm aiming at, Dobbs Dillard. It's very simple: survival. That's my goal. And Spalding fits in with that plan perfectly."

Dobbs rarely looked angry, but that afternoon she did. "I feel sorry for you, Perri. You live by the invisible rules of your society, and you're afraid to step one toe outside of that perimeter. You're desperately trying to go back to how things used to be. But you can't ever get that back."

Her words stung, and I lashed back at her. "I just wish for once you could be happy about something good that has happened to me. You're a great friend when I need sympathy and condolences in hard times, but you are a pretty awful friend when I need congratulations. That's all I wanted to hear from you tonight, Dobbs. I just wanted to hear you say, 'Congratulations.'"

I left her standing in her bedroom and hurried out to the Buick. I drove to Club Drive with my heart hammering in my chest. Dobbs was the best friend I had ever had precisely because she refused to play our society games. She had tried to tell me the truth, and sadly, I would not listen.

Mamma's reaction to my being pinned was the complete opposite of Dobbs's. "Why, that is wonderful, darling. He's such a fine young man."

Barbara begged me to let her hold the SAE pin, and Irvin put a record on the Victrola, and we danced and laughed and celebrated. No one mentioned engagement or a wedding, but I knew Mamma was thinking that at least one of her children would marry well and be cared for.

Later that night, I went to tuck Irvin into bed, as had become my custom. "You like him an awful lot, don't you, Sis?" he asked.

"Yes, quite a lot."

"But you won't run off and marry him yet, will you? You'll stay here with us for a while, won't you?"

I hugged him tightly. "Oh, Irvin. Of course. I'll always be here for you. Always."

I tiptoed out of his room, feeling that familiar weight of responsibility on me. I found Mamma in the kitchen.

"Mamma, you think Spalding's a fine boy, right?"

"Yes, I've been impressed with him. He has impeccable manners and was a great help to us during the move."

Finally I said, "Mary Dobbs doesn't like him. She thinks he's all wrong for me."

She reached over and patted my hand. "Perhaps she's just jealous. You took her under your wing and helped her find her place in Atlanta. She's probably just afraid of losing your friendship, or having it be diminished because of your time spent with Spalding."

"But, Mamma, usually Dobbs has a lot of insight."

"Everyone makes mistakes in judgment, Perri. Mary Dobbs is no different."

"Why do you say that?"

Reluctantly Mamma told me about the stolen items that Mary Dobbs claimed to have seen in my father's toolbox and of how she told her aunt about this. "But when Josie and I found the toolbox—right where Mary Dobbs claimed it had been—it only contained your father's tools." Mamma cleared her throat. "It was such a strange thing, Perri. I've wondered if she took those things from the toolbox and sold them for her poor family. But if she did, why would she have told us about them? And the fact that she found them there would mean that someone else had stolen them and hidden them in your father's toolbox. I tend to think she made that story up to try to help out the Chandlers' servants." She sighed. "I'm sorry to tell you, Perri, but I'm afraid I don't trust her. That's it. I can't imagine why she would make up such a story, especially when you two are such good friends."

When Mamma said that, I shivered. Maybe I could not trust anything that Mary Dobbs Dillard had told me in the past.

Then again, maybe I could. And that's what worried me the most.

Mr. Robinson had said that desperate times caused people to do desperate things, like gambling. *"Among other things."* He had pronounced those words, and suddenly I wondered if "other things" could mean stealing. Could Daddy have stolen things to get money?

I hurried out to the little garage, not even bothering to put on a coat. On shelves to the right side of where the Buick was parked, Mamma had stored some things of Daddy's that she couldn't part with—like the toolbox. I found it there and knelt down on the frozen pavement—teeth chattering and my fingers shaking from cold and fear. I lifted the lid, removed the top tray, and stared down at the tools underneath. Daddy's tools. Nothing more.

I thought back to the day when Dobbs had helped clean out my father's closet, tried to remember her reactions, tried even to imagine seeing pearl-handled knives and jewelry lying inside this very box. My father stealing things from the Chandlers was as unthinkable as his gambling away money we didn't have.

But the things Dobbs supposedly saw were not found later. Was Dobbs lying? Was Mamma?

I shut the lid on the toolbox, returned it to the shelf, and left the garage, feeling absolutely numb and confused.

Dobbs

On the last day of school before Christmas break, Perri showed off her SAE pin with great flourish and pride. But every time I saw that pin, I thought of Spalding in the room necking with another girl and I felt sick to my stomach. The way I saw it, Spalding wanted to have the prettiest girl in Atlanta as his girlfriend, but he had no intention of remaining faithful to her.

I had to tell Perri what I'd seen. I waited until she was working in the darkroom that evening.

"We need to talk," I said.

"You better believe we do," she replied. Her green eyes were flashing. "Mamma told me that you made up a story about finding all the stolen stuff in Daddy's toolbox! Oh, Dobbs! Why would you do that to us? Does some colored woman you barely know mean more to you than me and my family? Is that it? I don't understand you, Mary Dobbs! I don't understand you at all."

Perri was more worked up than I had ever seen her. She didn't even let me respond but continued her diatribe. "Why do you have to keep making up stories? I never did believe all those stories you told us. But this is the worst! You want to ruin my family's good name!"

"Perri, I've never made a thing up. I promise they're all true. Even about the stolen items. Don't you know me well enough to see that the only reason I didn't tell you about the toolbox was to spare you further pain?"

She didn't answer me, and I couldn't tell if she believed me or not.

I didn't want to tell Perri the other thing I had seen, but I loved her too much to keep my mouth shut. For as much as I had felt a conviction that she didn't need to know about the toolbox, I was certain she needed to hear about Spalding.

"Spalding's not right for you, Perri. He's a womanizer. I've seen him being intimate with another girl. He'll only make you miserable. Please, Perri. Please, listen to me. I promise I'm telling you the truth."

To my astonishment, she threw down the photos she was holding in her hands and actually screamed at me. "Quit telling me the truth, Mary Dobbs Dillard! Do you understand me? Leave me alone! I am tired of hearing the truth."

Distraught, I said, "But, Perri, this is your life. You're throwing it all away for the sake of appearances. You can't do that. You are so much . . . so much . . ."

"So much what?" she spat. "Better? Deeper? Than that? Than my society? Well, you're wrong. I'm not! I hate the way you come waltzing into my life and criticizing everything that matters to me. Stop telling me that my life is wrong and bad."

"I've never used those words. I'm just pointing out the inconsistencies in your life. You have the potential to do so much more with your life than just becoming a society lady. I think you want more."

"Well, you think wrong! I know exactly what I want, and I'm going to get it. And I don't trust you anymore. Please, please leave me alone!" She rushed past me, out of the darkroom and the barn, slamming the door shut behind her.

I felt as if she had yanked the little rug I was standing on out from under me and I'd fallen flat on my face. Anne Perrin Singleton had made her choice, and I was not a part of it. I had the desperate feeling that this was the end of our friendship.

Perri had left the darkroom in a mess, running out to the Buick and not looking back. I began cleaning it up, thinking of Perri's accusations as I did and feeling completely exhausted. Parthenia found me there. "I's done finished all my chores, and Papa said I could come see you. Kin I take a peek at all the photographs?"

Parthenia often came to see the new photos Perri had taken. Perri had, in fact, begun to show her how to use the camera, which pleased the little girl immensely. Normally, it warmed me inside to watch her examine them, her little face intent and studious.

"Of course. Just don't touch anything, you understand?"

She nodded. Slowly she walked around the room, peering at the black-and-white photos hanging by clothespins from a wire.

I was busy leaning over the vat, finishing the last batch of negatives, when Parthenia let out a blood-curdling scream. She startled me so much that I dropped the negatives in the solution and twirled around.

"What in the world is the matter, Parthenia?"

Her eyes were wide with fright, but she said, "Nuthin'."

"Parthenia, something has upset you. Tell me what's the matter."

She turned her head down, not looking at me. "I know what I seen. I jus' knowed it."

"What are you talking about, Parthenia?"

She grabbed me around the waist and buried her head in my chest. "I know it ain't proper for a colored girl to be hugging a white lady, but my mama ain't here, and I's afraid."

"*Shh,* now. It's okay." Wondering what had given her such a fright, I sat down on a bench and held her in my arms. "Are you afraid of something you saw?"

She nodded, her head still buried in my lap.

"A mouse? Did you see a mouse? Or a rat?"

She shook her head.

Then I had an idea. "Was it a photograph that scared you?"

Immediately, her head went up, and she nodded, "How'd ya know?"

"I *don't* know, Parthie. But tell me."

"Kain't or it'll be worse and worse for my family."

"Why?"

"Somebody stole them things, and I knowed it."

Gradually I was catching on. "You saw a picture of the person you think stole the silver knives?"

Another nod.

Carefully I lifted Parthenia's head so that she was staring right at me. "Listen here, Parthie. I need to know who you're talking about. It's very important for your mother. Show me which picture you mean."

She clung to me as if for life itself. "No, no! I'm too scared to tell ya, Miz Mary Dobbs. I kain't do it. Don't want nobody killin' my family." She held me even tighter. Then in a whisper I could barely hear, she said, "But I saw him at that party, I did. And he saw me. He held on to me so tight, and he said if I ever done mention a word of what I seen him do, he'd have my whole family sent away or worse. He'd have us all hanged."

I held the terrified child in my lap and stroked her hair until she fell asleep. Cornelius came looking for her and picked up his little sister from out of my arms and carried her to their quarters.

I searched through the photographs Perri had just developed. They were from a debutante party held at the Piedmont Driving Club. Perri had taken closeup shots of loads of people. Hanging from the wire were over thirty individual photos of finely clad men and women. I didn't know most of the people, just the Chandlers and the Robinsons and the McFaddens and Dot Singleton and several people I'd met at St. Philip's. Then I came to a photo that sent fear zipping up my spine. I was standing in the exact spot where I had found Parthenia when she screamed. The photo directly above was one of none other than Spalding Smith.

Perri

Two days before the Alms Houses Christmas Tea, I parked in front of the Chandlers' residence and walked back to the barn. I was just beginning to develop some negatives when someone knocked on the door. "Yes, who is it?"

Dobbs stuck her head in and asked, "Need any help?"

I made my face hard and said quickly, "No. No, I don't need your help at all." I saw the enthusiasm drain right out of her face. For once, she seemed unsure of what to say or do, so I added, "Please go away."

She closed the door and disappeared, and I fought back my tears.

Mary Dobbs Dillard rescued me from the worst of myself; she came to me as a gift, and we spent that time in a bubble. I asked myself why the bubble burst—or more precisely, if it had to. Was I destined to retreat back into the pain of my world instead of pressing forward with Dobbs and the one thing that she offered me—an unchartered life of guaranteed adventure that would take me far, far outside of myself? I could not let her convince me; I would not believe her.

With everything in me, I wanted to know that Dobbs's accusations about Spalding were unfounded, that she had not seen him kissing another girl. I could not prove her wrong, so I made her leave.

———

The next evening, Mamma and Dellareen fixed a special meal for Spalding and me. While we were busy cooking, Spalding helped Jimmy and Ben with odd carpentry jobs around the house. Irvin tagged along, and I caught sight of Spalding handing my little brother some kind of wrench and showing him how to use it, just like Daddy used to do. My heart flooded with relief. Spalding cared about me and my family. He was a fine young man.

After dinner, Spalding presented early Christmas gifts for the whole family. He gave Barbara a whole set of the latest movie star magazines—*Screenland* and *Movie Mirror* and *Silver Screen* and *Movie Classic*. Each had the photo of a famous actress on the front, and Barbara's favorite was Bette Davis on the December 1933 cover of *Motion Picture*. When she saw it, she leaped off the floor and gave Spalding a spontaneous hug. Then they both blushed and Mamma and I laughed. When Irvin unwrapped a stack of baseball cards, he exclaimed, "This is the best present ever!"

Then Mamma opened Spalding's gift to her, and she teared up, in a good way. It was a beautiful silver frame into which I had put a photo of Barbara and Irvin and me.

"It's from both of us, Mamma. I set up the camera and Spalding took the photo."

"It's beautiful, Perri and Spalding. Thank you."

My gift from Spalding was a gorgeous sapphire necklace that must have cost him a fortune. It took my breath away. "I thought it would look very nice with the dress you wore to the SAE formal. We'll find another occasion to wear it. Okay?"

Barbara rushed to look at it. "Leapin' lizards! It is the most gorgeous thing I've ever laid my eyes on!"

"It is absolutely divine," I said and stood on my tiptoes, giving him a kiss on the cheek. "I'm afraid my gift is very humble in return."

I had gotten Dobbs to take several closeup shots of me, and she'd helped me pick out the best one. Cornelius had made a lovely wooden frame for it. I watched Spalding's face carefully, and I saw it soften as he unwrapped my gift. "It's perfect, Perri!" He seemed genuinely pleased. "It's a fine photo, and I must say, it comes close to representing your real beauty."

He stayed with us that whole evening, and somehow, having a man in the house again was a great comfort to us all: the fire blazing in the little den, everyone having filled up with good food, Irvin and Barbara hanging onto Spalding, and Mamma's face reflecting something akin to hope.

At the end of the evening, I finally got up the nerve to ask Spalding about what Dobbs had told me. How I didn't want to spoil the beauty of that night. To my great relief, he laughed and said, "Is that what Mary Dobbs said? She has never liked me, Perri. You've seen that. But why she would make up a story like that, I have no idea. Yes, of course I had a date. With Virginia Hopkins—just as I told you. But we weren't doing anything inappropriate. You can ask Virginia yourself. Or one of my frat brothers."

Then he hugged me tight. "You won't find Spalding Smith two-timing his one and only." And he kissed me on the lips to seal his promise. Then he took hold of my shoulders and looked me square in the eyes. "Perri, I've told you before, and you didn't want to hear it. I'm wary of Mary Dobbs's influence on you. She's such a strange girl. I know you care for her a great deal, but please be careful about believing everything she says."

I snuggled into his arms, reassured.

I lay awake that night, thinking back to all of Dobbs's stories. Had she made up those about her father's revival services, just as she had made up the stories of the missing silver and jewelry found in Daddy's toolbox and Spalding necking with Virginia Hopkins? The beginnings of doubt trickled into my mind, gradually filling it up with real suspicion until I felt I could not trust her.

But one thing was true. I missed Mary Dobbs Dillard. I missed her terribly.

Dobbs

Perri let go of our friendship. That's the only way I could describe it. I awoke the next day with a feeling of dread in the pit of my stomach. She had chosen Spalding instead of me. I had failed to convince her about his character. Had Spalding really stolen those things and hidden them at the Singletons'? I wrestled with these thoughts without an answer. One thing I did know—Parthenia had been genuinely scared in the darkroom.

Aunt Josie took me shopping the next day for Christmas presents for my family. "You simply must have a few things to take back to them."

My aunt was at her best, her happiest, when she could do for others. Her generosity touched me deeply. She picked out a darling red wool coat with black fur trim for Coobie, along with matching gloves and hat. For Frances, she purchased a whole selection of makeup and nail polishes and perfumes and a lovely sweater. For a while, I forgot about Perri, imagining how wonderful spending Christmas with my family would be, and how safe and loved I would feel in Hank's arms.

As we shopped, I asked her, "How many fancy galas do you have each year?"

"Oh, heavens, a dozen or so, I suppose. Normally." She studied me. "Except for this year. After the Valentine's party . . . Well, you know." She sighed. "This year has been different."

I understood all too well, but I wanted other information. "Do any Tech boys come to the parties?"

Aunt Josie smiled. "Of course, dear Mary Dobbs. Loads of college boys come to the parties. Don't worry, we'll get you a date for the next one. Or perhaps you want to invite your Hank down. That would be splendid."

"So Andrew Morrison and Spalding Smith have come to your parties?"

"Yes, of course. They're both fine boys. Uncle Robert loves his alma mater and invites the Tech boys to many parties. Both Spalding and Andrew have come to quite a few."

I digested the information, and it burned going down. Spalding Smith had attended Aunt Josie's parties and had the perfect opportunity to steal the knives. But why?

I tried to push it from my mind as Aunt Josie and I continued shopping. We returned home with enough gifts to fill two suitcases. "Thank you for your kindness. I can't begin to thank you enough."

"My dearest Mary Dobbs, it is my pleasure." Then she caught me by the arm as I turned to go. "Remember, my dear. Don't try to figure out things that are too hard, past our knowing."

I blushed and nodded. My aunt had seen through my questioning. I longed to explain everything to her, but one look at her face and I knew again, she did not want to hear.

———

Mechanically I went through the motions of putting finishing touches on the Christmas tea. On Saturday, the whole Phi Pi sorority drove out to the Alms Houses. We sang Christmas carols out on the lawn in front of the White Alms House, and little by little the tenants from both the White and Black Alms Houses came out of their rooms, shawls and coats pulled around them to ward off the chill. They listened in a childlike way.

Then we all gathered in the foyer of the White Alms House and played two rounds of bingo. Mrs. Clark came forward and said, "We are ever so thankful for your generosity, girls." The residents clapped in their feeble way. I saw Anna sitting stiff as a board in the back of the room with several other colored women. It hurt to think she wouldn't be spending Christmas with her family.

Mae Pearl, Peggy, and Lisa handed out little bags we had filled with goodies—homemade cookies, a new toothbrush and paste, knitted socks and mittens, and a little Gospel tract that Father often used during his revivals. The tract explained how to make peace with God.

What I wanted to know was how to make peace with Perri.

I was thankful for the joy on the residents' faces. It helped that feeling of dread subside for a little while. Perri kept busy snapping photograph after photograph, completely ignoring me. I thought it ironic that I had encouraged her to pursue her passion and now she was using that camera to hide behind, as a type of shield from contact with me. I felt a slow ache throughout my body, and I was thankful that in two days I would leave for Christmas break and would spend ten days in Chicago with my family.

How I missed Perri.

———

The night before I was scheduled to take the train home to Chicago, Becca came by the house with her two little boys. Aunt Josie and Uncle Robert were thrilled to have their grandsons and whisked them off to the barn to see the horses and the cow and the pig. Becca slowly climbed the stairs and stood in the doorway to my room, where I was busy filling the two bags Aunt Josie had lent me with gifts and clothes. Becca was breathing heavily, and I brought the desk chair over for her to sit in. She looked beautiful, in spite of her fatigue, her thick hair falling loosely to her shoulders and her belly protruding under a shimmering blue-and-white dress.

"Hello, Becca."

"Mary Dobbs," she said, taking a seat.

I had no idea why she had come upstairs. "When is your baby due?" I asked, to make conversation.

"Mid-March. Yesterday wouldn't be soon enough for me."

"You're terribly uncomfortable?"

"Yes. That's putting it mildly."

I searched for something else to say. "Your children are adorable."

"They're a handful is what they are." She paused. Then, "Listen,

Mary Dobbs, please don't try to placate me with compliments. I came over tonight to talk to you."

My heart started thumping in my chest. "Talk to me?"

"Yes." She took a deep breath, rested one hand on her stomach, and said, "Mother told me that you claimed to have found the stolen items at the Singleton house. She's asked you to leave it all alone, but you keep nagging at her, bringing it back up. You've got to stop it, you hear? Your family has caused us enough trouble. Please keep your mouth shut and leave it all alone."

Taken aback, I asked, "What do you mean about my family causing you such trouble? What have we ever done to you?"

"You father, my dear Uncle Billy, is responsible for single-handedly sending my grandparents to their graves! His gallivanting around with prostitutes, using up their money, fathering children when he was barely your age. I can't—"

"What are you talking about?"

Becca's face went white for just a moment. "Never mind. It's the pregnancy. Sometimes I don't know what I'm saying."

I didn't believe her for an instant. "Becca Chandler Fitten, you can't tell me my father fathered children and then erase it without a blink. Why would you say such a thing?"

She regained her composure, gave a deep sigh, not unlike those of Aunt Josie, and ran her hands through her hair. "Because it's true. Why do you think my grandparents sent him off to that religious school? To get him away, before he spent all his father's fortune and more. Goodness! Anyone can see what was going on in those years. And then he gets all religious and breaks their hearts again."

I was too shocked to comment.

"Your father has hurt us enough, nearly killed my mother and father too, with worry." She took a breath and her face lost its harsh appearance, and she looked vulnerable for one brief moment. "I'm sorry to say it this way. I didn't realize that you weren't aware of . . . of all the details of the past, Mary Dobbs. But please believe Mother, believe me, and leave the present situation alone. I beg you, Mary Dobbs. Leave it alone." She stood up with difficulty, gave another sigh, and left the room.

As soon as I heard her heading downstairs, I went to her bedroom and took the photo albums from her closet. I was looking for something I had seen before, something that all of the sudden seemed important. Lying on my bed, my bags only half packed, I leafed through the second album, the one I had perused months ago, turning page after page without my father in the photos. His wild years, Aunt Josie had called them. But as I turned the final pages in the second album, I stopped short at one photo. The Chandler house was decorated with candles in every window. The whole family was out in the front yard along with dozens of guests. My grandparents were in the middle, Aunt Josie was with Uncle Robert, and Father was there, too, with a young woman. Her head was turned, almost as if she didn't want to be photographed, so I could only see her profile partially. But as I peered carefully at the photo, I recognized her, and my heart skipped a beat.

Irene Brown. Jackie's mother.

Suddenly, I knew. It all made sense—our charity to Jackie, her mother coming and going, leaving the child, my mother caring, and Father adoring her.

Jackie Brown was my half sister.

I closed my eyes, sitting cross-legged on the floor with the album in my lap. . . .

We were at the beach. Jackie, Frances, and I were building a sand castle. Baby Coobie kept crawling over and messing it up. At length, Frances picked up her sandy sister and began tickling her as she waded out into the ocean. Jackie and I repaired the castle, giggling and whispering as we worked. I grabbed her hand and said, "You're just like a sister to me, Jackie. Better than any sister."

She looked at me in a funny way and started to say something. But just then Frances had come running back over to us with Coobie.

Now I knew what Jackie had wanted to tell me that day—*I am your sister, Mary Dobbs. I am.*

CHAPTER
21

Dobbs

The next morning Hosea took me to the train station, parked the Pierce Arrow, and retrieved my bags. Then he motioned to the back seat. "You got some mail that came for you yesterday. I guess ya didn't see it." I picked up a letter and a small box wrapped in beautiful paper and put them in my handbag. We made our way to the train, and Hosea got me settled in the right car.

"You have a good Christmas, Miz Mary Dobbs."

"Thank you, Hosea. I'm sorry Anna won't be with you."

"We'll be all right."

I rested my head against the window and watched the steam billow up as the train left the station. My mind felt as foggy as the air outside, clouded with images of both wonderful and horrible scenes of the past months in Atlanta.

I had hardly slept at all the night before. Faces kept parading through my thoughts—Becca's, with her revelation about my father's past, Parthenia's little black face seized with true fear, and Perri's, with her see-through green eyes narrowing. "*Leave me alone! I'm tired of hearing the truth.*"

Oh, so am I! I thought to myself. Truth might just destroy all of us. How ironic when Father always said the truth would set us free.

I carried my newest hurt inside without a way to find solace. Jackie was my sister. I had loved her like one, had accepted her. But Jackie remained the crack in my spiritual armor. Now I wondered if her death was Father's punishment for his past sins.

Did God punish that way? I suddenly did not know.

I only knew that I felt flattened out and wiped clean, like the photos. I was heading home with a broken heart. My best friend distrusted me, I alone held strong evidence about thefts, and now I felt betrayed by my parents.

Hank. Thank goodness for Hank.

And yet, even that was fuzzy. I fingered my short hair and wondered what he would say. I thought of the dances with Andrew Morrison and the way he looked at me. I only pretended not to see how much he cared.

I wanted to have both lives, and suddenly it seemed as if I had neither.

From down inside I felt it surging up, threatening to surface, that vile poison of doubt. I tried to calm the voices that whispered fearful things in my head. *Your God didn't provide. He let Jackie die. He let your sister die.*

I fought to erase those thoughts and remembered the beautifully wrapped present in my handbag. I took it out, carefully removed the bright paper, and found a small box with an envelope on top. *Mary Dobbs* was written on the envelope in handwriting I didn't recognize. Intrigued, I opened the flap and retrieved a single piece of stationery.

> *Merry Christmas, dear Mary Dobbs,*
> *I hope you have a fine time with your family. I want you to know I have enjoyed our dates this fall. I thought this would look lovely with your new hairstyle.*
> > *Yours affectionately,*
> > *Andrew*

I lifted the lid of the box. Sitting on folds of tissue paper was a beautiful red-and-violet porcelain clip for my hair. The newest rage in Atlanta fashion.

I felt my face burning as I held the clip in my hands. The red matched perfectly with the day dress I had chosen for my trip home. I reached up, brushed it through my hair, and clipped it in place. I was smiling. Then quickly I removed it. What if Hank asked me where I had gotten such a thing?

I reached in my handbag for the letter, immediately recognized Frances's handwriting on the envelope, opened it, and began to read.

> . . . I miss Atlanta! We're all excited about having you with us for Christmas in just a few more days.
>
> Coobie is always up to her mischief. Last week she got called to the principal's office for slugging a boy on the playground. She told the principal that she wasn't one bit sad because the boy deserved it. He was calling her names.
>
> Right now she is acting a little calmer because she's been under the weather. It's the bronchitis, as always, and now Coobie has a deep cough, and Mother is making her take some wretched cough syrup. I hope I don't catch it. . . .

I set the letter beside me and felt the faith in me dying.

It's amazing how five ordinary words can change you, strike fear in your heart, remind you of the darkest days of your life, and fill you with dread.

Frances wrote, "Coobie has a deep cough."

If she'd written a cough without the adjective deep added in, I might have passed over it without another thought. But Jackie had struggled for years with weak lungs and bronchitis, and the last time, the bronchitis progressed quickly into a deep cough that eventually killed her. Mother had said it was due to a congenital defect. It ran in families, the doctor had told us. My new bit of information, that Jackie was my sister, sent chills down my spine.

Did Coobie have the same congenital defect?

I could picture it perfectly: Coobie and Frances and Jackie and me playing on the beach of Lake Michigan and the sun streaming down on us, hundreds of people mingling in the unusually warm weather of May. Jackie had on her bathing suit. Mother disapproved of it, saying that even with eighty-five-degree weather, May was not the month to put on bathing breeches. The lake water was so cold it made us scream, goose bumps breaking out on our arms as we dipped our toes in the water.

Then we were headed home from the beach, laughing, and Mother and Father were all filled up with love and plans for the summer revivals. And that's when we heard it again. The deep cough.

Nothing to worry about. She'd had it before, and the doctors had gotten rid of it. But four months later my precious friend, my Jackie, was dead.

Somewhere in the middle of Frances's paragraph about Coobie's illness, somewhere in between her pretty slanted cursive, those perfectly spaced words *Coobie has a deep cough* and *I hope I don't catch it*, I stopped believing.

I felt the fury pulsing in my temples, and I rushed out of the train compartment and wobbled down the narrow hallway. I opened the doors between the cars and stood out on the platform in the freezing air, balancing on the moving grated steps. I almost wished I could plunge myself off the train into nothingness. Instead, I gripped the railing until my knuckles turned white, and I yelled over the racket of the squealing wheels, "I hate you, God! It's a sham! It's not true! You aren't good."

"The LORD gave and the LORD hath taken away . . ."

"You may *not* take her away!" I screamed, watching the countryside fly past in a blur of speed and tears. "I won't allow it! You may not kill us again. Haven't we suffered enough for you? Haven't we?"

In my mind, I heard Perri, my lost friend, yelling at me. *"Why do you have to keep making up stories . . . ? I don't have time to wait on your God to somehow miraculously provide for me and my family. . . ."*

On and on the voices taunted me, and I held myself there, daring God to save me if I let go. I closed my eyes and pictured myself tumbling under the wheels. I loosened my hold on the rails, imagining it again.

"Ma'am!" A rough hand grabbed me around the waist, pulling me away from the railing and steps, pulling me back into the safety of the compartment. The controller, his face red, scolded me. "You could get yourself killed like that, young lady!"

I felt dizzy and nauseated, and my face was chapped from where I had cried and the whipping wind had dried the tears. My hands, too, looked split and chapped. I barely mumbled, "I'm sorry. I needed some fresh air."

He led me back to my compartment, and I fell into my seat. Several other passengers stared at me warily.

I closed my eyes, and my whole body began to shake, yet I felt completely numb. I drifted off to sleep with only one thought in my mind. *Life is a bottomless pit of sorrow, and I don't know why almighty God made it this way.*

————

In Chicago, I found myself playing a role I had never practiced in my eighteen years—a pretender. I pretended to be happy to be home. I hugged my parents and Coobie and Frances, and on the ride home from the train station I told them stories of the Alms Houses and the sorority Bible study. But something had died inside of me.

In a fog, I joined my family in our little apartment, which looked pitiful and dingy to me. Coobie proudly announced that Hank had cut down an evergreen tree in the forest and set it up for them in the den. It was leaning to the right, adorned with paper snowflakes and a string of popcorn and berries. Several presents, wrapped in the funny pages, were under the tree.

I unpacked the beautifully wrapped gifts from Aunt Josie, and they seemed incongruous with the apartment and the little tree and the cheaply wrapped presents.

Coobie gave a yelp of delight and gathered the packages in her arms. "I knew Aunt Josie would get us presents! I knew it!"

I glanced at Father. His smile never wavered. He gave his belly laugh and grabbed Coobie and said, "Goodness gracious, what in the world do we have here?"

Both Coobie and Frances were down on their knees, scrambling with their fingers to open the tags on each box. "There are three here for me!" Coobie announced triumphantly.

"Same for me," Frances said, and gave Coobie a slight shove.

Mother wrapped her arms around Father. The warmth in the apartment was palpable, and yet I felt cold, chilled to the bone.

Hank came by later in the evening and grabbed me in a big hug, swinging me around in his arms. "Boy, have I missed you!" he said, and Mother and Father and my sisters watched us with affectionate approval. I closed my eyes, and for one brief moment I was swinging around with Andrew Morrison at the SAE house, laughing in a carefree way. I thought of his Christmas gift and blushed, and I was thankful Hank did not notice.

He was dressed in those dirty, worn-out overalls, and his hands were rough and his knuckles scabbed over. I ran my hands over them.

"I picked up a job unloading heavy boxes on some big trucks—kinda menial work, but I'm mighty thankful to have had it. It wasn't much, but it was good for three days of pay."

"You've torn up your hands," I said.

"Oh, Dobbs, it's nothing worse than at the steel mill. Hands heal." He gave me his lopsided grin, but I turned my head so that he wouldn't see the way my heart plummeted with the knowledge that he hadn't found another steady job.

Ever since the World's Fair closed in November, Hank had spent his mornings waiting in long lines with hundreds of other men for jobs that rarely materialized. He still worked at the church in the afternoons and evenings for no pay. I imagined us always struggling, just as Mother and Father had, and that ugly feeling of doubt crept through me into every corner of my being: doubt of my faith, of my parents, of Hank.

I could not bear for Hank to see my turmoil, so I pressed my face into his chest and let him hold me there until I could quiet my heart. Quiet the voices.

Eventually, my parents shooed my sisters back to our bedroom to get dressed for the Christmas Eve service. Mother busied herself in the kitchen and Father went back to their bedroom where he had his desk so that Hank and I were alone in the den.

"I'm heading up to Ma's house tonight after the service," Hank said. "I'll spend Christmas Day with her and my sibs. I'll be back the day after that, but I wanted you to have your gift tonight." His face got beet red when he took a small rectangular box out of his pocket and placed it in my hands. "I want you to wear it and know how much I care. It's not valuable—took more time than money—but I put all my heart into it. Merry Christmas." He kissed me softly on my cheek.

I took off the top of the box, and inside was a finely braided necklace of different metals—nickel and copper and bronze. The metals caught the lamplight and gleamed brightly. "Hank, it's lovely!" I said, but it was a calculated statement, not my usual enthusiasm, and I was thinking of Andrew's beautiful and expensive hair clip.

"I made it from the scraps at the steel yard. My superintendent let me take some when I was laid off. I hope you'll wear it and know how much I think of you, even if I'm just a hillbilly city boy." He gave me a squeeze and then fastened it around my neck. I swallowed hard as his fingers brushed my skin. "Your hair looks real swell like that, Dobbs."

My heart was hammering so hard I thought I was going to burst into tears. Part of me wanted him to take me in his arms and part of me wanted to run as fast as I could back to Atlanta.

"Thank you," I managed. I recovered enough to get my gift for him from beneath the tree. He opened it and his face wore a perplexed expression. With Aunt Josie's prodding, I had chosen an expensive Waterman pen-and-pencil set that I had paid for with some of the money I'd made helping Perri with photography. I blushed, realizing how very inappropriate it probably seemed to him. "I thought you'd enjoy using them when you wrote your letters to me," I said feebly.

"I'll use them, Dobbs. I promise." He peered at me in the way that usually made my heart skip a beat, but all I felt was confused. "I think we need to take a walk," he announced, and the awkward strain was broken.

Once outside, he said, "What on earth is the matter, sweet Dobbs?"

I shook my head. "I can't even begin to tell you, Hank. It's so complicated and horrible. I feel like I'm completely losing my mind. It would take hours to explain it all, and we don't have time. You've still got to get ready for the service."

He took both of my hands and said, "Whatever it is, it can wait two days. We'll have time after Christmas. It'll be okay, Dobbs. You know that, don't you?"

I could not even meet his eyes to nod yes. He took me in his arms and held me there—strong, gentle Hank. I rested my head on his shoulders, but on the inside I felt weighed down by that one heavy word: doubt.

At the Christmas Eve service, Hank and Father both looked handsome dressed in suits from Holden Singleton and Uncle Robert that Mother had altered. Together they led the small congregation in the candlelight service with the beauty and simplicity I used to love. The church was nearly full, families sitting together, dressed in their finest clothes and wrapped up in the celebration of eternal love coming down to earth. The evening passed in sweet victory for Christ, but it did not fill me up with excitement as it had before.

Hank kissed me good-bye after the service, and relieved to feel that familiar tugging in my heart, I shed real tears. Surely I still loved him. Surely I did.

My family was all asleep, and I tiptoed into the bathroom. I stared at myself in the mirror and brushed my hands through my short hair. I fingered the necklace, leaning into the mirror to examine Hank's handiwork. It was delicate and finely wrought, to be sure, but as I touched it, I felt a slight disappointment. Life with Hank would be this. A good man with good intentions giving me cheap, handmade gifts.

I took it off and put it on the sink. Then I got the beautiful hair clip from out of my handbag and fixed it in my hair. It perfectly matched my dark red tea dress, and I looked sophisticated, even lovely. Another wave of disappointment washed over me. I had nowhere to wear it in Chicago. I would never dare, anyway. But back in Atlanta, it would look divine with this dress, and I dreamed of the next dance with Andrew.

I leaned over the sink, my stomach cramping. Why would I think such things?

It came to me immediately: escape. I was like my friends in the sorority. I was desperately trying to fill up on something that could replace the dread and fear that were eating their way into my soul.

————

The next morning, Christmas Day, I awoke to Coobie leaning over me. She kissed my cheek, and I grinned up at her. "Hey, Sis!"

Frances was still asleep on the top bunk.

"I'm glad you're home," she said.

"Me too."

Then she wrinkled her brow and said, "I found this by the sink." She was holding out Hank's necklace. "Don't you like it?"

I sat up quickly. "Oh yes. It's beautiful. I took it off last night to wash my face."

Coobie studied me for a minute. I don't think she believed me. "And where in the world did you get this?" She produced Andrew's hair clip in her other hand.

I cringed. "Back in Atlanta."

"It's so, so pretty. Did Aunt Josie give it to you? She gives the best gifts!"

"No. It was another friend." I took it from Coobie and felt again like I was being pulled in two.

I helped Mother fix the turkey and got my hands all gooey from the homemade corn-bread dressing I stuffed inside it. Mother hummed a Christmas carol as she set the table, using her finest linen tablecloth and the china she had inherited from her grandmother. She lit two white candles and placed them in the silver candleholders. The table looked festive, but I kept thinking of the gorgeous homes in Atlanta and of those tables set with fine china and sparkling crystal and sterling silver and all the parties given with such seeming ease and such abundance. Mother used her most precious things, but I watched her set them out with a feeling of anger and jealousy. We had so little. Why couldn't we have the beautiful furnishings of the Atlanta homes? I found myself missing it all.

After opening our gifts, the five of us took our seats around the table, which was laden with the golden turkey and a delicious winter squash casserole and sweet potatoes and tender green beans and homemade rolls—the fragrance enticed us all. Father's voice boomed out the blessing. "Holy Father, as we celebrate your advent, we humbly thank you for the bounty you have given us, the love of family, and the love of Christ. And thank you, dear Lord, for bringing our Mary Dobbs home for Christmas."

I murmured "Amen" with the rest of my family, but still I felt cold inside. In my mind, Father was a young man, standing beside my grandparents and Uncle Robert and Aunt Josie. And Irene Brown. It stabbed at me so that my stomach hurt.

I managed to eat my dinner, but what I kept noticing was how thin Mother was and how Father's hair had turned almost white and how Frances and Coobie had long since lost their summer tans and what deep circles were under Coobie's eyes. Her face was pale, and she had the thick throaty cough from her chronic bronchitis. Every time she coughed, I felt the pinpricks of fear. This year, it sounded like a death sentence.

Father sat back in his chair after we'd eaten dessert and said, "I do believe we need to take a family walk. Coobie, why don't you try out that pretty red coat and hat, and Frances, that sweater?"

My sisters, delighted with their gifts, hurried to change.

Mother said, "Mary Dobbs and I are going to straighten up a little. We'll meet you in the park in thirty minutes."

"So be it!" Father said, and he pulled on a wool overcoat that I recognized as another of Holden Singleton's possessions.

"See ya soon!" Coobie said, twirling around in her red wool coat.

"You look marvelous," Mother said.

Coobie beamed, then coughed and left the apartment with Father and Frances.

As soon as the door shut, I said to Mother, "She sounds just like Jackie did when she got sick the last time!"

Mother set down the plate she was washing and turned to me. "What would make you say that, Mary Dobbs?"

"Because it's true! She's got the same condition, doesn't she, Mother? It's congenital. It runs in the *family*." I flung down the dishrag and hurried from the kitchen.

Mother found me in our bedroom. "Darling, what are you saying?"

"You can't deny it, Mother. I know. I found out."

She grabbed me tightly and held me for a long time while I sniffed and whispered, "There are so many bad things, Mother. I'm so very confused. I've found out things about our family, and about Father. About Jackie." My eyes welled with tears.

She held me tighter, if that was possible. Then she sat me down on my bed and said, "Tell me it all, everything, Mary Dobbs. I'm not budging until you get it all out."

She sat across from me on the floor, leaning against Coobie and Frances's bunk bed.

"Did you know everything about Father when you married him?"

"I knew he'd had a very rough past. I didn't know all the details."

"Did you know about Jackie?"

"No, not at first. Not until Irene showed up at your father's parents' house when we were there."

"How did you stay with Father after all he had done? You had to take in his child, Mother. His bastard child! The child of a prostitute!"

Mother gasped. "What are you saying, Mary Dobbs! I loved Jackie! You know I did. We all loved her. She was a blessing—not a curse."

"How can you say that, Mother? He made you suffer time and again for his past. He made you live with it all, didn't he? You took her in and you raised her and you gave her a real home, and then she died. Why didn't you tell me she was my sister? And now Coobie has the same illness, and she will die too."

Mother rarely looked angry, but she silenced me with one glare. "Mary Dobbs Dillard, you stop it. Right now. Stop that twisted reasoning. Stop your mind from going that way. You understand me?" I saw in her eyes that rock-solid determination that had characterized her for all my life. "You don't pronounce that on Coobie. You hear me?" Then more calmly, "Your father had his reasons for keeping his past from you. I've told you that before. You must talk to him. Why are you afraid of facing him? I want you to talk to him."

I shook my head. "I can't."

She lifted my chin and said, "You certainly can. And you will." Then she relaxed her shoulders, and her eyes softened. "Mary Dobbs, when you love someone, you love every part of him—the past and the present and the future. You accept it all. I have a good man who loves me, and I love him, and I would not trade that for anything in the world.

"When you love, it will hurt. You have to choose to forgive, again and again. But it's worth it. That's the crux of human relationships, Dobbs. The sweetest thing. Loving deeply. And forgiving. Your father loves you so much. Talk to him. Ask him your questions. Don't be afraid of your anger and your hurt."

She stood up. "Now I'm going outside to find your father and your sisters."

I nodded but didn't budge, and she left me there.

The evening slipped away as my sisters worked a jigsaw puzzle with Father, and Mother put the finishing hemline in the wool skirt she had made for Frances. I sat beside her on the sofa, my stomach in knots. Every time Coobie giggled, it was followed by a cough, which brought to the surface again the surge of fear and doubt and anger.

Later, as I tucked my sisters in bed, Frances whispered, "Merry Christmas, again, Dobbs. I really like the makeup."

Coobie hugged me around the neck and said, "The doll is my favorite ever."

I kissed her, but the words of my sisters didn't fill me up. I looked at Coobie, lying on the bed, pale as the new moon, and I saw Jackie in that frail face. I shuddered, and left the room quickly.

I walked into the living room, where Father was standing by the window, staring out into the night. I went over to him and whispered in a hard, desperate way, "Where is the money? What have you done with it?"

He turned to me; his expression was beyond startled or shocked, his round, red face grew pale. "What money, Mary Dobbs? What do you mean?"

"The money from the inheritance! The thousands and thousands you inherited, just like Aunt Josie! There must have been money! Where is it?"

Now my father actually gave a low groan—his knees buckled and he sat down with a thud in a threadbare chair. "That money? Why, Mary Dobbs, that was years ago. Many years ago."

"It was twelve years ago, and your share had to be a lot of money. So why are we barely scraping by?"

His face lost all its color, and Mother, sitting across the room with her sewing in her lap, turned a grayish color, and I thought I saw her head shake, as if she were begging me to stop my questions. But I paid her no heed.

"Answer me, Father! Don't hide behind some holy excuse."

"I have no excuse, Dobbs," he whispered. My father, whose voice could fill a stadium, could barely choke out the next words. "It's all gone. Was spent long ago. That money is not here. Mary Dobbs, believe me, if I had that money, I would use it to—"

"How can it be gone, Father? How?" I felt anger throbbing in my temples, and I choked on my words. "What did you spend it on?

Gambling? Women?" My voice broke, and I began to cry softly. Mother had scooted close beside Father, her arm resting on his. "You spent it long ago so we could starve today! So Coobie could die, just like Jackie! Just like my *sister*, Jackie! My sister who you hid from me! How many other sisters are out there? Are you hiding them? Are you spending your money on them? Is that it?

"Here we are, begging for food, and you would hide behind the guise of God's provision. You're a hypocrite, Father, and all you care about is some pitiful religion that doesn't even work."

I was standing in front of my parents, my eyes blazing with emotions I had never in all my life allowed to escape. "Well, I care about my family," I continued. "I'll take Frances and Coobie back with me. Aunt Josie will see that Coobie sees the finest doctors and has warm clothes and plenty to eat. I'll take care of them. You go ahead with your godforsaken calling!"

I spun around and fled the apartment, leaving the front door to the apartment wide open. I ran down the steps, tears flying in all directions, and out into the bitter cold of Christmas Day in Chicago.

Perri

Somehow we got through Christmas Day. Instead of traveling to be with Mamma's family down in Valdosta, we stayed put in that little house on Club Drive. Two of Daddy's siblings sent us gifts, as they did each year, and my grandmother called us long-distance, sounding disappointed not to have us, but Mamma said she didn't have the strength to pack us up in the Buick and drive four hours south.

Bill and Patty Robinson brought us over a beautiful baked ham and presents for every one of us. Dellareen and Jimmy, bless their souls, didn't take the day off. Instead, they came over with all the kids and fixed us a Christmas feast. Dellareen told my mother, "You gotta do somethin' different to git through this first holiday, Miz Dot." So we played games, and Irvin spent the afternoon trying out a pair of stilts that Jimmy had made for him, and Barbara spent an hour fiddling with her hair and putting on the makeup I'd given her, and then I took photos of them out in the backyard.

A few days earlier, I had received a letter and package from Philip Hendrick. I opened them both on Christmas Day.

> Dearest Perri,
> We're getting along fine. The Fair's business gained us quite a reputation, and we've been busy during the Christmas holidays with sittings for these family photo Christmas cards. I believe it will become a Christmas staple.
> Thinking of you and your family and praying you are well.
> Your fellow photographer,
> Philip

He'd sent me a Christmas card that acted as a frame for a photo of Luke and him. Across the top he had written *Merry Christmas, Perri!* The package held something he called "the newest gadget for your business." It turned out to be a cable that, when attached to the camera, would allow me to activate the shutter from a distance so that I could be in the photographs with Mamma and Irvin and Barbara. That tickled us so much, we couldn't stop laughing for the longest time. Afterwards, I got Jimmy and Dellareen and their kids to come in the picture with us, and I think we all forgot about Daddy for just a little while.

In the evening, after supper, Irvin came to me, his face somber, and whispered, "Can we take a little drive, Perri? Just you and me?" Then he lowered his voice even more. "I want to go by our real house."

Seeing his pinched pale face, I wasn't about to turn down his request. "Of course we can go."

Mamma didn't protest at all when I told her I was taking Irvin out for a ride in the car.

I drove Irvin down Club Drive onto Peachtree and straight out four miles to where I turned right on West Paces Ferry Road, driving past the Chandlers' house. It was lit up, and five cars were parked in front of the house.

I fleetingly wondered if Dobbs was doing all right in Chicago with her family.

I wound along the streets and turned onto Wesley Drive. We drove up the long winding drive in silence and around toward the front of the house.

Irvin noticed it first. "Someone's here." Sure enough, I saw a light coming from inside the upstairs bedroom. Irvin hopped out and ran to the backyard and stood staring at the garage and the stables.

Spalding's sporty car was sitting in front of the garage.

"What's he doing here?" Irvin whispered.

I hadn't the foggiest idea. I went to the back door. Locked. Walking to the front porch, I tried that door. Locked also. I banged on the door. No answer. Finally I called out, "Spalding! Yoo-hoo! It's us!"

At last he opened the door. He looked, for one moment, startled, and then recovered his smile. "Perri! Irvin! What a surprise! Merry Christmas."

Irvin walked past him into the empty foyer and looked around him. "What are you doing here?"

"Good question. Wouldn't you know, dear ol' Dad sent me over here. He said he has a client interested in seeing the house tomorrow and he wanted me to make sure it was presentable."

"You're kidding!" I blurted out. "Your father's selling the house for the bank? Mr. Robinson didn't mention that to us. I thought your father worked for Coca-Cola."

Spalding shrugged. "Dad has other interests, too, such as real estate. I didn't know Dad had anything to do with this house either until he asked me to come over here tonight. I've learned not to ask questions and just do what Dad says." He punched Irvin playfully. "What brought you over here?"

"I wanted to see my old home," Irvin said.

"Of course. Of course. Hey, listen. I've got a football in the car. Why don't you and I practice some passes?"

Irvin's face brightened. "Sure." Then, "But it's awful dark."

"I'll fix that." Spalding brought his car to the front yard and turned on the headlights, leaving the engine running.

I watched them tossing the football back and forth beneath the naked oaks and hickories with the chill in the air. Then I walked through the empty house, the sound of my pumps echoing on the wooden floors, and my soul felt as cold and barren as my former home.

Dobbs

Father found me out in the park. He'd brought my coat with him and put it around my shoulders. "We must talk, Mary Dobbs."

"It's too late for talking. I already know it all now."

I turned away from him, but he caught me by the arm. "No. No you don't. Please. Please give me a chance. One chance."

I didn't answer.

We walked side by side, toward the lake, his arm occasionally brushing against mine. He spoke in a low voice, all his natural enthusiasm completely drained out. "When I was thirteen, I got in with a rough crowd at school. Hung out with them for several years. I got involved in terrible things, just what you said—drinking and gambling and fooling around with women. I put my parents through a dark tunnel whose end was hell." He let out a long sigh that reminded me of Aunt Josie and even Becca.

"And then Christ found me and my life changed. I eventually moved up to Chicago, and it looked like my past sins were not only forgiven but forgotten.

"But there was Irene Brown. She showed up at my parents' house in 1915—ironically, right after you were born. Irene knew their house—I'd made the mistake of taking her there once or twice."

I thought of the photo I'd seen in the album where Irene looked as if she were intentionally trying to hide her face.

"She had a sickly child and claimed I was the father. Threatened to cause a terrible scandal if my parents didn't help her out. At first, bless their souls, they bailed me out, just as they had done so many times before. They didn't even tell me about Irene's visit—and of her blackmailing them—until much later, when you were about two. Your mother and I had taken you down to see the family in Atlanta. Irene came to the house for money, and that was the first time I heard her story and found out that I was Jackie's father."

We had reached the shore of Lake Michigan. Father stopped and stood staring out at the wind rippling across the water. His hands, which so often moved around expressively during his sermons, were thrust deep into his pockets.

"As you can imagine, it was quite a shock. It nearly destroyed me when I learned how she'd been getting money from my parents and all the heartache she'd caused them." He glanced over at me. "But I want you to know that I loved Jackie from the first time I laid eyes on her.

"I worked out an arrangement with Irene. I'd pay her a monthly allowance for Jackie if she promised never to go to my parents' home again. She agreed.

"I told my parents how sorry I was and begged their forgiveness, which they gave, once again. But I couldn't forgive myself. And they never knew of the deal I had struck with Irene. I wanted them to think it was all behind me.

"We didn't get down to Atlanta very often. Money was so tight. Oh, Papa offered to help us. I was too proud and too ashamed. And I couldn't bear to tell him that every extra nickel was going to Irene."

"Poor Mother," I said. "How she must have suffered."

"Yes. Your mother was a saint. She never complained or blamed me. Just took a job as a seamstress and worked so hard." Father got lost in some thought. The wind increased, and I watched it pick up a strand of his hair and twirl it about his balding head.

"In the spring of 1919, Irene found us in Chicago. Jackie was sick, and Irene claimed she couldn't care for her anymore. Of course we took Jackie in. Off and on, Irene would take Jackie back, but Jackie's ill-health kept her out of school a lot and prevented Irene from working. She said she had to work—she owed money to a lot of ugly men. So your mother and I ended up caring for Jackie for longer periods."

"You should have told me she was my sister."

"Perhaps. You loved each other like sisters—that's for sure." Father looked at me, his whole face sagging. "Irene was so unpredictable. Your mother and I thought it would be better for you girls not to know. Less painful."

"It wasn't less painful. And now it hurts even worse."

"I'm so sorry, Mary Dobbs. I didn't mean it to be this way."

I glared at him for a long moment and then turned my gaze to the lake. Father stood by me, breathing hard, as if the telling of this story had completely worn him out.

"I didn't want my parents to be pulled back into my problems, so I cut ties with them. I shouldn't have done it the way I did, but zeal isn't always tempered by wisdom, Mary Dobbs. There are so many things I regret.

"When my parents died, Irene got wind of it and begged me to help pay off her debtors. She said they were threatening to kill her. So, with your mother's consent, we used a good portion of my inheritance to cover her debts and send her away to start a better life. The rest was used on Jackie.

"I thought what I'd kept would get us along and still pay Jackie's doctors' bills. But—" here he faltered and gave another heavy sigh— "Jackie took a turn for the worse, and the bills increased, and . . . and we found ourselves with nothing. No money left over, and no Jackie.

"Sin'll do that to you, Mary Dobbs. Tangle you up till you can't see any way out. I broke ties with my family—I thought it was for their good. I hurt my parents, caused them untold grief. Hurt Josie and Robert too. I can never take that back. My parents went to their graves tired and broken."

It began to snow, large pristine flakes falling around us as my father confessed his sins. For an instant, I thought he might start bawling, as he had done all those years ago at my grandmother's funeral. I didn't want to see that. I didn't want to feel any tenderness toward my father. He had answered my questions, but I found no solace in them. I had only one question left. "Does Coobie have the same condition as Jackie?"

Father's face fell. "Yes. Yes, she does."

I turned away from him and hurried toward the lake, leaving my father standing in Holden Singleton's wool coat with hundreds of snow-flakes landing softly on his shoulders.

I ignored my father for the rest of the evening, filling up the time in the apartment with my nose planted in a book. Mother watched me without a word. For some reason—divine wisdom, she'd doubt-less claim—she did not reprimand me. She went about making our home just the same warm and safe place as always, and miraculously, I thought, my sisters did not wake up and notice that I had brought a sheet of ice inside.

When Hank came by the next evening, my heart was far, far away. He showed up in the suit Uncle Robert had given him, smelling fresh and clean. The Waterman pen was in his lapel pocket. His hair had been trimmed, and my heart melted, just seeing him standing there. He held a lone red rose in his hand.

I had not dressed up to see him. I blushed. "I'm not presentable." Truthfully, I had not expected to need to dress up. "Can you please give me a moment?"

Coobie hopped on Hank's back, and he cantered around the den like a bucking horse while she giggled and coughed, giggled and coughed, singing out, "Giddyup, you! Giddyup!"

I hurried to the bedroom and put on a sunset-colored evening dress I had brought to Chicago, just in case, brushed my hair, and searched for the necklace. I fastened it around my neck, and the pretty braided metals glistened and picked up the color of the dress.

"You look absolutely keen," Frances said. "Would you like to borrow some of my makeup?"

I caught her in a hug. "Would I ever!"

Hank took me to the Walnut Room at the Bismarck Hotel, one of the fanciest restaurants in Chicago.

"How in the world will you afford this?" I whispered when we walked inside.

He looked at me with such love, such admiration. "Remember the envelope you brought me from Uncle Robert? He said his Christmas gift to us was a meal here."

I watched Hank studying the menu. Normally so self-assured,

he wrinkled his brow and stuttered once when we ordered. Then he glanced at me, shrugged, and we laughed together.

The orchestra played slow romantic ballads, and after dinner Hank led me to the floor and held me close. "I'm not good at this at all, Dobbs," he whispered. "But I want to try. For you." He took big awkward steps, and I had a fleeting thought of Andrew and other Atlanta boys who were such swell dancers.

"You're doing great," he said.

"I learned a little in Atlanta."

Finally, back at our table over dessert, Hank took my hands and said, "You said you had so many things to tell me, hard things. I'm ready to hear them now."

I had told Mother what I had discovered about Jackie, but I had told her nothing of the other problems in Atlanta. Now I poured out everything in my heart to Hank: the truth about Jackie and my reaction to my father's confession, the whole fiasco about the stolen items, my fears about Spalding and how Perri had chosen him over me, and finally the train ride and Coobie's cough and my terrible doubts. The only thing I didn't mention was about Andrew Morrison.

As I talked, it struck me that, though the circumstances were different, my problem was the same as I'd had that day two years ago when Hank had sat in front of me in the pew of our little church: doubt.

"Why does it always have to be so hard, Hank? Can you answer me that? Why?" I ventured a glance at him and whispered, "I don't believe anymore, Hank. I don't."

We sat in silence.

I continued. "Maybe my parents aren't doing everything right. Maybe there's no such thing as repentance and salvation. Maybe their whole life has been doing everything wrong! And God is punishing them. Oh, you'll say He's trying to teach them a lesson. Well, I don't want His lessons. I don't want to watch my family starving or Coobie dying from a horrible disease. Maybe God showed up before, or maybe we just pretended it was God and it was all a coincidence, but this time I'm not waiting on Him to act. I'll do just fine on my own. I'll figure it out."

A chill zipped through me, and I realized that I sounded just like Perri Singleton.

I saw the worry and pain flash across Hank's eyes, the understanding and the hurt. When I finished, he tried to pull me close, but I resisted. "Holding me won't make it better, Hank. Nothing will make it better now."

He looked as if I had slapped him across the face, and that stung my heart. He put his chapped hands with the cracked fingernails over mine. "I can't answer your questions, Dobbs. Life is just plain hard. It is."

A terrible falling sensation struck me, everything inside me tumbling down and down and down. Hank knew of life's unfairness. Losing his father when he was ten, he had suddenly been thrust into the role of man of the house. He had worked so hard; he had struggled and kept going.

And he loved me. He loved me in spite of my pettiness and doubts and vacillations between Chicago and Atlanta.

"I'm scared to go back," I whispered at last.

"I know." He clasped my hands, then gently put one hand under my chin and lifted my eyes to meet his. "Remember two things, my lovely Dobbs. First, God is bigger than all your doubts. And second, after you've asked every question in that mind of yours, I'll still be here, waiting for you. I promise I will."

Perri

I divided my time during the Christmas break between the darkroom and Spalding, thankful that Dobbs was still in Chicago and that I didn't have to deal with avoiding her. Twice Spalding took me to our old house, let us in with the key that I suppose his father had given him, and walked through it with me.

"I'm going to get it back," I confided to him on the first visit.

"Somehow, I'm going to get it back. Don't let any one else buy it, Spalding. Please."

"You've got enough determination to do it, Perri. I swear you do."

On the second visit, I asked Spalding to leave me alone for a while. I went into my father's empty study, sat down on the cold floor, and pretended he was there with me. I imagined that we were sitting side by side at his desk and he was going over the financial records, teaching me about stocks and bonds.

"You've got a good mind, Perri," he had often told me. *"I can see you at Wellesley in a few years, top of your class."*

I had wanted with everything in me to please Daddy. When I understood the books and conversed about his life at the bank, he seemed to relax. Even as a young girl, I had seen his down moods. I loved the way my laughter and attention could pull him out in a way that even Mamma couldn't do. Sometimes he would take me in his lap and hold me ever so close. I'd lay my head on his shoulder and smell the crisp starch in his shirt and the faint scent of his cologne.

I closed my eyes and could almost conjure up those very same smells. *Oh, Daddy. I would give anything to be a little girl again, sitting in your lap.*

I sat cross-legged on the floor and thought of these things. I filled my mind with them, and Spalding, for all the times he enjoyed talking, left me there in my private grieving. Alone.

———

I rushed back into the school activities with a type of relief, a way to find stability amidst all that had been taken away. Dobbs honored my wishes back at school. She made no overt approaches to talk with me, even discreetly slipping away when I joined a group that she was part of. Sometimes I watched her out of the corner of my eye, and was surprised at the change in her. She looked cute and sassy with her short hair, but all the fire in her eyes was gone. I pretended not to notice because I didn't want to feel any guilt about that. But I knew

Mary Dobbs Dillard better than anyone else at the Seminary, and I could see she wasn't doing well.

It is hard to have a superficial relationship with your former best friend, but we tried. Although I never let on, I was worried about her. Neither Mamma nor Spalding trusted her. Once Mamma said, "I almost feel sorry for Mary Dobbs and the way she seeks out attention with her strange stories."

When Mamma said that, I got a knot in my stomach, wondering again if all of Dobbs's stories were made up. I honestly could not imagine Mary Dobbs Dillard lying about so many things. And even if she could, would she?

Dobbs

Back in Atlanta, Aunt Josie peppered me with questions about my Christmas in Chicago.

"Oh, they all loved the presents. You made it such a lovely Christmas for all of us, Aunt Josie." I told her of how much fun I'd had with Frances and Coobie and how wonderful it was to dance with Hank at the Walnut Room.

"But something didn't go so well." Normally all business, Aunt Josie had followed me up to my room and now leaned against the doorframe while I unpacked my suitcase.

"Why do you say that?"

"Because you're acting just like Billy used to after he received bad news."

My mouth fell open. "I am?"

"Neither your father nor you are extremely discreet, Mary Dobbs." She looked serious but flashed a quick smile. "Your face has gone pale and your eyes are dim—they've lost their light."

I didn't want to hear that I resembled my father in any way. I busied myself hanging up my dresses in the closet and said, "The night before I left for Chicago, Becca told me about Jackie. About my sister." I mashed my lips together. "She let it slip and . . . and so now I know."

"Ah. Well, then." She folded her arms over her chest. "Yes, now you know. And you carried that information with you to Chicago."

I nodded and then sat down on the bed. "I confronted my father—asked him about the inheritance he should have received and why we have no money."

Aunt Josie was shaking her head, as if she knew the rest of the story.

"I was quite horrible to him. But he explained it all—his past and the way your parents were blackmailed by Irene Brown and then how Jackie came to live with us. And the way sin tangled him all up—that's how he put it. He didn't even tell your parents when Irene started demanding more money."

Now I was lying on the bed, my head turned toward my desk. Aunt Josie had taken a seat beside me, and she reached over and patted my back. "And then when Irene found out about the inheritance, she begged him to help her—said her employers were going to kill her if she didn't pay off her debts. So he paid them for her. Did you know that?" I glanced up at her.

"Yes. I learned of that afterwards. Dear me, it's a rather sordid tale, worthy of a novel. And then with that poor child dying. God rest her soul."

"Why are things so very complicated?"

"You know, it's not an easy thing to have money, Mary Dobbs. It allows one to do wonderful things, but it also carries a huge responsibility. People want what you have. There are so many legitimate ways to help with money. But there are many people who are deeply jealous and looking for ways to take it."

"Like Irene Brown."

"Yes. She was a desperate woman with a sick child. But her—" Aunt Josie searched for a word—"her *employers* were horribly ruthless, and I believe they would have killed her." Stout Aunt Josie shuddered with the thought.

"I don't think Father has ever forgiven himself for all of it."

"No, bless him. But there was a lot to forgive. Billy made some foolish mistakes in his youth, which, unfortunately, entangled him with some pretty wicked people."

"But you've forgiven him?"

"Heavens yes. Oh, I've been angry with him. But I love my little brother." She stood up, reached over to pat my shoulder, and said, "I'll let you finish unpacking." Before she left the room, she turned around and said, "I imagine it is pretty rough on your father to have his daughter at odds with him."

———

I followed Aunt Josie's not-so-subtle advice and wrote Father, apologizing for my loathsome behavior, but it didn't take my doubts away, nor my worries about Coobie's cough. A letter from my father arrived the same day as I posted mine to him. My heart skipped a beat. Father never wrote letters; he was a man of the spoken word. I felt a softening around my heart as I read the letter. Again, he apologized fervently—as Aunt Josie said, everything about Father was passionate—and spoke of his love for me, for all of us. Then he ended the letter with:

> My dear Mary Dobbs, please be assured that your mother and
> I will take every precaution necessary for Coobie to make sure
> the cough does not worsen.

But it did.

Hank wrote me twice a week, and I could read, in between his encouraging and loving words, a deep down worry for my little sister. Two letters from Mother described several trips to the doctor.

Then Mother actually called me from her mother's home, telling me that Coobie was hospitalized. Everything became a déjà vu for me, and I wanted to curse God for giving me the strange gift of knowing something ahead of time. I did *not* want to know this about Coobie.

The best doctors in Chicago were on Coobie's case, but Mother soon wrote: *Every doctor agrees that Coobie needs a warmer climate when she is stable enough to travel.* That phrase turned my blood to icicles, and I sat numb in my room with Mother's letter frozen in my hand.

Perri

Without Dobbs to challenge me, I went about life as I wished, attending loads of parties and dances with Spalding. Dobbs and I remained cordial to each other, but we spent no time together. Though my friends were obviously aware of this, only Mae Pearl dared to say something.

"Have you noticed the morose mood of dear Mary Dobbs? Why, she hardly speaks up at all in class or at Phi Pi events, and last week she announced the Bible study was canceled for the next month, due to what she called 'unforeseen circumstances.' Whatever is going on with her?"

I shrugged. "Maybe she's gaining a little common sense and deciding to keep her opinions to herself."

"Why, Anne Perrin, that doesn't sound a thing like you. Are you upset with Mary Dobbs? Don't you see her anymore?"

"Oh, sure, I see her. I'm over at the Chandlers' several times a week, working in the darkroom."

Mae Pearl shook her head. "That's not what I mean, and you know it. Y'all aren't close anymore, are you?"

I shrugged again. "Maybe you could just say that we're taking a break from each other."

"Well, I think that's a mighty shame. And it's obvious she's all torn up about it."

I had no patience with Mae Pearl's do-goodism. "Look, you don't know all the details. I'm sure it'll blow over."

She looked a bit miffed and said, "Well, until it does, I swear it's real chilly around here."

———

On a blustery Saturday afternoon, Spalding and I had a double date with Mae Pearl and Sam Durand. We went to see a movie at the Buckhead Theatre and then walked across the street to Jacobs' Drugstore to get a hot chocolate.

Mae Pearl's white cheeks were stained a pretty soft pink from the wind, and she giggled on Sam's arm. Inside the drugstore, she took me to the side and whispered, "Sam has agreed to go to the Alms Houses with me in a little while. He wants to meet Mr. Ross and some of the other residents. You could bring your camera and take photos, and Spalding could meet people too."

"That's a wonderful idea, Mae! Tell it to Spalding."

Spalding was still at the counter ordering our drinks, and Mae Pearl went over and shared her thoughts with him.

"Sorry," he said, without even giving her suggestion serious thought. "We've got other plans."

"But, Spalding dear," I said, embarrassed. "Nothing too important. We could all go there for a little while. It would mean so much to the residents."

He took my arm and held it in a tight, possessive way. His smile never faded. He simply held up his car keys in the other hand and said, "Mae Pearl, what Perri sometimes has a hard time remembering is that I hold the trump card. Always."

Mae Pearl looked astonished. A flicker of worry crossed her brow, and then she said in her soft little voice, "Well, I'll let y'all decide between you," and she sat down at a table with Sam.

Spalding's hand tightened on my arm. "My dear, your memory is slipping today."

I shook myself free of him. "Spalding Smith! What horrible manners! Can't you see I want to go to the Alms Houses with Mae Pearl? If you can't take time from your schedule, well, so be it. I'll get a ride with Mae Pearl."

He fingered the SAE pin that hung on a chain around my neck. "Perri, we are not going to the Alms Houses today. We can plan it for another time." He seemed to calm down. "Go if you wish, but"—here he tilted his head and gave me his best disapproving look—"you did promise to go by and see my mother. She's looking forward to it."

My anger faded. Though we had not arranged a specific time to visit his mother, he was right about our having prior plans. I felt a tinge of guilt and acquiesced. "That's true. All right."

We sipped our drinks at the table with Mae Pearl and Sam, trying to ignore the first few moments of awkward silence. But then Spalding and Sam began talking about football and then baseball, and Mae Pearl and I listened, both pretending to be interested. At length we went back to our cars.

As Spalding started the engine, Mae Pearl hurried over to the car. I doubted she could have missed the disappointment on my face, even though I tried to mask it. She said, "We can't get you two to change your minds?"

"I'm afraid not," Spalding said briskly.

Mae Pearl brushed her hands through her hair and wrinkled her brow. "Okay then, kids. Have fun."

I nodded in a stiff, wooden way and wondered briefly if my life was going to be a continual submitting to the desires of Spalding Smith.

Dobbs

Perri all but ignored me at school. I took to sitting at a lunch table with Lisa and Macon and some of the younger Phi Pis. I carried a perpetual ache inside so that I only nibbled at my food. I could not pray; my Bible was left unopened. I felt as if I had lost all the faith inside of me.

I cringed with the memory of Aunt Josie's words. *"You're acting just like Billy used to after he received bad news."*

Now I understood why my father hated sin so much. It had ruined his life. It was ruining mine.

Uncle Robert and Aunt Josie knew the cause of my angst, and I survived that month because they cared. Aunt Josie let me call Mother at her mother's house every week, and we followed Coobie's progress as if it were episodes of *Amos and Andy*.

I shared the news with Parthenia, too, and her little face was often drawn into a frown as she worked. Occasionally I heard her mumbling to herself, "They betta bring her down here fast where she kin git well. They betta do it if'n they know what's good for 'em!"

My friends noticed my mood and tried to cheer me up. Brat told her jokes, and Lisa and Macon recounted the latest gossip from parties, which I listened to numbly. In spite of my heartache, I was thankful to go to school, to have homework, to be forced to stay busy.

I watched the Seminary girls in a different way, socializing with more of them now that I spent no time with Perri. It had taken me almost a year to realize, but finally I understood that they had plenty of work to do right here in their society.

ELIZABETH MUSSER

And they were doing it. I had been so blind. I had ignored their service.

People in this part of Atlanta were not poor like the people on the streets of Chicago or the ones in Oklahoma who had their homes blown away in clouds of dust, or the ones in south Georgia who had to eat their animals.

But many families, like the Singletons, had lost so much and had little money with which to purchase necessities. Common human goodness was helping people survive in Atlanta, just like in every other part of the country. The fruits and vegetables that Frances and Coobie and I had canned with Parthenia over the summer now were handed out to families in need. Whenever hobos showed up at the house, which happened a lot that winter, Aunt Josie invited them in and served up a plate of food.

I once overheard my aunt and uncle discussing the huge number of unpaid bills from Uncle Robert's customers and how every month or two, my uncle burned the bills. He said it wasn't worth sending them out, since people couldn't pay anyway. My aunt and uncle's goodness humbled me, convicted me, and the hole of sadness I had fallen into seemed only to grow deeper.

I attended the Phi Pi meetings halfheartedly, and early in February, Mae Pearl shocked me by saying, "Mary Dobbs is going to tell us a story at Bible hour tomorrow afternoon, so everyone be sure to come."

"It's about time!" said Lisa. "We've gone nearly two months without a story."

"You just make up all those stories, don't you, Mary Dobbs?"

I found Mae Pearl after the meeting. "I don't have any more stories," I told her.

"I know good and well that isn't true! You haven't ever told them about the lady whose son died or the mangy dog or . . ."

"I don't want to tell any more stories, Mae Pearl."

"Goodness, Mary Dobbs. What's the matter? It's Perri, isn't it? She's off with Spalding all the time and never sees you."

"It's not just that, Mae Pearl. It's other things too. Things that I can't talk about. But thanks for caring."

"Well, can't I help? There must be something I can do."

I looked at Mae Pearl, her pretty blue eyes just oozing sweetness, and I said, "*You* could tell the story tomorrow, Mae Pearl."

"Me? I don't have any good stories."

"Tell them a Bible story, Mae Pearl," I said without enthusiasm.

She brightened. "Why, that's a great idea! Yes. I'll tell them a Bible story, and I'll pray. I'll pray for you, Mary Dobbs, just like you always do for us."

"Thanks, Mae Pearl," I mumbled, and then, seeing her standing there with such concern on her face, I added, "Pray for Coobie. She's been real sick, and it worries me."

"Oh dear. Not Coobie!"

"I'm sure she'll be okay," I said, without a shred of conviction, and hurried off.

I received two visits from Andrew Morrison at the Chandlers', each time accompanied by a beautiful bouquet of flowers. I asked him to go to the Phi Pi Valentine's Dance with me, telling myself that if Hank truly knew what was in my heart, he wouldn't want me to be his girl anymore. No matter Hank's proclamations, no matter the letters he wrote me twice a week, I convinced myself that I was no longer worthy of him. He needed a strong woman of faith, and mine had evaporated.

I had not written to him since I'd returned to Atlanta.

Mother's letters tried to reassure me about Coobie, but I had heard the cough, and I knew the truth. I remembered exactly how Jackie sounded in the months before she died.

Perri

To my great surprise, Mae Pearl led the Bible lesson on Tuesday, and Dobbs did not even attend. Mae Pearl confided to me that she had stayed up half the night preparing, and as she talked her cheeks grew pink, and I heard something strange in her soft voice—passion, belief, conviction.

She finished her teaching, closed the Bible, wrinkled her brow, and said, "There's this verse in Scripture where Jesus is telling a parable, and at the end, He says, 'For unto whomsoever much is given, of him shall be much required; and to whom men have committed much, of him they will ask the more.'

"Girls, think of all we've been given. We have families and houses and food and clothes, and we have churches to attend, and we have this fine institution where we can get a top-notch education. Remember how back in December Mary Dobbs asked us if we tended to be Pharisees or publicans? Remember? Well, I went home and made a vow to be a better person. And I told that to Mary Dobbs, and she said, 'Mae Pearl, we can't be better on our own. Not really. We need Jesus in us to be better.'

"So anyway, I thought about that, and then I was thinking about all we've been given and how sometimes we complain. But hey, listen, we live okay, even with horrible things, and I think we just have to keep on helping the poor around us and giving gifts to the children and going out to the Alms Houses. It may not seem like much, but I think it *is* something, and I think when we do it, in the right way—you know, how Mary Dobbs says—well, I think God must be awfully pleased, and so . . ." She stopped, blushed, and finished timidly, "So that's all I have to say today, and thank you ever so much for listening."

She sat down next to me, and I saw how much her hands were trembling.

Lisa stood up and asked, "Does any one know where Mary Dobbs is?" She looked straight at me.

I felt the heat rise in my face, but I shrugged and shook my head.

Mae Pearl answered, "I think she's just awful sad, and I don't know all the whys, but I promised we'd pray for her, like she does, ending every meeting with prayer."

To my astonishment, fifteen girls bowed their heads and sat in what Mae Pearl called "a few minutes of silent prayer for our dear Mary Dobbs."

Finally Mae Pearl finished by saying, "Lord God Almighty, you sent us Mary Dobbs to help us learn more about you, and now she is sad, and so we pray that you will comfort her in her affliction. And help her sister get well. Amen."

I caught up to Mae Pearl as she was leaving the classroom. "What's the matter with Dobbs's sister? Which one?"

"She didn't tell you? Coobie's been real sick, and she's worried about it. She didn't tell me any more than that."

I frowned at the news. I knew how protective Dobbs was of her little sisters. But to Mae Pearl I simply said, "You did a good job."

"I was scared stiff, but it went okay. I'll have to tell Mary Dobbs."

I watched her leave, and it was as if my focus was sharpening, just as it did behind the camera. I ached inside. Even if Dobbs's revival stories were made up, the things she taught from the Bible weren't. I had to admit she was making a big impression on some of my friends. In fact, it looked to me like Mae Pearl was on her way to becoming devout like Dobbs.

———

I missed seeing other boys. I longed again for lazy afternoons with loads of boys coming by the house. I found myself bored at times with Spalding's constant banter. At other times, I shivered with the way it seemed he wanted to possess me. In those times, Dobbs's voice whispered around me, *"He's not right for you; he'll only cause you heartache."*

At least I had told Dobbs the truth about one thing: I wasn't in love with Spalding Smith. And I no longer believed he was in love with me. He liked me a lot, but he wanted me to behave exactly as he desired, and I knew I could not keep up that charade.

I was too proud to admit that to Dobbs, so I took my photographs and developed them in the darkroom, alone.

At night, I thought about Philip Hendrick and the letters he sent me every week and the way he signed them and our shared interest in photography. Right before I turned out the light, I read from *Patches from the Sky*. I wondered how I could distance myself from Spalding and find a freedom that I needed like fresh air. I began gasping for it until at long last I could admit that more than money and stature in the community, more than surviving our particular tragedy in the midst of the Depression, what I wanted was to know that somehow, somewhere, with someone, I could be safe.

I had said it before. I wanted peace.

Occasionally at night, cuddled in bed under plenty of covers, I whispered prayers into the dark, whispered them with great fervency, because I wanted, and desperately needed, help. And every time I whispered them, what came back floating in the air were Dobbs's words about faith and God's provision and the way we were all trying so hard to fill ourselves up on something so that the desperate void and pain of the present would subside for just a while.

———

I was leaving school on a Friday afternoon when Lisa caught up with me in the hall. "Perri! Wait up. I was going through a folder with old photos from last year's *Facts and Fancies,* and I came across these for you." She handed me an envelope with my name across it.

"Thanks, Lisa."

I walked outside, shivering in the frosty air, opened the envelope, and took out three photographs. I remembered having lent them to Lisa the year before, in case she could use them for the yearbook in a section entitled *Back When We Were Young*. The photos had been taken by a professional and were from Lisa's birthday party when she was six or seven. In one, we were all sitting at our dining room table with party hats on. Mamma and Mrs. Young were both there with us. That was the year we'd offered to have Lisa's party at our house because her house had caught fire and was under repair.

The next picture was of Lisa and me making silly faces.

I looked at the last photo and felt chills run from the top of my head all the way down to my toes. Five of us little girls were crowded around Daddy's desk. We had sneaked in there and surprised him by bringing him a piece of Lisa's birthday cake. The other girls were smiling their toothless grins at the camera, but I was not looking at the camera at all. I was snuggled tight in my father's lap.

I gave a little gasp, remembering my plea in my father's study.

"Oh, Daddy. I would give anything to be a little girl again, sitting in your lap."

It was windy outside, curling the edges of the photographs I tightly gripped. I stopped and stared at that photo of me in my father's lap.

No one else in the whole wide world knew the plea I had voiced alone in Daddy's empty study in late December—another chance to sit in his lap. But it was what I wanted more than life itself, and here, in a strange way, my plea had been answered.

Just as quickly, another scene flashed in my mind. I was accusing Dobbs of her God never providing, and she said, "I'm praying that one day God will provide something for you, you alone, Perri Singleton, in a way that you won't be able to doubt it is from Him."

"Daddy!" I began walking faster, now seeing the men's faces on that dark street in downtown Atlanta and then hearing someone calling my name and feeling that my father was somehow right there beside me. Then it rustled by me gently, a breeze across my face. Not Daddy, but a father nonetheless, *the* Father in heaven that Dobbs talked about. He had been present that night, and He was present now.

I forgot about meeting Barbara after school or waiting for Jimmy to pick us up. In a blur of excitement, my heart racing, I walked to the streetcar stop, hopped on, and rode it all the way down Peachtree, near the corner of Wesley. I hurried off and ran the half mile to our old house, our *real* house, panting as I climbed the steep driveway. By the screened-in porch I noticed that two purple crocuses had pushed their way out of the ground, and there was a faint smell of spring in the air. In our backyard, I spread my arms out and turned around and around, giggling as if I were Mary Dobbs Dillard. I finally stopped, out of breath, sat down on the back steps, looked again at the photo of me cuddled in my father's lap, turned my eyes upward, and whispered one word. "Thanks."

———

Two days later, I was sitting in the pew at St. Luke's, like I did every Sunday morning, with Mamma beside me. She had on her light pink suit and the pink straw hat with the little pink see-through veil that came down just over her eyes. Mamma kept dabbing her white-gloved right hand, in which she held a tissue, under her left eye to remove tears. Occasionally, she'd even bring the tissue to her nose and dab softly underneath and give a tiny polite sniff.

The preacher was talking about joy after weeping, and when Mamma reached over and squeezed my hand, tears blurred my eyes too.

And then it happened. Something. I couldn't explain it then or later in any way that made much sense, but I felt a peaceful settling in my soul.

The closest thing to describing it was a memory of something that happened a few days after Daddy died. Exhausted with grief and the details of the funeral and everything else, I'd fallen asleep on the sofa on the screened porch. Being March, it was chilly outside, but I was just too tired to get up and find a blanket. I was cold and had goose pimples on my arms. All of the sudden, as if she could read my mind, Dellareen tiptoed out on the porch and covered me up with the beautiful old quilt that she had made for me when I was born. It was worn through in places and smelled of baby powder and years of love. She wrapped it around me in the gentlest way—and Dellareen wasn't always gentle—and whispered, "You go on and sleep a little bit, Miz Perri. You need some rest."

I slept for a long time cuddled under that quilt, a sleep without nightmares, without tears. Peaceful.

That's what happened that Sunday in church. I felt warm and

comfortable and peaceful. And something else. Sure. I trusted that we were going to make it out of this horrible mess of our lives, but it wasn't up to me. That revelation took my breath away and warmed me at the same time. The crushing heaviness of responsibility seemed to roll off my back, as if Mamma had taken her scissors and cut the strings that held it there.

I felt free. I believed. I believed in that moment what Dobbs had told me for so long. Faith. Truth.

God was going to get us through. Jesus would do it, just like Dobbs always had promised, just like her stories always illustrated.

Just like God had proved to me.

Yes, I had proof. I had the photo of me sitting in Daddy's lap.

I felt loved and comfortable and reassured and excited and beyond exhausted all at once.

And forgiven.

I had said that I wanted to know that somehow, somewhere, with someone, I could be safe.

Now I knew.

But no one else did.

One day, I'd tell Dobbs. I still had way too much pride to do it right away. But someday I'd tell her.

There was one person, though, that I had to tell. Immediately.

Spalding came to our house for Sunday lunch, and afterwards, standing in our little den when Mamma and Irvin and Barbara had gone outside for a walk, I tried to give him back his SAE pin. He listened to me in that way he had of seeming to care, of projecting sympathy. He pulled me close to him, gently, and patted my hair and my shoulder. "It's normal to have the jitters."

"It's not the jitters, Spalding. I know it isn't right. We aren't right for each other. I mean it. I want to break up."

As I spoke, his arm got tighter around me until he was clutching my arm. His eyes narrowed, and drawing me even closer, he whispered to me, "You don't always get what you want, little miss-spoiled-society-girl. You know that. There is no way you are breaking up with me. Do you understand?"

I didn't look up at him, so he took my chin in his other hand and forced it up. "Do you understand?"

I felt terror hammering in my heart, almost like I'd felt when the two men had mugged me. Spalding's look was so calculated and cruel. Why had I not seen it before? How had Dobbs known?

That was the first time I saw his anger, uncovered. His face turned a darker shade. He grabbed me again and said, "You're mine and you'll go where I want to go and do what I want to do." He fingered his SAE pin on the chain around my neck. Then his hand tightened on the chain and he pulled me toward himself and kissed me soundly on the mouth.

I shivered slightly. I was furious with him. And then the fury was replaced by cold fear. "Don't say such things, Spalding! You're making me afraid."

"There's no need to be afraid, Perri dear"—his hard smile was back—"as long as you do everything I want."

In a flash, I saw Dobbs before me, warning me again and again and again. *"He's not right for you. He's a womanizer. I've seen him being intimate with another girl. He'll only make you miserable. Please, Perri. Please, listen to me."*

Why didn't I listen to you, dear Dobbs?

I stamped my foot and yanked away once more from his hold on my arm. "I am breaking up with you! You've made me mad, and I have no desire to be with you right now!"

I turned to get away, but he stepped in front, put both hands on my shoulders, and said, "Don't you dare, Anne Perrin Singleton. If you leave me today, the rest of your family will suffer."

"Are you threatening me? Why would you say such a thing, Spalding?"

"You can call it whatever you want. But you better pay attention."

It was at that moment I realized the absolute truth. I had thought that Spalding Smith was fitting into my plans, but I was wrong. He was carefully fitting me into his plans, though I did not know what they were.

My heart was pounding and my head sizzling with an ache.

"You hear?" He let me go so abruptly that I staggered backward, caught myself on a chair, and collapsed into it. He pointed at me with one outstretched finger, turned on his heel, and left the house. I heard the door to his sports car slam and then a squeal of the wheels.

My one thought was *I have to find Dobbs and tell her. I have to.*

I hurried to the Buick and hopped in, killing the engine three times before it finally caught. I drove, blinded by my tears and real fear, to the Chandlers'. I ran into the house, not even greeting Parthenia, who was in the entrance hall.

"You shore is in a hurry, Miz Perri, for a lazy Sunday afternoon."

I took the steps two at a time and pushed open the door to Dobbs's room without knocking. It was empty.

"She's out in the darkroom, Miz Perri," Parthenia called up to me. When I rushed down the steps, Parthenia added, " 'Bout time you come lookin' for her. With all the sad things in her life, and here she he'pped you when you needed it most."

I barely paid attention to Parthenia's reprimand but went into the stable and past Dynamite's stall. I opened the door to the darkroom and found Dobbs sitting in the lone chair, a photo in her hands.

She glanced over at me. The look on her face, one of pure grief, halted me in my tracks. Then, gradually, I came beside her. The photograph was one I had taken the past summer of Dobbs and Frances and Coobie. They were all three in swimming bloomers. We had just returned from the club. They had their arms around each other, and Coobie had that look of mischief in her eyes.

"She seemed so healthy then," Dobbs whispered, but not really to me, more as if she were convincing herself. "I knew it. I hate knowing things. I knew this time her cough sounded different."

I knelt down in front of her and said, "Oh, Dobbs. Mae Pearl told us something was the matter with Coobie. What is it?"

Dobbs turned a tear-stained face to me. "She has the same disease. The same one as Jackie. The very same one."

"What are you talking about?"

"Remember I told you about my friend Jackie and the congenital disease that took her so quickly? Well, Coobie has it too."

"Oh, Dobbs. How can it be? You said the disease is so rare."

"It runs in the family."

I just stared at her.

"Jackie was my sister. My half sister, from my father's 'other life.' I found it out before I left for Chicago. Becca told me."

Those words catapulted me outside of myself. Dobbs had carried this wound inside her for so long, and where had I been? On a selfish, foolish detour.

"She was three years and nine months older than me." She said this to herself, as if she had forgotten I was there. "We were the best of friends. But she came to us sick—always had been sickly. Her mother couldn't help her. Mother and Father took her to all the fancy doctors—I didn't realize how hard they tried to help. But in the end, there wasn't a thing to be done. She died two weeks before she turned nineteen."

At last Dobbs looked up at me, her face destroyed. "Coobie's got the same disease, and there's nothing left to do."

I don't know how long I knelt there on my knees, the bare earth pressing its imprint into them, trying to share a tiny bit of her deep pain and cursing myself for my selfishness. After a while, I managed to say, "I'm sorry, Dobbs. I'm so sorry I've been horrible to you. You were right. You've been right all along."

She didn't even acknowledge my words. She simply said, "I don't believe anymore."

"What?"

"I don't believe anymore."

I frowned. "I don't understand what you mean, Dobbs. What do you not believe anymore? About Spalding? About the stolen things?"

She shook her head slowly. "I don't believe. I've lost my faith."

Nothing could have shocked me more than hearing her pronounce those words. "That's impossible. Impossible."

"It's true." She finally turned to look at me. Her eyes were pools of black water. "I've stopped believing."

I plopped down on the floor and tried to digest this confession, but I couldn't. And more than that, I didn't want to digest it. "You can't do that, not when I need you. You can't leave me all alone."

"Alone?"

"I believed you and then I believed Him."

"Him?"

"Your God."

I had hoped to see a flicker of light in her eyes, maybe even a smile of approval or excitement. Instead, she looked forlorn.

"You cannot tell me it's not real, Dobbs. Why would you do that?"

"I don't know."

Her lethargy scared me, and for a moment I forgot her pain and thought again only of myself. "Is it what I've always said, Dobbs? All your crazy stories weren't true, were they?"

She didn't reply. I watched her profile, the way her short hair fell onto her forehead and the fine slope of her nose.

"Why did you make them up? Was it just to convince us of that crazy Sawdust Trail?"

"I never made up one thing. They are things that really happened to my family. I was there, and I saw it—I lived it. I wasn't lying. You can ask my parents or sisters or a hundred other witnesses. Those stories are absolutely true, just as I've told you before. I promise."

I narrowed my eyes at her and said, "So you're telling me that all those miraculous things really happened to you, that God kept showing up and providing for your family and for all the poor people, but now you don't believe it anymore? That's impossible! How could you see miracles and stop believing?"

"People change. Things happen. You doubt; you wonder. It's not impossible."

I felt myself deflate before her eyes. "If you don't believe anymore, who in the world can have real faith? If yours wasn't real, with all your enthusiasm and fervor, what hope is there for anyone else?"

She shook her head. "I don't know. I'm sorry, but I have no answers." She paused. "It's just what I said. I stopped believing! I just stopped. I didn't mean to or try to. It just happened, on the train from Atlanta to Chicago. It flew right out the window, and there was nothing I could do to stop it."

She stood up and replaced the photograph in one pile and reached for another, this time of Coobie and Parthenia. "I will not sit here and watch Coobie die. God cannot take her too. "

"Oh, Dobbs, we'll get all the girls in the sorority to pray so hard for her. I'll tell them right away."

"Do what you want." Her voice was resigned. "It might help; it might not. No one knows the ways of the Lord." A slight sarcasm had crept into her voice.

"But you know He'll care for y'all. He'll provide. You've said it a hundred times. You've seen it with your eyes. Oh, Dobbs, don't stop believing. You can't! You're the one who convinced me; you're the one who made the Bible seem so real, so relevant, who told us those marvelous stories and who gave us hope in the worst moments. You're the one who knew how to keep me living when Daddy left. You told me—"

"Stop it!" she cried out, and for a brief second, passion flashed in her eyes. "Stop telling me what I've said. Don't you think I know it, Anne Perrin? Don't you think it's tearing me up inside to admit the truth? I don't need to be reminded that I'm the worst hypocrite in the world." Now tears were streaming down her face. "But the thing is, Perri, if you had known your father was about to take his life, you would have done everything in your power to stop it.

"And I know Coobie's dying, 'cause I watched it happen to Jackie. I have to do something to help her. I don't have time to wait on God." Dobbs stood up unsteadily and braced her arms on a table. She looked thin and weak, almost faint. "They're hoping to bring her down here if they can get her fever under control."

I grabbed Dobbs in the fiercest hug I had ever given. "I am so sorry, Dobbs. I am so, so sorry. We'll think of something. We will."

She let me hug her, but she didn't close her arms around me. She just stood there with her head down and mumbled, "I'm sorry I've disappointed you, Perri. I'm sorry I don't believe anymore."

That night I didn't tell Dobbs about Spalding or about the intricate way her God had answered my prayers or anything else about me. I just held her in the darkroom, and after a long, long time, she rested her head on my shoulder. When I reached up and touched her forehead, I realized it was burning hot.

CHAPTER
24

Dobbs

It turned out that Coobie wasn't the only one with a fever. I had one too. Perri called out to Hosea, and he came in the darkroom just about the time the room started reeling around me. I slumped into his arms, and he carried me across the expansive yard, and as my head hung down, I noticed the first shoots of the daffodils peeping out of the soil.

Hosea brought me into the house, upstairs to my room, and laid me gently on my canopied bed. Aunt Josie appeared from somewhere and, completely flustered, cried out that she should have recognized how weak and flushed I was. I listened to them in a deep fog; all my strength was gone. Maybe it had started as being heartsick, but it had turned into something else.

Aunt Josie brought me a thin chicken broth that evening, made especially for me by Parthenia, and Perri fed it to me, spoonful by spoonful.

In spite of everything, I gave a weak smile to see my friend perched beside my bed. *She's back,* I kept thinking again and again.

Parthenia sneaked upstairs to see me and sat right outside the door, knees gathered up to her chest. I dozed off and on, and once when I awoke I saw Perri sitting on the floor beside Parthenia. Their heads were bowed, and it almost looked as if they were praying. At length, Parthenia stood up and curtsied and turned to go down the stairs, and Perri said to her, "It's going to be okay. Somehow it will."

Later, the doctor came to the house and listened to my chest. He took Aunt Josie aside and consulted with her. Before he left, though, he came back to the room and said, "Miss Dillard, you rest now, you hear me? And you eat. You can't help your family if you're sick in bed."

Perri finally left my side late that evening. But before she left, she whispered to me, "One time you told me, Dobbs, that in the darkest moments, we can't pray ourselves. We're too torn up with grief, but God puts other people around us to pray and hold us up and keep us going. They believe for us when our faith wavers.

"That's what you did for me, and it worked. And now, my sweet, faithful friend, I'm going to do that for you. I'll pray. Mae Pearl and I will be like those two men holding up Moses' hands. We'll believe for you. It's gonna work out. God will provide."

I didn't know what to say to her, so I simply whispered, "Thank you."

She put her hand over mine, and for the rest of the night, as I drifted in and out of slumber, I kept hearing Perri's voice saying, "My sweet, faithful friend." I held on to that. Only that.

Perri

I drove to Mae Pearl's that night. Mrs. McFadden opened the door, wearing her robe. "I'm ever so sorry to appear at this late hour," I apologized. "But it's very important, and I need to see Mae Pearl."

Mrs. McFadden let me in. "I hope it's not bad news, Perri."

I shook my head. "It's a little bit of everything mixed up into one, but I believe it will be okay."

"Go on upstairs."

Mae Pearl was curled up in her bed, reading a magazine. "Perri! What on earth brings you here at such an hour!"

"It's Dobbs. She needs our help!" And I told her about how bad off Coobie was and about Dobbs's fever and how she had lost her faith.

Mae Pearl got a gentle flush to her cheeks and gave her beautiful sad smile and said, "Whatever do we do now if Mary Dobbs has stopped believing?"

"We carry her," I said with a strange conviction in my voice. "We help her somehow."

"But how?" Mae Pearl set aside her magazine and motioned for me to join her on her bed.

I went into my most efficient organizational mode. "Tomorrow you get all the Phi Pis together again and tell them all the details about Coobie. Ask the ones who feel inclined to pray that Coobie's fever will lessen and that she'll be strong enough to make the trip down to Atlanta so she can receive treatment here. And for Dobbs to get stronger—she's got a bad fever too."

"How in the world will Mr. and Mrs. Dillard pay for treatment here?"

"I don't know. I'll ask Mrs. Chandler, and then maybe we can organize a way to raise money for Coobie."

"A fund-raiser? During the worst year of the Depression?"

Annoyed, I said, "If the almighty God could provide for all those poor people who were planning to eat their pets, well then, surely He can provide the funds for Coobie."

"But how?"

"That's not my problem. It's God's."

"Wow, Perri. You sound just like Mary Dobbs."

It was past eleven o'clock when I got back to Club Drive. I had warned Mamma I might be late; still, she looked relieved when I came into the house. "Where have you been? We've all been worried."

"I'm sorry, Mamma. Coobie's real sick, and Dobbs is so torn up about it that she's sick too."

In my room, I picked up *Patches from the Sky* and hurriedly flipped through the pages. I couldn't find the verses Dobbs had quoted to me about God providing.

Irvin found me in my bedroom, haphazardly pulling out books from boxes we had not unpacked.

"Whatever are you doing, Sis?"

"I need to find a Bible."

"Why?"

"I don't know. I just need to. For Mary Dobbs. For me."

My little brother, up way past his bedtime, sat down on the floor beside me, yawned, and then gave a sheepish grin. "Mamma got to fretting about you, and she plumb forgot to make us go to bed." He opened another box and began removing books. On the fourth box, he announced, "I found it!" and triumphantly held up the black book.

"Oh, Irvin! Thank you." I hugged him, took the leather-bound Bible, and started thumbing through the gold-rimmed pages. The thin paper made a rustling sound each time I turned a page.

"How do you know where to look in the Bible?"

I flipped to the Gospel According to St. Matthew. "I don't know, really. But it's something Jesus said about not fretting and God taking care of us. And see, in this Bible, everything Jesus says is in red."

Irvin was peering over my shoulder when Barbara came in the room. "What on earth are you two doing? Mamma'll have a fit seeing all these books spread all over the place."

"We're looking at the Bible for Mary Dobbs," Irvin explained.

Barbara gave us her best disinterested fourteen-year-old face, but she sat down beside me and said, "I thought you were mad at Mary Dobbs."

"I never said that."

"No, but you stopped seeing her."

"Well, that's over now. She needs our help."

I hadn't gotten very far in the gospel of Matthew when the verses leapt out at me. "Here they are! Right here." Irvin and Barbara crowded beside me, and I started reading to them. " 'Therefore I say unto you, Take no thought for your life, what ye shall eat, or what ye shall drink; nor yet for your body, what ye shall put on. . . .' "

I kept reading Jesus' words with my little brother and sister peering over my shoulder, and occasionally Barbara would announce, "Oh, I've heard that verse before."

"See, it says God is going to take care of us. And that's what we need to remember for little Coobie. God is going to take care of her."

Mamma came in my room and got a sweet look on her face, seeing us scrunched together on the floor looking at the Bible. "It's way past your bedtime," she said at last. I handed her the Bible, and she held it open to that page, and I swear she was reading those words of Jesus too, and I almost think her worry lines disappeared for just a while.

Dobbs

I didn't go to school for three days. Aunt Josie practically forced me to stay if not in bed, at least in my room. I took to sitting in a chair by the window and staring out into the backyard. Sure enough, the daffodils kept pushing themselves out of the ground. Father always loved the coming of spring, with all its spiritual metaphors of new birth and regeneration. As I watched the February sun shift through the trees, I thought briefly of the snow falling around Father and me on Christmas night. My heart was cold, frozen over.

I marveled at Perri's profession of faith, but in a detached, distant way. She came over after school on Monday, the first day I stayed home, and told me all about how God had done something for her that was so personal and real and secretive that she had no doubt it came from the Almighty. "Just like you prayed for Him to do, Dobbs! He even did it in the way I could understand best—through a photograph."

I got chills that had nothing to do with my fever as she told her story, but I did not have the strength or faith to show my usual excitement.

Still, we found ourselves in that comfortable position of friendship, giggling and wiping tears—back and forth, catching up on each other's lives.

At last, she said, "Here I am jabbering away when I want to hear more about you. Tell me everything about Jackie and what happened on that train ride to Chicago where you said your faith flew out of the window."

For an hour or longer, I talked on and on about my anger at my father and all I learned of Jackie's past and my terror at hearing Coobie's cough. I showed her the hair pin Andrew had given me and described my meal at the Walnut Room with Hank. The telling of it to her was a balm. It didn't restore my faith, but the shadows lifted a little.

"What about Hank now? Does he know all about how you feel—you know, about your faith?"

"I told him. He just keeps writing to me, but it's not going to work for us, Perri. I started thinking about how hard life will be all the time, forever, for Hank and me. And I can't do it. I've gotten used to luxury. Granted, things are hard for everyone, but it's a lot easier here than in Chicago. I'm going to write him and break things off; he deserves a girl who is a lot better than me."

"But, Dobbs, he loves you so much!"

"You said it before—what does love have to do with it?" As soon as I pronounced those words, I heard in my mind Mother saying, *"Love is the crux of human relationships; the sweetest thing."* I pushed away the thought and added, "He still hasn't found a steady job, and anyway, he's going to need a strong woman of faith."

"I'm awful sorry to hear it, Dobbs." Silence drifted between us, but it was almost back to that easy silence of friends. At last she brought up Spalding. "You were right all along. He's not right for me. For a while he acted like the grandest gentleman." She explained about finding Spalding at her old house on Christmas Day. "Sometimes he's so kind. Why, he's let us visit our old house several times since then."

I stopped her. "Why in the world was he at your old house on Christmas Day? How did he get a key?"

"I guess his father gave it to him—he's the one selling it and had him check it out before showing it to a potential buyer."

"I thought his father was an important man with Coke and now he's selling your house? Is he in real estate too? And Spalding shows up on Christmas Day? That seems awful strange to me."

"It does?"

I shrugged. "Maybe it's just my imagination, but don't you think it's odd that he was there?" I tiptoed up to the subject. "Remember how I saw the stolen things in your father's toolbox and then when Aunt Josie and your mother went to look, they were gone? And Spalding has a key to the house?"

"What are you saying?"

"Maybe Spalding is somehow involved in the thefts." I told her about Parthenia's reaction to the photo of Spalding she had seen hanging in the darkroom.

Perri got those deep red spots on her cheeks and covered her face with her hands. "I've been so incredibly blind, Dobbs! I refused to see any of it, even when it was staring me in the face." She stood up and started pacing around my room. "Yes, that would make sense. It would. On Sunday, after I'd had those experiences with God—that photograph and then at church—well, I just knew all of a sudden that Spalding and I weren't right for each other. So I tried to tell him, but he got so angry. It scared me. He even threatened me, Dobbs, saying I can't break up with him. What am I to do?"

I honestly had no idea and just said the first word that came to my mind. "Pray."

That night after Perri left, I brought up the subject of the thefts one more time with Aunt Josie. This time, I felt it merited discussing. "Please, Aunt Josie, let me just tell you one thing—I think the thief might be someone from your society."

Aunt Josie busied herself beside my bed, checking my fever, fluffing pillows. "In the times we are living in, people are desperate, Mary Dobbs. People have had plenty and now they are on the verge of losing it all." She looked at me. "So they steal."

"Do you mean you know who's been stealing things? Parthenia does too."

"Not so fast, Mary Dobbs. I saw what being blackmailed did to my parents. I wasn't going to go through it again."

"You're being blackmailed?"

"Threatened. We've received threats on our servants' lives, on our lives too."

That one word took me back to my discussion with Perri. Spalding was threatening her. "Parthenia said she was threatened. She saw who stole the knives, and he grabbed her and threatened her."

"I don't doubt it."

"But she's terrified to say anything."

"She's right to keep her mouth shut."

"But Anna is innocent!"

"Of course she's innocent. That has never been in question." Aunt Josie put a firm hand on my shoulder. "And she is absolutely safe in that Alms House. And Hosea and Cornelius and Parthie are safe here—where we can watch them. Do you understand?" Aunt Josie's face became hard, protective, almost fierce.

In that moment, I did understand. "Someone has stolen things and framed Anna and threatened to hurt her family if anyone denounces him."

"Exactly. So Parthie is absolutely right to keep quiet. Don't try to get anything out of her."

"Anna will be at the Alms House forever."

"She is well taken care of, and no one can get in and harm her. She's safe. Mrs. Clark is well aware of the situation."

"But Parthie knows who did it!"

"Perhaps she knows, but we have no proof. And without proof, what she knows could get her killed." She rubbed her hand on her forehead, and suddenly she seemed old. "When you told me of finding the stolen things in Holden's toolbox, I felt it would be a step toward locating the thief and setting this horrible mess to rest. But, as you know, when we looked, the things were no longer there." She pronounced "no longer" in a tone that reassured me.

"Anna is not in danger at the Alms Houses, I assure you, Mary Dobbs. And Parthie, bless her soul, she can complain all she wants about her work, but she must keep on doing exactly that, so no one will suspect that we are still trying to find the evidence."

I grabbed Aunt Josie in my bear hug. She patted my back, as usual, reserved in her display of affection. "I'm sorry I've been such a pest."

"*Shh*. It's okay. Just realize this is not a penny mystery to solve. It is very serious, and grown-ups who know what they're doing are working on it. Slowly."

"Have there been more homes with articles stolen?"

"Many."

"Then it is most likely a group of people. A crime ring."

Aunt Josie brought her face within inches of mine. "It is absolutely none of your business, you hear?"

This time I understood. "Yes, ma'am."

———

Tuesday afternoon, Perri came by the Chandlers' with other Phi Pis and somehow convinced Aunt Josie that I needed company. Ten girls sat crowded on the floor in my room, jabbering about all the preparations for the Valentine's Dance. Finally Mae Pearl hushed them and said, "Well, girls, we thought it'd be good to do the Bible hour here with Mary Dobbs, since she's the one who got us started on this good habit."

Perri stood up and leaned against the poster of the bed and said, "I have a story to tell you all." In a wavering voice, she recounted being accosted and thinking she had heard her father's voice and seeing the man who rescued her, and then she explained how I had kept assuring her that God would provide and how I'd prayed He would show up in her life in a very personal and dramatic way that could only be Him.

The girls' posture changed as Perri spoke, from a relaxed nonchalant lounging on the floor to sitting up straight and then leaning farther forward with every phrase. When Perri got to the part about Lisa giving her that old photograph and how she had wanted to be in her father's lap more than anything else in the world, Lisa let out a little cry and Mae Pearl started sniffing, and even Macon and Brat and Peggy were dabbing their eyes.

Perri kept on talking—telling of her experience in church on Sunday—and then she said, "And girls, I've been terribly selfish and stubborn and just plain foolish, and I took out my anger on Dobbs." She came and stood beside me and took my hand and said, "And I'm ever so sorry. I really am."

I gave her a nod, and then she read from Matthew, chapter 6, those beautiful verses where Jesus says, "Consider the lilies," and all the while the girls listened, enraptured.

Perri ended by sharing about Coobie's illness and the need for prayer and practical help.

I was thankful that they all considered me too weak to participate, because I had nothing to say. I listened to them as if it were a dream, and I thought about how unfair life was and the irony of being surrounded by a dozen girls whom I had considered merely floozy socialites, hearing enthusiasm in their voices as they talked about God's provision. Even Peggy seemed excited.

But now the topic left me indifferent. Almighty God would not get me back so easily, by convincing a few friends to act excited about Scripture—not even with Perri's amazing story.

As I listened to them, though, I thought of my father and the horrible grief he must harbor inside, along with anger and fear. He'd passed on deadly genes to two of his daughters, and he was being forced once again to watch one die. How in the world would my father get through this?

A momentary warmth of compassion for my father flooded through me, and I was astounded.

————

After two days in bed, I was grouchy, and I took it out on my aunt. "Whenever will Coobie make it down here? They should have tested her sooner. They should have left her in Atlanta last fall!"

"Your parents believed it was wiser to have her at home with them."

"Well, they were wrong. Chicago winters are dangerous. Now look what has happened!"

Aunt Josie got that hard look on her face again, not angry but definitely annoyed. "Mary Dobbs, you are your father's daughter. You're going too fast. The doctors at Piedmont ran tests on Coobie when she was here last summer. The results were compared with those of the doctors in Chicago. Everyone agreed that she needn't stay in Atlanta for the fall, but rather, if her condition weakened, she would come back down south. Your parents worked it all out with me."

"When?"

"When they were here for the revival in June. Your father and mother have been very vigilant about Coobie." She gave her famous sigh. "Now I understand their reasoning. They knew that if you found out about Jackie, you'd start assuming things about Coobie. You're bright; you see things. And sometimes"—here she gave me a wink—"you jump to conclusions. They wanted to spare you that pain. They hoped the different treatments would cure her."

I felt very small in my room that night. I had let myself distrust my parents and blame them for horrible things. Yet all the while, never defending themselves, they were working and planning for Coobie to get the treatment she needed. They had protected us girls so that we wouldn't carry a burden too heavy for our ages. I, most of all, remembered the suffering of Jackie. My parents had seen my deep grief, a grief that never really healed, and they wanted to protect me from projecting the same fate on Coobie. They had known what my reaction would be if I found out that Coobie had the same disease as Jackie, and my responses in Chicago proved them every bit right. Now that I knew, I feared the worst.

Perri

It distressed me greatly to see Dobbs without faith. I knew what she needed, no matter if she declared otherwise—a visit from Hank. As soon as I left the Bible hour on Tuesday, I drove to the post office and sent him a telegram.

> Hank—Dobbs very down. Needs you. Can you come surprise her? Maybe take her to the Valentine's Dance? Please consider it.
> Yours truly, Perri

I visited Dobbs the next afternoon but didn't breathe a word about my telegram. Instead, we talked about Spalding. Dobbs recounted her conversation with Aunt Josie—how someone was threatening her uncle and aunt, how they were protecting Anna by keeping her at the Alms Houses, and how everything seemed to point to Spalding.

With each detail Dobbs revealed, I got angrier and angrier, until finally I said, "I'll stay with Spalding. I'll call him up and apologize and go to the Valentine's Dance with him. I'll pretend I still like him, and I'll figure out a way to prove him guilty! And when that's done, I'll be rid of him forever. I can play my part, and at some point we'll catch him, and maybe other people too. I'm only too happy to help out."

Dobbs was not convinced. "Oh no, Perri. It's dangerous. I saw it on Aunt Josie's face."

"We need proof to stop him, and I'll get it."

"But, Perri, you said you got downright scared when he was mad. There's no telling what he might do if he figures out you are just playing a game with him. And I bet he's working with other people."

But somehow I didn't feel one bit afraid, just convinced of what had to be done. I didn't say it to Dobbs, but I knew something else— I had a Father now who would protect me, wherever I went.

Dobbs

On Saturday afternoon, Mother and Coobie arrived in Atlanta at Terminal Station, and Hosea drove my aunt and uncle there to meet them and take them directly to Piedmont Hospital. I wasn't allowed to see my little sister on account of my recent illness. Parthenia and Cornelius had to practically hold me down to keep me from borrowing the old Ford and driving to the hospital myself. I paced around the house like a pent-up stallion.

When Mother finally got back to my aunt and uncle's house in the late afternoon, we collapsed in each other's arms.

"Sweet Dobbs, I've been worried about you."

"Oh, Mother, I was just a little sick. What matters is Coobie. How is she?"

Mother brushed my hair back from my forehead and took my face in her hands. "You're pale as a ghost."

"Mother! Tell me about Coobie."

"She's weak. The doctors will be observing her for a few days to determine if and when she can start the experimental treatment."

The first words out of my mouth were "It'll cost a fortune!"

"God will provide. He always has, Dobbs."

Before she left for the hospital, she turned to me with a twinkle in her eyes and said, "You have fun tonight."

I wondered what in the world she meant. She had no idea about my date with Andrew Morrison that evening. I had not even had the courage to tell Perri. Honestly, I had thought I would have to cancel, but now I eagerly anticipated the dance—getting out of the house, seeing people, dressing up.

Perhaps because Becca had in a sense been the catalyst to my spiral of despair, she had become kinder to me and insisted I use her dresses for any of my social events. I put on a beautiful deep violet gown that was tight-fitting around the waist and scooped around my neck but cut low in the back. I fastened the pin Andrew had given me in my hair, applied my makeup carefully, and surveyed myself in the mirror. I liked what I saw.

When the doorbell rang, I rushed down the steps, thinking only of how much fun I would have dancing with Andrew Morrison that night.

Uncle Robert opened the door and said in his booming voice, "Well, if it isn't Hank Wilson! What a very pleasant surprise! I had no idea. Come on in!" He gave Hank a pat on the back and left the room.

I froze on the bottom step and felt the color drain from my face.

Hank stood dressed in Holden Singleton's perfectly tailored gray suit, holding an armful of red roses. He grinned as he held them out to me and said, "Happy Valentine's Day, my dear Dobbs! I hope I haven't shocked you too much. You've gone all white."

Mechanically, I took the roses from him. He kissed me softly on the cheek. "You sure look beautiful."

I stared at him, speechless. "Why are you here?"

He stepped back, gave a slight frown, and said, "Perri set it up. She didn't tell you? I guess she wanted to keep it a surprise 'til the end." He shrugged and grinned again. "You must have suspected something because you've gotten ready."

"No, she didn't tell me a thing. I . . . I had no idea."

Then it registered for Hank. "You have another date, don't you?"

I swallowed hard, looked down at the gorgeous roses, which must have cost him a whole week's salary that he didn't have. I swallowed again. "Yes. Yes, I do."

His face fell, and I wanted to rush to him and hug him and hold him tight, but I just kept gripping the bouquet. "I'm sorry, Hank. I didn't know. I had no idea."

"Perri thought you were doing so poorly that I might be able to cheer you up. I see she didn't understand the situation at all. I've embarrassed you. I'll be going." He turned to leave.

"Wait! Hank! Don't go!" I called down the hall, "Parthie! Parthie, can you help me?"

She hurried into the foyer, saw Hank standing there, and turned her eyes down, a smile spreading across her face. "Nice ta see ya, Mista Hank." She curtsied.

"Good to see you too, Parthenia." But he was distracted.

I handed the flowers to Parthenia and instructed, "Please take these roses and put them in a vase."

"Ooh, yes'm, Miz Mary Dobbs. They's bee-u-tee-ful."

When she left, I said, "Hank, thank you for the roses. I don't know what to say." I felt dizzy again, but not from the fever. Hank seemed miles away.

"It wasn't what I thought, was it?" he asked. "You weren't missing me. You're over me, aren't you? That's why you haven't answered my letters."

My heart was beating so hard that even in my confusion I knew for sure I wasn't over Hank Wilson.

"I told you I was afraid of losing you in Atlanta," he said after a moment.

I touched my forehead, which was prickling with perspiration. "Then why did you encourage me to come here, Hank? Why didn't you beg me to stay in Chicago? I would have done it, you know. For you. I would have."

"It wasn't my right to do that. I felt God had something more for you, and if we were meant to be together, the relationship would survive."

"Well, you've been all wrong! I'm way far from God right now and I'm far from you too. It's all been a mistake, and yet, I don't want to go back. It's all so confusing."

"Dobbs, the story isn't over yet."

I heard a car door close, and knew Andrew was approaching. "I can't promise you anything. I just don't know what's going on inside of me. I'm losing my mind, my faith. It's scary. But it's exciting too, to think I can act outside the realm of what I have always believed. I'm sorry for such a horrible confession."

"I'm not sorry. You're being Dobbs—speaking your mind, running ahead with your plans and your dreams. I figure if the Good Lord wants me to catch up with you, He'll speed me up or slow you down. But I know one thing—I'm not trying it on my own."

He held out his hand, took mine, and squeezed it softly. It actually felt like he was squeezing my heart and it was fluttering around. I longed for him to stay, or even to pick me up, sling me over his shoulder like a sack of potatoes, and carry me back to Chicago. But Hank was not one to force himself on another, no matter his convictions. I had always admired that about him.

And so I watched him turn around in the Chandlers' foyer and leave.

CHAPTER
25

Perri

I was no actress, but somehow, I convinced Spalding that I was still crazy about him and willing to follow him wherever he wanted to go. So we attended the Valentine's Dance at the Capitol City Country Club, entering the ballroom hand in hand, as if all was well between us. When Dobbs appeared on Andrew Morrison's arm, I left Spalding and walked across the long ballroom to where Andrew was removing her coat. "I'll be right back," he said and went to check it in the valet room.

I looped my arm through hers and pulled her off to the side of the ballroom. "What in the world are you doing here with Andrew?"

Her face was pale, and she looked like she was on the brink of tears. "I invited him weeks ago."

I gripped her arm more tightly. "Oh, Dobbs! I've messed everything up! I invited Hank, and he came down here, and now, poor thing, who knows where he is. I—"

"He came to the house first, with a bunch of roses, the most beautiful roses you ever did see." Now Dobbs did actually start to cry.

"I'm so sorry. It's my fault! I thought if he surprised you, it'd make you feel better, just to have some time with him."

She was nibbling her lip and wiping a finger under her eyes. "I've hurt him, and I don't know what to do."

"What happened?"

"I was so shocked, and then he figured out real quick that I had another date. And so . . . and so he left, and it was horrible. Him walking down that long driveway, crossing shoulder to shoulder with Andrew as he came up to the door."

I thought she might collapse in my arms. "Dobbs, take a seat. You're still weak." I guided her to one of the lavishly decorated round tables. In a flash, I had made my decision. "Don't think about anything. You just enjoy the dance with Andrew."

She had found a tissue in her purse and was dabbing her eyes and nodding halfheartedly.

I hurried to the bar area, where Spalding was getting drinks. Andrew was there too, and was saying to Spalding, " . . . And I showed up at the house right when her beau, Hank Wilson, was leaving. A very awkward moment."

"Henry Wilson is here? Well, yes, that is strange. And she didn't know?"

"I'm the guilty party," I confessed.

Spalding frowned at me, and Andrew gave a shrug.

"Well, the gentlemanly thing to do is to find Henry and invite him to the dance," Spalding decided.

"Yes, I suppose you're right," Andrew conceded.

"That is precisely what I was thinking too!" I announced. "Will you help me find him, Spalding? I'm not sure where to start."

He narrowed his eyes and then shrugged. "Why not?" He then addressed Andrew. "You just stay with Mary Dobbs."

It actually didn't take long to find Hank. We went to the casual dining room downstairs at the Country Club, where I knew the Chandlers were having dinner with my mother, figuring they could give us an idea of where Hank was—and we found Hank smoking a cigar with Mr. Chandler in the Men's Lounge.

I rushed in and began to apologize to Hank. Mr. Chandler stood up and led me out of the room—women were forbidden in the Men's Lounge—while Spalding took a seat with Hank.

Mr. Chandler chuckled. "Oh, the traumas of youth! Don't you worry about Hank, Anne Perrin. I figured since he came all the way down here, I might as well introduce him to some of my buddies at the club. We might just find him an interview at Coca-Cola. Don't you worry."

"But Dobbs wants him at the dance," I whispered.

Mr. Chandler shook his head. "I can guarantee you that Hank has no desire to be there."

"And Hank's supposed to stay with you this weekend. How terribly awkward."

Mr. Chandler patted me on the back and said, "Anne Perrin, don't worry your pretty little head over this. We men will take care of it."

Spalding left the Men's Lounge, calling over his shoulder, "See you tomorrow, Henry," and then he took my hand and led me back upstairs to the ballroom.

That night Dobbs looked beautiful in the deep violet gown, doubtless another treasure from Becca's closet. We smiled as we danced side by side, but we knew each other perfectly well. We were both completely heartbroken, longing to be with someone else.

Dobbs

The house was quiet when I got home from the dance. I told Andrew good-night under the porte-cochere entranceway, and he kissed me lightly on the lips and thanked me for a delightful evening. I climbed the stairs to my room, feeling very confused. Parthenia had put the vase with Hank's roses on the dresser in my room. Seeing them there, I flopped on my bed and groaned, reviewing the evening in my mind. I'd managed to enjoy the dance with Andrew and danced quite a lot with other boys, but I kept glancing toward the entrance to the ballroom, hoping against hope that Hank would appear and take me away.

Now, I thought of him just downstairs, sleeping in the guest room, and again I longed to tiptoe down the steps and find him there and tell him my heart. But what was in my heart? Only doubt and confusion and other things that would hurt him. I lay awake most of the night, retracing every moment I'd spent with Hank over the past two and a half years. I finally fell asleep around dawn.

"Mary Dobbs! Yoo-hoo! Breakfast time!" I awoke to my aunt's

cheerful voice, but I doubled over with cramps. How in the world could I sit across from Hank at the big table, laden with scrambled eggs and bacon, biscuits and gravy, with the rest of the family looking on, and act as if everything was all right?

"I'm not ready, Aunt Josie! Please start without me. I'll be down in a jiff."

When I got to the table, Hank was not there. But Mother was. "Did you have a good time last night, Mary Dobbs?"

"Yes, Mother. It was okay." From the look on Mother's face, I knew my aunt had filled her in on the details.

"Where's Hank?" I asked.

"He's in his room getting ready for church," Uncle Robert said. "He wants to hear the new preacher at Westminster Presbyterian, Peter Marshall. He's taking the Ford over there."

Hank came back in the kitchen, dressed again in Holden Singleton's suit. "Good morning, Mary Dobbs." His tone was formal and guarded.

"Hello, Hank." It seemed like a hundred awkward years passed between us as my mother and my aunt and my uncle looked on. Finally I jumped to my feet, knocking over my glass of orange juice, and said, "May I please go with you to church, Hank?"

Aunt Josie covered her mouth with a napkin, but I saw her smile.

Hank looked surprised and then shrugged. "Why sure, if you'd like to."

"I'll be ready in three minutes." I dashed upstairs without even offering to clean up my spill, but I don't think the grown-ups minded a bit.

"I'm awfully sorry about last night," I said when we were in the car.

"Don't worry, Mary Dobbs. It wasn't your fault."

"Yes, I know, but—"

"You don't have to explain anything. It's okay." Then Hank changed the subject and began talking about Peter Marshall.

All through the service he sat next to me, never even touching my hand or brushing his shoulder against mine. He seemed mesmerized by the young preacher, whose sermon was powerful and moving—he preached on the subject of overcoming doubt—and several times, I got a chill. It seemed as if he were preaching directly at me.

I could almost imagine Hank standing in that very spot, delivering an eloquent sermon. I wanted to grab his hand and tell him that, but instead I kept mine folded in my lap, and honestly, I think Hank forgot I was sitting next to him.

When the service finished, Hank said, "Someday, Dobbs, I pray the Lord will give me the poise of Peter Marshall and the ability to communicate God's Word in such a powerful way. It's what I want with all my heart."

And I knew it was absolutely true. I did not doubt Hank Wilson's sentiments for me, but I knew his real love was the living God.

After Sunday lunch, Mother went to Piedmont Hospital to be with Coobie. "I'll come back later in the afternoon, and if the doctor says she's strong enough, you can go see her."

Mae Pearl, Peggy, Perri, and I went to the Alms Houses. I asked Hank to join us, but he said, "No thank you, Dobbs. I have some things to talk over with your uncle. But it's a mighty fine thing you girls are doing."

Mae Pearl drove us there in her coupe, following along behind Hosea and Cornelius and Parthenia in the Ford.

Perri had her camera with her, and she spent the afternoon photographing what she called "spring around the corner," using the new film Philip had sent her—brought down by Hank—to take many photos of nature. In the fields, the first little wildflowers were dressing the grass in yellow and white, and buds were forming on every tree.

Peggy and Mae Pearl found Mrs. Clark and talked to her about another project that was percolating in Mae Pearl's mind, and I felt strangely out of place, with nothing to do.

I found my way to Anna's room at length and stood outside, watching her cuddling Parthenia in her lap. Hosea had his hand on her shoulder and every once in a while, he'd reach over and brush her cheek lovingly. Cornelius was busy trying to repair something on Anna's shelf.

After a few minutes, Anna noticed me and called out, "Come on in for a visit, Miz Mary Dobbs."

"Anna's safe at the Alms House," Aunt Josie had assured me. Yes, she was safe and somehow satisfied. Parthenia bubbled over with stories of how Perri was teaching her how to take real photographs. Then she told about Hank bringing me the prettiest bouquet of roses that she'd ever seen.

When it was time to leave, Anna placed her calloused hand on mine, looked me in the eyes, and said, "Don't you worry none about us. Miz Chandler knows jus' what to do, and I trust her with all our lives."

"Yes, ma'am. I know."

Late in the afternoon, Hosea drove Mother and me to Piedmont Hospital.

Coobie looked so small in the hospital bed, her pale face peeking out from under the crisp white sheets. Her black curls hung limply around her, and there was a sickly yellowish hue to her skin. But when I walked in the room, her face lit up and she cried, "Dobbsy!" Then she immediately collapsed in a fit of coughing.

Mother went to her side. "Remember, whisper, honey. Whisper."

I stayed with her for several hours. We played game after game of Old Maid, and I tried so hard not to see Jackie sitting in the bed. Once in a while, I even shook my head to get rid of the image. We didn't talk much, but nothing could have covered up Coobie's deep, throaty cough.

I watched my mother with Coobie, admiring her gentleness as she wiped Coobie's forehead with a cool cloth or patted around Coobie's mouth after one of my sister's coughing fits. And I remembered the same mannerisms with Jackie. I wondered how Mother had held up through the excruciating pain of accepting Father's child, growing to love her, nursing her through a terrible disease, and watching her die.

Later that evening, sitting with my mother in her room at the Chandlers', I said, "I'm so sorry you have to do this again, Mother."

She knew exactly what I meant.

"I keep asking God over and over again, Why? Why?"

Mother's voice was a bare whisper. "That's not the right question, Mary Dobbs. You'll drive yourself crazy asking that question."

"So what are you supposed to ask?" I said bitterly.

Mother shrugged. "Honey, I've learned to ask not *why* but *what?* 'Now that I'm in this impossible place, Lord, what do I do next?' "

"Does God always tell you what to do next?" I asked incredulously.

She gave a little chuckle and nodded. "I usually have a pretty good idea, if I take time to listen." She gathered me up in her arms the way she used to do when I was a child, on the old sofa at home. "It's okay to ask questions, sweetheart. You're going through some rough waters. God is bigger than your questions. Don't you worry about that."

I nestled in my mother's comfort and thought about my father. His life was a paradox of sin and forgiveness, faith and unrelenting penitence, and a zeal that had led him straight into sin and back out again, but had left a complex trail of broken relationships with his sister and parents.

There was no middle ground for my father, and Aunt Josie said I was just like him.

There I was, swinging wildly on a branch, like a monkey at the zoo. On the left was over-the-top religious zeal, and on the right was a young woman who was cynical and bitter and so very angry.

I wondered if there was a flat, stable place where faith mattered most but didn't swing precariously on emotions and events. Mother had a faith like that. So did Anna.

I found myself wanting it too.

———

The doctor met with Mother and me on Monday after school was out. He spoke gently as he went over Coobie's treatment, but his words sounded sterile and cold to me.

"As you know, Mrs. Dillard, there is no known cure for your daughter's disease. The treatment we are proposing is experimental, begun only a year ago. It lasts for two months. For the first month, your daughter will be in a completely sterile room. Only family is allowed to visit. Of the five children treated last year, two have gotten remarkably better, with almost no signs of illness remaining." He gave us a stiff smile.

Mother nodded.

I blurted out, "And the three others? What has happened to the other three children?"

The doctor cleared his throat twice. "The three other children succumbed to the illness, I am sorry to say."

"They died? They died within a year of the treatment?"

He nodded.

"Could it be the treatment itself that killed them?"

"Mary Dobbs," Mother whispered, "lower your voice."

The doctor's face relaxed. "It's all right. I know this news is very upsetting. The truth is that we only took children who were in the final stages of the disease. So honestly, we don't know if it was the treatment or the disease that killed them."

"And the cost?" This Mother whispered.

"Two thousand dollars, initially."

Mother reached out and took my hand to steady herself. He might as well have said two million. No one had that kind of money in the middle of the Depression. Even my aunt and uncle had very little cash, just land and animals and gardens and generous hearts.

Regaining her composure, Mother asked, "And when would you hope to begin the treatments?"

"Immediately."

The doctor nodded his head and left us there in the hospital waiting room.

"We'll get the money, Mother. I know we will somehow."

"Yes, of course it will work out." But her voice was raspy with raw emotion. "Your aunt and uncle are paying for the hospital stay right now."

Hosea drove us back home in silence. I don't know what Mother was doing, but I was calculating in my little mind, thinking about the Phi Pis and their prayers for Coobie and wondering if their brand new faith was strong enough for this kind of trial.

Perri

Hank and Dobbs appeared at my house late on Monday afternoon. Dobbs's face was so pale and distraught when I met them at the door that I knew she didn't have good news. When she fell into my arms, I looked up at Hank for a hint of what was happening. He was wearing my father's suit, and that took my breath away.

"She's just come from seeing Coobie at Piedmont. The doctor wants to start the treatment immediately." He waited for Dobbs to chime in, but she had pulled herself from my arms and stood woodenly, almost as if she were pasted there, like a paper doll. "The treatment is cost prohibitive. They need to come up with two thousand dollars by the end of March."

I kept hearing Dobbs telling her stories. *"God will provide. He always provides."* And then I saw her during the long past week. *"I don't believe anymore. He didn't provide for Jackie, and now he's ripping us apart again with Coobie. I don't believe anymore."*

Hank took care of her as if she were his little sister, but long ago I had recognized the depth of love he had for Mary Dobbs Dillard. I prayed she would come back to her faith, and I prayed she would come back to her Hank.

After they left, I went into my room, took the tin of pennies and turned it over on the floor, listening in a trance to the crash and then

325

jingle of the copper and nickel and silver, watching them spinning and twirling and finally settling all over the floor. Hundreds and hundreds of pennies, now interspersed with nickels and dimes and quarters. Barbara and Irvin and Mamma, who had been listening to the radio in the little den, heard the noise and rushed into the bedroom.

"What in the world . . . ?" Mamma began, but then she saw the determination on my face, and she smiled at me, put her arms around my siblings, and said, "Let's finish listening to *Little Orphan Annie.*"

I began to count the pennies and then the nickels and the dimes and the quarters. I knew at that precise moment, like Dobbs used to know things, what I was supposed to do with the money in the tin and the money I still had from my earnings at Mr. Saxton's and from my own photography sales—I'd give it all to Dobbs to help pay for Coobie's treatment.

So I stayed on the floor counting the change and scribbling figures in my little notebook and then letting the coins slip from my hands back into the tin. By the time Barbara came into the room, ready for bed, I had reached a hundred and forty-three dollars. It was a start.

I stared at the four framed photos of our old home, which now hung on the wall in this room. I brushed my hand over them and figuratively waved good-bye. I let the dream of once again owning the house my father and grandfather built die softly beside me. But somehow, it seemed like a very sweet death.

———

On Tuesday, I told the Seminary girls about the Dillards' predicament. Peggy immediately called a special meeting of the Phi Pis after school; she was at her best leading troops into battle, planning strategy. "Okay, girls, I propose we set up a dance marathon on a Saturday in March to raise money for Coobie."

"Oh, that is just a perfect idea! It's all the rage now!" said Macon, and to illustrate, she started dancing around the room with a make-believe partner, shaking her red hair and moving her hands all around.

Gradually the other girls joined in, giggling and twirling around and around. Later, they buzzed with ideas for other projects they could set up during the month to help raise money, and Mae Pearl leaned over and whispered to me, "Perri, you were right. It just might work."

Dobbs

Hank stayed in Atlanta all that week, looking for a job. Every day I greeted him at breakfast and we chatted together at times, but it seemed so very artificial, as if we were both on our tiptoes, trying to decipher the other's thoughts, the other's heart. Every day, I measured Hank against Atlanta, Andrew Morrison, Georgia Tech, and the country club.

I had wanted both worlds, and then, suddenly, it seemed as if I could have them.

It was on the last Saturday in February—a glorious day, sunny and unseasonably warm, spring perfuming the property. Hank found me helping Parthenia in the kitchen. "May I borrow Mary Dobbs for a little while, Parthenia? I need to talk to her."

Parthenia gave a big, openmouthed smile, curtsied, and said, "Why of course you kin, Mista Hank. She's only here keepin' me company. I kin fix lunch all by myself."

His expression told me he had something serious on his mind. It scared and excited me at the same time.

We walked toward the lake, side by side, and when we got to the bench where we'd sat the first day Hank was in Atlanta, he motioned for me to sit down. He stood there in front of me, a half frown on his face. "I've been offered a job," he began. "With Coca-Cola. Here in Atlanta."

I gave a little gasp, and my eyes got wide.

"Your uncle's done so much for me, setting me up with interviews, and well, it looks like they want to hire me. It won't pay much at first, but there's opportunity to move up in the company."

"Oh, Hank! That's wonderful! It's the best news I've heard in a long, long time!" I almost got up to hug him, but then I realized that he wasn't smiling. He still had that serious look on his face, and I didn't know if he even heard me.

"So I wanted to know what you're thinking about us, Mary Dobbs. About you and me. I won't lie to you. This job isn't what I want the most, but it is a fine opportunity, and I'll take it, if . . . if you're thinking of staying down here. I've heard you're considering college." His voice cracked the slightest bit. "What I'm trying to say is that I'm still mighty fond of you, Dobbs, and I told you I'd wait for you, and I will. Only, if you're not interested in me and you're not staying in Atlanta, well, I don't think there's much here for me."

Miss Emma had asked me twice to consider attending Agnes Scott College in Atlanta. Now it would all work out so well. I could stay with my aunt and uncle, go to college, and still have Hank right beside me. "Oh, it's perfect. Perfect! I was so afraid we'd be poor forever, but if you work for Coke and stay in Atlanta . . . it will be divine!"

He gave me a stiff smile, and then I realized what I'd said. "Not divine, Hank. But it would be mighty fine."

He sat down on the bench beside me, and I kept imagining our life with money, with friends, us living close to Perri. Hank in Atlanta. Hank listening to Dr. Marshall. Hank influencing the important business people. Hank with me. I reached over, squeezed his hand, and thought to myself that some things were working out right after all.

———

"Isn't it over-the-top wonderful, Perri? Hank's gotten a job with Coca-Cola. He's staying in Atlanta, and it's got all kinds of potential to turn into something big."

"That's a good thing, I suppose," Perri said, but she didn't sound one bit excited for me. "I never got the feeling that Hank was very interested in making a lot of money."

"No, he's not, but he's needed a job, and he wants to be with me, and now that I'm thinking of staying in Atlanta next year and going to Agnes Scott, well, it just makes so much sense."

"It doesn't make a lick of sense to me."

I was shocked. "What do you mean?"

"Isn't he going to Bible school up in Chicago? Is he just gonna up and quit?"

"No, no . . . I guess he'll just postpone his studies." Honestly, I had not given that a thought.

Perri was unconvinced. "I don't know much about religion and people having a calling from the Lord—isn't that how you've always put it?—but I've seen Hank with those kids at the revival, and I've heard him preach and seen the fire in his eyes, and if he isn't a called man, I don't know who is."

I flinched the slightest bit. "He can still preach on weekends if he wants. And he mightn't work for Coca-Cola for years and years. Just for a while."

"He's decided to stay in Atlanta. For you."

"Yes, I told you—he said that he wouldn't take the job if I wasn't still interested in him. But I am. I love him. You know that, Perri. I've always loved him."

"Yes." She crossed her arms over her chest and tilted her head. "Only, this doesn't seem like love. It seems like something else. It seems, I don't know, calculated—like how I used to be."

Her words stung. "No, Perri. It's not like that. I promise, it's not."

She took me by the shoulders and stared straight into my eyes with her see-through-green ones, wrinkled her brow, and said, "You know I just want what's best for you and Hank. That's all."

Perri

Little by little during the next weeks, the pennies and nickels and dimes and even quarters came in as the Phi Pis went to work raising money for Coobie. Mr. Saxton gave me film, and I took more photos than I thought possible. My photos of the girls at Washington Seminary became so popular that two other schools asked me to photograph their students. On both occasions Parthenia accompanied me. She'd wave to the students and motion them to come over to our little booth and then point to the handwritten sign she'd made that said *Cash for Coobie* and go on and on about what a wonderful little girl Coobie was, and before they knew it, those students were posing for a photograph and paying me a dime.

Macon had the swell idea of asking the boys to pay a nickel for each cookie or brownie they ate while pop-calling at the Phi Pi homes. Andrew, Sam, and even Spalding spread the word, and our houses—even mine—were overflowing with eager college guys who wanted to help a sick little girl.

Hosea brought over a bagful of cash that he'd gotten from the people at his church, and one Sunday St. Luke's took up a special offering for Coobie.

At a Phi Pi meeting, Peggy said, "Didn't you tell us that Dobbs's mother is a genius seamstress? What if we hired her to make our May Fete gowns instead of going to Rich's? That money would help Coobie."

And before Peggy could bat her fake eyelashes, every senior Phi Pi went to Mrs. Dillard and asked her to make formal gowns for May Day. So Dobbs's mother sat in the chair by Coobie's bed during the day and at the Chandlers' house at night, all the while sewing beautiful gowns for us.

The dance marathon on a Saturday in mid-March brought boys from Oglethorpe, Tech, Emory, and Boys High and girls from Washington Seminary, North Avenue Presbyterian School for Girls, Girls High, and Agnes Scott. We charged a dollar per person to enter, and Lisa got loads of sponsors to give money. Mae Pearl and Sam danced for five hours, and Spalding and I lasted for six and a half, but many other couples danced straight through the day and night. We also auctioned off dates to every imaginable thing, and to my great surprise, I was "bought" three times. Spalding did not protest. In fact, his father contributed three hundred dollars to the Cash for Coobie fund.

There's nothing like uniting for a common goal to draw girls together. While we baked brownies and set up for the dance marathon and collected money during pop-calling, a sweet camaraderie formed between us all, and there was no jealousy or rivalry or pettiness. We were focused on getting two thousand dollars for Coobie.

As the end of March neared, Lisa counted the money and announced, "One thousand two hundred twenty-one dollars and fifty-two cents. That's not counting the money we owe Mrs. Dillard for our dresses, which comes to four hundred and sixty dollars. And the Chandlers have already paid three hundred dollars to start the treatment, so . . ." She paused and calculated. "We're only missing eighteen dollars and forty-eight cents."

The girls let out a huge yelp, and I ran to tell Mary Dobbs. God had done it! He had done something seemingly impossible.

Dobbs

The treatments made Coobie violently ill to the point where she couldn't even talk.

There were days in school when I could barely concentrate on my lessons. Mother spent every day with Coobie, and after school, I relieved her so that she could go back to the Chandlers', where she sewed dresses for lots of the Seminary girls. I knew the money was trickling in, but honestly, I was too tired to notice.

All I noticed was my little sister wasting away before my eyes.

Hank started his job with Coke and, for the time being, stayed at the Chandlers'. We passed each other in the house and ate meals with the rest of the family just as if Hank had become my protective big brother. No romance, no complicity, just a shroud of worry beating down on us all. He'd come home in the evenings, all sweaty and worn out, and then he'd go out to help Hosea in the fields or Aunt Josie with household affairs. He was everywhere and nowhere, taking care of us from behind the scenes.

When Becca's baby finally arrived, a little girl, her safe arrival perked up the spirits of Aunt Josie and Uncle Robert, and Mother, who went right to work sewing her an adorable dress from leftover pink material from Macon's May Fete gown. For several days, my aunt and uncle and mother navigated the halls of Piedmont Hospital, going from the maternity ward, where life began, to the ward where terribly ill children awaited death.

One day, Parthenia found me in the darkroom, staring again at that photograph of me with my sisters from the summer. She curtsied, holding her hands behind her back, and approached me cautiously. "Ya know Miz Chandler done let me keep a good bit of the jars of peaches and jams and otha' things that we canned this summer for my family, and I hope you won't think it's wrong, but Dellareen had a sale for Coobie ova' at Johnson Town, and I done took all those jars that was left and then some of the women baked things and we had a fine turnout and sold jus' 'bout everything." She brought her hands from behind her back and handed me a handkerchief that she'd gathered into a pouch. "It's plum full of nickels and dimes, Miz Mary Dobbs. Ain't a lot, but it's all for Miz Coobie's treatment."

"Oh, Parthie! Thank you so much." I could not get out another word. She let me hug her, and I just held her for the longest time.

Then she turned her dark face up and pleaded, "I know there's no way I kin go an' see Miz Coobie, but I's written her this letter. Kin you please take it to her? I miss her awfully much."

"Of course, Parthie. Of course." And I hugged her again.

———

They stopped the treatments for five days, and we were thrilled when Coobie gained enough strength to talk again. I was alone with her one afternoon when she asked me, "Am I dying, Dobbsy? Is that what's happenin' to me?"

Taken aback, I tried to make my voice sound light and unconcerned. "Of course not, Coobs. The doctors are giving you a treatment to make you well."

"It's jus' making me real sick. Feels like I'm dying."

"I'm so sorry. Sometimes we feel worse before we feel better. But it's a treatment to cure you."

"Only it might not work."

"Why do you say that?"

"Just seems like that might be the case, is all."

"You don't need to think that way, Coobs."

She reached over her little hand and covered mine and said, "You don't need to pretend I'm getting better. I know I'm not. I can feel it way down in my bones."

I swallowed hard and could not make my mouth open to pronounce some reassuring word.

"But don't worry, Sis. If I die, I'll go be with Jesus. It's just like Father always says, 'For to me to live is Christ and to die is gain.'"

Tears puddled in my eyes, but I refused to let them slip out. I mashed my lips together and turned my head to look at the blank wall. But my spirit was screaming for all it was worth. *No! No, no, no, no, no! It won't happen like that. No!*

———

The payment for the treatment was due on March 30. The day before, Perri had grabbed me at school and reported all the money that had been raised in the course of five weeks. I was overwhelmed at the generosity and ingenuity of these girls. And the sacrifice. I knew what Perri had done, even though she never breathed a word to me. I thought of her years of saving pennies and of the countless photos she'd taken in Atlanta. I knew all about her tin of pennies and her dreams to buy back her house, and here it was being spent on my little sister.

My little sister who wasn't responding well to the treatments. My little sister staring hollow-eyed at the blank white walls.

I took the slip of paper that Perri had given me up to my room and looked at the carefully scrawled figures.

$1,221.52—*raised through the dance marathon and other Cash for Coobie monies*
$ 460.00—*paid to Mrs. Dillard for dresses*
$ 300.00—*paid as an advance to Piedmont by Chandlers*
$1,981.52—*grand total*

Below the final figure, Perri had written *God has provided again!*

My heart started beating hard, hurting, cramping. I got out Parthenia's handkerchief of loose change and dumped it on the bed. I began to count the coins, slowly, methodically, almost resignedly. I knew what the amount would be, and I was right.

$18.48.

A God who provides down to the last stinking penny.

"God showed up in a way I could understand—through a photograph. Just what I needed."

"And you're showing up for me in a sack filled with pennies."

I tore the paper with the figures on it into tiny bits and scattered them on the floor, and I let the hatred in my heart all come flooding out at once. Not a warm stream of love and provision but of hate.

I screamed into the room, "You didn't provide! It's all a lie. Everyone's worked so hard, and Mother's worked her fingers to the bone, and we don't sleep, and people pray and Father and Frances call every day with worry in their voices, and we're going to pay all this money for nothing."

Now I was sobbing. "For nothing, Lord, because she's dying! Why! Why in the world would you let this happen? Why would you bring in the exact amount of money, only to let her die?"

"Don't ask why, *ask* what.*"*

Mother.

I sank to my knees and buried my head in my hands and in a

whisper, I said out loud, "Okay, then. I give up. You win. You're bigger; you're stronger; you can do whatever you want. So *what* am I supposed to do, Lord? If you can provide exactly two thousand dollars for my little sister's treatment, surely you can let me know what I'm supposed to do next."

I stayed on my knees for a long time, until all the hate and disappointment and fury had finally leaked out. I felt like Jacob, wrestling with God's angel, and at the end of the night, there was only one word from God Almighty. *Believe*.

Perri

There's something about new faith that makes everything seem easy.
After God showed up and provided for me, and then for Coobie, I
floated into April on a cloud of fluffy optimism. Coobie was going
to be fine, and Dobbs was going to be fine, and somehow Spalding
would be found out, and God would even get our house back in a way
I could not imagine.

It seemed to work that way in all of Dobbs's stories.

I guess God gives us naïve belief at first so that we'll march ahead
in our fresh trust. The adrenalin that pumped through all the Phi Pis
after the success of raising money for Coobie made us feel powerful
and indestructible.

So when Dobbs greeted me in the hallway of Washington Seminary
on April 2 looking pale and sunken, I couldn't understand her. God
had showed her through Parthenia's pennies that everything was going
to be all right.

"Coobie knows she's dying," she whispered to me after English
class. "She keeps talking to me about it. At first, I reassured her that
the treatments might make her feel worse, but they would ultimately
make her better. But now . . ." Her face was all drawn and hollow,
and I felt alarmed, a little prick of fear, like when a siren screamed
too close to home, and my heart took a little leap and then twittered
inside for a moment.

"No, but God's going to heal her, Dobbs. He's shown you that."

She gathered up her books and held them tight against her chest,
and we walked outside, squinting in the brilliant sun. "He didn't show

me that He'd heal Coobie, Perri. He just reminded me that He is God, and I am not."

"Oh," I said, surprised by the squeak in my voice.

"I can't do this, Perri. It's too hard to watch her waste away. It's just too hard."

I felt this deep, piercing dread, like a bolt of lightning stabbing through the clouds, and just as quickly, I saw Daddy's dangling legs. Then we both dropped our books on the manicured lawn of Washington Seminary, fell into each other's arms, and wept.

Dobbs

It was a horrible thing to watch someone I loved dying and to know that it was in part my fault. Atlanta was killing Hank. He'd been working at Coke for just over a month when I realized something. He wasn't smiling anymore. He wasn't teasing Parthenia or picking on Irvin and Barbara when we went over to the Singletons'. He wrote notes to Coobie and had me deliver them to her, but they weren't silly like I would have expected. He talked at dinner with Uncle Robert about Coca-Cola, but there was no passion in his voice, no excitement, and when he looked at me, I felt a horrible longing in his eyes, but something else too. Something like death.

At first, I reasoned that with him getting used to his new job and me spending so much time with Coobie, it was no wonder things with Hank seemed a little strained. But gradually I admitted the ugly truth. I was a selfish, prideful girl who wanted Hank to take a job for me and my happiness and to fit into my plans. Me, me, me. When I finally got up the nerve to ask him about it, his honesty cut me to the quick.

We were walking down by the lake on an afternoon in early April. There were three little ducklings, tiny, squawking as they followed their mother, making miniscule waves on the smooth water. A weeping willow hung over the water, the big gnarled roots twisting up and around, and the willow's leaves made a perfect canopy over the bench where I stopped. I squinted up at Hank through the kaleidoscope of colors the sun made in the leaves.

"You don't like your job, do you, Hank?"

Hank stood opposite me, his legs braced against the back of the stone bench. "No." He turned his blue eyes toward mine. "But I want you, Mary Dobbs, and I guess I'd be willing to do just about anything to get you. I thought I wouldn't. I thought I'd be able to live okay without you."

I guess his words should have made my heart soar. Instead, it plummeted, and as it hit the ground, I saw the truth. "You'd give up your calling for me? Even if it went against all you felt God was asking you to do?"

"Love is a mighty powerful force, isn't it, Dobbs? People sacrifice all kinds of things for love." Then he whispered, "Love is strong as death."

I swallowed hard. Hank loved me enough to give up the very thing God had called him to do. So I could have everything I wanted: not the opportunity to tell others about God, nothing lofty like that anymore. I just wanted comfort and Hank. Was that right?

Perri's words came back to me then. *That doesn't seem like love. It seems calculated.*

"You can't do that, Hank. I won't let you give up what you really love, for me. You love God; you love preaching His Word; you love explaining truth to needy kids."

"Can't imagine any of it without you beside me, Dobbs. That's the thing. That's the bare truth."

I thought of that photograph of Perri in her father's lap and of little Parthenia handing me a handkerchief filled with coins and of the voice of the Lord last week that whispered to me, *Believe.* And I knew. I knew it as much as I had known that Atlanta would change me, and that Perri and I would become best friends.

"This isn't where you belong, Hank. I was wrong to encourage you to take this job. I've been so horribly selfish."

The look he gave me was one of profound sadness and intense

relief. "It wasn't just you being selfish, Mary Dobbs. I was the one who decided to stay. I wanted you back, so I went against my good sense, went against what my Lord was saying."

"You belong in Chicago."

He nodded, very slowly. "You're right, Dobbs. This isn't my place. I need to be back at Moody, back at the church."

I had a huge knot in my throat, and I couldn't swallow. It seemed like every spark between us had fizzled and died in Atlanta.

"I 'spect there's a whole lotta fine young men in Atlanta looking for a job at Coke. And your uncle says I can most likely get on with them again up at the World's Fair in Chicago in May."

"You've already talked to Uncle Robert?"

"He's not blind, Mary Dobbs. He knows this job's not for me, and if you know it too . . ." He shrugged. "Well, you can't blame a fellow for trying as hard as he could."

Wait for me, Hank! Wait! I wanted to scream, my heart beating so hard it hurt. "It's Coobie. It's everything. I'm so confused."

"I know it. It'll be better for me to be gone. One less thing on your mind."

And despite his many declarations of love for me, I knew what he meant. He was letting me go, and it was right. Horribly right.

He left on the train for Chicago a few days later, and no one tried to talk him out of it. "His heart wasn't in the job here," Mother said. "His place is in Chicago."

"He tried it for me," I said numbly.

"I know. And then he saw that you weren't ready."

"I've been awful to him, wanting him to wait until I made up my mind about so many things."

"One thing at a time," said Mother. "One thing at a time."

———

Father wrote to us almost every day. We received thick envelopes in which he included a letter for Mother, one for Coobie, and one for me. Often Frances had written a letter too. Father was different on paper than in real life. I guess I would have expected his letters to be filled with bold, brash statements about God's power and punctuated with exclamation points. But it wasn't that way at all. He wrote to me about how Aunt Josie dressed him up and dragged him around the property in a wagon when he was a little kid, and then about ramblings of his life as a boy, and about how beautiful Mother was—"like a mirage," he wrote—the first time he laid eyes on her. And he said his five women—that's what he called us—had made his life the happiest, richest in the world.

He never preached a sermon to me, never mentioned how horrible I'd been to him, or asked repeatedly for forgiveness for his past; in fact, I don't think he said much about God at all. What I read was a man reflecting on his life and family, but not in that penitent way that became overbearing and pity-filled. And he didn't sound worried for Coobie—those thoughts I'm sure he saved for Mother. But he did tell me that as soon as Frances's school was out, they were coming to Atlanta to stay indefinitely.

Up until then, *indefinitely* did not seem to be a word in Father's vocabulary. He was a man of action and purpose and planning, and he stuck inexorably to his schedule. But not now. He was impatient to come, impatient to see Coobie. He did not say this, but I knew—he wanted to be with his daughter before she died.

———

Coobie's questions about death broke my heart, but they also plunged me into action, action I desperately needed to keep my mind from hopping around between Hank and Andrew and college and stolen things and Coobie's fate. Determined to give my little sister something better to look at than drab blank walls, I got Cornelius to make a big wooden board onto which I thumbtacked all kinds of photographs—ones taken during the summer of Frances and Coobie and me, several that Parthenia had taken recently, and one that Perri had clicked of Hank with Coobie on his back when Hank first came to Atlanta last year. When I tacked it on, I just stared and stared at the photo—Hank's back hunched up and his arms in the air, and Coobie giggling, her arms thrown around his neck. *Hank*.

I even wrote out several Bible verses that were happy and hopeful and tacked them to the board too.

When Aunt Josie saw the board, she said, "Why, Mary Dobbs, what a marvelous idea! And that gives me an idea too." Then Aunt Josie cut flowers from the garden so that Coobie would no longer stare at the bare white walls but at vases brimming with gardenias and roses and hydrangeas, white and blue and deep, bright pink.

The nurse balked at first when I arrived with the vases and photo board. She went to find the doctor and returned with a startled look on her face. "The doctor says she can have flowers now."

"You seem surprised."

She shrugged. "It's not normal protocol for this treatment." She cleared her throat, gave me a sympathetic smile, and added, "But it's all experimental. Take her flowers. And the photos."

I put the vases on the windowsill in Coobie's hospital room and propped the photo board on a chair right by the bed, and I would have given anything to have a photo of the expression on Coobie's face. For just a second, she got her wonderfully mischievous look in those dark eyes, eyes that sparkled in that magical moment. A smile twittered on her lips, and she brought her skinny little arm out from under the sheets and pointed to the photo of her on Hank's back and said, "He's the best bucking bronco ever!"

And then she said something that made me want to twirl around like Ginger Rogers with Fred Astaire. "Dobbsy, I can't wait to go out in the backyard with Parthenia, down by the lake, and count the fireflies when the sky gets dark. She says it's just about as delicious as ice cream."

I gave her hand a quick squeeze and said, "Won't that be swell? In no time at all, I'll bet you'll be down there together."

Before I left, she asked me to tack up her letter from Parthenia along with three she'd received from Father. As I waved good-bye, she was staring at the board with a soft expression on her face. I think it was a look of faith, hope, and love, all mixed in together.

That evening Aunt Josie came into my room, and in her way of immediately getting down to business, said, "Uncle Robert and I want to give you a party for your graduation."

I had been fiddling with my hair—which desperately needed trimming—and staring out the window toward the barn, thinking of Coobie. I turned from the window. "A party for me?"

"Yes. It's the custom for all the Washington Seminary senior girls. It would bring me great pleasure."

"But the money!" Those were the first words out of my mouth. Then, "You and Uncle Robert have already helped so incredibly much—letting me stay here, buying me clothes, paying for Washington Seminary. And now you're helping with Coobie's hospital expenses and keeping practically the whole family here and—"

"We would be honored to do it." The way she said it made me slow way down in my argument. She pronounced those words as if they were really important. "Mary Dobbs, you've become like a daughter to me. You are so full of life and hope and goodness, and you've just spilt it all over the house. Your uncle and I think a party would liven things up a bit for everyone, and we mentioned it to Ginnie. She likes the idea." Aunt Josie smiled and added, "As I knew she would."

I gave a half smile, imagining very well Mother becoming enthusiastic about a party.

I said, "Okay, Aunt Josie. I would be delighted for you and Uncle Robert to give me a graduation party."

———

The next day, as soon as I returned from school, Parthenia came galloping up to me, all excited, her little bare black legs sticking out from her dress and a whole bunch of wildflowers in her hand. "She's done put on her spring frock, she has!" she announced to me gaily.

"Who, Parthie?"

"The pretty little hill down by the lake! She's all dressed in violets, and it's the most beautiful thing you could ever hope to see."

She grabbed my hand, and I found myself traipsing beside her, past the barn and the servants' quarters and down the little hill to the lake, and then she said, "Turn around and look for yourself."

Sure enough, the hill was covered with tiny delicate purple flowers and a smattering of bright yellow dandelions and bluebonnets. From a distance, it did look like an enormous skirt, billowed out over the green backdrop.

Parthenia started twirling around and giggling and saying, "She's all decked out in her finery, and we're giving a party! It's been so long since there's been a party here. Ever since they accused poor Mama. But now . . . ! Now we gonna decorate and make it all so lovely."

Then she got a sly look on her face. "And Miz Perri says that I can take photos with her camera—that's what she says. I'm going to three other graduation teas, too, and taking the photos. So by the time your party comes along, well, I'll practically be an expert."

I thought of the photos that Parthenia had taken and which were now in Coobie's hospital room. "You do have an eye for photography. I'm glad Perri is giving you this chance."

But all that I really wanted in the whole world was for Parthenia and Coobie to be frolicking around the grounds of the Chandler house, hand in hand, with Mother and Father and Hosea and Anna looking on. I wanted God to provide in that way.

Perri

All during the second half of April, in addition to being invited to all the senior Seminary girls' graduation parties—teas and soirées given in honor of each graduating girl—I also got hired, through Mr. Saxton, to be the photographer at many of these affairs. Spalding was always my date for the soirées, but I often left him, to take photos. I learned to be inconspicuous at the parties, taking candid shots of people. In truth, I had another reason to go unnoticed. I kept my camera poised, ready to snap a photo of Spalding or anyone else who happened to slip a silver fork or spoon into his pocket.

Mrs. Chandler allowed Parthenia to go with me, and she was a quick learner and a great help. Everything I had taught her when she watched me in the darkroom and at the Alms Houses, asking never-ending questions, she applied when we were with our clients. And Parthenia provided entertainment, bantering with the girls about all the wonderful things Cornelius built or how pretty my photographs of her were, so the girls were always in the best humor for their photos. And when the colored servants at those parties passed by with silver trays filled with tiny sandwiches and petit fours and offered them to Parthenia, she got "tickled pink."

On the way home from the parties, she'd be all bubbling over with enthusiasm, and then she'd say something like, "But jus' you wait, Miz Perri. Not a one of these fancy parties will hold a candle to what Miz Chandler's got planned for Miz Mary Dobbs. You jus' wait and see if I ain't right."

Dobbs and I were in the darkroom one evening, developing the photos from Brat's graduation tea. "Would you look at this," I said, as I finished one roll. "These are Parthenia's photos. I let her use my East-man Kodak at Brat's party. She's got talent for such a young girl. And about as much mischief as Coobie. Why, she snuck right up to Brat's brother and his steady and took a picture of them kissing in the woods. And they never noticed a thing."

Dobbs grinned. "I'm not surprised."

I held up the photograph to prove my point. Parthenia had been lying on her stomach, under a bush, she claimed, and had shot the photo from the ground up so that the young couple looked elongated, their legs wider and their bodies narrowing and their heads so small, they were completely out of proportion. But they were kissing for all they were worth, and that made the photo seem just right.

———

A letter from Philip arrived, and I felt a quick flush come to my cheeks when I read it.

> *Dear Perri,*
>
>   *Mary Dobbs has invited Luke and me to the graduation party that the Chandlers are giving for her at the beginning of May. We were hoping to come down for it. If I could be so presumptuous, I wonder, would you be my date? We could take pictures together and maybe share a dance or two.*
>
>   *Your photographer friend,*
>   *Philip*

I could think of nothing I'd enjoy more than being Philip's date for the graduation party. But I was still pretending to be pinned to Spalding, and so I wrote to Philip on the back of a postcard photograph of me and Parthenia that we'd printed for our business:

> *My dear fellow photographer friend,*
>
>   *How delightful to hear that you will be coming to Atlanta soon. I look forward to seeing you and Luke. And I appreciate your invitation more than I can say. Unfortunately, I've already got a date for the Chandlers' party, but if you are staying for a few days, I'd love to show you around Atlanta. Maybe we could go for ice cream at Jacobs' Drugstore.*
>
>   *Shooting away!*
>   *Perri*

Dobbs

April was another paradox for me—divided between Piedmont Hospital and parties, the smell of anesthesia and rubbing alcohol and perfume and rich foods. When I was with the Phi Pis at the fancy tea parties for us girls and our mothers and grandmothers, I felt buoyed up by their enthusiasm. They talked of the future and they talked of

Coobie and they had absolute faith that the treatments she was undergoing would be successful.

Twice, Mother accompanied me to a tea party, and she fit in perfectly with the other mothers, wearing a beautiful deep blue suit that she had stitched for herself. Aunt Josie had insisted that Mother and I both go to the beauty salon, and Mother emerged with her long hair bobbed and styled like mine, and she was fairly glowing with the pleasure of it. When the hair stylist had commented, "You look more like sisters than mother and daughter," she gave the sweetest laugh, a light and happy melody in my ears.

Andrew Morrison took me to every single soirée. There was something intoxicating for me about putting on the lovely party dresses—some from Becca and a few that Mother made me from material Aunt Josie provided. I savored the feel of the cool satin and the soft silk and the crisp cotton. I liked how Andrew's eyes lit up when I walked down the stairs at the Chandlers' house in my gown, and I liked being with him. He had a serious side, and we talked about faith and our dreams for the future, but he also had the power to make me forget my worries and fears for Coobie for a few hours while I was swinging around in his arms and he was smiling down at me with his eager eyes and a boyish grin that melted my heart.

But only for a while.

Then I came back to Coobie, and every time I walked into that hospital room, reality took my breath away. Coobie was not getting better.

One day when Mother and I entered her room, Coobie was lying on her side. I thought she was asleep, but she heard us and whispered, "I'm awake." A cough. "Could you help me write—" another cough and she tried to sit up in bed—"a letter to Parthie?"

Slowly, with a breath between each word, sometimes each syllable, she dictated. "Dear Parthenia, I miss you. Thank you for your letter. I read it every day and I pray the same prayer too. I can't wait to count the fireflies and see the wildflowers on the hill with you. Love, Coobie."

How I wanted Coobie to see that field of flowers with Parthenia!

I wondered if maybe, perhaps, the doctor would allow Coobie to leave the hospital—if only for one brief hour. The letters and photos cheered her up. Wouldn't time in the sun with all the flowers around her do much more?

That night, when Uncle Robert and Aunt Josie had left to go see Becca's little baby girl and Mother and I were sitting on the screened porch, I dared to whisper, "Mother, if anything happens to Coobie, I'm afraid I'll hate God and stop believing forever." I sat on my hands, swung my feet like a nervous little girl, and whispered, "Won't you too?"

I watched her closely, wishing I had not let my doubts escape. Mother's skilled hands set down the pale blue dress she was hemming, and she stared out into the dusk, where crickets were making their strange, persistent music and fireflies gave tiny explosions of light. She scooted closer to me on the little loveseat and looked me straight in the eyes—black eyes staring into black eyes.

"My dear Mary Dobbs, faith doesn't work that way. You don't just believe when you get everything you want. That's not our choice. We share in the sufferings of others, Mary Dobbs. We bear the burdens together. We take what comes, and we believe. It's not down here that it will all be equal and okay. It's later. Here, well, the Lord promised us sometimes we will have hardship and suffering. He also promised He'd never leave us. His presence, His holy presence is with us here.

"And later, *there*, that's when the tears will be wiped away. Later."

I hated Mother's answer, but I knew deep down it was the absolute truth. "I don't understand God at all!" I whispered, a little ferociously. "He provided for all those poor people in Georgia that I didn't really care a thing about. He gave them food through us, Mother, and He won't heal Coobie. I just don't understand Him at all!"

Mother smiled over at me, that winsome smile of wisdom and patience and, I thought, heartbreak. She cupped my chin in her hand and said, "Mary Dobbs Dillard, never have you pronounced a truer statement. Our part is to get to know God, as a Father and a friend. But to understand Him? His ways are far past our understanding. Infinitely far." Then she took me in her arms and held me against her. And in a broken voice, she said, "We trust Him because He loves us, even when we don't understand."

Later that evening, I took out my Bible, turned to Genesis 22, and read the familiar passage about God asking Abraham to sacrifice his only son, Isaac. And Abraham had obeyed, but just as he was going to slay his only son, an angel hollered down and said "Stop," and Abraham saw a ram caught in the bushes.

I always thought of God like that—providing in the nick of time— believing in Him got me something: a miracle, or at least help. God owed me something.

But with Coobie, it wasn't working. The money had all come in, but she wasn't improving. And finally it hit me. Selfishly, I wanted a formula to fit God into, something that could be explained the way Perri helped me in mathematics class. It had seemed almost easy—the way He'd provided for us so many times before. But Mother was right. God was past understanding, and He was asking me to trust Him as a good God and Father before I knew there would be a ram.

Mother and Anna and Father were completely convinced that God was at work wherever they happened to be—an Alms House or a hospital or a tea party or a revival filled with destitute people. And it wasn't so important that everything worked out the way they wanted—they just needed to trust that God knew what He was doing.

I kept thinking back to the first thing Anna told me—that after they'd tried everything, she figured the Good Lord had her at the Alms Houses for a reason.

God could provide—no doubt about it—but would He?

I dropped down on my knees, and I gave God my little sister— figuratively, but as well as I knew how to do. "I trust you to know what is best."

Down on my knees, by my bed, immobile, it seemed nonetheless that I moved one inch forward in what Father called "the wisdom that cometh from above."

I was still on my knees when I whispered, "Don't leave me, Jesus. Please don't leave me now."

Perri

As usual, along with the parties, April was devoted to preparations for May Day. The entire school was involved in writing skits and rehearsing the dances all around the theme of the seasons of the year, borrowed from Greek mythology. I thought that Dobbs would brandish her Bible and scold us for reenacting mythology, but she had truly changed, and she participated as one of the maidens in the Winter Dance. Mae Pearl got the main role, and as she practiced and practiced, she indeed looked like a movie star and a ballerina, leaping and pirouetting and spreading spring to everyone as she tossed handfuls of rose petals across the stage.

She was also voted to be on the May Court, which came as no surprise to anyone. The May Court was all about beauty, just as sororities were about good looks and personality. Such things had mattered so much to me for so long, and often in past years I had dreamed of being on the May Court. So when Peggy announced that I was Queen of May Day—she smiled and lifted an empty hand, as if she held a champagne goblet in it, and said, "I toast you, Queen Perri, our dear girl of a thousand dates"—I should have been over-the-top, deliriously happy. But things had changed. What had once seemed so important did not anymore.

There was enthusiastic clapping, and I thanked the girls ever so much, but my cheeks were on fire, and I wondered what Dobbs would say.

"It's marvelous, Perri," she told me the next day at school. "You're all around the most beautiful girl in our class, and you deserve it."

Seeing my frown, she narrowed her eyes and said, "It's not the most important thing in the world, granted, but you should enjoy the honor." Then she twirled a strand of her short black hair around a finger, a habit she'd developed ever since she'd had her mane cut, and said, "I've been thinking a lot about what Jesus says about laughing and weeping. And, you know, Jesus loved a good party. Weddings were His favorite, but I think He'd be okay with May Day, Greek mythology and all."

To my relief, she didn't say a word about how Jesus viewed weeping, because I didn't want her to think about poor Coobie, who according to Dobbs, was nothing more than skin and bones and limp black curls.

Dobbs

Every day Parthenia, holding the letter Coobie had written her, asked me how much longer until Coobie could come see the wild-flowers, and every day I tried to think of something positive to say. But finally exasperated, Parthie said, "I don't see how those doctors know nothin' 'bout what's good for her. Why, if you leave her cooped up in bed for two whole months, she shore will get weak and pale and ever so grouchy and tired. Didn't they eva' read *The Secret Garden?* Miz Chandler let my mama borrow that book, and she read it to me when I was five, and now I read it myself two more times. You kin learn a lot from a book, and here's what I done learned. That wild boy, Dickon, knew about how to make that sick boy, Colin, well—he sho' nuf did—and waddn't letting him stay all sassy and mad in his bed. Uh-uhn. He needed to go outside.

"And that's what Miz Coobie needs—sunshine and air and flowers and even . . ." Here her eyes got wide and sparkly. "Even horse manure. Did you know Coobie likes the smell of horse manure?"

I did not know that, but it didn't surprise me a bit.

———

The next time I saw the doctor alone, I decided to follow Parthenia's advice. "I know it's not protocol, but, sir, she doesn't seem to be getting better—worse, really—and could a few hours of sunshine hurt her? You said the treatment lasted two months. It's been two months. What are your plans from here?"

"Miss Dillard," he said and gave a very long sigh, "your sister is quite ill." He rubbed his hands across his eyes. "Very weak."

Then, to my intense relief and amazement, after a thoughtful pause, he added, "But perhaps you're right. Perhaps the sunshine and familiar surroundings will do her good. All I know is that I've run out of options for the time being."

He glanced around as if what he was about to say was secretive. "We'll have more effective treatments for this disease in five years, ten years at the most. We're making progress. I'm so sorry that we're not further along for your sister."

"Maybe love will keep her alive."

He shrugged. At last he said, "It can't hurt to try, Miss Dillard."

"So we can take her for the day?"

"No. Not the day. I'll discharge her. Tomorrow. For right now, I'm afraid we've done all we can. Give her sunshine and flowers," he said. Then he added, "And love."

————

We brought her home on Tuesday at noon. Hosea drove so slowly it was as if he thought a bump in the road might kill her. Coobie lay in Mother's lap, covered with a blanket. When we got to the Chandler house, Aunt Josie and Uncle Robert and Cornelius and Parthenia were standing out under the trees, waving.

And right beside them were my father and Frances.

Parthenia rushed up to the car, leaned in the window, and thrust a handful of wildflowers into Coobie's lap. Neither little girl said a thing, but they grinned at each other for a long, long time.

Then Father came and lifted Coobie out of the car, and she buried her head in his chest.

"I've missed you so much, my Coobie."

"I've missed you something awful too, Father." And it seemed like the most natural thing in the world for me to lace my hand through Father's arm and hold on tight as we walked into the house.

I don't even remember one thing about exams. I took them, we all did, but my focus was on getting home every day, and going out on the porch where Coobie was stretched out on the chaise lounge, lying under a crisp cotton sheet, and Parthenia was curled up on the floor beside her, both little girls whispering and giggling. The cough wasn't completely gone, but it no longer sounded like a death sentence.

On those afternoons, I often found Father sitting outside under an oak tree, discussing politics with Uncle Robert or walking hand in hand with Mamma around the property or even working out in the garden right beside Aunt Josie and Parthenia and Hosea and Cornelius. Sometimes I'd even blink a few times to make sure of what I was seeing—my father looking happy and comfortable and at home at his sister's house in Atlanta.

One afternoon, I asked him, "Father, whatever happened to Irene Brown? Did she really use the money to pay off her debtors? Did she move from Atlanta and start over?"

Father shook his head. "She paid off her debts and moved up to be closer to Jackie. But she never found steady work and eventually fell back into her former occupation. Her health deteriorated. Your mother and I went to visit her whenever we got the chance, but she never got over losing Jackie. I think she gave up. She died one year after Jackie."

"I'm sorry, Father. Sorry about it all."

"Me too."

I waited for him to say something about sin, but instead he just put one arm around my shoulder and held me there.

I knew Coobie was getting stronger when she asked me one day, "Why'd Hank have to go back to Chicago?" She was propped up in

Becca's bed with five different pillows surrounding her. "He told me in his letters he got a swell job here with Coca-Cola."

"He did. But then he decided that wasn't the best thing. That he should be back at Bible school and preaching at church."

"You don't love him anymore, do you, Dobbsy?"

"Oh, I do. I care very much about Hank."

"Caring for somebody isn't necessarily loving somebody, and Parthie says you weren't behaving properly to him. She said you were ignoring him when he went an' got the job for you. An' now you're spending all your time with that other boy, the one who gave you the fancy hair clip."

"Coobie!"

"That's what she said, and I believe Parthenia."

What could I say to that?

I had invited Hank to the party my aunt and uncle were giving for me—how could I not invite him? But he wrote to say that since he had been back in Chicago for less than a month, he did not think it wise to come back down to Atlanta, for "many different reasons." I knew he was right, and I suppose I felt relieved, but it hurt to see it in writing.

Coobie was furious with me when I told her Hank would not be coming to the party. "If anybody can make me feel better, it's Hank! Why'd you have to go and chase him away?"

That tugged at my heart a lot, because more than anything else in the whole wide world, I wanted Coobie to get better.

Cornelius repaired an old wheelchair that my grandmother had used during her last year of life. Coobie sat in it and Parthenia pushed her down toward the lake. From a distance they could have been Dickon and Colin, reincarnated out of the pages of *The Secret Garden*, on their own quest for health and life, looking at the wildflowers on the hill.

Lisa Young's parents gave a party—a hayride at their farm—on the evening before May Day. Perri had begged for Andrew and me to ride to the party with her and Spalding. They showed up at the Chandlers' right on time, Perri calling out to me. "Hey, Dobbs! Andrew? Y'all here?"

Parthenia and Coobie and Andrew and I were sitting on the screened porch, sipping iced tea and playing Old Maid.

"Come on out here," I hollered.

They found us on the porch, and Perri went over and gave Coobie a kiss on the forehead, and then she said, "Hey, Parthenia."

Parthie gave her classic curtsy and smiled up at Perri. "Hello, Miz Perri. You shore does look mighty pretty tonight."

"Thank you, Parthenia. Have you met Spalding?"

My breath caught a bit when I realized Parthenia might fall to pieces as she stood face-to-face with Spalding, but she simply batted her eyes, gave her coquettish smile, and curtsied again. "I have never had the pleasure of meeting you, sir. But I've seen you sometimes at parties."

Spalding laughed and said, "Well, it's good to meet you, Parthenia. I've heard all kinds of nice things about you."

Parthenia got embarrassed and put her hand over her mouth to hide her huge smile.

Perri rolled her eyes. "We need to go."

"Okay, y'all go on," I said. "I'm coming in a sec." When Andrew and Perri and Spalding had left the porch, I knelt down in front of Parthenia and looked her straight in the eyes. "You've seen Perri's boyfriend before?"

"Oh yes, ma'am. Loads of times. He's almost always at the parties. I've even taken his picture some. He is the most handsome young man I believe I have ever seen." There was not a hint of fear in her eyes.

I thought about this for a long time as I sat beside Andrew in the back of Spalding's red convertible coupe. If it wasn't Spalding Smith's photo that had scared Parthenia, whose was it?

Perri

Spalding and I rode with Dobbs and Andrew and three other couples in a wagon overflowing with hay and pulled by two mules. We laughed and made light conversation as the mules toured us around the Youngs' plantation. Then we ate barbecued pork and corn on the cob and baked beans and peach cobbler topped with homemade vanilla ice cream.

Stuffed and content, Dobbs, Lisa, Brat, Peggy, and I lay down on the quilts that were spread out under a huge tent and gabbed about May Day while the boys sauntered off to play some kind of game.

When the band began to play, the boys came back and found us. Right away, I noticed the smell of alcohol on Spalding's breath. Ever since Prohibition had been overturned in December, it was lots easier to sneak beer and spirits into the parties.

"You've been drinking."

He smiled. "Not much. Let's dance."

The band was marvelous, and for thirty minutes, maybe an hour, we danced with all the other couples, and I felt safe there, in the crowd. Parthenia had politely turned down my offer to come to this party to help me photograph, preferring to stay with Coobie, and Dobbs seemed distracted by so many other things, so I asked Mae Pearl, and she agreed. We took turns—she'd dance with Sam while Spalding went and got us drinks and I snapped photos, and then we traded. Mae Pearl thought it was "simply over the top" to take photos, even though she hardly knew a thing about it.

As Spalding and I were slow dancing, I glanced over to where she was sitting. She lifted the Zeiss Contax, put on a flashbulb, and pointed it straight in our faces, and boom! She and I caught each other's eyes and laughed, and then Spalding pulled me closer, but I pretended for just a moment that I was dancing with Philip, who'd be coming down to Atlanta in just three days.

"I'm burning up, Perri," Spalding said. "Too many people under this tent. Let's take a walk."

"I'm tired, Spalding. I don't feel like taking a walk right now."

He put his face next to mine. "Come on, girl. Just for a minute."

He grinned, his eyes just the slightest bit drooping, his speech a little slurred. "I hear they have the biggest pig in the county over in the barn."

Reluctantly, I followed him away from the crowd. The music from the band still reverberated loudly as we walked inside the barn. Several horses nickered, and I heard the clucking of chickens. As we walked farther back, sure enough, enclosed in a stall was the biggest pig I had ever seen. "He's kind of disgusting," I said. "And it stinks in here. Let's go back."

Spalding laughed a bit too loudly, and that's when I knew he was truly intoxicated. "Oh, not yet, Perri. The fun's just beginning." He put one arm around my waist and, with the other, began to unbutton my blouse.

"Stop it! You're drunk!" I shoved his hand away.

"I'm not too drunk to know what I want. I want it now." He pulled me closer to him.

I struggled away. "Stop it! You do not own me, Spalding Smith, and I'm not afraid of you."

Now he was gripping my wrist so tightly that I gave a little yelp of pain. "You should be."

"Why do you say such horrible things? Are you insane or is it just the liquor?"

"I've got my reasons. Very good reasons."

It struck me then that Spalding had lost all inhibitions, and that perhaps I could get the truth out of him. "What reasons?"

"Reasons," he slurred. "I have mine and you have yours. You've known it all along. Our life together is a compromise. One big compromise."

"You don't really care about me at all, do you?"

He leaned over me and the smell of alcohol hit me in the face. "Of course I care, Perri." He fingered my blouse again. "I have a great affection for you."

"Just as you do for your car and your golf clubs."

"Something like that."

"Why have you done this?"

"Perri, I've only done what you wanted."

"No. It's not true. I didn't seek you out. You came to me at my house, right after Daddy died. Why did you come? Tell me."

"I needed you, Perri." He held me close. "We needed you. We needed your house."

"My house!"

Spalding grabbed for my shirt again.

I scooted away from him, wriggling free of his grasp. "What are you talking about?"

Spalding shook his head a little, as if trying to clear his mind, then he leaned toward me and whispered, "Those with a keen sense of business can see these things coming."

"What do you mean, 'see things coming'?"

"It doesn't matter."

Then I said, "I know! You're the thief. You're the one who stole all those things from the parties. And then you hid them at our house! Anna didn't steal those things, did she? It was you!"

This Spalding had not expected. He yanked my shoulders and began shaking me. "Shut up! Shut up, you spoiled little tramp."

From out of nowhere, a flashbulb went off, and there was sweet little Mae Pearl, trembling like a leaf, her pale blue eyes wide as Mamma's demitasse saucers. She was clutching the camera in her hands, fumbling with a new flashbulb.

She clicked the shutter, and again the flash went off. "You leave her alone, Spalding Smith!"

Spalding began to laugh. "Mae Pearl, put that thing down."

"I won't. I've heard what you said. You're horrible, Spalding!"

He let go of me and took a step toward her. Mae Pearl started backing toward the barn door. He swung his arm around and hit her hard in the face, knocking her to the ground. The camera fell beside her. "You heard nothing! Nothing!"

I screamed and knelt by her side. "Mae Pearl!" Her eyes were closed, and a tiny trickle of blood was on her left temple. "What have you done, Spalding? You've hurt Mae Pearl!"

That seemed to sober Spalding up, and he bent down. "I'm sorry. I didn't mean it, Mae Pearl."

I buttoned my blouse. "I'm going to get help."

But before I could budge, Sam Durand appeared. "Hey, have you guys seen Mae Pearl? She just disappeared, and I—" He saw her lying on the ground. "What happened?"

I looked at Spalding as we both leaned over Mae Pearl. His eyes were so hard that I shivered. He turned to Sam. "Perri and I were taking a stroll and heard Mae Pearl scream. She must have tripped in the dark and fell. She's got a bad bump on her head."

I was too stunned to disagree.

Sam lifted Mae Pearl's head and tried to revive her. Her eyes fluttered open, and Spalding bent down over her and said, "Are you all right, Mae Pearl? Goodness, you gave us a fright." But I knew he was whispering some threat, too, as he helped her stand.

I tried to break away from him, but he never let go of my arm. When Sam continued toward the Youngs' house with Mae Pearl, Spalding held me back and whispered, "You keep your mouth shut! She fell. You hear me? She tripped and fell."

"You're a monster," I seethed. "Let me go."

"You better do what I say." He released my hand and said, "It would be a mighty shame if anyone else were to have an accident."

I hurried up to the Youngs' house and found the only real thing injured about Mae Pearl was her pride. She whispered to me from where she lay on a chaise lounge, "He doesn't scare me one bit! You develop my photos, and we'll see who's afraid of whom."

In spite of the circumstances, I could not help but smile.

Seeing Spalding's condition, Andrew drove him home, and Dobbs and I got a ride with Sam and Mae Pearl. We didn't say much on the ride home, but when Sam let us out at the Chandlers', Mae Pearl called after us, "I'll see you tomorrow. And bring those photos with you."

I had called Mamma to inform her I'd be spending the night with Dobbs, and I rushed to the darkroom, with Dobbs on my heels. "What in the world is the matter with you, Perri?"

"You'll see. You'll see."

As we developed the photos, I explained the whole incident to Dobbs. "He practically admitted he stole those things and that he somehow knew that Daddy was going to commit suicide. It's so horrible." An hour later, the photos lay in the tray, gradually turning into reality, and there it was, blurry, out of focus, but nonetheless truth. Spalding holding my arm, shaking me, and me wincing.

Dobbs looked at the photos and said, "I'm so very sorry it happened, Perri. And it was sure brave of Mae Pearl. But all this proves is that Spalding has a bad temper when he's drunk."

The next morning, Mae Pearl showed up at school with a small bandage on her temple, but otherwise, she pronounced herself fine. In the rush of preparing for all the May Day activities later that afternoon, she and I had no time to talk alone. I watched her to see if she looked afraid, but her pretty eyes sparkled with something more like resolve.

She played her role in May Day perfectly, and every time someone asked her about the accident the night before, she repeated the same story. "I saw Perri and Spalding leave the dance floor and I had the silly idea of following and getting a few candid shots—that's what Perri calls them. And I had that old bulky camera in my hands and wouldn't you know, I tripped right on a big ol' root and fell flat on my face."

And because Mae Pearl was an actress, everyone believed her. Only, I thought to myself, if they'd been thinking straight, they'd have known that graceful Mae Pearl had never tripped on a thing in her life. But she told her story and played her part in the backyard of Washington Seminary, which was once again brimming with guests.

The afternoon light was perfect as they crowned me May Queen and the Maidens danced around me and put a laurel wreath on my head. And I smiled as everyone applauded. I smiled and swallowed and breathed and batted back any tears that threatened. But the only person I really saw the whole afternoon was Spalding Smith, his gaze following my every move. And he didn't look mean or cruel. He looked absolutely terrified.

Later I realized that Mae Pearl's performance at May Day was of little importance to her. She saved her best performance until that night, when the grounds were empty of guests and all the Seminary girls had made their way home. Alone with me, she asked, "Did you get to develop the film?"

"Yes, Dobbs and I did it last night."

"Then let's go now to the police. I've made up my mind. I'll tell them everything I heard."

"Spalding will deny it, and he's threatened more accidents."

"I told you I'm not afraid of him."

"Mae Pearl, this whole affair is very dangerous. It could turn out badly for the Chandlers' servants if we aren't careful."

"But Spalding won't know what we're doing! He's heard me repeat my story loads of times today. He won't suspect anything." Then she turned to me, hands on her hips, and said, "Anyway, you've been saying it lately—we don't have to be afraid, because the Good Lord is watching over us."

I just nodded, wide-eyed, at Mae Pearl.

So I drove us to the police station in the Buick, and Mae Pearl and I repeated our story to the policeman, Officer Withers. He had a funny look on his long, skinny face, much of which was taken up by a thick moustache. I couldn't quite interpret what I saw in his eyes, but it worried me nonetheless. We showed the photos to him and told him about Spalding threatening me and hitting Mae Pearl and our certainty that Spalding was involved in the thefts. Officer Withers nodded and listened, and when Mae Pearl was through, he said, "I'd like to ask Miss Singleton a few questions alone."

Mae Pearl furrowed her brow, and I shrugged, and she said, "I'll wait for you out at the entrance."

Officer Withers took me into an office, closed the door, offered me a cup of coffee, which I refused, and said, "Miss Singleton, you and your friend, Miss McFadden, claim that Spalding Smith is responsible for a series of thefts that occurred last year, items stolen from the homes of families who were hosting parties. Is that correct?"

"Yes, sir."

He took out a cigarette, lit it, and leaned back in his chair. "I'd like to ask you a few questions. Do you have a problem with that?"

"No, it's okay."

"Were you at the Valentine's Dance at the Chandler residence in February 1933?"

"Yes, sir."

"Were you at the party given a week later—" he shuffled through a few papers—"at Becca Chandler Fitten's house?"

"Yes, sir."

"I know you have been through a particularly traumatic time this past year after your father's death. I understand that you and your father were quite close and that he often confided in you about financial issues."

"I was used to doing finances with my father."

"How would you describe your father's state of mind in the weeks preceding his death?"

I frowned and wrinkled my brow. "What do you mean?"

"Was he overly concerned about finances? Worried? Desperate?"

"Desperate people do desperate things." Mr. Robinson's words slithered into my mind.

I thought of Daddy's drawn face, the way he looked worried most of the time. "He was as concerned as everyone else in America, I'd say, sir."

"Desperate for money, perhaps?"

"No!" I was beginning to feel a little panic creeping up my spine.

"I find this all extremely interesting." He crushed out his cigarette, leaned back in his chair, and put the fingers from each hand together, making a bridge. "You see, Miss Singleton, earlier today I had a visit from Mr. Spalding Smith."

That caused me to sit up straight.

"Strange, isn't it? His story was quite different from the one you and Miss McFadden related. He also told me about an argument you had with him last night, over stolen items. Mr. Smith claims that both you and your father were stealing costly items from homes during social gatherings; he claims your father hid these things in your house and that you knew where. Is this true, Miss Singleton?"

I felt my pulse throbbing in my temple and stared at the policeman. "That's preposterous! No one has ever found the missing items—certainly not at my house."

Except for Dobbs, in Daddy's toolbox.

The policeman bent down, retrieved a shoe box, and opened the lid. Inside was what appeared to be every single item stolen from the Chandlers—the pearl-handled knives, the jewelry, the silver. I thought I might faint.

"Is it not true that Mr. Smith has been asked by his father to watch over your house? He claims he found all this as he was helping your family clean out the house but didn't come to the authorities immediately so as not to deepen your shame and grief."

"He's lying about it all! He stole everything—not my father."

"Miss Singleton, Mr. Smith has an airtight alibi. He has never been to Becca Chandler Fitten's house. Mrs. Fitten has confirmed this. Nor to three of the other parties where other thefts occurred last February. But either you or your father was present at each one."

He looked down at his notes, ruffling papers around on his desk. "Spalding Smith says you will do anything to protect your family name, to get your house back. He feels that other stolen goods are hidden somewhere on the property, although he has not been able to find them."

I kept staring at the pearl-handled knives.

"Mr. Smith hoped you would come forward and confess to your father's crimes. He says he didn't want to rush you but has been trying to convince you to turn in these items that were found where you'd hidden them—in your father's toolbox. He says you were arguing with him about bringing the stolen things to the police last night."

"It's a lie!" I felt dizzy and couldn't imagine how this man could believe such a crazy story. *Perhaps it's no crazier than your own.*

Daddy did not steal things.

Was he desperate? Yes? Was he in danger of losing everything? Yes. Did he steal things? No! Impossible.

I stood up quickly. "I would like to go now. I won't answer any more of your questions until I have a lawyer." I needed to talk to my mother. "You have no proof of these things!"

"Not yet, Miss Singleton. Not yet."

When I told Mae Pearl about the interview and the accusations, she said, "The nerve of Spalding! Well, we'll just have to prove him wrong, that's all. He's desperate, making up lies, trying to cover his hide. We'll think of something."

"I've never seen you like this, Mae Pearl. You're so . . . so—" I searched for the word—"unafraid to confront."

"Heavens, I'm surprising myself and I can't believe it's me talking. But I do know we have to prove what Spalding has done."

Before I let Mae Pearl off at her house, I said, "Please don't say anything to Mary Dobbs yet. We'll talk to her after her party. I don't want her worrying about me right now. I want her to enjoy everything tomorrow night."

Back on Club Drive I pulled Mamma outside, and I paced back and forth, back and forth, as I frantically told her everything about what Spalding had said and done at the hayride and then about Mae Pearl and my visit to the police station and of Spalding having gone down earlier and of the way he accused Daddy and me.

Gradually I saw an unfamiliar emotion install itself on Mamma's face. Anger. When I finished, she said, "Good heavens, Perri! And here I thought he was a charming young man. Why didn't you tell me of your suspicions earlier?"

"You liked him, and I wanted it to work out, for it to all be okay with him. I thought he cared for me, and I thought we were congenial."

Mamma narrowed her eyes. "You thought he had loads of money and would provide for us?"

"Yes."

"Perri, I never expected you to carry everything. Goodness, what made you feel this way? Your father would be deeply grieved to know that you felt you had to provide for us. We work at this together." Mamma took me by the shoulders and shook me lightly. "Have I ever asked you to solve the problems?"

"No, Mamma, but I thought it was too hard for you."

"Too hard? Of course it was too hard, but we do what we have to! Did you not see how thankful I was for your salary this summer and fall? Did you not understand it was enough? We all contributed. All of us. It wasn't up to you, Perri. It's never been up to you."

I thought back to my first reaction after Daddy's death: *Nothing will ever be okay again, unless I make it okay. It's up to me now.*

"I'm so sorry, Mamma."

I fell into Mamma's arms, and I let her hold me tight with the moon looking down on us, the crickets chirping, and I thought I even heard a nightingale singing its sweet song of love.

Later, as we sat in the lawn chairs, I asked, "Whatever are we going to do?"

I felt an immense relief in asking her that question. I had always viewed my mother as fragile and weak, but now I realized that Mamma had been the one to hold Daddy together for so many years, and she had gritted her teeth and held things together for Barbara and Irvin and me once he was gone.

She calmly said, "We'll call a lawyer, and I'll get in touch with Bill

Robinson. He'll explain what Spalding's father is doing with the house. He'll explain it all. Goodness, to think that boy was sneaking around stealing things. And I suppose dear Mary Dobbs was telling the truth all along."

"I think so, Mamma."

She wrapped her arms around me and held me for a long time. "I'm sorry I let you carry this burden. I didn't mean to."

"It wasn't your fault, Mamma, it was mine. I thought I could do it all. I can't." Then I added, "Only, Mamma, don't talk to the lawyer and Mr. Robinson yet. Let's get through Mary Dobbs's party tomorrow. I can't bear to spoil that."

"Will Spalding be there?"

"Not as my date—that's for sure. And I can't imagine that he'd show up after all that's happened, but don't worry, Mamma. In case he does, I've got a few ideas of how to handle him."

"Anne Perrin Singleton, you remember what I said. We're in this together. You understand?"

"Yes, ma'am."

I think I looked at my mother for the first time that night, looked past the image I had formed of her to who she really was: a very brave woman, a survivor. I had seen glimpses of the truth in the past year, but now I breathed it in and accepted it.

Daddy had been my confidant, so when he died, I just took his role upon myself. I tried to let Mamma be the sweet socialite with not a problem in the world. How completely foolish! She had loads of problems, and she sought help from Mr. and Mrs. Chandler and Mr. and Mrs. Robinson and plenty of other adults.

We are in this together.

I had made a huge mess of everything. In trying to save my family I was closer than ever to ruining us all.

Dobbs

I spent the day getting ready for the party, forcing myself not to think about Hank. In fact, I had decided that I would think of nothing sad on that evening. I owed it to my aunt and uncle, to everyone, to enjoy the party.

Parthenia seemed skittish all day long, flitting from one thing to another but not really paying attention. Twice she spilt a bowl of condiments that Aunt Josie had prepared, and the second time it happened, she looked as if she might burst into tears.

"Whatever is the matter, Parthie?" I asked. "You don't have to worry. It's just a party."

She nodded at me, chewed on her lip, and said, "Yes'm, Miz Mary Dobbs. I guess I'm jus' too excited, all nerves and such."

Coobie was determined to stay outside for the whole party, so Cornelius decorated the wheelchair with balloons and bright pillows, and then he took a chaise lounge down by the lake and found a shaded spot where Coobie could lie on it and still be in the midst of the guests.

Mother had made lovely pale blue gowns for Frances, Coobie, and herself, and for me, a strapless black satin gown that hugged me around the bodice and fanned out wide down to my ankles. Along the top of the dress she'd sewn a beautiful pearly material, and Aunt Josie let me wear her necklace of real pearls and little pearl earrings.

Father wore his best suit, and his shirt was already soaked in perspiration before the night had even begun. That made me smile, reminding me of him at the revivals. He came up to me before the party and gave me a beautiful corsage made of little white rosebuds and tiny purple flowers. "Josie said it's proper etiquette for the honoree to have one, and I wanted to do the right thing."

I stood on my tiptoes and kissed my father on the cheek.

Hosea and Cornelius were dressed in black tuxedos, and Parthenia had on her black servant's outfit. Jimmy and Dellareen had even come over to help, and they were wearing their fanciest uniforms. Andrew came early, too, and helped install the tables for the guests and set up another table with food and drinks in the little white cottage down by the lake.

It was a lovely party, something from another world. All my friends were there with dates. When Perri came in with Spalding following her, I got a quick chill. She caught my eye, and motioned with her hands for me to stay calm. Then she smiled so sweetly and looked so pretty, in a strapless pale yellow chiffon gown, that I made myself concentrate on the other guests. Spalding had on his signature Madras pants and white loafers, but something about him didn't look confident or charming—more distracted.

Becca arrived with her husband and her two little boys and the baby, and she greeted me warmly and actually said, "You look lovely, Mary Dobbs." She even went over and gave my father a hug and Mother a kiss on the cheek. At first they didn't say much, but the next time I saw them, Becca and her husband and Mother and Father were all sitting at the same table. Father had one of the little boys on his knees and Mother was holding Becca's baby and they all were chatting happily.

Mrs. Singleton had a date with a man I had seen at St. Luke's, and she looked to me that night how she must have looked before Mr. Singleton's death: pretty and petite, green eyes, so much like Perri's, sparkling. There was a lightness about her, as light as the material on her strapless green gown. Barbara looked all grown up in pink taffeta, and she was wearing loads of makeup, but it suited her. The moment she arrived, she grabbed Frances and they went over and talked to several of the boys from Boys High.

Mr. and Mrs. Robinson and Mr. and Mrs. McFadden were there, along with several couples from St. Luke's and parents of Washington Seminary girls. Oh, there must have been a hundred people spread out across the back lawn and down by the lake. There were tea lights on every table, and the food was marvelous.

Although Andrew was my date, I hardly spent any time with him. Every time we started to take a walk by the lake or sit at a little table or even chat with Mae Pearl and Sam, Aunt Josie came to introduce me to another person. Andrew, who didn't seem to mind one bit, would greet the guest, listen for a while, and then squeeze my hand and whisper, "I'll be back in a little while."

Philip and Luke Hendrick showed up around eight o'clock, both of their faces about as red as their hair. Philip handed me a bouquet of flowers and said, "I'm sorry we're late, Mary Dobbs. We missed our connection on the train this morning, but don't you worry. We'll make up for it and take some swell photographs."

I had no doubt they would.

As often as not, Perri was with them. They'd come over and instruct me to "smile for the camera," my arms around my parents or Coobie and Frances or other guests. One time Perri stood beside me, and we both stuck little wildflowers in our hair, and Philip took a photo of that.

Coobie was lying on the chaise lounge, Parthenia and Mother watching her like hawks as people stopped by to wish her well.

After the dinner had been served, the orchestra switched from classical music to big-band tunes, and people got up and danced under a beautiful white tent.

Andrew and I were dancing when I heard Coobie shriek. At first I panicked, but then I looked around, and there was Hank with Coobie on his back. Stunned, I left Andrew on the dance floor and ran over to Hank. "Whatever are you doing here? You've surprised me again."

He saw how flustered I was and said, "It's okay, Dobbs. This time I came for Coobie. She's my date tonight. She needed me to be here."

I just stared at him, unable to think of a thing to say. "She wrote me a letter. Who can resist Coobie when she begs?"

Father and Mother looked thrilled to have Hank at the party. With Coobie on his back and Mother, Father, Frances, and Parthenia walking beside him, he paraded around, greeting the guests. The Washington Seminary girls kept telling their parents, "That's the little girl we were raising money for." I heard it whispered again and again.

Maybe it was my imagination, or maybe it was the Lord Almighty opening a window for one night, but Coobie's face had lost its yellowish tint, and she didn't cough one time—at least I didn't hear it. And my heart just about burst for joy when she broke into a huge smile every time she got to tell someone that Hank Wilson was her date.

It was nearing the end of that magical evening, and the night sky was salted with a million stars. I felt like everyone was giving a happy sigh, some sitting at the tables by the lake and others swaying to the music as the singer crooned out the words to a popular song.

> "Love is the sweetest thing
> What else on earth could ever bring
> Such happiness to ev'rything
> As Love's old story . . ."

Then, in the matter of a few seconds, the peace was shattered. Hosea came running over to my aunt, his eyes all wide with fear. "Miz Chandler. There's smoke coming from up at the house." He and Cornelius took off running, and in a blink, several other men followed. Sure enough, smoke was billowing above the trees. Before anyone could think straight, Father and Uncle Robert were yelling, "Water! Get water from the lake! There's a fire!"

And then I saw tongues of fire leaping into the night air like hundreds of fireflies all lit up at the same time. When I got to the top of the hill, I realized it wasn't the house or the garages or even the servants' quarters that were burning—it was the barn. I heard the horses' terrified whinnying and felt the heat rushing toward us.

Cornelius came from the barn, holding on to Dynamite's lead shank, trying to calm her as she reared. Hosea followed with the ponies, and Uncle Robert dashed in to get the pig and the cow. Andrew held on to Red, and then the horse bolted toward the lake.

Someone got buckets and pots and pans and metal tubs, and the men threw off their coats and made a long assembly line, passing buckets brimming with water from the lake all the way up to the barn.

From around the back of the barn appeared Philip and Luke and two other men, holding on to Spalding and dragging him along behind them, Luke yelling, "He started it. Spalding Smith started the fire! I have it on film!"

Spalding's face was red and covered in perspiration and his eyes looked wild. He was straining against the men's hold and saying, "It wasn't me. It wasn't me."

For a few seconds, it seemed the crowd, in unison, forgot the fire and turned as one toward Spalding.

Uncle Robert bellowed, "Take him up to the house and call the police, boys, and the firemen! Get the firemen." Then he rushed along with a bucket of sloshing water, and the commotion broke out again and everyone's attention was back on the fire.

Suddenly Cornelius dropped the metal tub he was holding and began rushing through the crowd of people. He grabbed me and began to shake me, pleading with his eyes, eyes that were lit up with terror.

The boy who had never said more than two or three words before in his whole life—and those, merely unintelligible sounds—gave a deep grunt and with great effort mumbled in a low gravelly tone, "Where's Parthie?"

Amidst the screams and the fire and the clatter, I had no idea.

"Where's Parthie?" he grunted again above the howling of the night.

Cornelius had tears running down his face.

I screamed as loudly as I could, "Parthenia! Has anyone seen

Parthenia, the little colored girl?" Soon people were calling out for her. Mae Pearl and Sam ran up to the house to check there, and Hosea and Cornelius rushed back into the servants' quarters, which were right beside the barn and fast taking flame and smoke.

Father was carrying Coobie in his arms, and she whimpered, "She shouldn't have done it. She shouldn't!"

I ran over to my little sister. "What shouldn't she have done, Coobs?"

She became almost hysterical, taking quick little breaths and then squeaking out, "Parthi took a photo of the man stealing at another party, and she was going to show it to you after this party. She told me so. But later she came up to me and said, 'He's here. He's here tonight.' She was real scared, and then she just disappeared."

And then I knew it. I just *knew*. "She's in the darkroom!" I cried and dashed toward the barn, which was one gigantic bonfire of flame. I was still fifty yards away when the heat knocked me down.

Hank knelt down beside me. "You can't go any closer, Dobbs." He stripped down to his undershirt, soaked his dress shirt with water, and pulled it down over his face like a mask, and before I could say a word, he trudged toward the barn. I was aware only later of my hot tears and my terror. My strange conviction was sending Hank into a pit of death.

Then we heard it—Parthie's high-pitched screams, screams of pure terror and pain. Hosea and Cornelius stumbled out of the burning servants' quarters, choking on the smoke, and stumbled across the lawn to the stable.

Everyone was running with buckets of water from the lake, the scream of sirens in the distance, and I felt more scared than ever before in my life as I watched the great orange and blue flames lick the sky, selfishly, hungrily, devouring everything in their midst.

Parthie's horrible screams had silenced.

And then we heard the crashing of wood and the barn imploded.

"Hank!" I ran in a daze toward the flames, but Father caught me, and right before I fainted from the blast of heat, I saw, as in a mirage,

Hank emerging from the barn, the fire chasing him, and in his arms, the lifeless form of Parthenia Jeffries.

Perri

The fire destroyed the Chandlers' barn and servants' quarters and a good part of the garden before the firemen finally put it out somewhere near two o'clock in the morning. But I wasn't there to see it. I was at the police station with Mrs. Chandler and Becca Fitten and Dobbs and Mae Pearl and Spalding and Philip and Luke.

Officer Withers interviewed each of us, so we stayed there half the night. But nobody was really paying much attention to his questions because every single one of us wanted desperately to be at Piedmont Hospital to find out the fate of Parthenia and Hank and little Coobie, whose tears got her into a fit of coughing so that the Dillards took her to Piedmont too.

Mae Pearl and I repeated our stories from the party at Lisa Young's house—Officer Withers had kept the photos that Mae Pearl took—and then Dobbs gave him a charred bit of a photograph that Parthenia had been clutching in her hands when Hank rescued her. Dobbs told the officer about finding the stolen items in Daddy's toolbox back a year ago and then how they disappeared. When Officer Withers showed her the pearl-handled knives and the jewelry, she exclaimed, "Yes! That's them! Where on earth did you find them?"

All through our testimonies, Officer Withers was writing down things, and then Philip and Luke came forward and told what they'd seen. Luke, face beet red, cleared his throat and said, "Well, um, yes, I saw Spalding Smith leaving the party, and I thought I'd follow him. He ended up at the barn, lit a cigarette, and went inside—and I have this all on film, sir, only we haven't developed it yet—and then he came back out, only he didn't have his cigarette any longer."

"What did you do after Mr. Smith left the barn?"

"I ran and told my brother, and he came back up with me, and by that time there was smoke, and we heard the cries of 'fire,' and so we thought we'd better find Spalding. And we did."

Luke grinned, turned his head down, glanced at his brother, and said, "We tackled him, we did. He's fast and a fine football player, but we tackled him."

"Did you see the child?" The officer looked down at his notes, "Did you see Parthenia Jeffries enter the barn?"

"No, sir, I didn't."

"That will be all, boys. Thank you for your time. You may all go home now."

"But what about Spalding?" I asked.

"Mr. Smith will be staying with me tonight, here at the jail, behind bars. I'll have a chance to hear his testimony tomorrow. He may be telling a different story this time. He's not going anywhere."

Dobbs

Aunt Josie, Perri, Mae Pearl, and I finally got to Piedmont Hospital at about two a.m. Hosea and Cornelius and Mother and Father were still there. Mrs. Singleton had come and taken Barbara and Irvin and Frances home with her. Uncle Robert was still at the house with the firemen.

"Any news?" I asked.

"Coobie's resting fine," Father said. "They got the coughing stopped, and she's asleep."

Mother took my hand and whispered, out of Hosea and Cornelius' hearing, "Parthenia was burned pretty badly. They're not sure the extent yet. They're trying to ease the pain, and the nurses haven't said much else."

"And Hank? How's Hank?"

Father had a queer look on his face. "They haven't said much about Hank, sweetie. I'm sorry."

"What do you mean? He's okay, isn't he? He was carrying her out of the fire. He's gotta be okay."

Mother looked over at Father and put her arms around me. "There's an awful lot of smoke in his lungs, they say. He's having a hard time of it."

"No!" I screamed and buried my face in my father's broad chest.

"They're trying hard to stabilize him. Hank's a fighter. He'll pull through."

I paced back and forth, back and forth. Perri tried to get me to sit down, but when I refused, she came and walked beside me, up and down the long hospital halls.

You learn how much you love someone when you think that person is going to be taken away. So while I paced the halls, I realized in a blink what life would be like without Hank Wilson. Meaningless. The slow ache I had felt in my heart ever since he returned to Chicago had not healed through parties or dates with Andrew or the prospect of college or financial security or anything else. It took a year's worth of life for me to realize the truth. I wanted Hank more than I wanted anything else on earth. He'd said, "Love is strong as death," and he was right. That was what I had learned.

I only hoped I had not learned it too late.

In those halls, I felt my heart come full circle—from zeal and belief to doubt and despair to belief again. But it was a different kind of belief. More mature, maybe. All I knew was that the waiting was agony, but it was an agony buoyed up by a supernatural peace. I had absolutely no way to explain it or even to try, but in the hospital, peace descended on me in a rush of fatigue, and I fell asleep right in my father's lap.

Later, I wondered if sleeping like a child in my father's lap in the midst of fear and uncertainty was not the perfect image of the trust the Lord wanted me to have toward Him.

While I drifted in and out of sleep, my aunt sat next to my father, their heads bent together, whispering away in the night. I caught snatches of the conversation—Father explaining some piece of Jackie and Irene's story, and how he stayed away from Atlanta because he was so very ashamed. It was the saddest story, but as he told it, Aunt Josie scooted closer to him, and when I woke up hours later, they were still talking.

I stood up and stretched and left them there, but I noticed that Aunt Josie had tears in her eyes, and I think that Father finally felt forgiven, finally accepted it from his sister and his God. Surely, it had been granted long before, but I guess sometimes it takes most of a lifetime to accept.

So when the nurse came to the waiting room and said, "They're gonna make it, all of them," the first thing that Father did was pick Aunt Josie up off the ground—no small feat—and engulf her in a hug, while he kept repeating, "Thank the Lord, thank the Good Lord."

I tiptoed into Hank's room. He was hooked up to some machine that looked like it was breathing for him. His eyes were closed. I went over and sat by the bed and took his hand. "Hank, it's me," I whispered. "Don't try to open your eyes. Just listen. Can you hear me?"

He gave my hand the faintest squeeze.

"I'm so sorry, Hank. I don't know what I was thinking during these past months. Maybe it took this horrible fire to make me grow up enough and realize I don't want to stay in Atlanta. All I want is to be by your side, in every moment of life, the soul-soaring times when youth respond to Christ and the times when we have nothing to eat in the pantry and we're down on our knees, counting on the Lord. I just want to be with you."

His eyes didn't open, but he squeezed my hand again and his lips moved a tiny bit, forming a lopsided grin.

Somehow I think that it helped Coobie to have the attention off of her for a while. The fact that two of her favorite people were in the very same hospital, and for the time being were in worse shape than she, gave her the perfect excuse to be mischievous. Twice on the second day, she sneaked out of her hospital room and pattered around the hallways, like a lost puppy, until she found Hank's room.

I was there when Coobie appeared.

"What in the world are you doing?" My tone sounded exactly like our neighbor's in Chicago when he scolded his dog for some misdemeanor.

Coobie padded over to me, feet in slippers, and climbed into my lap. "Bored stiff. Looking for company. Needed to see if my date was okay."

I tickled her a little, and she squealed, and Hank actually opened his eyes for a few seconds, turning his head toward us and holding out his big hand for Coobie to grab on to.

Next, Coobie wiggled her way into Parthenia's room—yes, I helped her find the ward for colored patients—and perched herself carefully on Parthie's bed, and Aunt Josie and Hosea did not object. Parthenia was heavily sedated, drifting in and out of sleep, but when Coobie started describing in minute detail everything she had observed about the fire, and added several lengthy phrases about how amazingly brave Parthenia was, Parthenia struggled to open her eyes and said, "Kin ya tell me that part of the story again?"

Parthenia's worst burns were located on her hands, her little hands that kept digging through flames and wood until she found her photos, photos that seared into her palms as she clutched them. Stubborn Parthenia! Her arms and torso were burned badly too, but somehow her face was not. She was often in great pain, but she rarely cried, just biting her lips and squeezing her eyes shut and moaning, "It hurts something awful, jus' awful."

Though she was soon discharged, Coobie spent hours and hours in Parthenia's hospital room, sitting by her bed and reading to her from *The Secret Garden*. When we told Parthenia that Officer Withers needed to talk with her at some point, she struggled to sit up a little in her bed and asked, "What's the matter with right now?"

It seemed that the thought of getting to talk to a "po-leece-man" perked her up even more than Coobie's visits. So a few days after the fire, Officer Withers came to Parthenia's hospital room. Hosea, Aunt Josie, Coobie, and I were there with her.

"Hello, Miz Parthenia," the officer said, pulling his chair right up by the bed, where she lay with her hands and arms swaddled in clean white gauze.

"Hello, Officer," she said in a tiny voice and tried to smile.

"I'm going to show you some photographs, and all you have to do is either nod or shake your head. You understand?"

She nodded.

He held up a photo of Spalding. "Is this the man you saw stealing knives at the Chandlers' Valentine's party last year?"

Parthenia's eyes grew wide. She glanced at Aunt Josie, who said, "It's all right, Parthie. You can tell the truth this time."

She looked at the photo, then forcefully shook her head. "No, sir, it ain't him. That's jus' Miz Perri's boyfriend, and he is shore handsome. Waddn't him that stole them knives. But he's mean as a wasp if he's the one that started that fire."

Hosea patted his daughter's forehead and said, "Parthie, you stay calm now, or I'll haveta ask Officer Withers to leave."

Parthenia frowned and nodded at her father.

Officer Withers then said, "The man in the photo you brought out of the barn was unrecognizable—the photo had pretty much been destroyed."

Here Parthenia let out a moan. "It kain't be! It jus' kain't be!"

"But I have another photograph, which I believe is of the same man." He held out the photograph for her to look at.

She stared at it for only a few seconds, and her face became a tight frown. "That's him. He's the one."

It was a photo of Bill Robinson.

"Bill!" cried Aunt Josie. "Oh, my heavens. It was Bill." She was standing by the window, and her face went pale—exactly as it had on my first day in Atlanta, when she'd gotten the phone call about Holden

Singleton. Hosea went to her side, and she held on to him and almost looked small beside big ol' Hosea.

"It's gonna be all right now, Miz Chandler. It's gonna be all right," he kept repeating to her as she collapsed in a chair.

Even though Officer Withers told her she didn't have to say anything else, Parthenia got riled up again and began talking in jumbled phrases, and no one could keep her quiet. "He's the one that done stole all those things. I saw him at the Valentine's party, and he saw me too. And he was real mean ta me—so mean, my legs done turned to jelly. And I neva' did breathe a word, 'cuz he said if I did, he'd hang us all, me and Mama and Papa and Cornelius—said he'd hang us from the hickory tree right by our house, and I believed him, I did. He looks all scrawny, but he ain't. He's worse than mean. He's evil. And so I's been waiting and waiting, 'cuz Miz Chandler said we hadda have proof.

"And then Miz Perri taught me how to take photos, and I went to those parties with her, 'cuz I said to myse'f that once there's a bad weed in ya—well, apart from the Good Lawd ripping it out—it's gonna stay. And that Mista Robinson, well, I was pretty shore he wuz full a weeds."

Parthenia seemed to forget the pain from her burns for a time, enjoying the attention of Officer Withers and the rest of her audience. "And sure 'nuf, at another party last week, well, I saw him again, and I followed him around all that night, and he never once saw me. He didn't. Until he started slipping things in his pocket—and that's when I took his photo. And he heard it. He heard the camera when I pressed the shutter, and he saw me, I'm sure he did. But he didn't come after me, 'cuz I was safe with Miz Perri."

I could perfectly well imagine feisty Parthenia crawling through bushes and hiding and waiting, biding her time until she could catch Bill Robinson stealing again, as she'd seen him do that first time at the Valentine's party in February of 1933.

"And I wuz so afraid of him showing up at Miz Mary Dobbs's party, but I wuz even more afraid of something happenin' to my photos. We developed them—Miz Perri and Miz Mary Dobbs and me—but they

381

wuz all worked up about the photographs they done taken at the otha' party, the ones of Mista Singleton, so as they didn't pay no neva' mind to my photos. I didn't breathe a word, but I wuz getting ready to tell Miz Chandler, wuz gonna do it after the party, and that's why I wuz all high-strung and such afore it started."

She paused, her voice raspy. Hosea held a glass of water to her lips, and she took a sip.

"So I had it, finally, finally, I had what they needed—the proof that Mista Robinson was the bad man who'd done all the stealin'. And when he showed up at Miz Mary Dobbs's party, well, I knew he wuz gonna hurt me good then, mebbe even hang me up by my neck. But he didn't. He didn't even look at me which-a-ways. Jus up an' ignored me completely.

"Then Papa come runnin' and sayin' about the smoke, and I knew what that awful man had done—started a fire in the darkroom. So I had to do somethin', didn't I? I had to git that photo. I jus' had to. For my mama."

Dear brave and brash Parthenia Jeffries ran back into the burning barn and into that darkroom to save the photograph. And it nearly cost her her life.

Miracles happen every day. They really do. They come in all different shapes: a rich lady feeling God's tug on her heart to feed a swarm of hungry people, or a photograph from years earlier appearing at the right time to convince a grieving young woman of God's presence, or a father saying he's sorry after so many years of silence, or a little girl giving a bag full of coins to me so I would come back to my heavenly Father.

But on the night of my party, the miracle was this: a mute boy saved his little sister's life by pronouncing two words. I don't know if Cornelius ever said anything else, but it didn't matter—the miracle was that on that night, he did.

Perri

Thank goodness Mr. and Mrs. Chandler were at the house with us when Mamma first learned about Bill Robinson. It was Mr. Chandler who broke the news to her. Mamma went completely pale, and she sat for the longest time in a trance, and then she reached out to Mrs. Chandler, and she cried for a good long time. Then she kept repeating, "He was Holden's friend; we trusted Bill. We trusted him with everything."

What we learned from Spalding's testimony and then from Bill Robinson himself—who broke down in tears in front of Uncle Robert and Aunt Josie and Officer Withers on the day he was arrested—was that Bill Robinson had been stealing from my father for several years. Very slowly at first, little by little, he changed the figures in Daddy's books. And because Daddy trusted him and it was just little bits here and there, Daddy thought he had somehow miscalculated.

Daddy had lost all his stock holdings in the Depression, but the rest, his savings and other investments, and eventually the house itself, were lost to Mr. Robinson, who was sucking Daddy dry and then making my poor father think he was the one slowly going crazy.

I don't believe that Mr. Robinson set out to have Daddy hang himself. I believe that Mr. Robinson was a very sick man, caught up in a terrible addiction and looking for a way out.

Mr. Robinson had said it to me. *Desperate people do desperate things.* How well he knew it.

———

The day that Bill Robinson went to jail, with cameras flashing in his face and his photo splashed across the *Atlanta Journal*, Mr. Chandler and Hosea went to the Alms Houses and brought Anna home. Only she didn't even stop by the Chandlers' but went straight to Piedmont Hospital to see her little girl.

Dobbs and Coobie and I were in the room with Parthenia when her mother walked in. Parthenia let out a weak squeal. "Mama! Mama, yore here! Look at ya, Mama!"

Before I left the room, I took a snapshot with the Zeiss Contax— I knew that Parthenia would treasure it later—of Anna there beside

Parthenia, her calloused hands on Parthenia's forehead and great big tears running down Anna's face, down through the crevasses and spilling onto her dress. Parthenia's face was lit up like a lantern in the darkroom.

Anna was humming hymns, and every once in a while, Parthenia would turn her head and smile at her mother, and once she said, "I got the proof for ya, Mama, so as you cud come home."

Anna had one hand gripping Hosea's and the other cradling Parthenia's face, and she kept saying, "Thank the Good Lawd, thank ya, Lawd."

I had known the first time I really looked at Anna Jeffries that she was a survivor. Gradually, I understood that she was a woman of faith, who worked out on that prison farm and prayed to her heavenly Father and fully expected Him to answer those prayers in His way and His time.

The Good Lord had done it; He had.

Dobbs

We graduated from Washington Seminary on May 16—from what I understood, it was usually the highlight of the year, but we had lived so many crazy emotions the previous week that none of us thought much about graduation. The talk all week was of the fire and Parthenia and Spalding and Bill Robinson. Rumors got mixed in with truth.

Perri had the idea first. "The best way to stop the rumors, Dobbs, is for you to tell the story, the whole story, as only you can."

So on an afternoon a week later, Perri and Mae Pearl and Lisa and Peggy and Brat and Macon came to the Chandlers' home, and we sat on the screened-in porch with Aunt Josie and Mrs. Singleton and Mother and Barbara and Coobie and Frances. Anna and Dellareen were there, serving us homemade peach ice cream. But as I started the story, Aunt Josie and Mrs. Singleton insisted that the servants stay with us on the porch. Parthenia, hands bandaged in white, snuggled in her mother's lap.

Hosea and Cornelius and Jimmy and Uncle Robert and Father and Hank were busy building back the barn—with a new darkroom—and the servants' quarters. The debris had been cleared away, and now we heard the sharp ringing of hammers and the buzzing of saws, and somehow, it seemed the perfect accompaniment for the story I was going to tell.

"Bill Robinson was a successful accountant who was well respected in Atlanta and very involved in the social life of the city. He and his wife were best friends with the Singletons and the McFaddens." I glanced at Perri and then Mae Pearl.

"But he was also a gambling man, although no one knew it at the time. And one morning, he woke up to the bitter news that his fortunes had slipped away, just like so many other people learned on that fateful day in 1929. Mr. Robinson was determined not to let this unfortunate turn of events beat him. It started out as a small thing—he corrected a paper for a client, changed one figure, and pocketed the cash. Then another adjustment, minor and unnoticed, and then another. Eventually he began changing other clients' statements and stealing little bits of money from them.

"He gambled more and more, had more debts to pay back, and so he took another step down that rocky road of sin. He began pocketing silver and jewelry at the fancy parties he attended, and then hocking them off to contacts who would buy the stolen things for a good price. His plan worked for a while.

"But Mr. Robinson had not counted on the sharp eyes of Parthenia Jeffries, and when she caught him stealing those pearl-handled knives at the Chandlers' Valentine party—" here, Aunt Josie displayed the knives for all of us to see—"he threatened her, said he would kill all of her family if she dared breathe a word.

"Shrewd Mr. Robinson put the blame for the thefts on Anna by planting a silver knife in Anna's home. Becca Fitten, searching for the missing items, found the serving piece in the servants' quarters and accused Anna, who was sent to the Alms Houses.

"Of course, the Chandlers didn't believe Anna was guilty, and Bill Robinson figured as much. So to keep them from talking, he sent them anonymous letters, threatening the Jeffries family and, eventually, the Chandlers themselves.

"Later, when Becca found her own jewelry and silver missing, she was more convinced than ever of Anna's guilt—until Aunt Josie showed her the threatening letters. The Chandlers were looking for the real thief, all the while acting as if they believed Anna was guilty. In truth, Aunt Josie and Uncle Robert were protecting Anna and her family by keeping her at the Alms House.

"Bill Robinson had been selling the stolen materials for quite some time, but knowing the incredible worth of the knives, he wanted to find the right buyer. So he hid the silver and jewelry in his good friend Holden Singleton's toolbox—a foolproof way to be cleared if the goods were found before the right buyer appeared.

"Bill Robinson never considered that Holden Singleton would go into his garage on a cold February evening, get out his toolbox, and find those stolen goods. It was the straw that broke the camel's back.

"When Holden went to talk to his good friend and trusted accountant about what he found in his toolbox, Mr. Robinson said words he would regret for the rest of his life—this Bill Robinson has confessed completely—'Holden, let me help you. Perhaps you need to see a doctor? Perhaps you should go to a place for those who are mentally disturbed.'

"Holden Singleton, suffering from depression, watching his money disappear, his money which Bill Robinson stole, found himself suddenly implicated in a crime he didn't commit. We thought he took his life, but I say he was driven to it; driven mad by his trusted friend."

I looked over at Perri at this point, and though she didn't breathe a word, I knew she was thinking about the note her father left her before he took his life. *I didn't do it*, her father had written. No, he hadn't stolen the items, and he hadn't lost all the money.

Mae Pearl was crying softly, and Aunt Josie had taken Mrs. Singleton's hand, and all the girls were clinging to one another. Perri came and sat beside me as I continued, but more softly now.

"No one was more surprised than Bill Robinson when Holden Singleton took his own life. Day after day, he went to the Singletons' house, trying to help them and yet, knowing, too, he had to find Holden's toolbox. He was never alone at the house to search, so he invited Spalding Smith to be his accomplice, knowing that Spalding had a reputation for being shrewd and charming. He also had evidence of Spalding's philandering and drinking and threatened to tell the authorities and the coaches at Georgia Tech, which would get him kicked off the football team and ruin his reputation. So Bill Robinson made a deal with Spalding—he must befriend Perri, search her house, locate the toolbox, and retrieve the stolen goods. Mr. Robinson would then sell the goods and split the money with Spalding.

"Of course, Spalding agreed—he didn't have a lot of choice. He spent lots of time with Perri, but he never found the toolbox. In the end, Mr. Robinson realized the only way to search the house was if it was up for sale. So he continued to adjust the Singletons' accounts, taking more and more money from them and inventing stories of gambling. Eventually Mrs. Singleton made the decision he was hoping for: she would sell the house.

"Then, while helping Perri clean out her father's closet, I found the toolbox with the stolen items. I was stunned and had no idea what to do, so I left the toolbox in the closet. Eventually, I told Aunt Josie about what I'd found. Meanwhile, Spalding had come to the house and helped Mrs. Singleton pack up, always with the goal of finding that toolbox—which he finally did. He took the knives and jewels and silver, and when Aunt Josie came looking for it, the toolbox contained only innocent tools.

"Mr. Robinson and Spalding decided to keep the items that had been in the toolbox for a while, in case they needed to implicate Mr. Singleton again."

"It's downright horrible!" Peggy said.

"Why would Mr. Robinson do such awful things?" Mae Pearl asked, crying again.

I thought of Father's words, and I whispered out loud, "Sin'll do that to you. Tangle you up till you can't see any way out." I looked over at Mother and Aunt Josie.

"But all along, the Chandlers were searching for the real thief, and Anna was praying and Parthenia was looking for proof, and finally, Mr. Robinson slipped up. He panicked when he found Parthenia snapping a photo of him stealing more silver at Brat's graduation soirée. He had Spalding start a so-called accidental fire in Perri's darkroom, to make sure the photos were destroyed.

"When Spalding was accused by the police of all the thefts, he immediately worked out a deal to get less prison time if he'd point them to the real thief. Then when Mr. Robinson was caught, he broke down. He had lived with so much guilt and grief mixed in with his cruelty that it finally all came out."

"I do believe that is the saddest story you have ever told, Mary Dobbs," Mae Pearl said.

I gave a little nod. "The good part is that Mr. Robinson and Spalding are both in jail now, and Anna is free and Parthenia's hands are mending and . . ." I paused and looked first at Perri and then at Mrs. Singleton. "We understand a little more of why poor Mr. Singleton made the choices he did."

I motioned to Coobie, and she came and stood by me. "And Coobie's cough is gone. It really is."

Now all the girls were crying. I didn't say that Coobie's cough was gone *for good*, because none of us knew the future. But right then she was healthy.

Hank came from the work at the barn, onto the porch, looking a bit lost in the midst of all the women and girls. He whispered to Anna, but we all heard it, "Could we please get some water? We're wilting in the heat."

It was the perfect time for me to tell the last part of my story. I turned to look at Hank—whose eyes, whose kind, kind eyes, were riveted on me with that crazy look of love in them—and said, "I've learned so much about myself and others here in Atlanta. There have been good times and really hard times, but it's just like my mother says, when bad things happen, don't ask the Lord why, ask Him instead what you're supposed to do. And when the fire happened, well, I all the sudden knew exactly what I was supposed to do.

"I thought I would be attending Agnes Scott College, but that's not my place. I'm going back to Chicago, girls. I'll miss you something awful, but I want to study at Moody and sit on the front row pew while Hank tells the kids about salvation."

Hank, blushing, came over to stand beside me and hold my hand.

Everyone stood up and stretched. Anna and Dellareen went to get drinks for the men, and Mae Pearl said in her soft, sweet voice, "Well, at least your story has a good ending, Mary Dobbs."

———

I think we loved Coobie back to life. The treatment didn't cure her, but it didn't kill her either, and when the doctor checked her in late May, there wasn't a rasp left in her throat. It could come back—Jackie's had. But it wasn't there then.

Hank's lungs cleared up pretty well, although the doctor said he might get short of breath on occasion.

Hank and all of us Dillards planned to head back to Chicago the next week. Parthenia, with her hands still in bandages, got to wailing as soon as we told her the news.

"Oh, for heaven's sake, quit your hollering!" Coobie told her with a gleam in her eye. "Father says that Frances and I are coming to Atlanta in the fall to go to Washington Seminary."

Parthenia gave a little yelp of joy and ran over and jumped up into Father's arms and said, "Thank you, sir!" Then she slapped her bandaged hand over her mouth and said, "I's sorry, sir. That ain't the proper way for me to be acting." But I could tell that Father didn't mind a bit.

Andrew Morrison came to tell me good-bye. He took my hand and said, "I'm gonna miss you, Mary Dobbs. I really am. But you've got yourself a good man."

"Thank you, Andrew." That was all I could say.

When it came time to tell my aunt and uncle good-bye, I got all choked up. Even Aunt Josie got tears in her eyes. She held on to Uncle Robert and said, "Mary Dobbs, I'm counting on you to take good care of my baby brother, you hear?"

I don't think that Father had ever really felt worthy of his calling, but when he finally accepted complete forgiveness for his past, well, he accepted other things as well. He agreed to preach at a revival with his classmate from Moody, whose face was plastered all over Chicago. Oh, he and Mother went to the Dust Bowl again. They would always feel called to the poorest, but he did a mighty fine job preaching to a real big crowd—over a thousand—on a humid June 1934 night in Chicago. I know, because I was there with Hank and Mother and Frances and Coobie.

Perri

For so long after Daddy's death, all I had seen was everything I had lost, but gradually, I began to see something entirely different. I had gained God, a protector and provider—just as Dobbs always said—who took all that was hard and wrong and somehow brought about good things in spite of it all. Beauty from ashes, I guess.

I had my dear friend to thank for that.

On the day before Dobbs left for Chicago, I drove out to the Chandlers' and parked the Buick.

"She's down by the lake, Miz Perri," Parthenia told me.

I ran through the grass, past the new barn and servants' quarters and down the little hill to the lake, that same lake to where I had followed Dobbs on horseback on the first day of our friendship. She was lying on her back and staring up at the blue, blue sky, arms outstretched, as if she were waiting for the Lord God Almighty to pick her up off the ground and carry her to himself.

The sweet smell of tender grass mingled with a sound of water tickling the banks of the lake. I walked over to where she was lying. Her eyes were closed and her hair fell across her face, shielding it from the sun.

I sat down beside her and said, "I'm gonna miss you something awful."

She turned her head and looked at me. "I know. I can hardly bear to think of it." She squeezed my hand. "But you'll be up in Chicago for the summer, working with Philip at the World's Fair, and I'll come back to Atlanta from time to time, now that Father's agreed to let Frances and Coobie attend Washington Seminary next year."

I handed her *Patches from the Sky.* "You take it back to Hank. It's helped me start on the path of grieving, and now that I have the Lord, I'll be okay. We'll all be okay." I got choked up but managed to say, "I wouldn't have found Him without you, Dobbs."

"He would have found you, Perri. He always finds His sheep."

I nodded and whispered, "I can't tell you how thankful I am that we got to be friends."

"Me too."

Then Dobbs laid the book in the grass and jumped to her feet and started twirling around and around. She grabbed my hands and pulled me toward her as she backed down the little bank and stepped into the lake. She let go of me and sent an arc of lake water straight into my face. I squealed and splashed into the lake beside her, and for a good long time we swam and laughed there together, getting our pretty summer frocks soaking wet.

———

Dobbs had once said to me, "Imagine that you are part of something big and wonderful, Perri. Imagine that you are going to help feed all the poor people in Atlanta."

I guess she said it to her aunt, too, because every Sunday night from June until October of that year, the Chandlers opened their home to the poor. Anna made the most delicious food, with Parthenia's help, of course. Dellareen and Mamma and Mae Pearl and I went to help too—we wanted to because of Dobbs's stories. Mrs. Clark brought over some of the residents from the Alms Houses, and other poor people from the streets came, too, and Cornelius built a dozen long picnic tables, and we'd sit under the trees by the lake, everyone eating together, and I'd take my photos of what Dobbs called reality.

We didn't get the house back—eventually, I realized I didn't want it, with all the horror of what had happened there—but nice folks bought the house, and every once in a while, in the evening, when the fireflies were out, Irvin and I would sneak over and sit on the grass and count the stars.

Perri—1939

If I had not met Dobbs during that hard time in my life, I don't know if I would have pursued photography in the same way. I do know that, because of her, I stepped outside of my world into another, following in the footsteps of Dorothea Lange. Philip helped me a lot, and he even encouraged me with a special dream I had, born from my days at the Alms Houses. From April of 1936 to May of 1937, I lived among the poor, tracking the people caught up in the Dust Bowl and others of whom Dobbs had spoken.

When my first book of photos was published in the summer of 1939, I knew who I wanted to receive the first copy, and so I set out with that book and my camera, leaving Philip to care for our photography store in Atlanta, and our little boy, Dobbson.

In a dusty town in the heat of July, I found her. I would have known her anywhere, that long black hair falling in gentle waves to her waist. Two small children were playing around her legs, and her Hank was talking to a farmer, one of the Oakies, I do believe. From far away I took the picture. It will always be one of my favorites.

Almost as if she sensed the snap of my shutter, she looked around, and then her eyes flew open wide, and she began screaming and running toward me.

I put down my camera and the book, and we grabbed each other and swung around, crying and laughing all at the same time.

"I found you."

"You found me."

"We're both doing what we were created to do, aren't we, Dobbs?"

She beamed at me. "Yes. Yes, we are. Come see Hank, and meet my boys."

I handed her my photo book. "This is for you."

She read the title, *"Hands of Time."* Then she ran her fingers across the cover photograph, the one I had taken all those years ago of Mae Pearl's and Mr. Ross's hands. "Oh, Perri, it's mighty fine."

When she opened the book, she read my dedication:

To Dobbs,
who first showed me that the eye is the window to the soul.

ACKNOWLEDGMENTS

When we moved my dear grandmother (now 97) from her apartment to a full-care floor in her retirement home in Atlanta, my parents found Grandmom's diaries from 1928–1932. I was, of course, eager to take a look. Thanks to my brother, Jere, who scanned all those diary entries, I was able to read them over here in France.

The diaries sealed the fate of my next novel: I'd write about 1930s Atlanta and specifically the life of two girls attending Washington Seminary (the real-life girls' school my grandmother attended that was eventually incorporated into The Westminster Schools—the school I attended).

As I researched that era and heard stories of how both the wealthy and the disadvantaged survived the Great Depression, I found my characters asking the question that I have asked (and heard asked) time and again: Does God provide in the midst of difficult circumstances?

Twenty years on the mission field watching Him provide for my family in original, creative ways lets me answer the question with a resounding "Yes!" But I have learned that the *way* in which He provides is as important as the provision—and that it is *His* way, not mine.

> "The steadfast love of the LORD never ceases; his mercies never come to an end; they are new every morning; great is your faithfulness. 'The LORD is my portion, says my soul, therefore I will hope in him.'" Lamentations 3:22–24 (ESV)

I'm indebted to the following people for helping me understand what Atlanta was like in the 1930s:

Ladies who attended Washington Seminary: Beverly Dobbs

Mitchell, Nan Pendergrast, and of course, my grandmother, Allene Massey Goldsmith, and Pat Ham, who attended Girls High.

Irvin McDowell Massey: my great-uncle, who provided fun little tidbits about Grandmom and confirmed that she was indeed the "girl of a thousand dates!"

Cathy Kelley: assistant archivist at The Westminster Schools, who opened up the archives to me on more than one occasion and provided me with very helpful information.

Two books about Atlanta provided invaluable help with my research:

The Poor Houses by Henry M. Hope—thanks to Jim Hughes for suggesting the book to me.

Buckhead by Susan Kessler Barnard

As always, I'm grateful for the support of my family, all of you: Jere and Barbara Goldsmith; Jere and Mary Goldsmith, Katie, Chip, and Chandler; Glenn and Kim Goldsmith, Will, Peter, and Jonathan; Alan and Jay Goldsmith, Elise and Kate; and the whole Musser clan.

In a novel about friendship, I cannot skip over the important role so many friends have played in my life and my writing career: again to Val, Marmar, Kimmie, and La—there are many "winks" in this story for you girls. Also a heart full of love and thanks to other dear friends: Heather Myers, Trudy Owens, Odette Beauregard, Cathy Carmeni, Cheryl Stauffer, Lori Varak, Marlyse Francais, Michele Philit, Dominique Cottet, Marcia Smartt, LB Norton and the list goes on. I am incredibly blessed with your friendships!

Thanks to Cheryl Stauffer, Cathy Carmeni, and Bob Dillon, who once again looked over a manuscript when it was at its roughest (and longest) and said ever so kindly—"Shorten it!"

I am so fortunate to work with a great group of people at Bethany House: A special *Merci* to Dave Horton for continuing to believe in me and my stories and offer advice—"You need to cut out 40,000 words"—and encouragement. And a big thanks to my new editor, Karen Schurrer—it's been a joy to work together. Somehow you made deleting all those words less painful! To the rest of you—bless you, bless you for all you do.

My agent, Chip MacGregor, is amazing—supplying me with wise counsel, a listening ear, timely information on the business side of writing, and lots of encouragement along the way.

My dear readers—I cannot adequately express my gratitude that, in this age of fast-paced *everything*, you took the time to pick up this novel—in whatever form you chose—and read my story. I pray it was worth it!

My husband, Paul—I'm so thankful we get to step into our new ministry adventure together—your love and support and wonderful good humor and joy keep me going. I am filled up to overflowing with your love. You are the best gift I have ever received.

Our sons, Andrew and Chris—how did you get to be young adults? I am incredibly proud of you and thankful for your faith and courage and sense of adventure, as well as for your love and encouragement. Thank you, Andrew, for choosing such a wonderful wife. Welcome to the Musser clan, Lacy!

And finally, thank you to my Lord, who inspires and guides me daily. The longer I live and journey with You, the more I learn that Your love is truly the sweetest thing.

Historical Note:

The Alms Houses, located in what is now known as Chastain Park, are still in use. The White Alms House has become Galloway School and the Black Alms House, the Chastain Arts Center. The Savannah School of Art and Design in Atlanta is housed on the original Washington Seminary property. The girls at Washington Seminary did not wear uniforms.

The book, *Patches from the Sky*, as portrayed in the novel, does not exist. However, I have a little light blue, hard-covered book called *Patches from the Sky* that is a collection of poems written by my great-grandmother, Elizabeth Fitten Goldsmith. For many years, when I was a child, that little volume inspired me to keep writing poetry.

The Singleton, Dillard, and Chandler families, and all other characters, except those of known historical importance, are fictitious, and any resemblance to real persons alive or dead is purely coincidental.

But . . . if you look around Buckhead, you just may be able to figure out where the Chandlers and Singletons lived all those years ago (in my imagination, of course!).

Merci!

ELIZABETH GOLDSMITH MUSSER, an Atlanta native and the bestselling author of *The Swan House,* is a novelist who writes what she calls "entertainment with a soul." For over twenty years, Elizabeth and her husband, Paul, have been involved in missions work with International Teams. They presently live near Lyon, France. The Mussers have two sons and a daughter-in-law. *The Sweetest Thing* is Elizabeth's eighth novel.

To learn more about Elizabeth and her books, and to find discussion questions as well as photos of sites mentioned in the stories, please visit *www.elizabethmusser.com*.

More From
Elizabeth Musser

Mary Swan Middleton has always taken for granted the advantages of her family's wealth. But then she meets Carl—and everything changes. In the midst of a tragedy that touches all of Atlanta, she seeks his help to uncover a mystery. And what she learns is more than she could have imagined.

The Swan House

Lissa Randall was speeding toward a promising future when a tragic accident brought everything to a screeching halt. Yet help comes from the most unlikely of places—and people. As she slowly sets out on a courageous journey of healing, she wonders if, just maybe, life isn't as random as she thought.

Words Unspoken